PRIVATE WORLDS

PHYLLIS BOTTOME

PRIVATE WORLDS

GROSSET & DUNLAP
PUBLISHERS   NEW YORK

Bear free and patient thoughts

King Lear, **IV**, **vi**

PRIVATE WORLDS

PRIVATE WORLDS

..

CHAPTER I

JANE EVEREST glanced about her sitting-room to see if she hadn't an excuse for moving about in it. But it was relentlessly tidy. The fire burned brightly, a tray with whisky-and-soda stood, equally ready, for triumph or defeat.

When Jane expected anything unusual to happen, she always tried to appear more than usually the same, as if by being a little subnormal herself she could reduce the element of hysteria in events. It was therefore disturbing to her to recognise that she could not fix her attention upon her thesis, until she knew who was to be the new Superintendent of the hospital. Lists of patients, with their individualised case histories and neat charts, were spread out intriguingly before her, but into the industrious accuracy of her consciousness had crept the disintegrating element of suspense. She pushed back her chair and ceased to struggle against her nervous tension.

What kind of an impression would Alec create? Would his easy brilliance and the pressure of his personality attract or repel a circle of humdrum business men, often irritably suspicious of specialised intellect? Would Alec—just because this job was one on which his whole heart was set—proceed to throw his chances away by some foolish, daring phrase or unconventional action?

Alec always believed that nothing mattered but a man's

work; but Jane knew better: what mattered was the man himself. His work was the fruit of his soul, but the tree came before the fruit.

If only she could have gone with him, to damp down his exuberance! His brilliance was his own, but she couldn't help knowing that the steadiness which had again and again saved his experiments from disaster was hers!

She hadn't grudged him the credit of their successes. The sympathy between them was too sincere for rivalry.

If Alec were made Superintendent of the hospital, to all intents and purposes Jane became Superintendent too!

Jane glanced at the clock. She found herself wondering that Sally hadn't run over to share their suspense. Sally knew that Jane was on duty and couldn't leave the hospital. Still, she told herself indulgently, it was only natural for a two months' bride to prefer to keep her husband's crisis to herself. She would have to wait a little longer, and then they would both come over together to set her fears at rest.

She had better get her rounds finished first so that she would be free for them when they did come.

Jane rose with a movement of relief, slipped on her long white linen coat, and felt in her pocket for her torch and keys. She had double rounds to do in Alec's absence; but fortunately nobody was very ill to-night.

She let herself into the women's side of the hospital first, and walked swiftly down the long, dimly lit, silent corridors. There was no one about. It was quite quiet. Nobody, Jane thought to herself, could have imagined that he was in a mental hospital! When she had first come here, even Jane herself had expected lurid nights, disturbed by shrieks; but she had soon found that disturbances were extremely rare. It was most unusual, after ten o'clock, not to find these hundreds of disordered private worlds peacefully asleep.

The door of the night sister's room was open. Sister Stanton came forward alert and compact, ready to exchange her usual confident quiet smile with her superior officer. Jane smiled too: it was always a relief to her when Sister Stanton was on duty. Each knew her business thoroughly, and need shoulder no responsibility for the other.

"Quiet to-night, Sister?" she murmured, with her hand on the door of the nearest ward.

"Oh, yes, Doctor, thank you, just as usual," Sister Stanton answered cheerfully. "Little ups and downs, of course, but nothing to speak of. I don't know that I care any too much for that new male nurse—Clarkson! When he's on duty the patients don't settle down as they should. He doesn't seem to have any tact: they're uneasy with him; and if a good man's on duty they aren't uneasy. They stay where they're put. Still he may improve with time, of course! New brooms aren't much good in a mental hospital, whatever they may be like at other jobs!"

"I think you're right," Jane said thoughtfully, "about new brooms in a hospital."

Her mind strayed off to the great decision. Would the Committee know this? Would they understand what they would gain by having a man, already beloved and understood, whose authority was unquestioned, and under whom staff and patients alike had agreed to flourish?

"Well, we'll have to keep an eye on him," Jane said, dragging her mind back to this minor business of Clarkson. "I think that I must order an extra night nurse for the Admission now that we have that buck nigger Jerry, and the sick Arab. They're rather unknown quantities at night."

She dismissed Clarkson from her mind. The new Superintendent would have to settle the question.

Strange how near all these matters would be to her, and how controllable, if Alec were to be the new Superintendent, and how completely beyond even the expression of a wish, should he be a stranger!

Nurse Stanton turned on her torch. The two women passed, silent as shadows, through the dark open dayrooms into the locked, dimly lit wards.

Jane stopped to look carefully over the covered verandah, where the new cases lay, staring out into the blown darkness. It was a wild autumn night. Leaves sped along the wind; trees bent and shrieked under invisible attackers. A pale lozenge of a moon, helpless as a drunken man, slipped and staggered through driven cloud-wrack.

Jane's practised eyes ranged swiftly from bed to bed. She guessed at a glance how the new patients were dealing with their hidden problems. Here was one with more courage; and there one with less. A new case lay confused and at the mercy of driving images. The one who had been there longest was nearly ready to be moved into the convalescent villa.

The stormy night had not disturbed them. Most of them were already asleep. It had been Jane's own idea to put the newcomers at once on the verandah, so that they could look into the open garden and not feel themselves captives. In front of them, without a visible barrier, stretched the wide, wind-blown, friendly world.

There was nothing that needed doing here, so Jane turned back into the wards again.

As they passed through the more impulsive wards, a patient or two shouted out ribald or angry words at the two white-clad figures; but there was no stress behind their uncontrolled utterances. Jane glanced round her, and went on without a pause.

In the last of the women's wards a staff nurse fluttered up to her, to ask if she might give a sleeping draught to one of the patients. "She's been bent double for four hours," the nurse explained, "and last night she never got off."

Jane stopped at the foot of the patient's bed. An oldish woman sat, her arms tightly clasped about her knees, her head pressed rigidly against them. What implacable self-torment was at the core of the tense, huddled figure? How could Jane free her, against her will, into a night's rest? She knew that this symptom was but a trick of the afflicted spirit, a channel of communication which the retreating mind kept open, as if it still wanted to be in touch with a more ordered universe.

Jane moved away from the bedside into the centre of the ward. "She mustn't be allowed to exhaust herself too much," she told the staff nurse. "Wait a little longer, without noticing her, then, if she still keeps herself tied up like that, give her a paraldehyde draught. Ask Sister to make a special report. I remember her case. She is an over-sensitive, who has been too much exposed to criticism. She mustn't find any kind of undue notice here."

There was nothing else to be seen in the ward, everyone else was quiet. The women's side was finished. They passed through the main corridor back to the farther side of the horseshoe, where the men's quarters lay. There were very few noticeable differences, only male nurses instead of women reported to them at the door of each ward. These were Jane's own patients, but their cases were scarcely more familiar to her than Alec's. Ward after ward was as still as a child's night nursery.

Finally Jane came to the most isolated of the admission wards.

Maclean, the nurse on duty, reported that an Arab, whom no one could understand, was more than usually irritable and restless, and asked if he might take him to a side room.

The Arab, crouched on his crossed knees, was tearing up his mattress. His figure was as thin as a skeleton. His long black beard jutted out aggressively, as if it held more life than ran in his impoverished veins. The bedclothes had already been put beyond his reach; but he went on tearing ruthlessly with his long black fingers at the bare mattress.

Out of his deep isolation he looked up at Jane, with pleading, angry eyes. She sent for a drink of water for him, but when it came, he flung it savagely on the floor.

Jane stood quietly by his bedside, thinking out his dumb desires. She could not always fathom them, but he could read in her eyes her wish to relieve him.

"You must remember," she said sternly to the male nurse, "that even if he were sane, no one here can understand him. To a sane mind this would be terribly irritating, and to an impatient sick mind it must be intolerable. It is not surprising that he should be fierce. I don't want him moved to a side room, where he might feel his isolation more. At least, where he is he can see other human beings with wants like his own. Better that he should tear his mattress than tear at himself!"

Her eyes went back to the Arab. He was already quieter. If only Alec were made Superintendent, they could get him back to Arabia! It only needed the control of funds and authority to put the case through! She stood by his side till he stopped tearing at his mattress, and, giving a long, resigned sigh, sank back on to his pillow.

Maclean, who hovered near them, showed signs of uneasiness.

"If you please, Doctor," he said at last, "it's that Jerry!"

Jane looked up quickly, and saw that the most ferocious of the seaport negroes was sitting up in bed, glaring across the ward at them with hostile eyes. Jane moved swiftly across the ward to his bedside.

"Good-evening, Jerry!" she said pleasantly.

"For God's sake, Doctor," muttered Maclean, "stand back!"

She smiled down, unmoved, at the great black paranoiac.

"If you disturb anyone to-night, Jerry," she said good-humouredly, "you won't be able to sing in church to-morrow! That would be a pity, because you have such a nice voice!"

Jerry's scowl faded. The doctor stood quite near him! He could have caught and strangled her with his bare hands! But his rising fury was relieved by her presence. She had come over to him, as well as to the Arab! His burning vanity was appeased, and slowly the truculence died out of his sick mind.

Jane gave him a friendly nod and left the ward.

The two women finished the night rounds in silence and paused once more at the door of the sister's office.

"To-morrow, Sister, we shall know for certain who is to be our new Superintendent," Jane said, after a brief silence. She felt a strange feeling, as if she wanted to be reassured by Sister Stanton's shared suspense.

"But, Doctor, there isn't any doubt about it, is there?" Sister Stanton asked anxiously. "I understand that Dr. Armitage only resigned after he'd got the appointment for Dr. Macgregor! Why, it would be too dreadful if we were to have some stranger! The hospital, if I may say so, runs so easily with the two of you! Dr. Armitage is a good kind old man, and we all liked him, but we know who did the work!"

Jane smiled, a cool friendly smile. She wanted to be nice to Sister Stanton, whom she deeply respected; but not even to Sister Stanton did she want to be too nice! Just because she was a woman, and might be expected to relax sometimes, Jane rigidly maintained, with the whole staff, the social gulf fixed between doctor and nurse. Fellow-feeling about work was one thing, but personal intimacy was quite another.

Sister Stanton knew better than to press her advantage. She had received a partial confidence. She had been allowed to see that her revered chief was human enough to feel anxiety. It was gratifying to know as much, even though a little surprising.

Jane nodded a brief but friendly good-night.

When the door shut behind her, between the hospital and her own quarters, the strength of her official position fell away from her and she became once more acutely aware of her own state of tension. She had not been reassured by Sister Stanton's confident expectations.

No doubt Dr. Armitage had done his best for Alec, and given him the highest recommendation in his power. But not even Dr. Armitage could tell, in advance, what the decision of the Committee would be.

Jane put her papers methodically away. It wasn't any use trying to go on with her thesis. Alec was overdue already, and Sally was far too thoughtful and considerate, not to run over at once, the moment she heard his news.

For an instant Jane fought with a strange feeling of resentment. For five years she and Alec had worked together. Their work—their whole future life—was at stake; but it must be Sally, his bride of a few months, not Jane, to whom Alec would turn first, to share his triumph or his despair! Still, this idea of being first in another person's life was not a helpful one! Jane had been in that proud position once; and lost it. Although she was only thirty-one, she had lost everything; her parents, her three brothers, and her young lover. The War had swallowed them all. For years, grief had fitted over her like a strong glass case, enclosing her from heat or air. It had been her only security. She had felt nothing, moving about in it, unintimate and numb. She hadn't minded poverty, nor the jealousy of competitors, nor being pushed aside by women less honest than herself, who cajoled and cheated the authorities. She hadn't really minded anything, except her work. She had lived on that. It had given her alike armour and interest.

It was Alec who had broken her glass case down, and let in the air and warmth of the outer world! She remembered that for a long time she had taken no more notice of him than she had done of her other colleagues. She had liked his work. She had talked to him sometimes about her own. Gradually something in her had thawed. She could not have explained the process. But her mind, dipping into the pools of memory, found this image of Alec clear and intact. It was the only personal image that she found there, since her world had been destroyed. Alec had made her touch life again; he had almost made her like it! The enormous warmth of friendship had grown in her till it tingled to her finger-tips.

His marriage had only deepened Jane's sense of security. From the moment Jane saw Sally she had loved her, with a separate, deep, and scrupulous affection.

Sally was as clear as crystal, and as harmless as good water. She was, as well as being Sally, a part of Alec.

"As if it matters in the least," Jane told herself contemptuously, "which of us he tells first! The only thing that matters is his getting the appointment!"

It mattered so much that Jane, who had all her life long trained herself to surmount disaster, tried to train herself afresh, to face Alec's possible defeat.

She sat down in front of the fire, and began to build up their life together under a new Superintendent. But imagination abruptly failed her. She could not see the new Superintendent; instead she found herself shivering with anxiety.

She was no longer a stoic and a scientist. She was a woman and a friend.

CHAPTER II

THE French window swung wide open. A man stumbled across the threshold, swaying as if he were drunk. His clothes hung upon him wet and disordered, and all the stormy garden streamed into the room after him.

Jane felt a moment of sheer panic.

Jerry's bloodshot eyes flashed into her mind. But it was not her body which was in danger of sudden violence. Alec, uncontrolled and defeated, stood before her. Her panic died down; but the fear which took its place was a deeper fear.

Alec dragged himself across the room and flung himself into his usual chair, burying his face in his hands and shivering.

Jane got up and shut out the storm. She poured him out a stiff whisky-and-soda, and, pulling his hands away from his face, pressed the glass into his shaking hands.

Alec looked up at her with eyes drowned in misery.

Jane met his look—steadily, but without visible pity. This was a hideous set-back, but she must encourage him not to think of it as a mortal blow.

She said quietly: "Well—the appointment has gone to somebody else then?" Then she drew back from Alec's defrauded, appealing eyes; and sat down quietly in her former place.

"I shan't stay on!" Alec exclaimed savagely, as if he were combating a course which Jane had previously urged upon him. "It's an insult to shove a fellow of my own age, with nothing to show for it, over my head! The Committee is a set of bloody swabs with the minds of rabbits! I shall chuck the whole thing—and go and make surgical instruments! What's the use of psychiatry, anyhow? If you've got enough mind, you don't go out of it, and if you haven't, you may as well be out of it as in it! It's no use your sitting there looking like a stuffed Madonna! I'm down and out! From the time I was a kid I dreamed of this job. I worked for it till I dropped. I coached poops at the University till I got my Tripos! I've always done some other pampered fellow's job, to pay for being allowed to carry on my own! What's the use of it all? What's the use of having waited five years for Sally, and kept clean while I waited? What's the use of all the slaving you and I have done here? Think what we've put into our patients! How we've badgered old Luke for money to finance our research work! How we've given up our free time so that we could give the patients occupational therapy! And now it's all got to go to a gutless ramrod of a fellow, who doesn't know the difference between a laboratory and a pigsty! We must resign and clear out, Jane, and let the hospital go to hell!"

Jane listened in silence. However brilliant your record might be, flinging up jobs was not looked at with approval in the mental hospital service.

What would Alec and Sally do without a penny? They had married on Alec's job, and had put the savings of five years into their new home.

Sally wanted a baby, and the sooner she had one the better. Alec was the kind of man who needed something helpless dependent on him, in order to rivet him. He couldn't take a prestige question as if it were a mortal wrong if he had a family to support. What could she suggest to hold him now?

His defeat burned in her.

Jane hadn't only been proud of Alec's work. She had been prouder of his pluck. She had deeply respected the harnessed energy, which made Alec disregard personal comfort and personal pleasure until his work was done. She couldn't bear to see him flinching under any blow.

"What is the man's name?" Jane asked drily. "And what has he done—up till now? He must have some kind of a record."

Perhaps if she could get Alec away from his wound, even if she made him angry, he might regain his judgment, and not force her into such pity that she would lose her own!

"His name's Charles Drummond," Alec reluctantly flung at her. "He was born in a mediæval Scottish castle, and has a head full of Highland maggots. He is an Edinburgh man, and has been at Broadmoor. No doubt he thinks in machine guns! Imagine our hospital, Jane, run by a reactionary, who treats the patients like criminals!"

Jane refused to imagine it. She forced her mind away from Alec's picturesque statements. After all, she told herself, this man, who was to be put over their heads, was as innocent as any other stranger.

"I remember the name," she said reflectively. "Who wrote that adrenal gland paper you liked so much in the *Lancet* a month or two ago? Wasn't that by Charles Drummond? If it was, he must have done some sound research work. We have no grounds for supposing Broadmoor psychiatrists to be any more reactionary than we are; and he must have held some other post. His name is quite well known. Perhaps the Broadmoor experience was only because he had an interest in criminology. Thirty-five is young to have reached his present position. I fancy he must be an exceptionally able psychiatrist."

"You wait till you've seen him, Jane!" Alec retorted vindictively. "I tell you this fellow is one of those brainless icicles they train on you from castles. He thinks he owns the universe and that the archangels were lucky if they intermarried with his family. What's the use of a career to him? What's the good of science. His name's Charles Drummond, and there's an end of it! I suppose he's got no money—and that's why he works at all. But he won't work really. He'll stamp all over us, and cut down our research work. He'll think it's enough to say, 'Lock 'em up and keep 'em quiet!' He and the Matron between them will run the show like a den of lions. The only things they will ever want to pay for, on our side of it, are drugs and coffins!

"Why don't you say something, Jane, instead of sitting there like a chunk of cold cucumber? You must mind our having to give up everything—and being driven back to school under a dud?"

Jane frowned. Of course she minded. But what was the use of saying you minded things? She hadn't ever wanted anything for herself as much as she had wanted this job for Alec. It would have been for both of them, and for the hospital under them, an ideal situation. But, after all, what particular right had they to count on ideal situations? They weren't any worse off now than most medical officers of their own age. They were even rather better off, for whoever they had for Superintendent, they shared their work with each other. A bad Superintendent couldn't spoil their work. He could hamper it, of course, by cutting down research, or by refusing to finance improved methods. But the treatment of the patients was their own affair.

"I mind all right," she said slowly, after a long pause. "But he mayn't be as bad as you think. Our disappointment is not due to him, nor need your future be kept down by any Superintendent."

"I shall chuck my job," Alec said sternly, with hard anger in his fiery brown eyes, "and I count on your doing the same. They've no right to force a man who isn't senior

to us over our heads. Besides, I haven't told you everything. This fellow hates women doctors. If you won't
resign, he'll make you. Even if I didn't mean to chuck
my job for myself, I should do it to stand by you."

Jane winced. She must express neither gratitude nor
tenderness for Alec's loyalty. Tenderness was Sally's job.
She owed it to Sally to make Alec as angry as was good
for him. All the more she owed it to Sally, since Alec had
come first to her!

Fortunately Sally was a sensible, loyal little thing, who
might be reckoned on to see things straight.

Alec gazed across the room at Jane with reproachful
incredulity. His eyes asked her insistently if she could
be going to let him down.

Jane reminded herself sharply that she was standing
by him, and that one of the ways of standing by him most
successfully would be by letting him think her as selfish as
he liked!

"Have you actually seen this man yet?" she asked him
dispassionately.

"Seen him!" exploded Alec contemptuously. "How like
a woman! What do the fellow's looks matter? Are we going
to run our pituitary research on the new Superintendent's
personal appearance?"

"I don't wish to know whether he's handsome or not,"
Jane explained, with unruffled patience; "I simply want
to know what grounds you have for speaking so adversely
of him. It is not like you to be unfair—but I think you
are being unfair about him—and about me, too, if it comes
to that. You know what I feel. It is unnecessary to make
me say it. You say you will resign if I am forced to. Well,
so would I resign if you were forced to—but not if you
force yourself!"

"I couldn't help seeing him," Alec replied in a slightly
mollified tone. "We were all three driven into a pen to-

gether—a fellow called Travers from Stone—a good enough oldish chap I could have swallowed if I'd had to—though I must say I think the Mental Hospital Service's appetite for fossils is distinctly morbid—this beast with the grand manner—thirty-six years old—and myself! He never said a word to either of us! Didn't even take the trouble to shake hands! Just walked in and out as if the place belonged to him—and looked at us down his nose!"

Jane was silent. Alec was always suspicious of class distinctions. It had taken him a year to forgive her her own manners.

"He can't help his birth," she forced herself to say at last. "But if he's only a few years older than we are, it has one advantage—he will probably want to work in with us, on modern lines. And, after all, it's the work that matters."

"You might just as well say," retorted Alec, "like old Armitage, 'All the patients need is plenty of good food!' You know as well as I do that personality enters into every damned thing. A staff run by a friend on friendly lines is going to be a good staff and react well on the patients, whereas a staff that's run by a rival and an enemy is bound to be a bad staff and react badly on the patients. What on earth's got into you to-night, Jane, to take this fellow's side instead of mine? You can't like a man that despises women?"

"I don't propose either to like or to dislike him," Jane said coldly. "I shall do my work, without letting him interfere with it or with me. If he can't govern his hostility sufficiently to overlook my being a woman, and lets it interfere with my work, I shall of course have to leave the hospital. But since I have neither a young wife to protect nor a new home to keep up, it's financially immaterial whether I go or stay. Still, if I am not asked to resign, I propose to hold on to my job as long as possible. Nor shall I allow myself to jeopardise my patients by treating the new Superintendent either as a rival or as an enemy! I've had to stand the Matron's determined hostility ever since I've been here. She has bored and aggravated and sometimes enraged you, Alec, but she's been really fond of you, whereas she would like my soul in boiling oil as an apéritif! Still, I can't say that it's ever interfered with the well-being of my patients. It is crooked thinking to speak as if this appointment were in itself bad for the hospital, when it lies with us not to let it become so!"

Alec sprang to his feet and moved irritably about the room.

"I can't understand you, Jane," he muttered irritably. "Sitting there as cold-blooded as any schoolmarm, sticking pins into me about duty! I thought we were friends? Ah, well! You know what I mean! Our friendship's been tremendous! It's been like bread! We've lived on it, Sally and I. Why, we could never even have married if you hadn't wangled the house and a bigger screw out of old Luke! I thought I'd stood pretty well by you too—only that's a matter of course. If we have to begin to rake up what we've done for each other, I shan't feel as if the ground were solid under my feet. I always thought what we've had—was better than that! D'you really mean you won't strengthen my hand by resigning when I do?"

Jane turned her head away from him. She could keep her speech colourless, but not her eyes.

"I came to you first, instead of Sally," Alec added in a climax of reproachfulness, "just because I was sure you'd stand by me, and help me to make her see why I'd got to chuck the job!"

"Even if I agreed with you—which I don't," Jane replied stubbornly, "I should have refused to play my wits as a card to help you against Sally. Of course she won't think you right to resign. Why ever should she? She has just put her whole future into your hands. Don't you realise that it's Sally's life as well as yours that's at stake? And that the only compulsion there is to throw up your job lies in your own pride? Why shouldn't you work under another man? You're only thirty-four. Heaps of good men never get a job like this till they're fifty, and women don't get it at all. If you really respect women as equals, you should have gone to Sally first, and let her make this decision with you. She has as much right to a share in it as you have. I dare say I sound very ungrateful—after the handsome things you've said to me to-night. I have my feelings too. I'm not going to risk not being honest with you. I should have been grateful if you had both come to me together—after your decision was made—but now——!"

Jane stopped abruptly. She hadn't meant to let herself go, and she didn't know quite why she wanted to. Had you got to be angry just because you felt it would be dangerous to be nice?

"But now—what?" Alec demanded in a curious voice. He stood in front of Jane, his eyes fixed upon her face. He was dangerously quiet.

It oppressed Jane that Alec should stand there in that challenging way, as if she were hiding something from him. What was there about the truth which could hurt either of them? But it needn't be forced. It could be left alone.

"Now," Jane said, trying to keep her lips from trembling, "you make me ashamed of our friendship."

He said slowly: "Is that what you feel, Jane—because I am defeated?"

"Ah, but you're not!" she cried, pushing back her chair and moving blindly away from him. "You're not defeated! And I won't defeat you! Thank God, I can't! Alec—it's only you that can defeat yourself!"

She went to the window and threw it open. She wanted

to get her whole body and heart washed clean of feeling. The cold damp air rushed into the room like a relieving presence.

She heard Alec's voice behind her saying, "Jane! Jane!"

She turned once more, to face him. He had a crestfallen, sheepish air.

"I'm sorry," he said; "I ought to go home, I suppose. It wasn't fair trying to pin things down on you."

Jane smiled at him. "Perhaps you ought," she said. "But don't be too upset. Take another drink and give me one. Probably I won't be given any choice about resigning—and then you'll think you're justified in resigning too!"

He poured himself out an even stronger drink, but forgot Jane's.

"I took for granted, Jane, that you'd see it as I did—about resigning, I mean," Alec said in a more natural tone. "As for going home first, I knew I was all in, and I didn't want to upset Sally. Besides, as far as that goes, I rather thought I should find her here with you."

"Well, she isn't," said Jane succinctly, "and the sooner you go home to her the better. Don't let her think you came here first to see me. I don't like prevaricating, but there are plenty of other things you might have come to the hospital for. And Sally has been waiting a considerable time in some suspense. She's a reasonable girl, but you don't want to give her more than she can stand—and one thing even the most reasonable bride can't be expected to stand is the part any other woman has to play in her husband's affairs! We've had a blow, all of us, but don't let's make it any harder than we need for Sally!"

"You admit it is a blow, then?" Alec aggravatingly asked.

Jane did not answer him. She finished drinking the whisky-and-soda which she had poured out for herself, put the glass back on the tray, and laughed. "I'm not a spirit drinker," she observed, "but I needed that whisky. Come over, both of you, to-morrow morning early—and let me know what you've decided on."

"I'm not going just yet," Alec objected, sitting down again. "There are a few things I must tell you about first. I told Sally I couldn't tell when I'd be back."

Gloomily, but without desperation, Alec launched himself into a narrative of the day's events.

Jane gathered that Alec had behaved with rather more self-control than she would have expected, and said nothing irreparable to damage his future.

Dr. Drummond certainly sounded, from this fuller account, rather a stick—but he might only have been uncomfortable and shy. His qualifications were much the same as Alec's, but he had two years seniority and had been a Superintendent before.

The Committee had showered gallingly ineffectual praise upon Alec's work, and hers. Luke had written testimonials that should have got them both into Paradise.

But something or other had intervened. That unforeseen hitch which can destroy the most handsome of prospects had destroyed theirs.

Still, Dr. Drummond was not bringing any staff of his own, and things might have been worse.

It would be time enough to deal with the new chief's prejudice against women, if he turned out to have any. After all, such things could easily be reported without the slightest foundation; nor was it final if he had such a prejudice.

Luke Armitage himself had faltered over the idea of a young, unmarried woman alone in male hospital quarters; and yet how well it had worked!

Sex, Jane thought to herself, looking indulgently across the room at her own familiar friend, didn't play nearly as great a part in a useful working life as was commonly supposed. Look at herself and Alec, for instance. Could two people have liked each other better, through the daily contact of five years' work, without so much as a flicker of passion on either side?

Jane let him go on talking uninterruptedly. She listened every now and then, but most of the time she just watched the anger and defeat fading out of Alec's eyes.

He was normal again now, and no longer oppressed by the drive of his uncontrollable pride.

"You're a beast, Jane," he told her, smiling across the room at her, "but a just beast!"

At last he got up to go, and held out his hand. Jane put hers into it. Afterwards she rather wished she hadn't. He crushed her rings into her fingers so that they ached for hours. But it wasn't the physical pain which Jane minded. She wished that they hadn't shaken hands until after Alec had told Sally.

CHAPTER III

THERE was a small looking-glass in the corner of Jane's office. Before she went to see the new Superintendent for the first time, she stood for a moment in front of it, to get an impression of her appearance.

Women's characters can be judged by their attitude to their own looks.

Jane felt dispassionate about hers; and unhopeful. Her head was well shaped. Her eyes were a nondescript grey-green, but they were a good size and clear. Her nose was a little too long. It was a face without brilliance of either colour or feature. It could easily have been thought hard, except when she smiled. For then her humorous mouth lifted like wings, her clear eyes sparkled, and people saw a face which Jane had never seen; because she had never smiled into a looking-glass.

"Anyhow I'm clean and tidy," she said to herself resolutely. "Unless he wants to loathe me, he has no excuse for it in my appearance, and if he wants the other thing, he has even less excuse!"

She pushed her soft brown hair into more rigid lines, and slipped on a fresh white linen coat.

She kept her appointment punctually. The voice which told her to come in was a guarded but pleasant voice, with music behind it.

The large, rather brilliant blue eyes into which Jane found herself looking had a curious expression; as if the new Superintendent had met and hoarded so many dis... ...ts in the course of his life that he would naturally ...bject to be added to them.

He rose quickly and drew forward a chair for her.

"You are Dr. Everest, are you not?" Dr. Drummond asked, bowing with a slightly exaggerated deference.

Jane returned Dr. Drummond's bow and sat down. Neither of them smiled.

It struck Jane that either she was going to dislike this new Superintendent more than she had ever allowed herself to dislike anybody, or she wasn't going to dislike him at all. She was going to find him disastrously nice.

He continued to look at Jane, with that dreadful look of guarded disgust, for quite a long time. At last he said in a low but very distinct voice:

"I have never willingly worked with a woman doctor. The medical profession is one which one finds not at all suitable for women."

Jane lifted her sensitive, slightly arched eyebrows.

"Do you not think," she answered, after a noticeable pause, "that people should be judged by their work as individuals, rather than by their sex?"

"I have had the opportunity of noticing women's work," Dr. Drummond murmured gravely. "It has given me no grounds for altering my opinion. I cannot, however, overlook the testimonials I have received about yours. I do not propose to ask you to resign. It merely seems to me fairer, in case you are considering any fresh plans, to put my views before you. I can well imagine that you would prefer not to work under a Superintendent who definitely distrusts the work of women."

"I have always observed the limitations of my freedom as a medical officer," Jane replied with determined mildness. "I am deeply interested in my work here. I should be sorry to leave, even now, unless your dislike of women doctors inconveniences them in carrying out their duties!"

"That would be most unfair," Dr. Drummond said quickly.

"Yes," breathed Jane.

Dr. Drummond flushed. Jane watched with concealed amusement, while his controlled fury turned his manner to ice. She had stopped being frightened now. It gave her a queer sense of reassurance to find that Dr. Drummond knew exactly what she implied, by what she didn't say.

He turned his eyes away from her.

"You would, of course, be perfectly free to carry on your work according to the regulations of this hospital," he said stiffly.

Jane bowed her head, and sat with it a little bent, looking down at the floor. It was odd, but without looking at Dr. Drummond, she continued to see his face.

"I understand that your work hitherto has been with Dr. Macgregor?" he asked, after a pause.

"I have worked under him for four years," Jane replied. "But a year ago I was put in charge of the men's side of the hospital, and I have run it by myself."

"Do you not yourself think," Dr. Drummond asked "that a woman in charge of the male side of a mental hospital is most unsuitable?"

Jane was silent. She did think it in some ways an unsuitable appointment. Luke had asked her to take it over during an emergency, and since she had handled it with extreme competence, he had asked her to remain. But her competency had cost her something. She had felt the work among men patients a great strain, and if there had been an equal post for her in the hospital, she would have asked to be relieved of it; but if she were to take a junior position again, after having been for over a year her own master, the whole hospital would know that she had been pushed back a step, and she would find that having done so would interfere with her promotion. If she resigned rather than accept a junior appointment, Alec would resign too.

"It is true," Jane forced herself to say at last, "that I think it usually better to have a male doctor on the men's side. But I have held this post for over a year and I have learned how to handle my male patients now, so that unless you have a better man in your mind for the position, I should greatly prefer not to be obliged to give it up."

"Please don't think that I mean to complain of your work," Dr. Drummond said with cold courtesy. "I understand that you have carried out a most difficult job with great credit. But I cannot ask you to retain it, because, in spite of your success so far, it seems to me dangerous and unsuitable, both for you and for your patients. I take for granted that you do not accept my initial objections, still I should be interested to learn what your own reasons are for feeling, since you admit that you do feel, the position is not an ideal one?"

Jane drew her eyebrows together. "They are certainly not very vital objections," she explained, "or I should have resigned my post. I don't think I've done the patients any harm. Men—out of their minds, I mean—make good patients for women! One can increase their self-respect and hopefulness. Certain of my patients have, of course, difficulties on sex lines, but they hardly affect me more unpleasantly than if I were a male doctor. Most discouraged human beings are heterodox rather than oversexed. There are a few patients who would be actually impossible for a woman to handle alone, but since a male nurse is always present, I find no insuperable objection to dealing with them. What I do find an objection is, that each sex understands its own better than the other, or rather, I should say the most primitive types of both sexes. Men doctors have been traditionally accepted by women, and have therefore the advantage of us. Men are not yet accustomed to women doctors. I find a certain proportion of my men patients shrink from explaining their troubles to me. Still, their earlier and more confused utterances are usually the key to their difficulties, and those one can study while they are still too confused to observe one's sex. What they say later is more in the nature of a defence-mechanism, and is therefore less important. When I am in any doubt, I rely on my junior medical to take my place.

"There are some ways in which I think the male patients have definitely benefited by having a woman in charge. But it is less easy to put these improvements into words, since they are rather intangible. The actual percentage of cures has been higher this last year, but one cannot take this as any true indication, since there may have been more recoverable cases than usual under my care."

Jane stopped. She felt surprised that she had expressed herself so freely and at such length, but Dr. Drummond made a good listener. She had been conscious of a candid, impersonal mind at work on what she said.

When he answered her, Jane noticed that his slow, restrained utterance had become curiously freed and quickened.

"Yes, I should have supposed your difficulties would have been something like that," he admitted, "only I should have thought you would have found more vital drawbacks as well, on both sides. It is interesting that you did not find them. For instance, many a man's self-respect would be definitely lowered rather than raised, by his case being put into a woman's hands. That may again be traditional, but men are not accustomed to rely on women. Forgive my saying it, but I should suppose no schizophrenic would open his mouth to you. It can't be the best way of handling the situation, and in all mental illness— I am sure you would agree with me that anything short of the best is bad: I should like to make an exchange between you and Dr. Macgregor, but I see a very grave

obstacle to its being feasible. If you were to take on the
women's side, since that is the larger, Macgregor would
feel a certain loss of prestige. This is, of course, more a
technical than a practical difficulty, since the work of
each of you is quite independent. Still, it is a difficulty,
especially as you have worked under him for four years.
Have you considered it?"

Jane had considered it. It had long ago prevented her
from suggesting the exchange. It had never occurred to
Alec. He simply hadn't thought it mattered which side
either of them held; but he would think it mattered now.
Whatever Dr. Charles Drummond proposed would be hideously suspect to Alec!

"I think it would be most difficult," Jane replied decisively, "particularly just now. Dr. Macgregor is a most
able psychiatrist. I do not know if you have followed his
career? He has a splendid record, both as a psychiatrist
and as a surgeon. He has his F.R.C.S. and was noted for
his brain surgery in London. It was supposed that on
Luke Armitage's retirement he would have been made our
Superintendent."

There was a short pause, then Dr. Drummond said, with
a return to his former coldness: "I should suggest that you
make up your mind either to resign then, or else to return
to the women's side and once more work as Dr. Macgregor's subordinate. I could then make a fresh appointment on the male side. I have no one directly in view, but
I would immediately see about discovering someone."

Jane kept her eyes down. She was astonished to feel
tears rising to them.

Dr. Drummond's sudden retreat made her feel exposed
and driven away. The trouble was—and Jane told herself
sternly that she had better acknowledge it once and for all
and get it out of her system—Charles Drummond bore an
unmistakable likeness to her dead lover Michael.

Michael had had those startlingly deep blue eyes, the straight nose, the clear-cut lips; even the cleft in Michael's chin belonged to Charles Drummond; and the way his hair, however obstinately brushed, curled back from the jutting line of his forehead.

But Charles Drummond's expression was not the same. There was no softness in his eyes.

It chilled Jane's heart to think of the colour and the soft light of Michael's face.

The man on the other side of the desk sat curiously still while Jane drove back her memories.

"If I resign," she said at last, when she was sure that she could use her voice without its shaking, "I am afraid that Dr. Macgregor would also resign. I should deeply regret this step on his part, both for his sake and for that of the hospital; but I could not prevent his acting out of a mistaken loyalty to a colleague. He has just been married, and has no private means. It is therefore vital to his interests that he should retain his job; but personal interests, however vital, would not restrain him. I think therefore, I have no alternative to what you suggest. I must stay on in the hospital, as his subordinate, if you will allow me to do so."

Jane did not look up, so that she could not see what lay behind Dr. Drummond's long, considerate silence. He might be merely bored, or he might be amused, that she had had to knuckle under to him, in order to save her friend.

When he spoke again, he only said: "Very well, then we will leave it in that way for the present."

Jane rose to go. Dr. Drummond rose also. She was conscious that he was holding open the door for her, and she went out of it with her head held high, carrying her anger like a decoration, down the long corridor. For Jane found that she was very angry. She told herself bitterly that she had every reason to be satisfied, but she was not satisfied

She had done exactly what she had intended to do. She had said what would help Alec to stay on, without lowering his dignity. Dr. Drummond had not been at all tiresome about Alec. He was going to be, Jane instinctively recognised, extraordinarily nice to him, and only nasty to her. She wouldn't have to leave the hospital, and she was going to go on working with Alec. She could carry out the orders of his brilliant wits, and safeguard the patients from his dangerous oversights. Like all good subordinates, she would learn to suppress any alien brilliance of her own.

She was annoyed by the hushed way the hospital staff greeted her. They seemed to expect her to be upset on this particular morning. Of course she was not in the least upset! She was a little more severe than usual in her manner to the nurses, that was all! To the patients, although they were men, she was just as gentle as if they had been women. Still Jane went so far as to wonder, with rather a grim smile, if she would have been so gentle with them if they had not been patients! It couldn't possibly matter to her what the new Superintendent thought of women, but she found that, for the moment at any rate, he had made her more critical than usual in what she thought about men.

CHAPTER IV

WHEN Jane came back from her morning rounds she was relieved to find Sally in her sitting-room. They exchanged a long straight glance, which relieved Jane still more.

Sally looked white and a little harassed, as if she had not slept; but she bore Jane no grudge. However upset she was by the crisis in their lives, it hadn't occurred to her to make it worse by nursing a personal grievance. Sally was a very nice child.

"I'm glad you came over this morning," Jane said quickly. "You know what I feel. It is worse for you than for anyone, because of Alec, but it's a blow for us all. Everyone in the hospital is upset this morning. The Matron's been crying, and has a temper which would take the skin off the mice in the wainscot, if she allowed any mice to be in her wainscots! It is the first time I ever found myself sympathising with her in one of her passions."

Jane's eyes wandered round the room. Sally hadn't only come, she had filled Jane's room with autumn leaves and berries. It was nice of Sally, after a bad night, to make Jane's room look beautiful. It was almost, Jane thought, too nice! It was as if she had wanted to make up for something in her mind which had been less nice. That was the worst of being a psychiatrist. You found yourself refusing to take things at their face value. Jane knew that Sally should have been thinking only of Alec unless she had confused her sympathy for Alec with a less reliable feeling towards herself.

Jane thanked Sally without effusion, and poured out tea. Sally came and sat down on a stool near Jane's chair

The French windows, which looked on to a green tennis lawn, were wide open. The storm was over; leaves were brushed up; the sky above the flat, rather dull landscape was the clearest robin's-egg blue. It was a nice day to get over things in, Jane thought.

She looked into the garden, for a long time, in silence, then she said: "Well—Sally——?"

She didn't want to say what she thought until she knew what Sally had been thinking.

"It's awful, Jane," Sally said in a low voice, "quite awful—because—he minds so much. I suppose he's got to mind—only—only we were so happy; and it's all there still, isn't it—what we were happy about? But to Alec it doesn't seem there any more. This new man—you've seen him, haven't you?—is he simply a loathsome beast? Alec's with him now. He was to see him after you'd come away. But unless Alec flares up, he won't definitely resign until he's talked it over with us again. I think, if the new man isn't too odious, Alec might stay on. He wants us to talk it over together—now—and that'd help him decide. But I know he really and truly wants not to stay!"

"The new man's not simply a beast," Jane said cautiously. "I don't think he's loathsome either, but I should think he might be rather old-fashioned and obstinate. He'll be nice to Alec, though. He awfully doesn't want him to resign!"

Sally put her teacup on the floor. She spoke in a still lower voice, twisting a piece of heather between her fingers.

"Jane," she murmured, "do you honestly think Alec had better stay? He hates it all so awfully now—his work —and everything. Won't his hating it just get under the skin of everything he does and poison it? If it wasn't for me, I know he'd chuck it. And we'd not starve! I mean— not really. Would we? We've got twenty-five pounds between us and all our new furniture. Of course we couldn't

live on that long, without work, I know. But Mother
would take me in again if I'd got to be taken in, and Alec
would get some kind of work in his old hospital, and a
job would turn up for him sooner or later, wouldn't it?
Of course there's our new little home and——" Sally's
voice trailed unevenly away.

Jane put her hand out to caress her, but thought better
of it and drew it back. Perhaps Sally didn't want to be
caressed. Jane put her gentleness into her voice instead.

"I'd stay, Sally," she said after a long pause. "I'd
stick it out. It isn't only you and the new home. That
mightn't be enough to keep him here—if you didn't want
it to keep him. But there's his reputation. He has no real
reason for throwing up this job. He's certain to get good
promotion, and soon—Luke Armitage will see to that!
He's got to think of his career. He can't afford to be
looked on as a man who throws up his work out of pique
because another man has been chosen as Superintendent
over his head. Can he?"

Sally didn't raise her head to meet Jane's eyes. Her
voice, when she answered Jane, sounded curiously forlorn
and flat.

"I suppose not. I suppose he ought to try to stick it
out. At least, that's what I kept on saying all night. I
suppose men have to care most about the things they do.
You see—it seems funny to me. I thought—what we had
together—was worth more than that! Last night—after
it happened—he didn't come to me—he came here! He
said he had to! Well—I suppose he had—but I'd waited
so long—and when he came back to me—it was different!
I'd thought of it both ways—his getting it and his not
getting it—but I'd thought he'd come first to me!"

So Sally had minded!

Jane sat quite still. She felt frozen to her chair. It was
a miserable blunder for Alec to have made. Could she

have stopped him? She stared into the sunny space in front of her, and saw him stumbling in, a broken, blinded figure, out of the storm. Could she have repulsed his dire need? She still hoped that Sally didn't know he had come to her! The hospital was bad enough, but she herself would have been worse!

She turned her head and met the eyes that Sally slowly raised to her face.

"Things sometimes happen in a hospital," Jane said gravely, "that are pretty critical. It's a hard profession for wives, and the hardest part of it for you is that Alec's main colleague is another woman. It would be too hard for you altogether, Sally, if you didn't trust that other woman."

"Ah, but I do, I do!" cried Sally. She plunged forward and buried her head against Jane's shoulder.

Jane looked down uneasily at the sweet-smelling, untidy mass of Sally's curls. She wished Sally wasn't trembling so. Sally was usually so fair and unemotional, like a sturdy little boy, who has never found other little boys whom he couldn't stand up to. It wasn't like Sally to tremble and plunge and look forlorn.

Even now Sally pulled herself quickly together. She returned to her cold tea and drank it bravely, before pouring them both out fresh cups.

"I'm a perfect fool, I know!" she said, rubbing the back of her hand across her eyes. "But I talked all night with Alec, trying to persuade him to stay on. I seemed to see he ought to then; and when I'd got him to promise that perhaps he might try—well, then I began to wonder if he had better not! You know the feeling. It's like hockey rather—in a match—when you're captain of your side—and you see a girl's nervous, had you better force her to make a try, when she thinks she can't? Sometimes, of course, it just puts it through—and sometimes—she makes a mess of it! You can force yourself, of course—that's different. But if Alec stayed on, and had a bad flare-up, wouldn't that be worse for his career?"

Jane hesitated. There was something in what Sally said. Angry men make occasions for flaring up. But on the other hand, Sally didn't know Dr. Drummond. Jane felt pretty sure that Charles Drummond wouldn't take any notice of Alec's temper, if he did flare up.

If he could help it—and Jane thought that Charles would be able to help it—he wouldn't let Alec flare up.

She couldn't quite explain to Sally that you could trust Charles. He might be a great many things you didn't like —even personally impossible—but if he meant to be nice to a person, he wouldn't give him a chance to let himself down, whatever he said to make it hard for him.

"One hasn't," Jane agreed at last, "any right to force anyone else—ever. I am quite sure you are right about that, Sally, but I think if one is a wife, one must take a share in a decision that concerns you both. After all, his career is your life, as well as his, now. He can't act as if he hadn't got a wife. Besides, I don't think Alec will flare up. He can control himself, and he's far too big a man to throw himself and his career away—out of pique."

Jane saw that Sally didn't like this. She rather wished she hadn't answered for Alec's strength. Only she knew he had it! He was a hot-tempered enthusiast with a manic drive. He went at everything, hell for leather, and left his judgment unprotected, for the Devil to snatch at; but he was no weakling and should be allowed to use what sense he'd got.

Jane had often noticed that wives—perhaps because of the intensity of their affections—were apt to distrust their mates. It was as if they thought that to exaggerate danger was a proof of their own devotion; but it is the spoilt child who throws away his toy instead of mending it, and Sally was trying to help Alec to be a spoilt child.

Jane, however, put none of these thoughts into words. She merely stroked the head that was close to her knee.

"People do live quite comfortably," Sally began again, "in old railway carriages. We have all that new furniture, and I can cook better than I did, Jane, can't I? Money isn't everything, is it?"

"Dear me, no!" Jane agreed. "It's getting to be less and less, thank God! But one's job is rather a lot."

She wouldn't say any more, even if she could. Sally was only a child. The railway carriage idea was like the gingerbread house which had so tempted Hansel and Gretel —till they found the witch inside! You couldn't get over it—gingerbread houses always held witches! But Jane told herself that it was Hansel and Gretel's business to deal with the witch.

Sally sat for a long time in silence, then she said in that flattened tone which was so unlike her usual thrilled eagerness:

"But I mustn't just think of him as a lover, must I? You know he is a very good lover! More of one all the time! Only—when you're a girl it's different. Alec always says it isn't—but, Jane, it is! He's all I've got—and he's got the hospital as well as me."

"And," said Jane briskly, "before you know where you are you'll have a baby as well as him!—and he'll be jealous of that! It's a mistake for us to suppose we aren't all jealous of something or other, the moment we get a chance to be. Look at me, for instance. I dare say I'm jealous of both of you, because you're in love and I'm not!"

Sally laughed for the first time. It was nearly her usual laugh.

"Have you never been in love, Jane?" she demanded.

"Not even a little passion like a schoolgirl—or a dance flirt? After all, you do dance beautifully, you know—and it's rather unnatural not to want to flirt, let alone not to want to fall in love!"

Jane got up and stood by the open window.

The patients were out in their own garden, as they ought to be, enjoying the sun, though they never seemed to mind the cold either, she reflected. Normal people mind cold. Was it a little abnormal, then, that she didn't?

"I was in love—once," Jane said, without turning round. "My lover was shot for cowardice in the War. I was nineteen and he was twenty. There was an attack and he ran away. They'd have let him off if he hadn't taken the platoon with him. My brother was his Colonel. I haven't been in love since then."

"Oh, Jane——!" Sally said in an awed voice.

Jane laughed. "It doesn't hurt now," she said cheerfully. "It was twelve years ago. And it made a psychiatrist out of me. That's a thing to be thankful for. I had an idea even then that it wasn't just his fault—as people like to say of a nervous breakdown, and now I'm sure of it It was worth finding out."

"Does Alec know?" Sally asked hardly above a whisper Jane shook her head.

"I don't happen to have told anyone," she explained "To tell the truth, I hardly ever think about it now. I just somehow or other popped back into my head to-day We used to hunt together as children. It was what peopl called 'a boy-and-girl affair,' but they can go quite deep Of course you can tell Alec if you like."

"No," said Sally feverishly, "I shan't, Jane! I shan' ever tell anybody! But I'm awfully, awfully glad you'v told me!"

Jane felt surprised at this, but she hadn't any time t find out why Sally should be particularly glad to hea

her ancient gossip, because they both heard Alec's precip-
itate footsteps.

He banged into the room in a fearful temper, and Sally
ran to him and clutched his hand.

It took a long time to get him settled. He had to swear
at Charles, and be petted and made much of by Sally.

At last Sally got him into a chair, and perching herself on the arm of it, ran her fingers through his straight
stubbly hair, and soothed him into the comparative calm-
ness of a cigarette. She lit it for him, and another for
herself, and they sat in a blue haze together with a bough
of scarlet maple leaves behind them. It warmed Jane's
heart to look at them.

"Jane, you're a damned fool," Alec said in his usual
voice. "Of course I'm not going to let you work under me!
Why on earth should you? Just to give that filthy fellow
the chance to crow over a woman! We'll exchange sides,
that's what we'll do. I can't think why I never thought
about it before. It's no use your shaking what head you've
got left! I dare say you had a bad time standing up to
him, but you'll have a worse if you try to stand up to
me. You should have seen his face when I told him that
we'd swop, and that you'd neither knuckle under, nor resign. I mean, of course, if I did decide, which I haven't
definitely yet, to stay on! If I don't—you're to get the
women's side anyhow. I saw to that. I never saw a man
give a wryer smile, when he'd agreed to it! It was worth
not having chucked my job—to see how sold I could
make him feel!"

Jane slipped her hands into her pockets and strolled
back into the room.

She had a curious amused feeling—had Charles's smile
been wry? No doubt he distrusted women, but she had an
idea that he didn't want to send her away.

She took a cigarette from the table, and considered

Alec between the puffs. It was going to be a nuisance, dealing with Alec. He had his generosity pointed like a weapon against her heart.

Would it work, this arrangement, if she accepted it? Had Sally been right, and would anything Alec did from now on—at the hospital under Charles—work?

"Don't you think," Jane asked austerely, "that you might refer this matter to your wife? I never saw such a determined sun-treader of a husband! You ought to shake him out of his stride, Sally! And kindly remember that I'm not your wife! You certainly won't get me to agree to such an absurd piece of conjuring. It's going to be a little too much to bear, if both you and the new Superintendent think that women haven't got minds, and that you must make mine up for me! Why shouldn't I work under you again? I've worked under you before, without any bones being broken."

"You needn't make a blasted doormat of yourself, Jane, even if you are a woman," Alec reminded her. "She's trying to do the dirty on me, Sally, by making a bloody sacrifice of herself! You know what I felt about your giving me your share of the cream on our honeymoon! It's enough to cause a divorce—a put-up job like that! Now here's Jane trying to pour her cream all over me as well! You haven't the excuse of a bridal passion either, Jane, so put that in your pipe and smoke it!"

Jane leaned back in her chair and smiled.

"What all this amounts to, Sally," she said, "when you strip it clear of agreeable rhetoric, is that I prefer that Alec, who is my senior by two years, should remain my senior. What he is suggesting is that I should climb over his head on the mere fact that I'm a woman. I hardly know which treatment is the more humiliating, to be ordered by the new Superintendent to give up the male side because of my sex, or to be ordered by Alec to take what is con sidered to be the senior M.O.'s job, also because of my sex. Really, on the whole, I think I prefer Dr. Drummond's frank contempt to Alec's crooked chivalry. But it appears to me that both these gentlemen are a little out of date. I don't know what you think about it, Sally."

Sally pressed her curls against Alec's head. She took for granted, Jane saw, that only Alec could really be a judge of anything—except perhaps himself.

"What is Jane to do?" she murmured into his ear.

"Her plain duty," said Alec with decision. "What she's trying to do now is to get round me by pretending that I'm being unfair to her. I dare say she tried the same trick first on that manikin upstairs with more success! I won't have you work with me, Jane! I told him so just now. I said, 'I may resign anyhow, but unless Jane gets the women's side, with the option of my taking the men's, I'll resign on the spot!' "

"I hope you didn't say 'Jane,' " Jane said, frowning; "it sounds so undignified. What did Dr. Drummond answer?"

"Of course I didn't say 'Jane' to him," Alec replied hotly, "I said 'my colleague Dr. Everest,' as stiff as any poker; and he said: 'I hope very much that you won't resign. Perhaps you will have the kindness to discuss the other solution with her—and let me have both your decisions to-morrow.' "

Alec mimicked Charles's manner to perfection, which ought to have amused Jane very much. It did amuse Sally. Then he said, "Ugh! the filthy fellow!" and that didn't amuse Jane very much either.

"Resigning is a retreat," Jane said coldly. "I hope none of us are going to be driven into it. If you persist in your suggestion, Alec, I may be driven! I am almost certain of a senior job in another hospital, since, if I resign, it will be because the Superintendent dislikes women doctors.

This is a creditable reason for a change, and Luke, who has a good deal of influence, could work it for me. If we exchange sides, you deliberately sink your prestige. You cannot expect me to put up with that. Nor, in the long run, do I think you and Sally would like your having done it!"

Sally suddenly, and most surprisingly, said: "Oh, nonsense, Jane! This is just your pride, and hasn't any sense in it. You've often told me that both sides were really equal, and quite independent. We aren't children, to mind who comes first. If you want Alec to settle down and be happy, take what he's got for you. That'll help him more than anything not to resign. And if Jane will take it, you'll not resign—isn't that good enough, Alec?"

"Bless the girl!" said Alec admiringly, "I'm damned if she hasn't got us both in a cleft stick! Come on, Jane, shake hands on it. I'm game if you are—and we'll drink to the sudden death of the new Superintendent. Get out what I left of the whisky last night!"

Jane got it out, and gave Alec a drink, but she didn't take any herself. She didn't want the new Superintendent to die, and she felt strangely dissatisfied with having to let Sally decide for them all. She saw the sense of Sally's decision. She saw that it had been her own pride which was sticking in her throat. Alec would feel better about settling down under the new Superintendent now that the *beau geste* had been his, but she herself—was she going to mind because she had to take—instead of to give? Was she to hanker after a *beau geste* as if life were a game in which you had to win moral approbation as a prize? And what would Charles think of her? Would he know that she had done this to save Alec from resigning, or would he think that Jane had given up the rights of a generous friend to come off best herself?

CHAPTER V

JANE put out the light and laid her head down on the pillow; but she suspected that this sane ritual would not be of much use to her.

She was ferociously awake. First the hospital and its duties rose up before her. She could deal easily with them —what problems she hadn't solved to-day could be solved to-morrow; or they must be left to destiny helped out by common-sense.

The fluttered curiosities of the staff were less easy to dismiss. They beat again and again against her tired brain. The Matron's studied rudeness, the simpering disloyalty of the two deputies, who took the attitude of being pleased at the new appointment and not pleased at the same time!—All that housemaid's drivel about Charles's looks—they had known better than to let it out to Jane, but she had seen it in their excited eyes!

Her heart hammered sullenly on. Alec and Sally rose up before her, reconstructing their destinies and her own. There was that little episode of Sally's arranging the flowers; and minding! How careful Jane would have to be, if Sally was going to start minding; and how wholly careless Alec would always be, whether Sally minded or not! A brilliant psychiatrist in his career, and a bull in a china shop where his own heart was concerned! Then all the figures got mixed up together, without Jane's being in the least more sleepy.

She found herself looking into the pit of living.

Thirty-one years stretched before Jane's eyes, turning in the dark, like falling snowflakes, without direction or purpose, towards oblivion.

Only her childhood continued to stand out as clear as day; like part of a landscape left out of a storm.

There was her father, who had the gifts and habits of his class, and their completely hidden, almost subsidiary, life of the soul. He was a man of indomitable physical courage, which all his children shared. It would have been inconceivable to any of them to funk anything.

He killed rabbits remarkably well, Jane remembered; and had taught her how to do the same. Still that wasn't what had made her want to be a doctor. The life of her mind had come later. It was her mother who had decided that Jane should have a profession like her brothers. No one in the family had agreed with her; but as her mother had a small private income, she had carried out her new-fangled notion, and Jane had been trained for the career of her passionate choice. She had been able to feel almost like her brothers. She could ride, hunt, climb, fence, swim, as well as they could; but she had not been allowed to die with them.

The youngest was three years older than Jane. He had been killed that first winter at Festubert. The second had been trapped and drowned in a submarine. Bertram, the eldest, the core of Jane's young heart, had been blown off the hard surface of the earth. Her parents had not long survived his death. After a year or two of broken life they too vanished. Their place went to a distant cousin, who had cut down their Gothic beeches, drained the small lake and started a market garden on the silvery smooth green lawns. Jane hadn't had to go back there; and she very seldom thought of it, except if she saw foxgloves standing out of a hedge!

There was nothing to make a fuss about. She was young and strong, and better off than most people whose House of Being had been overturned by the same hurricane. Her mother's sister had been good to her; and she had four hundred a year of her own.

She went on working at the hospital where she had started training. She had made up her mind that the only way of keeping Bertram alive was to do what he would have expected of her. Her feeling for her eldest brother had never been a complete subjugation, but it had come perilously near it. If he thought Jane in the wrong, there was no reprieve; if he thought her in the right, there was nothing left which could daunt her! About Bertram Jane might be said never to think at all. You did not think of breathing.

To-night his image stood clear before her eyes, although he would not speak!

Jane wanted him to tell her how she was going to stand by her friend Alec, and help him to keep impersonally true to his work, if her own heart played truant and left impersonal truth behind it. She wanted Bertram to tell her what she must think of Charles, who had her dead lover's face.

The darkness grew as hideous to Jane as a grave.

"I've been in love once!" she said fiercely into the pillow. "Ah, God—not again!"

The images and even her thoughts left her. She found herself once more alone with her dead lover.

He must be shot at dawn—shot for running away!

She had known nothing of it till it was all over. Space and time had run through her heart implacably, without a hint of warning! She had waked up to find him gone.

She had learned not to mind his running away; but what she minded still was that she couldn't explain to him why she didn't mind it, and with his head against her breast, free him from his bewildered shame, into a death fit for their shared pride!

Bertram had trusted her enough to send her Michael's last letter.

He had known that she had a right to it, and that not to have had what Michael thought in her own mind, as well as in Michael's dying mind, would have driven her mad.

Jane knew the letter, as people say, by heart. Sometimes in desperate emergencies—during critical operations or at lonely death-beds—the words ran clear as if she were reading them off a tape.

"This is the best thing that could happen to me now. I'm glad—and not glad of it! I can't want to see your eyes again; but I can't want to die without having kissed you! That's silly, because the whole thing's silly! I don't know why I ran away. I'd been in tighter places and hadn't! The other fellows said not to tell you—they'd all say I died awfully well, and all that; but Bertram said, 'Tell her the truth—she's worth it.' So I'm trying to—only there isn't any. They got Martin—and then the trench crumpled up—and we ran. I was in command, and I think I kept saying we mustn't. It was like being driven back by a wind. Bertram's been awfully decent to me. I won't tell my people. You'll do what you think best about that—and about everything. Knowing that's something! I can't believe you'll always be ashamed of me. Do you remember——"

He'd stopped there. Perhaps it was the Dawn which had stopped him. Perhaps he had thought he oughtn't to ask her to remember. Perhaps he knew that she would always remember everything.

Jane buried her head deeper into her pillow, to make the darkness swallow his young beauty; and then, instead of Michael's face, she saw Charles's sterner, older face.

Charles must have been through a few months of the War himself. He had in his steady eyes the look of a man who has lost all his securities, except one. Charles couldn't have run away.

CHAPTER VI

WHEN Jane woke, after a short uneasy night, she had an instinctive feeling that something horrible was going to take place. Her first conscious thought was the challenge of Charles's faintly disgusted eyes. Then she remembered Alec's anger. She couldn't do anything about either Charles's eyes or Alec's anger. She would have to put up with both of them, and neutralise their activities by being as pleasantly passive as if she hadn't noticed them.

She was late getting down to breakfast. Dr. Barnes and Dr. Harding, the two junior medical officers, were already at the breakfast table. This deepened Jane's sense of discouragement. She liked to get down early and have her breakfast alone.

Neither of the two men rose when Jane entered the room. Both growled into teacups.

Dr. Barnes's growl was one of affection. He had a dumb tenderness for Jane, and Jane, if she had to have tenderness from men at all, liked it to be dumb; but this morning even Dr. Barnes's solicitous silence annoyed her. She didn't want to hear him speak, and she greatly resented his looking tenderly at the butter.

Dr. Harding's growl annoyed Jane even more, because she saw that he meant to be nasty. He was a vain young man, with a great many cheap attractions; and he couldn't understand a woman who didn't notice them, or, if she were forced to notice them, was not attracted.

He had offered with alacrity to serve under Jane, knowing that he could get the better of most women, only to discover that Jane was impossible to bluff and dangerous to defy. If as much as a hair went wrong, or an order miscarried, Jane had to know why, and Dr. Harding had had to tell her why. Every nerve of his masculine vanity had been stung by his three months' enforced subordination. He couldn't look at Jane without wanting to hit her.

Dr. Barnes had shrunk from working under a woman at all, but when his turn came, he had found that whatever differences there were took the form of improvements. Jane subtilely heartened his diffidence. She recognised his conscientious efforts, and helped him to make light of his blunders. Dr. Barnes wanted to die for Jane, even at the breakfast table.

Being hindered from presenting her with this ultimate proof of his ardour, he had kept her toast warm by clapping it between the folds of his napkin.

"Thank you, I never eat toast," Jane said acidly, and opened her newspaper.

Dr. Barnes, like an ingratiating dog trembling with eagerness to be noticed, flung his favourite bone at her feet. He told her the result of the Test Match between England and Australia. Jane made a faint sound that might have passed for acknowledgment. She had never felt less interest in how her fellow-countrymen played cricket.

Dr. Harding said airily: "Well—! I don't know if you two have made up your minds yet about the new Superintendent, but personally—I don't mind saying that I have no use for him whatever!"

Jane's eyes flickered dangerously over the folds of her newspaper.

"One wonders," she remarked icily, "if the question shouldn't rather be, what use has the new Superintendent for you!"

Appalled at this sudden descent into acrimonious personalities, she wished that she had bitten her tongue out rather than spoken. Never before had she given Dr.

Harding such an opening. His small moustache bristled
with eagerness to take it. He shot an impudent glance at
Jane.

"I hear the new man isn't any too fond of women colleagues," he said insolently; "that will be a change for
some of us! Macgregor will have to mind his *p*'s and *q*'s,
and not expect to have his chestnuts pulled out of the fire
for him!"

"Macgregor's grand!" Dr. Barnes sharply—far too
sharply—intervened. "He may be a little on the unconventional side, but we'd all have been proud to work under
him. Wouldn't we, Dr. Everest?"

Jane had to say "Yes," but she said it as if she were
parting with a tough piece of meat which she found it
hard to swallow.

"Well—we wanted fresh blood," Dr. Harding said with
a derisive grin, "or I did, anyhow. I know you two always
went hand-in-glove with him, but I'm bound to say I'd
rather have even Macgregor than this fellow! He looks as
if all he had in his veins was a little iced tea!"

Jane, with a valiant effort, recovered her passivity. She
looked as if she thought it didn't matter what either of
the two young men thought about anything. She poured
herself out a cup of coffee, drank it, and got up to leave
the room.

"You've eaten no breakfast!" Dr. Barnes pathetically
whimpered.

Jane let him whimper, and, opening the door, which
neither of them had dreamed of opening for her, left the
room. She wondered, as she slipped out into the corridor
why she should notice a lack of manners, for the first time
for years.

Halfway to the hospital Jane was brought up short by
the solid form of the Matron, barring her way.

"Good-morning, Doctor!" said the Matron, drawing a deep breath as if to say that there was going to be a good deal more to it than that. "Well—I suppose you've already seen the new Superintendent? He's young—and of course one isn't used to them like that! I should say myself that he'd make no impression on the patients whatever, except the bad females, and they'd better be kept in the background, for a bad girl is a bad girl, call her mental or call her moral, and they always break out at the same spot! Although I dare say it's not my business to remind you of it! Dr. Drummond won't have Dr. Macgregor's way with the staff, that's quite certain! But he doesn't look like one that will have favourites, which is always something! I hear he thinks women doctors quite a mistake, but I dare say you're used to that by now, and don't mind it! You had your interview with him yesterday, I take it; and poor Dr. Macgregor too! But it's no use quarrelling with your bread and butter, is it? I did hear that you might be going to leave us! But then! I never pay any attention to second-hand reports!"

The Matron paused. Jane's cool grey eyes met hers, and rested upon her speculatively, as if the Matron were a train which she didn't have to catch.

"I think that very wise," she said with a faint lift of her arched eyebrows.

The Matron, defrauded of her deepest hope, fell back swiftly on her second line of attack.

"Dr. Drummond," she went on brusquely, "is what I call a dark horse. He may turn out to be a blessing in disguise, if you know what I mean; or then again we may find him one of those you can't do anything with!"

Jane guessed that the Matron had never seen anyone quite like Charles. She always got on with men whom she could either bully or flatter. No doubt she had tried flat-

tery upon Charles; but she hadn't been able to find out
if he were vulnerable or not.

Because Charles's manner was cold, the Matron would
have thought him shy. You had, Jane thought, to be a
trifle like Charles yourself, to realise how deeply he could
evade the remotest human contact with a woman like the
Matron, far too deeply for her to realise that he was
evading it.

As the Matron once more paused to lure her adversary
out into the open, Jane looked at her watch.

"How fortunate it is for us both," she said, "that the
question of how the new Superintendent will turn out is
none of our business!"

Before the Matron had time to gather her forces together to reply, Jane slipped past her; but she was not
elated by her verbal victory. It was the second time that
morning she had found herself saying something which
she had no intention of saying!

It was a curiously sordid and ignoble day. The patients
were more than usually fractious. The nurses showed no
tact. Everyone felt on edge, aware of changes which
might affect them, and of futures which might be curtailed. Jane had to run the gantlet of continuous curiosity, sometimes veiled and sometimes unveiled. Even her
work went less well than usual. The Arab obviously meant
to die without affording a medical excuse for it.

"One really doesn't want a death just now!" the ward
sister complained to Jane with deep self-pity. "It doesn't
look any too well to a new Superintendent, to have patients dying the moment he arrives! I always have said
that black men are the most inconsiderate of all our
patients!"

Just as Jane had finished with the wards and was about
to make her morning reports to the new Superintendent

a new male patient arrived and refused to enter the hospital.

Jane loathed putting pressure upon an adverse will; but since the men's side was not yet taken away from her, there was no evading her responsibility. Getting a fractious new male patient in was just the kind of thing that Charles would expect a man to do better than a woman! Charles's office overlooked the drive, and it was more than a possibility that Jane would have his critical eyes upon her efforts.

From a big stationary car in front of the main entrance an arm waved frantically.

Jane ran down the steps towards the car.

"I don't want—! I don't want to go in!" a distracted voice protested.

It was a dull grey morning; dry leaves hissed and rattled over the gravel drive. The big stone hospital stood, massive and forbidding, under a lowering sky.

Jane laid her hand upon the window of the car.

"It's nearly lunch time," she said in a friendly voice. "Won't you get out of the car by yourself—and see what it's like?"

She motioned to the attendants to leave the patient alone.

She would not add to the agony of the young man's resistance by hurrying him, or even by noticing that he had any resistance. Her manner was that of a diffident hostess welcoming an honoured guest.

The wind ruffled her soft, nut-coloured hair and long white linen coat.

The two attendants in the car watched her uneasily. Maclean stood behind the open door, in case of trouble; but Jane did not anticipate trouble, and she had forgotten Charles. Her whole mind was concentrated now on serving this distraught, unhappy boy, with his fixed grudge against life.

For a moment or two the big hulking young man looked as if he meant to go on fighting; but finding no direct challenge to his strength, he got out instead, and looked confusedly about him.

Jane's mind ran over the points of the case, which she had just received by telephone. The young man was in an acute stage of dementia præcox. He was the badly pampered only child of a widowed mother. During his mother's lifetime he had spent her savings, refused to work and snatched or stolen his pleasures. When his mother died, no one cared about him any more. He came to an end of her money; and after a brief struggle and a short term of imprisonment, he had found the world too uninviting a place, and gone out of his mind altogether.

Poor little mouse, brought up in a trap stocked with cheese, no wonder he turned fierce, now that there was nothing for his teeth to meet on but the bars!

The young man made a threatening movement toward Jane. "Isn't this a mad-house?" he demanded furiously "I won't go inside! I tell you I won't! They shan't make me!"

Her eyes smiled at him without pressure.

"No one shall make you," she said gently. "No one can if you will come with me of your own free will. This is hospital, and you are not well. We will do our best help you to get better, and as soon as you are well enoug you can go wherever you like!"

The cold wind slapped at them, a dash of rain spatter big drops over Jane's hair. She took no notice; but s felt how cold, how wasteful, and how lonely life itself w for this trapped and desperate boy! She showed him pity, but the quiet friendliness of her manner relieved t worst of his tension.

"They won't touch me!" he muttered. "You won't let any of them touch me!"

She saw that he wanted to be reassured that at least his physical manhood was his own.

"If you will come with me, no one shall touch you," Jane said firmly.

Once more he looked about him, with stunned, bewildered eyes. In his face was such a sick distaste for life that had there been any means handy to end it, he might have taken them. He looked at the world about him as if he were saying good-bye to an enemy; then he followed Jane slowly and suspiciously into the hall of the hospital.

This, too, his haunted eyes seemed to say, might contain an enemy! But Jane herself was too neutral to rouse his hostile fears.

He went with her, through the hospital and into the ward for new admissions as a leaf follows the path of an invisible wind.

CHAPTER VII

When Jane entered the Superintendent's office, Charles stood with his back to her, looking out of the window which overhung the drive.

Alec sat glowering over the reports spread out on the table.

"You're late!" he said grudgingly.

"I'm sorry," Jane explained breathlessly. "I had to receive a new patient."

Charles turned round.

"Did you get the fellow in all right?" he asked her in a manner that was nearly human.

Jane nodded.

She sat down opposite Alec and wanted to smile at him, but finding Charles's eyes on them, she suppressed her friendliness.

"Dr. Drummond knows our decision," Alec announced truculently.

Jane wished that Alec hadn't said "our decision." There had been two decisions. One was Alec's and one was hers. They should have been kept separate.

Charles murmured politely, "The hospital is to be congratulated on retaining both your services."

Alec snorted. He hated politeness, and if there was one form of politeness which he hated more than another, it was impersonal politeness. The blood beat in Jane's ears. She looked down at her report and waited.

There was a long, torturing silence. Charles broke it at last by saying, "May I have your report, Dr. Everest?"

It was, of course, what they were there for, but it was hard for them not to remember how different it used to be with old Luke twinkling away at them, Alec dramatically leading a conversation full of pungent phrases and acute observations, while Jane, amused and at her ease, watched the work expand before them without the slightest fear of a personal hitch.

Charles sat behind the shelter of his desk, erect and formal. His face was quite expressionless, and he seemed to have discovered a way of being there, and not there, at the same time. Still Jane had a suspicion that the new Superintendent was the most nervous of the three.

She started reading her report, uneasily conscious that there were things she might have put better. She disliked the sound of her own voice and was startled at the difficulty she found in reading her own handwriting. She felt as if nothing would ever be comfortable again. Still it did not matter, Jane told herself, comfort and ease were not what they were there for.

Charles did not interrupt her by a single remark. When Jane had finished, he asked her a few questions, to which she had only to reply, "Yes, sir," or "No, sir." She felt as if by some mysterious sleight-of-hand, she and Alec had been changed overnight from high officials full of responsibility and dignity into the helpless insignificance of infancy. It was not wholly Charles's fault, in spite of his grand manner; it must have been rather hard for him to feel so irretrievably unwelcome.

He did not look at Jane, even whilst he was questioning her on her report, but perhaps he might have liked to be more human, if Alec had not sat, clenched to the table, determined to let nothing out of himself except antagonism.

When both their reports were over and had received Charles's comments, he opened what perhaps he had meant for a discussion on the patients' diet. He was evidently deeply interested in bio-chemistry and relied on it as one of the curative agents in mental diseases. Vitamin B was a point, Jane thought, that they might all have agreed upon. As Alec would not say anything at all, Jane felt that it would have been an act of disloyalty on her part to say very much. Still she went so far as to murmur a faint agreement. She did think it a good idea to improve the quality of the patients' food while limiting its quantity. Overloading the body could hardly be a short cut to improving the mind.

"What do you think Dr. Macgregor?" Charles insisted.

Jane feared the look of reckless mischief which sprang into Alec's hot brown eyes. "Well," he said grimly, "if you ask me, I have always noticed that gelded cats, not having any pleasure except their stomachs, eat enormously, and, as mindless people are more or less on the same basis, I should not grudge them fairly hefty meals. In my opinion most of the patients have no palates. The senses are always less acute when the nervous system is deranged. Of course they get constipated, but how much of that is due to bulk and starch, and how much is a protest against control, I have never made up my mind. Grodeck considers constipation is entirely due to habits of parsimony, and there may be something in it! Patients, after all, don't have much they can have their own way about, so it is not at all surprising if they want to hold on to their own insides!"

Jane could have shaken Alec. She saw that he was being fantastic, and off the point, entirely to annoy Charles; but he was also letting down the seriousness of their profession. This was not the time—in the middle of a hard morning's work—to air fanciful theories from Vienna. She glanced at Charles's face, but there was nothing to be gathered from his mask of cold, indifferent courtesy.

When Alec had finished speaking and switched his chair back towards the table, in a way which might easily have broken one of its legs, Charles said quietly: "One cannot, I think, be sure how far nervous derangement goes. All sorts of trifling differences may act as signals to the submerged consciousness. Pleasure should be the foremost and is the most helpful of these signals, and food is usually considered the most elemental form of pleasure. I have found it useful to experiment on these lines and by lightening, and varying, diet, I have observed that satisfactory physical results follow." Charles spoke to Alec, with an air of mingled diffidence and determination, which Jane rather liked. It was obvious that he meant neither to impose on Alec nor to ignore him; and still less did he propose to be cowed by Alec's smothered truculence.

Nothing more was said about food. Charles changed the subject to exercise and occupational therapy. These were Alec's favourite hobbies, the finest work in the hospital, on these lines, had been his own creation. But he was not going to share any of his enthusiasm with Charles. He remained obstinately silent. Alec's expression said that Charles could find out for himself. He would answer questions if they were forced upon him, but he would initiate nothing. Jane found herself obliged to speak for both of them. She told Charles what had been done and what they still hoped to do. Even the most non-social of their patients had some form of occupation to break into the perpetual weariness of their self-torment. Destructive patients could tear up rags to make paper, and the more co-operative could find in the workrooms, and on the farm, an outlet for their greater energy. Charles listened, and approved, and suggested. He actually said things which Jane and Alec had said to each other, but Alec never changed his expression of forbidding isolation.

He sat with his chair slightly hitched away from Charles, his head flung back, with an expression like an animal's that has just been slapped in the face.

Charles, after a glance or two at him, rather naturally addressed the brunt of his conversation to Jane. She met his remarks, as well as she could, torn between the desire to help him feel at home in his new surroundings and an equal desire not to let Alec feel more out of it than she could help.

Charles's voice grew more strained as he went on under the challenge of Alec's inimical silence. Obviously he had made up his mind what to say upon the chief aspects of their work and meant to go through with it. But it was equally obvious to Jane that to have to force his opinions upon unwilling hearers was torture to him.

Jane longed to show him greater co-operation and friendliness, but she did not dare. Alec's silence was odious, but to risk another of his derisive explosions would be still worse.

At last Charles's voice dragged itself to an end. A long and petrifying silence took its place. A little sunshine in the room, Jane thought, would have been some help, but it was raining as if it meant never to do anything else but rain.

Charles pulled himself together for one more effort. "Perhaps," he said politely, "you could make your change over next week? Would Monday be convenient to you?"

Alec spoke at last. He said sullenly: "One time is just about as convenient to me as another. I will change to-morrow if it suits Everest."

Alec never took administrative details with sufficient seriousness, but he need not have advertised this to Charles on the first possible occasion! They could not possibly make so instantaneous a change. Jane said hurriedly, "A week would be better, I think." Charles nodded. She rose; Alec rose; Charles stood up, behind his desk, and looked at them with a dignified but baffled helplessness which Jane found touching.

He wanted to be nice to them; indeed, as far as facts went, he had been nice to them; but he did not know how to make his niceness palatable.

You could not, as Jane knew from experience, be friendly if you were shy, unless someone else was so friendly that you forgot you had to be, and just enjoyed yourself.

It was Alec who could have warmed the atmosphere into instant comfort if he had wished to do so. Instead of which he had deliberately forced it below zero.

Charles's hands, not quite hidden from Jane by the angle of the desk, clenched and unclenched themselves.

"I hope——" he said stiffly, and stopped short. Jane smiled encouragingly at him, and then, remembering suddenly that she was a woman, and that Charles probably disliked encouraging women, ceased to smile.

Alec made an impatient movement, as if he were going to dash out of the room in front of her, but decided upon something still more tiresome, and, flinging open the door, shepherded Jane out of it, as if he were protecting her from assault.

Jane could not prevent it, she had to leave the room, while Charles, with half of his kind sentence congealed into silence, was still struggling to finish it.

Alec shut the door loudly behind them both, and burst into a flood of decorative profanity.

Jane did not wait for him to finish. She cut through one of the most gorgeous of his phrases. "You simply make bad—worse!" she told him angrily, and fled down the passage to her work.

In and out of a flurry of new emergencies and decisions, Jane found herself wondering what it was that Charles had hoped; and wishing that she could have helped him to produce it.

CHAPTER VIII

ALL the men on the verandah were asleep, except the case which Jane was watching.

Sleep had called off the pitiless sentry of their consciousness, and for a few hours at least their unquiet minds were at rest.

The air was still and keen. The stars glittered like frozen splinters from the sinking moon.

The garden Jane looked into seemed filled with a deep design of tranquillity.

The new patient talked to himself in a low, rapid voice. It was a never-ending, rambling attempt to justify himself against the normal world. From time to time there flashed out from his confused mutterings some signpost on the road his soul had taken; and Jane jotted it down, for Alec's future guidance.

Every now and then she could hear Dawson, the male nurse, moving to and fro on a night errand. Sometimes a sleeper would throw up an arm, or shout out suddenly, caught in the grip of some pursuing dream; but for the most part there was an unbroken silence over the whole hospital.

The young man Jane was watching lay there before her eyes, helpless and savage. His splendid frame was unused; his mind in utter revolt against the laws of his being; his heart empty.

Nobody else was punishing him: the judge he could not escape was at the root of his own being. There was no love in him for anyone else; no sane activity; no human fellowship! And because of the lack of these things, he was now hounding himself out of the possession of all his faculties. They could not function in the wilderness he had made.

His delirious monotone checked itself suddenly. He raised himself on an elbow, looked round him uneasily, and fixed his eyes on Jane. "Who are you?" he demanded truculently. "You let me in here, didn't you? I'll do you in for that!"

"What is the matter?" Jane asked gently; "aren't you comfortable here?"

"Ah—comfortable!" he said gloomily. "A fat lot anyone cares whether I'm comfortable or not!" Self-pity swept over him in a softening flood. The sense of injury was so perversely sweet to him that his anger lessened.

He turned his fierce, disappointed eyes away from Jane, and sank back into dramatic recitative. In it he ruled everyone. He came out triumphant. He had what he wanted.

Jane listened with a faint smile to the interminable hymn of his self-praise.

She knew where his pitiful delusion of heroism came from; and the depths of fear which it was there to support. Since this poor life-belt, to which he clung so desperately, had failed him, how was she to substitute for it, in mid-ocean, that simpler lesson of learning how to swim?

Fear is like an insect that lives on dirt. If you cleaned out your soul there was nothing for it to feed on. The man in front of her had supplied his soul with more and more dirt for fear to feed on. Now, filled with irritation and distress, he was trying to work his anger off on outside objects. Jane had a curious feeling that somewhere lately she had been watching a similar struggle in a saner mind nearer her own. She was used to these sudden juxtapositions of consciousness, to finding here and there among the patients one whose conflicts resembled her own,

or Alec's. It was Alec who had first pointed these likenesses
out to her. "I have the manic-drive," he had told her, "and
you the schizophrenic's sly retreats." Was the man before
her a caricature of Alec? Alec, submerged and shorn of
all the glory of his brilliant intellect? Was this fear Alec's
—and this desire to triumph, in order to compensate himself for fear? How could she get Alec to see that both
were false? In this new situation between himself and
Charles there was no real ground for rivalry. The hospital
was large enough for all of them. Each doctor had his individual duties, and each one the satisfaction of his work.
Even if Charles had to be inimical to them, and to their
desires, they could avoid the painfulness of a personal attitude.

She had her own private difficulties to surmount in this
new situation. She was haunted, as Alec need never be
haunted, by Charles's cruel likeness, and unlikeness, to her
dead lover; but this, too, she could train herself to ignore.
Charles could not be expected to be nicer to her because
he looked like Michael; and as long as she reminded herself of the complete stranger he was, the treachery in her
heart would be as idle and ephemeral as a dream. "One
can check a morbid fancy," Jane told herself, "as easily
as a morbid symptom, once one has found its cause."

"I'm going to do you in!" shouted her patient truculently into the black night. No one answered him. The
other patients slept on. Perhaps she might give him a
draught, and let him too have a little sleep? She had
learned as much of his circumstances and influences as
either she or Alec would need.

Jane rose slowly to her feet and looked down at him
compassionately. Dawson came round the screen from the
back of the ward, and stood beside her.

"Do you think he's going off, Doctor?" he asked in an
anxious undertone.

Jane shook her head. "I doubt it," she said quietly; "but I think we'll give him a draught and let him have a little sleep. He finds himself pretty poor company just now. Go and get it while I stay here."

"I don't hardly like to leave you alone with him, Doctor," Dawson protested.

"It'll be all right," Jane said soothingly, though she was not sure how she knew that it was going to be all right. A strange sense of peace flowed through all her being. It was so great that, standing by the bedside of her restless patient, she was aware that he too felt it.

Dawson obeyed her unwillingly. The patient tossed to and fro, grumbling and muttering his half-hearted threats.

Jane stood motionless, looking away from him into the quiet night. The moon had sunk behind the garden wall, only the stars glittered on through the unwavering darkness.

When Dawson came back, Jane stooped over the patient and gave him the draught.

"Are you my mother?" he suddenly demanded.

Jane smiled and shook her head; but as she left the ward she had a feeling that in a sense she couldn't define, and which left her strangely bereft now that her task was over, she had been used as a mother.

Perhaps this leaving of the men's side of the hospital was not so good a thing as Charles had thought it was. Perhaps he had overlooked that the insane are children, and that back of their wild minds is the child need, to be reassured of its integrity, by that Power which should have given its own integrity to the child.

"But I shall never be able to tell him anything like that," Jane thought to herself in shocked surprise, "even if it's true."

CHAPTER IX

JANE had not remembered that it was her last day on the men's side till evening; then, as she was doing the night rounds with Sister Stanton for the last time, it flashed through her mind: "This won't happen again like this! When I come here again, I shall be only a visitor!"

"I don't think I shall turn in just yet," she said suddenly to Sister Stanton. "Go back to your office, Sister. I should like to take a final look at my Arab. He's very low to-night!"

"It's very late already, Doctor; you'll get no night at all," Sister Stanton pleaded.

Jane shook her head with a smile of dismissal. She did not want a night, she wanted a fixed and final vision of her work. It had been her first sole charge. For eighteen months the care and protection of these three hundred men had been the intense preoccupation of her life. She did not want to take leave of the men individually, except automatically in her mind. What she was taking leave of was herself—that part of her which she had used on them because they were men, and which she would not need again when her work was among women. In all Jane's dealings with the men, she had been as near sexless as a woman can be; but she knew there was no such thing as complete sexlessness. What she had given her men they could not find in Alec, and what she had taken from them she would not receive from her women patients. She thought to herself: "What is it I shall take away? What is it I shall lose?" But she found no answer.

The hospital was completely still. She barely glanced

into the long dim wards in turn; smiled at their quiet
guardians and slipped out again unseen.

At last she came to the most distant ward, where the
most uncontrolled and impulsive patients were cared for.
She unlocked the door and braced herself afresh to meet
the familiar tension of the unexpected.

The new nurse Clarkson came forward to greet her.

"Why are you on duty here alone?" Jane demanded. "I
ordered a 'special' to share night duty with you!"

"Yes, I know, Doctor, but Matron, she said it wasn't
necessary and she wasn't going to have her wards clut-
tered up with specials. I don't think it's a one-man job.
There's half-a-dozen of 'em in this ward here that seem
up to any mischief!"

"That depends upon the man in charge!" Jane said
drily. "Why are those screens round the Arab's bed?"

"The new Superintendent ordered it. He's in there with
him now," Clarkson explained. "Talking his own lingo
to the Arab, as far as I can make out, Doctor! But what
with the Black the other end, and the new boy with the fits,
I haven't much time to listen!"

Jane had told Charles about the Arab, but he had not
said that he spoke Arabic.

The Matron had had no business to give such an order
to Clarkson. It was a flagrant instance of her interfer-
ence. No doubt she was trying it on, to see what Charles
would let pass under the new régime.

The test would have had to come sooner or later. Jane
decided to accept it. She would report the Matron to
Charles; and leave the hospital if Charles did not uphold
her authority.

"You must carry on for to-night," she told Clarkson
briefly.

She moved silently forward through the dimly lit ward

between the lines of the restless sleepers, and pushed back one of the Arab's screens.

Neither of the two men heard her. Charles knelt by the Arab's bed, his fair head bent over the withered blackness of the dying Arab. Jane saw Charles's face, as if for the first time—without self-consciousness. A man may lie to others; he may lie to himself; but when he is not thinking of himself, he cannot lie.

Charles, stripped of all his defences, was worth looking at. The soul that looked out of his eyes into those dying eyes was both brave and kind.

She put down the injection she had meant to give the Arab on the night table. It was too late to bother him with it. She saw, at a glance, that the end was near. The Arab's face was covered with that blanched darkness which spreads over the face of waters at the coming of night. His cheeks had fallen in; his breath came in quick, shallow gasps. His fiery eyes burned, like pits of flame, in the clenched gravity of his face. He knew that he was dying; but the agony of his long loneliness was broken at last. He understood Charles.

Jane watched the wonder and joy rise in his eyes, and for a time hold back the pressure of death. The soft long syllables were strange to her, but they evoked, even in her heart, strange images of the desert, and of an alien world.

Charles paused for a moment; then very slowly and distinctly he gave the desert form of greeting and farewell. "Go with God!"

With a long sigh, which seemed to shake the soul out of his body, the Arab answered it, and went upon his way.

In the timeless moment that follows the extinction of life, Jane was conscious that the guarded look came back to Charles's face. The Arab, deprived of his soul, looked

inconceivably dried and empty, like the husk of a dead
locust. A shadow flickered upon the wall behind Charles's
head.

Jane wanted to slip away before Charles had time to
notice her, but something in the flickering of that shadow
fixed her attention. She turned to see what was causing it.

With a cry of warning she sprang forward and seized
the arm of the black paranoiac. The fingers that would
have been round Charles's throat fixed themselves like
talons into her shoulder. She heard Clarkson's belated cry,
"My God, Doctor—it's Jerry!" The lamp overturned;
but Charles was on his feet beside her.

She shouted for Clarkson to pinion Jerry from behind;
but she had no faith in his doing so.

She was being whipped to and fro like a piece of chaff
caught in a machine. She remembered that Jerry's trick
was strangling.

"Mind your throat!" she gasped feebly to Charles.

The only answer that came was the sudden pressure
of Jerry's thumb on her own windpipe. But the great
hand had no time to fix itself before it was flung off again.
The grip on her shoulder relaxed. She found her feet and
could have freed herself, but she hung on to the massive,
heaving arm with all her strength. The three of them
moved in long, uneven jerks, like slow motion pictures on a
screen. The scrambling, grunting, ding-dong struggle in
the dark seemed to go on for ever. Jane's ears were filled
with the sound of hoarse breathing, but through it she
listened for the even more ominous sound of the ward rising behind them.

She was not conscious of fear, but somewhere in the
back of her mind she recognised with a cold clarity that
if Clarkson did not reach the alarm bell in time, neither
she nor Charles would leave the ward alive.

It came at last, sudden shrieks and chuckles of maniac

laughter, and the quick, pattering rush of bared feet.

Close to her ear she heard the unmistakable snap of a breaking bone.

Charles cried out: "Let go! Let go, you little fool!"

But of course Jane didn't let go. Jerry, unhindered, would make short work of Charles.

The alarm bell began to ring, peal after peal. Light ran over them, a blinding, dazzling ally.

Sister Stanton's voice rose implacably above the tumult.

The ward filled rapidly with nurses and attendants. Someone pinioned Jerry's arms from behind.

Jane was free now. She was conscious of something like breath whistling through her throat again.

Charles laughed down at her. "You see," he said, with exultant, dancing eyes, "I was right! It isn't a very suitable job for women!"

Jane ignored Charles; she brushed aside a bevy of nurses who wanted to know if she wasn't hurt. She moved forward unsteadily, to tell the attendants not to be rough with Jerry. He was still shouting and struggling while he was being hauled off to where he could carry on his fight, innocuously, against padded walls. Dangerous patients had already become terrified children and were scrambling back to bed.

There was something else in Jane's mind besides Charles's laughter. She turned and looked at him. He was standing where she had left him, holding his wrist with his other hand.

"*That* was the snapped bone, then!" Jane said. "You had better come to the theatre at once and have it attended to!"

Charles followed her obediently; but he was still laughing.

Jane did not speak: for one thing, her throat still felt

stiff; and for another she thought Charles's laughter, after such a scene in the ward, was out of place.

She was exasperated by such a thing happening before the eyes of a new Superintendent in the part of the hospital of which she was in charge. It never had happened before—it never should have happened! It was inexcusable.

The theatre, empty, hot, and immaculate, was a momentary relief to her.

She gave a quick glance about her, fixed the Röntgen ray behind Charles's wrist, and clicked off the light.

There was something friendly in the spluttering, hissing darkness.

Jane could see exactly where the shadow lay over the split bone. The plate showed up his wrist beautifully.

"A simple fracture," she said with relief.

"If it had been a compound one, would you have been angrier still?" Charles rather unexpectedly murmured.

Jane made no answer; but she felt it difficult to go on being angry with a man whose bone she was setting.

Nor could she forget Charles's face, bent down to meet the dying Arab's. However angry they might both be in the future, it would be difficult not to remember that they could rely on each other.

Jane turned on the light without answering Charles; but she was conscious that the sternness had gone out of her face.

"It would never have happened," she explained a little breathlessly, "if you had not put screens round the Arab's bed. Jerry cannot bear anything to be kept from him. And of course he knew that you were the new Superintendent, and resented doubly your interest in his rival. Black patients are specially sensitive. Still, if Maclean had been on duty, he would have known how to nip the trouble in the bud. There would have been no such rising. That is the worst of using a new man alone on night duty.

I shall have to report to you that Clarkson was on duty in that ward by himself against my express orders. I had asked for a 'special.'"

"Who disregarded your orders?" Charles asked her.

Jane fastened his splint carefully before replying.

"Clarkson," she said, when she had finished to her satisfaction, "told me that the Matron had ordered him to take Maclean's place, while he was away on an emergency visit, and had refused him the assistance I had ordered. She has no such authority. Such a disturbance has never occurred before in my whole five years' experience in this hospital. Nor should it have occurred now, though no doubt it will be difficult for you to believe this."

"So far I have found no difficulty in believing what you have told me," Charles said, with a faint smile. "It is certainly not the Matron's business to set aside a doctor's orders, nor to refuse specials for your bad cases. I will see that this is put before her. I gave the order to isolate the Arab myself. He was dying—and I thought that much was due to him. I found out he was a desert Arab, and they are lonely fellows."

"I did not know you spoke Arabic," Jane said in a low voice.

"No—?" said Charles. "Well—I served for a year, when I was seventeen, in Egypt. My uncle was working under Lawrence, and got me out there. I stayed on another year and learned Arabic."

Jane said nothing further. Charles made a good patient. He stood stock-still, and in difficult moments kept his mouth shut.

Jane knew that she had made a good job of his wrist, and been no longer about it than she could help. She must have hurt him; but he would know that she had not hurt him more than she must.

"By-the-way," Charles said, rather more stiffly, while

she was making a sling, "I am aware that you saved my life to-night. I shouldn't have cared to have my breath choked out of me by that black rascal's thumb. I'm really much obliged to you."

"Oh, well," Jane said, finishing off his sling and turning away from him to tidy up the theatre, "if it comes to that, I suppose you saved mine; so you needn't be annoyed by my small share of the shindy!" She was glad to get away from that handsome, dishevelled figure leaning against the table.

"I'm not at all annoyed," Charles assured her. "I'm grateful!"

"Well, nothing could be more annoying to you than having to be grateful, could it?" Jane allowed herself to demand, with a hint of laughter.

To her surprise Charles laughed too, rather a nice amused laugh.

"We're quits, then," he admitted. "I don't know whethe you noticed that your head hit the bedpost? You migh put some iodine on it before you leave the theatre. I'r afraid I can't assist you, because of my dud wrist."

Jane glanced casually into the small theatre mirro Her coat was torn to ribbons; her hair was in wild di order; one of her temples was badly bruised, and Jerry purple thumb-mark stood out unmistakably upon h slender throat.

With a pang of horror she realised that she had nev rung for the night sister! What could Charles ha thought of her? To be guilty of such a breach of etiquett on the top of being responsible for such a catastrophe!

"I'm terribly sorry," she said humbly, "that I forg to ring for Sister! I'm afraid that I must have been mo shaken than I realised. You should have reminded me."

"Oh, well, you know, I preferred it," Charles rath surprisingly murmured.

They walked in silence out into the corridor, but when they reached the turning where Charles should have left her, to reach his quarters, Jane found that he was still walking beside her.

It was an unexpected relief to her not to have to face those long, dim corridors alone.

Charles came with her to her sitting-room.

She gave him a stiff whisky-and-soda, and to please him drank a milder one herself. He stayed a very short while, only long enough to ask her casually if she supposed Barnes and Harding had got back yet. It was three o'clock in the morning, and Jane told him there was no doubt that they had.

After Charles had gone, it suddenly occurred to Jane that he had come back with her simply to make sure that she was not alone in the quarters.

To do you a service without putting you under the obligation of noticing it was, she thought, Charles's way of being kind.

CHAPTER X

IT WOULD not have been true to suppose that Charles had no affections. He liked tortoises, and when he came to King's Norton he brought Billy, his favourite tortoise, with him. To be surrounded by a hard shell, to put your head in when approached, to snap when taken by surprise, to wear rather wrinkled baggy trousers, were all traits which endeared themselves to Charles.

Charles could be, and generally was, rigidly tidy; but he considered clothes to be a form of domestic tyranny which he could not control and did not want to be controlled by. Clothes were the kind of thing his sister Myra liked.

But on the night of his first dinner party to his colleagues, Charles had decided to dress properly. He even wore a white tie and tails, in honour of Sally's being a bride. His studs were milky black pearls, and his links matched them.

When he was dressed, he walked about his new room with more appreciation than he cared to show. He liked his new home, and his new job, and he wanted to like his new colleagues.

There were plenty of bookshelves in the room, a deep heather-coloured carpet, a divan or two, and long bare outlines of chairs made of steel bands and black webbing. These chairs did not look comfortable, but when you sat in them, you found that they exactly fitted you.

After several well-executed family rows, Myra had reluctantly effaced a cocktail bar.

The walls and ceilings were the faintest possible rose

colour seen through clouded white. If you felt imaginative you could see yourself standing on a heather-covered hill at dawn; if you felt practical, there was a large kitchen table in an alcove, where you could work in peace.

An oak-panelled slip of a room behind the studio held a long, narrow Last Supper-ish oak table, decorated with scarlet leaves, crystal and old silver.

Charles was not fond of pictures, but he put up with a Lawrence and two Raeburns which were family portraits, and let them hang above the dining-room table. The silver was polished into the white sharpness of frost. Only Myra's temper used on a plastic parlour-maid could have achieved such a triumphant result.

Looking up, Charles saw Myra standing in the doorway, watching him. Her mass of red-gold hair rose up like a wave above the beautiful outline of her forehead.

Charles was never quite sure what Myra had done to her eyes and eyebrows, but they weren't quite the same as he remembered them to have been in the nursery. Perugino's Madonnas wore the same softly sceptical smile. Charles had often thought that no woman could be so serenely mild as Perugino's Madonnas looked.

Myra was dressed in silver and white. She carried three flame-coloured ostrich feathers in her hand. She was trying herself out against the hardened blankness of Charles's eyes. Her curved, childlike lips were just touched with a deeper pink than nature cares to supply. Charles knew that men liked kissing them, but he had never been able to understand why.

"These damned people are certain to be on time," Myra softly murmured, moving forward slowly into the room. She flicked a leaf or two on the table into picturesque disorder. "So I had to hurry. You look rather dressed up, Charles! It will be amusing to see who you've dressed up for! Not that untidy little schoolgirl—Mrs. Macgregor—

with a husband like a village blacksmith, surely? I can't see why I have to know such people at all. It would have been far more amusing if you'd invited six of your patients to dinner with us instead."

"You have only to be polite to my colleagues for an hour or two," Charles reassuringly explained. "They will, I fancy, realise that you are not their sort quite as readily as you realise that they are not yours. They may look like village blacksmiths and untidy schoolgirls, but you'll find they've got wits."

"Highbrows!" murmured Myra contemptuously. "That makes everything worse! A little primitive fun is far less boring than anything that hag in a starched piqué coat I saw the other day could put up! Leaking brains at every pore—dreadful woman!"

She had guessed whom Charles was dressing up for!

Myra tried the effect of a silver basket full of purple grapes in the middle of the table, then she turned and trailed away into the studio, leaving a whiff of wild geranium scent behind her.

Charles found himself wondering, if Myra meant to do him any more harm, how was he going to prevent it? Not that Charles thought Myra did altogether mean to do him harm. She had ruined his life, as near as it is possible for another human being to ruin anyone else's life. But all she had set out to do, as she had often explained to Charles, was to live her own life in her own way!

Charles had devoted his entire fortune to preventing Myra from being hanged. She had never, he knew, forgiven him for knowing the truth about her. She called it putting the worst construction upon an innocent act. The revolver had somehow or other got into Myra's hands and gone off, and Peter—her husband—had fallen backward down the stairs; and been picked up—dead.

Charles had not forgiven Myra either. In the abstract

Charles had had no objection to Myra's being hanged, but hanging does not take place in the abstract.

Fortunately Charles had never had another friend for Myra to kill.

His first guests arrived punctually on the stroke of eight. Sally wore her wedding dress. It was a pity that Myra's dress was white too, it made Sally's white dress look lumpy and childish.

Directly afterwards came Tom and Bertha Hurst, the research workers. Charles thought he might be going to rather like his research workers, though he wished they were not married to each other. They were intelligent, simple people, who hardly ever put their best clothes on; and this was what their best clothes looked like.

Jane, who had to do double rounds before she came over, was rather late.

Charles saw that Myra thought Jane was late on purpose, but on the whole he knew that she would despise Jane rather less than if Jane had been punctual.

He barely glanced at Jane himself, when she did at last arrive, but he was reassured by what he saw. Dr. Barnes, a rather awkward, lonely young man, came with her. Dr. Harding, whom Charles disliked, was on duty in the hospital.

The introductions took place without any of Charles's colleagues realising that they were being introduced to the famous Myra Anderson, who had barely been acquitted for murdering her husband.

Not that Myra would have minded if they had guessed who she was. She often told people just for the fun of annoying Charles. But to-night Charles thought—unless Myra got drunk—she wouldn't let any of them know.

Charles took Sally in to dinner. On his left sat Bertha Hurst; beyond her was Alec; then Myra; Tom Hurst; Jane and Barnes.

Charles liked Sally. He wished she were not quite so shy, but her shyness made him kind; and when Charles was kind, he was so nice that Sally was in danger of forgetting how much she ought to hate him.

Charles knew that Sally would have to hate him, for Alec's sake, and he liked her the better for it. Still he found Bertha Hurst easier to talk to. He enjoyed laboratory work more than any other part of his profession, and Bertha lived for it.

Charles thought she knew rather a lot for a woman, but he wished that she wouldn't talk with her mouth full and had given rather more discriminating attention to her teeth and hair. It was a pity that nice women did not know how important such things were—since less nice women always did!

Charles let his eyes stray across the table. He found himself wondering whether Jane were a more, or less, nice woman.

She wore a dress of fuchsia and very pale lilac, and her long amethyst earrings matched it. She wasn't talking at all when Charles looked at her. She was listening, with an expression she often had, as if she liked taking things in better than having to give anything out. There was a kind of restrained sparkle about her. She looked as if she appreciated good clothes and well-cooked food, but not to the point of exaggerating their importance.

Myra was speaking in a high, slightly metallic voice. She thought that talking at all—to such people—was very considerate of her and should rouse their instant, and absorbed, attention.

"I am sure bimetallism is what we really need," Myra asserted. "It stands to reason that if there isn't enough gold, we should use silver too. It's so silly of all those clever men not to do anything about it. I think taxes should simply be done away with altogether. As for the unemployed——"

Charles sighed gently and gave attention to his soup. It was a subtle, asparagus soup, made with cream and a drop or two of sherry. How sophisticated Myra's soups always were, and how infantile her mind! It was enough to put one off one's own beliefs to hear Myra sharing them!

Charles returned to Sally. Sensible child, she knew where roads led to! Charles was an earnest motorist and he liked to talk about roads.

Sally didn't tell him too much at once, nor did she mix her facts, but she did rather drag Alec in! Still Charles hardly expected a bride of a few months' standing to avoid that particular failing. If Alec were not directly responsible for the favourable upkeep of roads, he knew the names of all the villages—and any dangerous cross-roads, or blind corners, within a radius of a hundred miles.

A faint, an almost tender smile, touched Charles's lips. He wondered what it would be like to have a bride, so wrapped up in you that you had to be served up with every course and enter into every topic! Did Alec, too, find Sally in the salmon croquettes, and a description of her applicable to the sayings of Winston Churchill—or was it by now Lord Beaverbrook? Charles knew that those famous personalities would, sooner or later, enter into Myra's conversation and lead the way to Mussolini.

They had already got there! He heard Myra saying that what England needed was a Mussolini or an Adolf Hitler! A few machine guns closely applied would remove the world crisis.

Alec grew restive. He flatly contradicted Myra. Myra's azure eyes expanded incredulously; but on the whole Charles knew that she liked men who began by being restive. No doubt they tasted, Charles told himself, better afterwards; like birds cooked while their blood is still warm.

Bertha began to talk about a new method of plant injection which interested Charles. He knew more about it than Bertha did, but he was too good a host to betray his own knowledge. He listened to her respectfully; and when he disagreed with her, he made his disagreement sound like a compliment.

Suddenly he heard Myra challenge Jane. She was saying, in that curious pert voice she often used to women who were more intelligent than herself, "Do you like your profession, Dr. Everest? I think it must be horrid, and rather coarsening for a woman, to have to deal with mad people."

"I find there is not much difference," Jane replied guardedly, "between sanity and insanity. The screen is out of repair in the latter case, but the light that comes through it is the same individual light. The course it follows is a logical course."

Charles liked Jane's answer. In the main he agreed with it. One might go even further and say that in most cases the screen was not even out of repair—the use made of the light was the trouble. But Jane had the sense not to go down into anything. She knew that what Myra wanted was to find her learned and dull.

"I don't think I know quite what you mean," Myra replied, turning plaintively to Alec. "Is she being frightfully clever, Dr. Macgregor?—do help me! I suppose women doctors always are—aren't they? I'm afraid I don't quite believe in medicine for women; nor does Charles, I know. I hope you don't mind my being so frank, Dr. Everest?"

"Not at all," Jane said, with a little sideways smile, which proved that she had a dimple in her cheek. "Why should I mind frankness? Many people disapprove of women doctors. Still, we exist, nevertheless, and increase. And one is rather glad to find that we are usually disapproved of by people who know least about us."

Myra directed a piercingly lovely smile at Alec.

"Oh, well," she murmured, "I suppose one never trusts other women really. Men are so much kinder, aren't they? —and fairer, too, I always think. It would be too awful, being ill and having to be told by another woman that it was all nerves, or that one ought to wear flannel next one's skin, and give up smoking!"

"All doctors, men or women," Alec assured her, "take nerves seriously now-a-days, as they should every other symptom of illness. Nerves are no longer looked on as things in the air; and if you are over-smoking, or insufficiently dressed, it would be any doctor's duty to tell you so."

Myra gave him a still more enchanting smile, which somehow or other left Jane entirely out of the discussion.

"But I'm sure if I were really ill," she murmured, "you'd be awfully sorry for me—much sorrier than Dr. Everest would be, for instance!"

Alec flushed. Myra's marvellously caressing eyes had gone deeper than her words. Sally's attention wandered from discussing roads with Charles.

Charles noticed that Alec behaved properly. He brushed aside his roused sensations. "A good doctor," he said stubbornly, "has only one way of being really sorry for his patients, and that is by being intelligent about them. Hasn't he, Jane?"

Did Sally like that sudden appeal to Jane any better than she liked Myra's caressingness? Charles leaned forward to hear what Jane would make of Alec's appeal.

"Unfortunately we have never yet discovered a thermometer for the emotions," Jane said drily, "so that I am quite unable to tell you how sorry one is for one's patients compared with the sympathy shown by a male colleague. The greatest consideration any doctor can show to a patient is in fighting his disease."

Sally, with the faintest possible sigh, returned to the quickest way of getting Charles on to the Great North Road.

A marvellous dessert came in, made of whipped cream, apples, walnuts, and jam. Charles heard Myra saying that she had picked it up from a brigand chief in Bulgaria. Charles knew that Myra had never been in Bulgaria, and he doubted if brigand chiefs have much inclination for whipping cream. He suddenly met Jane's eyes for the first time. Did she, too, suspect that the dessert had come from some less romantic source? There was a sparkle in her grey-green eyes, which, when they met Charles's, turned to silent laughter.

Myra caught Bertha Hurst's attention, and led the way back into the rosy cloud of the studio.

They all tried Charles's queer chairs, and liked them except Myra, who picturesquely sank upon a black divan exposing a most beautiful line of thigh. This probably meant that she wouldn't play bridge.

Charles thought it a mistake. They had talked enough for people who do not know each other and have not the same conversational standards. But there was no use doing anything about it. If Myra meant to subjugate Alec any kind of obstruction from Charles, however passive, would merely hasten the process.

Coffee and liqueurs came in, and Charles reminded himself that Jane was the proper person for him to talk to now.

But when he had taken a chair near her, he found that neither of them had anything to say to the other.

He couldn't say that he was surprised to see that Jane

had such a pretty foot, although that was all which keeping his eyes on the ground put into his head.

Jane did not seem any more intelligent. At last she said: "I hope your wrist is better?"

Myra unfortunately overheard her.

"How did Charles have that nasty accident?" Myra demanded. "He says he fell against something at the hospital. He must have been dreadfully clumsy!"

"What he fell against was Jerry," Alec tactlessly informed the room. "Jerry had one of his tantrums and tried to do you both in, didn't he?"

Alec glanced across the room at Charles as if he were sorry that Jerry hadn't succeeded. Even after a fortnight of Charles's most perfect consideration, Alec had to be belligerent whenever he looked at Charles.

"Not really!" Myra exclaimed delightedly. "Now that sounds really thrilling! Do tell me more about it. Charles, why didn't you let me know what happened? I thought you said that lunatics were always perfectly safe?"

"Not quite," Charles murmured wearily. "I think that I may have said that if properly handled they were very seldom dangerous."

He wondered how Jane had known that he wanted to smoke a pipe. She had managed to help him light it, so inconspicuously that it was hardly necessary for him to thank her.

"I wish I'd been there!" Dr. Barnes groaned. "Just my luck that the only time the alarm bell was rung had to be my night out! Sister Stanton said she'd never seen such a hefty brawl!"

"Ah!" said Myra significantly. "You must take me to see Jerry, Dr. Macgregor. I want to go all over the hospital. Charles won't take me, but you will—won't you?"

Charles sighed. He did not intend that Myra should enter the hospital; and up to now she had never expressed a wish to enter it.

"I am sorry," he intervened between the puffs of his pipe, "but what you suggest isn't possible, Myra. You are neither a friend nor a relation of any of the patients, nor have you any official business in the hospital. Ordinary visitors are not admitted."

"Sally runs in and out whenever she likes," Alec said aggressively. "Any of the medical staff can take a visitor over the hospital if they choose. I see no reason for your sister not seeing over it if she wants to come."

There was a pause. Everyone felt uncomfortable, but nobody felt as uncomfortable as Charles. He smoked on.

"I am sorry," he repeated quietly, looking across the room at Alec, "but I must ask you not to take my sister into the hospital. I don't consider it suitable."

No one said anything. They all looked shocked; and they disapproved of Charles.

Charles was used to being put in the wrong by Myra; and he saw that he had now been put thoroughly in the wrong. Everyone knew how near Alec had been to holding Charles's appointment. Everyone thought Charles was being tyrannical, and discourteous to rub it in. Well, then they must go on thinking it! Better that Myra should ruin his first party than his first big job! She had never wanted to see over Broadmoor. Perhaps she guessed how very nearly she might have had to see it from the inside!

But had she ruined his evening? Not everyone disapproved of him. Jane didn't. She had the sense not to show her approval, but Charles knew with a sudden dazzling distinctness, more real than sight, that Jane agreed with him. He looked up and met her eyes. They glanced away from him, but not before he had caught their gleam of complicity.

Charles looked cautiously round him. No one else had caught it. He found himself wondering what his tortoise did when it was simply pleased.

CHAPTER XI

JANE seemed rather surprised to see Charles, but she was too polite for him to guess whether she was pleased or not.

It was a cold evening, and she sat on a footstool in front of the fire, looking rather small and lonely. She wore pale yellow, with red amber beads round her slim throat. Earrings to match them dangled against her cheeks. The shape of her head was like one of Sir Joshua's delicate ladies.

Charles sat down, rather stiffly, at some little distance from the fireplace, where he could watch Jane's face without appearing to notice her.

He could not remember having felt so comfortable since his mother died.

It was difficult to define what he felt comfortable about, but he suddenly knew that though Jane might be shy, or might still be disappointed with his having taken Alec's place, yet, deeper than her shyness and far deeper than her disappointment, she agreed with Charles! Perhaps Jane didn't know that she agreed with him, but Charles knew it!

He rested his long nervous hands on the arms of his chair; and leaned back, as if an inner tension had suddenly relaxed.

"I hope Macgregor will enjoy his holiday," he said after a short pause.

Jane replied "Yes!" and then, as Charles looked past her into the fire and said nothing, Jane added: "He is sure to!" in rather a cold, resentful voice, as if it had nothing to do with Charles whether Alec was pleased or not.

Charles asked her if she minded pipes, and she said that she did not.

Charles couldn't remember when he had last thought about a woman without pain or annoyance. Not since Myra's trial, he supposed. That had rather knocked the subject of pretty girls out of his head.

Jane was not pretty; but she was fastidious and unaggressive, with the kind of distinction Charles liked in women. Still, Charles reminded himself, many fastidious women are as common as dirt! How often beneath the screen of the most finished physical refinement women were slovenly and mean! Or, if their souls were tolerably clean and decent, they had the most banal minds! He told himself he must be careful of this woman, who made him feel so comfortable. He did not want his heart touched or his pocket picked. He had always thought the hunger of the flesh like any other hunger; not much prettier; and fortunately not quite so necessary to satisfy.

Charles liked his physical existence; and he liked keeping it to himself. He owed no woman anything. His body was thoroughly healthy and hygienically controlled. He could therefore afford friendship with a woman who attracted him, up to a certain point.

Jane didn't look as if she were the kind of woman who would try to attract him beyond it; and she wouldn't find it much use if she did.

Charles's eyes ran relentlessly over her. Her nails were short and clean; her ankles neat. She hadn't any superfluous flesh, and her skin, though not at all dazzling, had a clean pallor. She had fought for his life with those rather capable hands. You could trust a woman's courage when she could quite easily have got off cheap, and let you strangle!

Besides, she had risked her life, not to save a man she liked, but a stranger whom she had some reason to dislike.

If Jane had liked Charles, he would have thought a good deal less of her for trying to save him.

She knew her job, too! That dementia-præcox case—how well she had handled it! She had got the fellow in without a row; and started his treatment with his poor confused mind unchallenged and unhostile! It was almost a pity having had to shift her from the men's side—but much more suitable! And now he'd got Macgregor off for a month, to give her time to settle down! A month, having a good time with his little bride, wouldn't do Macgregor any harm either!

"Mrs. Macgregor," Charles said slowly, puffing contentedly at his pipe, "is rather a nice woman, I should think."

"She and her husband are my best friends," said Jane defensively, as if Charles were making some kind of attack on them.

Charles did not blame her for feeling annoyed. She would keep quiet about it.

That was the comfort of dealing with a person who was of your own sort. There didn't have to be any explanations.

A little thought on Jane's part—and she was capable of thinking—would help her to adjust her conflicting loyalties.

Charles need do nothing about it. He crossed his legs and looked about the room with his mind at ease.

Jane had a few good etchings, nothing else on the walls no ornaments in the room; plenty of books.

You couldn't see what kind of woman she was from her room, it was too impersonal; but you could easily see what kind of woman she wasn't. She wasn't untidy, nor had sh got one of those cluttered-up minds with soft spots in them.

She said, a little grudgingly, after a long pause: "It was kind of you to send the Macgregors off just now—on account of Dr. Armitage's illness they never had a proper honeymoon."

"Oh, well," Charles hastily explained, "a friend of mine can come to-morrow, for a month. It worked quite easily. Not exactly a friend, but a man I've worked with. His name's Hatchard."

Charles felt that he had told Jane quite a lot about Hatchard.

"Broadmoor?" Jane asked.

"Oh, no!" Charles said, and felt as if he had told Jane quite a lot about Broadmoor.

It would be curious if he began to tell Jane quite a lot about things!

She got up and offered Charles a whisky-and-soda, asking him how much whisky he took, and then pouring in the soda-water to save his wrist.

She drank nothing herself, but when she sat down on her little footstool again, she lit a cigarette.

Charles saw that her anger had gone now, or, at any rate, she had disposed of it conveniently enough for conversational purposes.

"Do you think you are going to mind working on the women's side?" he asked her.

Jane gave the funny little smile he liked, the one that had first shown him that she had a dimple, and said: "Oh, you know I like women! No! I shan't mind when I'm used to the change. At first it's puzzling, and I'm rather like a cat—I notice new things as if they were shocks—but I get used to them. I've got a case now I'm particularly puzzled over. You couldn't, I think, get anything quite like it in a man. I should like your opinion upon it."

Charles shifted his eyes to hers.

Jane's eyes were a bluer green than he had remembered; not a hard or bright blue, but a little misty, like wood smoke on an autumn day.

Charles never had liked shining eyes.

He gave a sympathetic grunt, to show Jane that when she had stated her case, she should have his opinion. He was not a man to give his opinion lightly, but probably Jane had already guessed that, and wouldn't presume upon his consent.

She seemed quite satisfied with Charles's grunt, for she went on after a slight pause, twisting her beads on her lap.

"She's a new patient, and she's been crying on end for four days and nights. I can't get her quiet. Her heart won't stand heavy drugging. It's not an ordinary melancholic case. She hasn't had any attacks before; and it is not involutional; she is only thirty. I wish Dr. Macgregor had seen her before leaving. She is the kind of case he reaches much better than I do. He is so much more electric."

Charles nodded. That was the mercy of Jane. She was not electric. Her presence no more weighed upon him than a summer breeze. Charles's mother had been the same. She could be in a room without Charles having to bother about it, and yet, when she left it, the room felt empty.

"Crying for four days and nights is rather an expensive bid for attention," Charles said slowly. "What type of woman is she? I suppose she has always been out for prestige and someone has let her rather badly down?"

"I think she's let herself down," Jane said consideringly. "I gather she's always been fearfully respectable and religious. She's a Roman Catholic of the most practising kind. She's been married ten years. Her husband is a tiresome kind of man; and drinks. But she seems to have been fond of him. Then one day—all of a sudden,

as it seemed to her—she was unfaithful to him. One act—
not premeditated. She doesn't care about the man she was
unfaithful with. It was like some awful accident. Now she
has gone to pieces over it, and won't go on living. I suppose she was too pure. And now she wants to get back
somehow, and be purer than if she had never sinned at all.
If she kills herself, she proves herself purer—or thinks
she has. For, after all, few people die from horror of their
sins. I don't think she's sorry for her husband. It's more
like having spilled something on a clean frock."

Charles enjoyed this simile. "Very like," he said drily.
"And now she wants to take the frock off and throw it
away. It would be interesting to know how many people
keep virtuous from vanity alone. Well, what have you
tried so far?"

Jane turned her full face towards Charles. The amber
earrings made a dark gleaming frame for it. She looked
more than ever like one of Sir Joshua's serene, immaculate
ladies.

"I asked her priest in to confess her," Jane told Charles.
"I thought her religion might be of some help to her. But
we couldn't get her to attend to him. Then I sent for her
husband, but the sight of him made her worse. She won't
hear of my sending for the other man. Lucretia couldn't
have had a greater horror of Tarquin, though I believe
the act was quite a voluntary one on my patient's part.
Physically there wasn't much I could do for her. I've had
her in a continuous bath; and I've given her sedatives; but
she doesn't answer to anything. So now I've got her back
in bed with a special nurse to watch her. At first she understood what we said to her, but I don't think she does
now."

"What did you say to her?" Charles asked. The question interested him. He rather wondered what a woman
like Jane felt about chastity, in herself, or in other women.

He was sure that it would be a question she would think out carefully, and act up to. She wouldn't just make a hash of it, or go about with an uncontrolled desire, like a man who sends a cheque to his bank with an overdrawn account against him.

"I said if she was really sorry she'd stop crying and go back to her husband," Jane told him gravely. "I told her I thought she was just angry, and unfaithful to her husband out of revenge. I said I understood that he had been very tiresome, and I thought that, without realising it, she had wanted to punish him for being tiresome—only she'd gone rather too far and punished herself instead."

Charles nodded. This was a line which he himself would have taken.

"Yes," he said reflectively, "I fancy if this lady were really sorry for letting down her husband, she'd go home and attend to cooking his meals. That fellow Nietzsche put his finger on the right spot when he said that remorse was always a dishonest business. Even God, though He agrees not to despise a broken and a contrite heart, has never expressed much satisfaction over one! People wash out their repentance with tears far more often than they wash it in."

Jane nodded ruefully. "I tried to make her see that," she explained; "but you see it would give her show away—and so she won't see it! She's quite intelligent if one could only break through her fantasy about herself. What she needs is someone to startle her—and I can't startle! If Dr. Macgregor were here, he'd do something so surprising that she'd have to attend to him!"

"And is that what you want me to do?" Charles demanded, knocking out his pipe.

He couldn't help smiling at Jane, she looked so ridiculously forlorn and shocked at her own failure. As if not to make unfaithfulness palatable to her patient was worse than being unfaithful.

Jane smiled back, rather doubtfully.

"I thought," she said hesitatingly, "that you might have a fresh idea."

"I think I'm rather like you," Charles murmured, looking away from her. "I don't find it at all easy to be startling. However, I'll come along and have a look at your patient, if you like."

Jane sprang to her feet. She slipped her white coat over her yellow crêpe-de-chine dress, but Charles was glad to see that she did not take off her earrings or her amber beads. She held herself well, with an easy, unstressed confidence. Charles, following her out into the corridor, thought that Jane would probably have a good seat on a horse.

They said nothing further till they stood in a small private room off the ward, and looked down at the moaning woman on the bed. Her sobs were mechanical, like a continuous hiccup. She seemed unaware of their entrance, or of anything which took place outside herself.

Jane dismissed the night nurse and stood behind Charles near the door. She seemed to know by instinct that he would like as little witness as possible to his being startling.

Charles bent over the woman and felt her pulse. It was stronger than he had thought it could be, but very quick and irregular. He couldn't be certain when a heart, thumping at such a terrific rate, mightn't chuck up its job.

She could hardly see out of her eyes, but Charles had an uncanny feeling that she was watching him.

He might try electricity, but would the heart stand it? Putting her suddenly into a cold bath was out of the question. Alcohol injections, while she was sobbing so violently, would be extremely dangerous.

He laid down her wrist. How far could he startle her without killing her? How long could she go on like this without killing herself? Her fixed will had taken her far beyond mere desire. Even if she wanted to stop now, she couldn't, unless something, from the world she had barred herself against, broke through to help her.

Charles put his right arm under her shoulders. He raised her with gentleness, but his voice when he spoke cut like a knife.

"If you don't stop crying," he said, "I'm going to lay you across my knees and smack you till you do! I shall count ten and then begin—and I shall smack hard!"

Charles wondered what he would do if the woman didn't stop crying; but his muscles were sure. His hands tightened on her shoulders. He began to count ten slowly. A long shuddering sigh broke from the woman. It seemed as if her life might go out on it. Then there was silence. Neither Charles nor Jane moved. The hiccuping began again. Charles's muscles tightened. His injured wrist hurt like hell, but by putting the chief pressure on his right arm, he could just stand it. Once more the sobs died down. Charles bent lower over the woman and looked into her dim, angry eyes. Was she capable of thought? He spoke quietly, as if he were speaking to a reasonable person.

"Well—now you know what's up, don't you? I dare say Dr. Everest will give you something to make you sleep. When you wake up you'll feel quite different. All that stuff about your husband is nonsense; and you know it's nonsense! When you get home again you let it be fifty-fifty! I dare say you're the better of the two, but you won't prove it by dying. That's a mug's game. If you're really sorry about what you've done, go back to your hus-

band, forgive his drink, and let him forgive your unfaithfulness. You'll find that'll work!"

She didn't say anything, but in her tear-sodden eyes
Charles saw a gleam that wasn't anger. He smiled at her
with sudden friendliness. "You keep a stiff upper lip!" he
finished, letting her sink back gently onto the pillow.

He felt sorry for the woman. After all, it took a kind
of misplaced pluck to die because you had robbed yourself of virtue; most people rob themselves more easily than
that!

It was wonderfully quiet in the little room. All this time
Jane had never stirred. Charles wondered if she was annoyed with him. He could not tell by her face. He went
out alone, and left her with her patient.

Sister Parsons, the ward sister, stood before him, eager
to know what had taken place; but Charles disliked eagerness. He stared coldly past her head, until Jane came out.
Jane said what she thought was necessary to Sister Parsons—not very much, Charles was glad to notice. She
made no comment to Charles until they reached the corridor, then she asked him in a low voice, "Would you
really have whipped her if she hadn't stopped crying?"

"Would you have forgiven me if I had whipped her?"
Charles demanded in return. He looked at Jane, but she
kept her eyes away from him.

"It is not my place to 'forgive' you," she reminded him.
"You are the Superintendent of this hospital. But I think
t would have killed her."

Charles felt, for once, rather pleased with himself.

"Well," he admitted ungrudgingly, "so do I, if it comes
o that. But you see she would have died anyhow if I
hadn't risked it. So it was worth the chance." Not even
Alec, he thought to himself, could have been more star-
ling! It seemed to him that Jane might appropriately
have thanked him, but she didn't.

"When one sees how successful the mere threat of whipping a woman can be," Charles said rather aggressively, "it seems almost a pity that the real thing doesn't get done a great deal oftener." He was thinking of his sister Myra; but Jane couldn't know that he was thinking of Myra.

They had reached her door. Jane stood in front of it, her hand upon the door handle. She was, Charles supposed, dismissing him. After all, he had saved her patient's life for her! She might in return have asked him in to smoke a final pipe!

The red amber earrings sparkled fiercely against her pale cheeks. She held her small head high.

She opened the door of her sitting-room without inviting him in.

"Yes," Jane said in a cool, even voice, "I notice that you, and your sister, seem to believe a good deal in physical violence. Thank you, though, for what you did for my patient. Good-night!"

Charles said: "One moment, please! Did you recognise my sister?"

He was so angry that he felt as if he were lightning and might strike Jane dead by merely looking at her. Perhaps he gave the same impression to Jane, for she gave a queer little gasp and said:

"I don't understand—what do you mean by 'recognise' her?"

Of course she hadn't! He'd been a fool—and very nearly given Myra away into the bargain! With anyone else he would have quite given her away, because they would have asked questions. But Jane would ask no further questions about Myra, either of him or of anyone else.

"I beg your pardon," Charles said with quick sincerity. "I thought that you were rather unfairly referring to something which I see now that you did not know."

That was enough for Jane. She still didn't ask him in; but she gave him her hand.

It was the first time that Charles had touched Jane's hand. He held it as long as he thought she wished it held.

The door shut quickly after her, and Charles stood for a moment, feeling rather lost outside it.

He almost wished that he hadn't stopped the woman crying.

CHAPTER XII

On a disagreeable morning, which Charles knew that he was going to make more disagreeable still, he sent for the Matron.

She came into his office like a pause in a hurricane. She knew what Charles had against her; but let him beware not to unleash the tiger!

Doctors must be catered for—Superintendents even indulged, up to a certain point; but the Matron always had her temper to fall back upon. Luke Armitage had trembled before it. Macgregor and Jane went out of their way not to rouse it. Nobody enjoyed the Matron's temper—except the Matron herself!

After she was seated, Charles leaned back in his chair, to give himself the fiction of ease. He found himself wondering whether—when the Matron took off her clothes at night—they did not stand upright without her.

"You have been here a long time, I believe," Charles began in what he meant to be a conciliatory manner.

"Fifteen years and six months," the Matron ejaculated, in a voice which had the timbre of a bell, startling an institution awake in the morning.

"That's a long time," Charles courteously agreed, "and I am sure you must have learned, during it, the full value of authority in such a hospital as ours?"

The Matron's rather untidy nostrils quivered dangerously.

"No doubt I have!" she said austerely. "I know when to put my foot down; and when down—it stays down!"

"Then I am all the more surprised," Charles suggested

"that you should so far have forgotten your duty as to infringe upon Dr. Everest's authority. Clarkson was not a suitable man to be left in sole charge of the admission ward at night. The Arab was dying and needed a special. Dr. Everest had given her orders accordingly. The result of your counter-order was, as you know, most unfortunate. It exposed the patients and several members of the staff to actual danger."

Charles watched the heaving of the Matron's massive breast anxiously. He wondered how much faster could it rise and fall, without endangering its artificial supports. It was like watching the last moments of a dam before it bursts.

The Matron managed to hold herself in till Charles had finished, then the floods broke.

"It's not perhaps surprising," she said in a rapid rush, "that the men come to me for their orders—however little I like it! I don't say anything against Dr. Everest—let her go to you the moment you arrive with her complaints! I know well enough what she's after—though I wouldn't lower myself by mentioning it! All that you'll learn in good time—if you stay long enough to find out. It's true I usually give Maclean the admission ward, but how could I help his mother dying just as we have a new mental nurse in? Those blacks have much too much done for them! Why a special, when my staff's short as it is? Clarkson's record is all that it ought to be, and you've only got to look at his shoulders to see that he's a match for any two excitables!

"Mind you, I gave no order! Send for Clarkson if you like and let him dare to tell me to my face that I ordered him to take it on alone. I may have said to him, in passing, when he came to me, as the men will do, for well they know real authority when they see it—and aren't to be taken in by a flaccid pussy-cat, sneaking her way through

gold medals and calling herself M.D.—I may have said:
'Well, I'm sure, Clarkson, you look strong enough for that
ward by yourself or any other!' A word like that may have
passed my lips—and have been taken more seriously than
it was meant. But I know—and no one better—not to give
an order beyond my province. All orders in this hospital
have to be written! I wrote no order!"

The Matron gazed triumphantly at Charles. He had a
feeling that, although she hadn't meant anything to happen in the impulsive ward on Jane's last night, she had
envisaged the possibility.

"Surely a hint from you is an order?" he dropped
gently. "Isn't it?"

The Matron bridled. "No one could be sorrier about
that broken wrist than I am, Dr. Drummond," she gra-
ciously observed. "Shocked if not surprised, as I said to
Sister Stanton the next morning. Of course you're new
to your job, and don't know which are the patients who
need to have an eye kept on them! Still, I should have
thought that with Dr. Everest on the spot—that black
Jerry might have been kept in his place! Nothing has
ever happened before my eyes, I can assure you! Not all
the while I've been here! If I go into a ward, the patients
stay in their beds, and if they want to rave they rave under their blankets. No wonder Dr. Everest tries to bring
the blame home to me. But there, I always have said—and
I always will say—that to have a woman doctor in a mental hospital is to tempt Providence! I was glad to hear
that you agreed with me."

Charles's hand tightened on the fountain pen he was
playing with. "I don't know that I do altogether agree
with you," he found himself saying. "Dr. Everest strikes
me as a most competent doctor. But her qualities have less
than nothing to do with the matter in hand. I have in-
terrogated Clarkson—and from his extreme reluctance

take charge of the ward, even after your order, I am forced to the conclusion that you refused him the assistance which Dr. Everest had ordered."

The Matron changed her ground.

"He is new, as you say," she admitted, "and from all I can see he is half-witted, as well as chicken-hearted! In my opinion he shouldn't be in the hospital at all. But there —as I often used to say to Luke Armitage, you doctors are no psychologists!"

Charles made one more effort to keep his temper. "Your methods, if you will allow me to say so," he began again, "are not my own—nor those, I gather, of my chief medical colleagues. As far as your work has to do with material objects, I am not finding any fault with it. It is flawless. But in a mental hospital all work depends on personality. There should be a very easy atmosphere—the exact opposite of any strain or tension. I have watched your work, and your control of your subordinates, and I am bound to tell you that I think it would be more appreciated in a different institution, run on more conservative lines. My idea for this hospital is the gradual introduction of freedom. I want the spirit to be that of ease and good humour, and every kind of encouragement. I want the patients to be allowed to do, in their own way, everything that it is at all feasible for them to do, even if this creates more wear and tear of material things. I want greater elasticity as to time, especially as to meals. I never wish to hear of a patient's being hurried. I am well aware that this involves harder work and great exercise of patience on all the staff; and far less regard for appearances. I know that you keep a very high standard of cleanliness, order, and economy, and I appreciate these things greatly. But I have a different aim; and economy, cleanliness, and order will perhaps have to be slowed up, for a time, to fit in with it. In the long run I hope they will benefit rather

than suffer by this new departure. But it will be difficult
for anyone to follow who has not the same aim as myself.
Do I make myself clear?"

The Matron drew a loud nasal breath with an intimidat-
ing reverberation.

"Clear!" she said contemptuously. "Well—I won't say
I don't know what you mean! I should know what a child
meant if it began to destroy the furniture! But it's difficult to believe you've ever run a mental hospital before,
or even walked through the wards of one, with a sister beside you to make things safe and tidy for you! Why, I
never heard of such a thing! Freedom, indeed! If patients
could be free, they wouldn't be here! And if you leave
them to settle when to get up and when to eat their meals,
why, they'd never get dressed or finish a meal between
daylight and darkness! Luke Armitage, who was a wise
man and a kind one, if there ever was one, used to say—
and, though coarse, it was the truth, as you'll find out for
yourself before long—'Fill their stomachs, empty their
bowels, and let the rest slide!' It's not my place to say
these things to you, I dare say, but you're a young man
with a new job, and if you take my advice, you'll go
slowly, and listen to those who have had this hospital in
their hands since you were a child, and know how to handle
it. Dr. Macgregor and Dr. Everest are modern enough
Heaven knows!—They're full of their krinkum
krankums; but even they've never gone so far as to expect
the patients to have their own way!"

"I haven't got as far as that myself," Charles admitted
with a faint smile, "but I have got as far as to wish the
way very slowly modified into a better way, and I have
my own ideas as to how this state of things can be accom-
plished. I have been fortunate enough to find that both my
new medical colleagues share my views. If you could have
seen your way to modify your methods and fall in with

our common aim, in spite of this one act of insubordination to Dr. Everest, I should not be asking you to send in your resignation to the Committee."

"I shan't do it!" said the Matron fiercely. "Resign, indeed! I should have thought this hospital had had enough changes by now—and on the wrong side! We all have our duties, young man, and no doubt you'll learn some of yours in time. But I think you'll find that dismissing the matron of a hospital isn't likely to be one of them. Why, if I were to go, the whole staff would go with me! If my work's, as you say, 'flawless,' that's enough. I'll take my stand on it. Of course I'll fall in with any plans of yours I can—that's quite a different thing. Any definite orders in this hospital that you issue, I'll see carried out. I know my place. There never was the faintest wish of Dr. Armitage's which I wasn't prepared to follow blindfold, as you might say. And even Dr. Macgregor will tell you, though I haven't always seen eye to eye with him, I've given in. Dr. Everest too—though God knows having a woman over my head as a doctor, who's never treated me like a human being once since she's been here—not a cup of tea, nor a quiet chat—nothing but cold little words dropped out of the side of her mouth which she might be speaking to her lapdog, if she were human enough to have one—even she can't say I've not known my business—and when she's clear as to what she wants, she gets it! I know that all doctors have their own little whims, and I expected changes. Anything in reason you have to suggest I'm prepared even now to listen to—but lunatics taking their own time over their meals, and not being brought up short to keep themselves clean—well, you try it! But not in my hospital!"

"I have no right to dismiss you," Charles admitted, "but I may report you to the Committee and leave them to ask for your resignation; and that is what I shall do.

I asked you in this morning in order to tell you what my report was going to be. I shall give you all the credit which I think is honestly your due, but I shall say that I think your personal influence upon the hospital is not a happy one; and that you have definitely failed to support Dr. Everest's authority."

The storm broke.

Charles, although he tried to appear as indifferent as a drifting iceberg, felt like a small boy being whipped. The Matron's ugly voice cut his nerves to ribbons and made him feel physically sick. He had to hear what she thought of him, what the sisters and nurses thought of him. The very patients themselves became his accusers.

Charles rose and stood silent, waiting for the storm to stop. Soon her breath must fail, or she would burst a blood-vessel. But the Matron had not quite reached her goal. There was something worse, which she had kept up her sleeve to the last. She hissed rather than spoke her final words at him.

"It's not likely, thank Heaven, seeing that your own sister's a murderess, that you'll stay very long in this hospital yourself! I found it out no later than this morning, from a friend at breakfast time, who wrote from Edinburgh. Well—by lunch time there won't be many in this hospital who haven't taken it in—sane or insane!"

Charles hadn't expected this exposure quite so soon; but he was never wholly unprepared for it. Sooner or later this particular knife could always be trusted to reach his vitals; and on the whole he preferred the shock of it to come at unpleasant rather than at pleasant moments.

He raised his head and looked at the Matron with his disgusted, burnt-out eyes.

"There is no secret," he said quietly. "My sister was publicly tried for murder and publicly acquitted. That you should speak of it is quite within your rights. It does not affect my work in this hospital."

"You wait and see if it doesn't," barked the Matron viciously. "We've got scandal enough here as it is. I know well enough why I'm being asked to resign! You've been got at by that slinking little harlot who calls herself a doctor! She was Macgregor's mistress, as the whole hospital knows, before his marriage, if she isn't since! A poor little thing, his wife—and can't face up to them! I dare say you're taking her on now—going in to visit her at all hours of the night already, and with all that criminal history behind you! Birds of a feather, as I've always said! I warn you that some day the very walls of the hospital will speak! I know why I'm leaving here—if I do go—but I shan't be the only one who knows! I warn you of that!"

A wave of uncontrollable anger surged through Charles. He took a sudden step forward.

"Don't you dare touch me!" shouted the Matron.

"Touch you!" said Charles cruelly. "My good woman, no man in his senses would touch you! But if you don't send in your resignation to the Committee in twenty-four hours, I think you'll find I can force you to leave this hospital!"

Charles saw her swollen, blazing face suddenly blanch.

He had shaken his fist at her, without knowing what he was doing.

Panting heavily, and still shouting, she rushed from the room.

Charles was left alone, with the incredible memory, not of her violence, but of his own.

CHAPTER XIII

CHARLES looked out over the sodden, flat, unenterprising earth, and hated it. He would still have hated it had it been greener and more enterprising.

The patients dotted about the hospital grounds seemed more than usually slouching and depressed. Each one carried about with him, as if it were visibly strapped to his back, the weight of his private hell.

They weren't conscious of the weather, or of the earth's changes. If you had put a bed of crocuses under their noses, their eyes would not have brightened.

An hour ago Charles had looked out on the same scene, and at the same figures, but he had not felt that dulled sense of defeat.

He had told the Matron that she could not spoil his work, but it was not true. She had already spoiled it. The objective life which was so dear to him would soon be muddied over with personal gossip. Every eye he met would judge him afresh in the light of this business of Myra's. Every order he gave would be accepted differently because of it. Worst of all, he would give his own orders differently because he was Myra's brother. He was not handicapped by his affection for her. If it hadn't been for his mother, Charles was inclined to think he would have let Myra hang. The whole point of the thing had fallen rather flat, for Charles's mother had died a few months after the trial was over.

The memory of his mother's death brought Charles's mind to an abrupt stop, as if he were pulling up a horse on the verge of a precipice.

He had not been aware that he had walked through the hospital grounds and into the private garden of the medical quarters.

The door of Jane's French window opened. He looked stubbornly away from it. He heard the window shut, and the gravel crunch under her feet. Her voice, close to his shoulder, sounded as if she had been running.

"I've got a couple of hours off," Jane said breathlessly. "Would you care for a run to the sea?"

Charles wouldn't even turn his head to look at Jane, he was so disgusted with her forwardness. She must know as well as he did that all invitations or advances must come from her superior officer. He would refuse in such a way that she would never dare to make such a suggestion again.

"Thanks," he said icily, "I'll come."

A moment later they were seated side by side in Jane's match-box of a car.

The wet road leapt up at them like a wild thing; the raw wind bit and stung their cheeks.

Charles liked the feel of the wheel under his fingers, but he didn't know where he was going. At intervals he heard Jane saying, "Right!" or "Left!" or "Straight ahead!" She didn't seem to mind how fast he drove. One moment there was the dulled light of the open road, a dirty white, then the dark blur of a car floating towards them. The shallow fields were wet and sodden, the hills cut off by mist. Road signs jerked faint warnings into his mind and out again.

The sun came out suddenly and fell upon the sea. High cliffs jutted forward on either side of the gap into broken water. The sea was the colour of a rusty apple, except where the cloud shadows made pools of purple and amethyst. Shafts of light from the drifting moisture filled the horizon with dim gold.

Charles pulled up, because he couldn't very well drive on into the sea. They got out and walked in silence up the nearest cliff.

Charles could hear Jane's clothes flapping against her figure like taut sails. The wind, and the sharp laughter of the gulls, filled the air with hurrying, intermittent sounds. Below them the sea hammered at the rocks. Edges of flying foam, caught by the sun, ran like broken rainbows along the ridges of oncoming waves.

Charles walked to the cliff's edge. He looked sheer down a wall of slate-black rock to a tiny cove. The dark water rose and fell with a curious smooth solidity against its side.

At the entrance to the cove the waves leapt upward, like desperate fingers snatching at the sky, to sink back discouraged into the wind-flattened sea.

Gulls beat up against the wind, tacking and veering with consummate skill.

Charles's eyes followed wistfully the reckless ease of their flight. They made the wind carry them, hanging for a moment as motionless as if they grew upon a tree, and then with the slight shift of a wing, their bodies glistening like silver lightning, they plunged into the sea.

Charles's heart plunged with them. By a tremendous effort he held his body back. Sorrow was upon him—the wild, clutching sorrow of his mother's death, which even now, after three years without her, could throw him into the Deep, as lightly as the ironstone rock threw off the foam of a breaking wave into the sea.

His mother had held the whole of Charles's heart, and she still held it.

There were moments when Charles thought of his heart as dead under her stiffened fingers; and others when the horror of it was that he knew his heart was still alive, and could not break away from the dead hands that were closed upon it. He knew now that his mother should never have held him. She, the most quietly free, the least possessive of women, had not known how to open her hands and set him free from her dominion.

She had understood him too well; she had spared him too much!

Charles neither blamed her nor himself. Neither of them had known any better, but he realised that at her death she had taken half his life away with her.

When these attacks of sorrow caught him, he had no redress. He could only let them play what havoc they liked, while his clenched will refused to act upon their mad beckoning.

Suddenly he felt a hand laid on his arm. He thought for a moment it was that dead hand, so firm and light was its pressure, but it pulled him back towards the solid earth.

"You are too near the edge, sir," Jane said quietly.

"It's all right," Charles murmured, moving backward a step. "I'm what guides call 'Schwindel-frei.' I hope I didn't frighten you!"

He wondered how long he had stood there forgetting Jane's existence. From the position of the sun he thought it must be quite a long time.

She was quite right, he had been too near the edge; but it was a good thing she had not spoken sooner, because Charles couldn't have answered her.

When his sorrow rode him, his jaws locked themselves together like stone. Nor did he hear when he was spoken to.

It must have been rather a terrifying experience for the poor girl. She looked white; but she didn't ask him any questions. She only told him they were near a farm where they could get tea.

They walked along the cliff's edge, side by side, the wind beating them back, as if they were trying to break into one of its secrets. They couldn't have talked against it if they had wanted to.

They came quite suddenly upon an exposed, wind-bitten little farm surrounded by stone walls.

An old woman, gnarled as one of the bent trees in her tiny orchard, opened the door to them. Her daughter had been one of Jane's patients and she couldn't do enough for them. For a long time she stood there talking, in a singing whine, rather like the voice of the wind. She brought them cream, and golden butter, and honey in the honeycomb.

Charles liked the sound of her voice; but he was glad when she went.

They were in a queer little room, furnished with slippery black horsehair, and full of sepulchral or insipid ornaments. But the fire was alight, and the tea was hot.

It occurred to Charles that he would like to tell Jane about Myra himself. Some officious person would be sure to tell her directly she got inside the hospital, and though he had never spoken of Myra to anyone, he had a feeling that he would prefer that Jane should know the facts from himself.

"I've had an amusing morning," he began with grim lightness. "I was trying to dismiss the Matron, and she dismissed me instead! But I don't know that I am going to go!"

Jane looked at him interrogatively, and stopped eating.

"She had her reasons," Charles went on. "There's been a scandal attached to my name, and she was lucky enough to find it out. She threatened me with exposure. It is quite a neat little case of blackmail. She didn't say that if I withdrew the charge against her she would let me off, but I presume that she would have done so. What should you advise?"

Jane said rather reprovingly: "Of course you are joking, sir! She could know nothing against you."

This amused Charles.

"On what do you base your theory of my complete innocence?" he demanded. "You know nothing about me!"

Jane flushed a little.

"There are certain rudimentary things," she murmured, "which one knows about some people. The Matron is very foolish if she supposes she can frighten you."

"The thing the Matron knows about me," Charles said, more gravely, "is definitely one that I should prefer kept quiet. However, it's not going to be kept quiet, so that I thought I should rather like to tell you what it is myself.

"About three years ago my sister's husband was found dead on the stairs. He was shot through the head, and the revolver was beside him; but there were certain indications that made suicide seem unlikely. My sister was alone in the house with him at the time of this occurrence. She was accused of murder—and after a long and rather notorious trial she was acquitted. I was the chief witness for the defence."

Charles paused. He looked across the table at Jane. Her curiously sensitive face looked like a landscape, shaken by a breeze. Her eyelids fluttered and her lips shook a little. She only looked hard when she had previously determined not to show her feelings.

Suddenly it occurred to Charles that Jane already knew about Myra, and that this was why she had dared to ask him to come out with her! The Matron must have gone to work even sooner than he had expected.

"It's quite atrocious!" she said quickly, "and so silly! You mustn't—either of you—give it another thought. The Matron can do no harm by talking of it—except to herself!"

"I think she can do harm," Charles said slowly, "but

perhaps not as much as at first I thought she could. The Committee, of course, already knew of the circumstances. They had hoped it would not become generally known. My sister changed her name, and she only lives with me for a small part of the year. Fortunately, she prefers Continental life. I took her abroad for two years after the trial. It suited me quite well; I wanted to study psychology in Vienna. When I got back to London, I tried for a job there, but that didn't answer.

"I was lucky enough to get a temporary post at Broadmoor; I held the Dartford appointment for two years, but that also was too near London. I was glad when this turned up—so far away from everything! You don't think it will hurt the work then—everybody's talking about us?"

Jane said: "Why ever should it? On the contrary, I should think it might help!"

Charles stared at her fiercely. "What d'you mean?" he asked. If she was going to dare to pity him——!

Jane laughed. It was an amused, friendly little chuckle, as if she thought Charles rather a joke. Charles, a little unwillingly, found himself smiling too.

"Well," she said, "I dare say you don't know it, but you are considered at the hospital to be rather too immaculate. If subordinates are to feel comfortable, their chief must have a flaw. I admit this is only a vicarious one, still perhaps it will serve. The question of your going is absurd. Don't go! What about the Matron—can you really get rid of her?"

Charles felt thoroughly relieved. He didn't want to go on talking about himself or Myra. He hadn't said that Myra was innocent. He couldn't lie to Jane, and acquittal sounded as good as innocent—except perhaps to Jane

"I think I can dismiss her," he said thoughtfully. "I didn't act hurriedly. You see, I've let more than a month pass since our dust-up in the ward. I made an official enquiry immediately, but I gave no decisions about it. I wanted to give her plenty of time to grasp our new methods—if she could grasp them! Nor did I wish to make a personal matter of her dismissal. But she gave me no alternative. I think she will resign, but if she doesn't, and the Committee don't dismiss her after the report I intend to send in, I shall resign myself."

"She'll go," Jane said quietly, but with conviction. "She'll see that she can't work with you, and she won't want to be dismissed. Give her twenty-four hours before sending your report in—and she'll resign."

"I hope," Charles said interrogatively, "that the Macgregors won't mind? I rather counted on the whole thing being over before they got back, and a fresh Matron installed."

Jane didn't answer. Charles noticed that she never answered for Alec; but there was perhaps an intimacy in not answering for him as great, if not greater, than if she had answered for him. Did she know that if she left Alec free enough he would always come round to what she wanted? But what did she want? She had said to Charles: "Don't go!" Yet surely, as Alec's friend, she must want Charles to go?

Why had she asked Charles to come with her to the sea after she knew Myra's story? She shouldn't act like a friend if she wasn't a friend! And could she be both his and Alec's friend?

"You're late!" said Charles, suddenly remembering the time. "Didn't you say you'd only got two hours?"

"Yes," said Jane airily, as if it didn't matter. "I am rather late, I know. Dr. Barnes will just have to carry on till I get back!"

She didn't offer to let Charles drive home, and Charles saw, not without satisfaction, that Jane had a good deal to learn about driving.

CHAPTER XIV

EVEN if Alec hadn't been happy, he would have driven well. His little car bounded along neatly at fifty miles an hour, stretching herself out to sixty on an open road. Other people had spills or perpetual repairs, they were blocked for hours behind hay-carts and lorries, but Alec, playing to his luck, generally got round obstacles before they had time to hold him up. An open road, a good car, a job of work, a chance companionship, went down, with him, as easily as a glass of milk. People with foresight handicapped this gift with anxiety. Alec took things as they came, and if they didn't come, he took something else instead.

He was so happy that he didn't want to talk. It was a late December day and the road stretched flat and dim towards the lilac line of hills. He wondered if frost, wood smoke, and sodden leaves had ever smelt so good to anyone before; or if ever a flat, familiar road could hold again this dim enchantment of a dream. He didn't want to talk and apparently Sally didn't either. She had passed into his blood and he was aware of all her wants. For the last month he had eaten, slept, waked, and breathed Sally. She answered to him as the faithful little car answered to his quick brain and steady hand. If anything went wrong she was ready to tumble out onto a muddy road and help him with it like another man. She took being benighted on a dark moor as a joke. Her love and laughter were the stops under his fingers.

Alec had looked forward to his marriage for years, but he hadn't known it would be as good as this. He had gone into it full of excitement and curiosity. Another human being had had the temerity to prefer him to anyone else. But once married, he found that marriage wasn't merely winning a prize. It was at once something more aloof and more intimate. He had opened the door of his heart to a fresh stream of life that ran through it, and was one with it, and yet separate. A mysterious transfusion was taking place all the time. The symbolic act of love which bound them was transcended by this deeper union. Their short honeymoon and the rush of his work after it had but pointed the way to a new, unhampered state of being into which they had now grown. If Alec stretched out his hand, without look or speech, to Sally, she put into it at once what he wanted. If she was cold he felt the little shiver down his back. If he was hungry Sally was quick to suggest food. When they didn't speak they were thinking to each other—quite as much as if they spoke out loud. To explain what they meant to each other would have seemed almost a retreat from a deeper communion.

Sally, silent, was a new creative power; Sally, speaking, was only an absurd and adorable child. She had been unawakened when Alec married her, but her response to his ardour had been unruffled and complete.

Alec knew that many women in love keep something back to enhance their charms, but Sally did not yield, and then make you pay for it by instalments! She gave him all she had. He was as sure of Sally as of the beats of his own heart. It wasn't as if she were merely biddable or slavish either. She had her own way of brushing her teeth, for instance, and wouldn't change it. She was dazzlingly clean, but hadn't a notion how to improve her physical appearance. She had a boy's honour and shyness, but she wasn't particularly tactful. She said what she meant, even when she had much better not say it.

The city rose up round them like a flat-footed beast

with a tough hide. It was a shoddy industrial seaport blasted by nineteenth-century ugliness; but the dusk hid its worst features. Mysterious jewelled lights broke the unsightly shops into fantastic palaces.

Alec enjoyed edging into cross-streams of traffic and picking his quick-witted way through the fumbling stupidities of the market town. A big square opened out of the drab flurry of streets. Dignified white buildings, with clean, unshortened lines, rose up, each set in its own wide grass space. The heart of the city, rebuilt since the War, was as young and beautiful as their new life together, as separate and as deeply interfused. Alec had a pride in it, and he slackened pace a little that Sally might share his pride. He wasn't sorry to be back again. The steady sunshine of his personal happiness would flood him safely over the rock of Charles.

He had talked a lot with Sally about Charles, and they had both agreed to push him out of their consciousness and just go on with the job.

Jane had been right about it. Let Charles dither about in outhouses, sign papers, and give orders; the minds and lives of their patients were still their own to deal with!

It suddenly occurred to Alec that it would be nicer to go straight to Jane's for tea than to their own cold little house, which would have to be reopened and settled down in. He felt eager for news of the hospital.

Jane hadn't written much, only two or three curt little lines about things he had asked her to do, or cases he'd begged for reports on. This had been all that he had wanted at the time, but he was conscious now that he couldn't hear quickly enough what had been happening to the hospital.

"Sally," he said to the Double Consciousness beside him, "let's run in to Jane's for tea."

He was instantly aware of a change. The consciousness ran single.

Sally said: "Oh—do you want to, Alec?" It was almost as if she had said "I don't!"

A sharp thrill of annoyance passed through Alec. The pleasant prospect of Jane's room became an irritating need.

"Well—why shouldn't we?" he asked impatiently. "She'll be expecting us. We've got to get our house open —and get tea ourselves, and all that. Besides, I want to hear what's up. You can't leave a thing like a hospital in a strange man's hands for a month and not find changes. Of course I shall hate whatever he's done, but I'd like to know what it is!"

"Well, if you'd hate it," Sally quite reasonably suggested, "couldn't we put off hearing about it till after tea? It'll be such fun opening house together and getting our own tea. I awfully want to see Jane, too, but we can run in later. It's horrid to have to start hating directly we get back!"

Before his marriage Alec had always done what he liked without a moment's hesitation. He had often not particularly liked it after he'd done it, but he had felt no constraint which wasn't common to mankind. He hadn't had to stay away from tea with Jane, whom he hadn't seen for over a month, in order to have tea with a girl who hadn't been out of his sight for the same period of time.

He said, directly the jagged edge of this thought struck him, "I want to go to tea with Jane!"

Sally answered quickly—but not quite quickly enough —"Then of course we will!"

The silence that settled down between them both beneath the friendly noises of the car was quite a different silence. To begin with, they no longer shared it. Sally had taken hers away from Alec; and he didn't know, and didn't want to know, what Sally's contained. His own was unpleasant enough without that. He had been cross to Sally, and she had given way to him, and let him see that she hadn't liked giving way to him.

What could be more exasperating than that? Why couldn't one have one's own way and yet not be given way to? If Sally didn't want to go to tea with Jane, why the devil shouldn't she go home and make her own tea? All she had to do was to put a match to the gas stove. Of course he loved Sally to distraction, but they'd have plenty of time to have tea with Jane, and get enough distraction in before dinner—let alone after!

The hospital buildings stood up suddenly out of the shadowy plain. It wasn't dark yet, only frosty and blue.

The hospital didn't really look like a prison, though of course Parkins, the lodge-keeper, had to see who you were before you went out or in. Still, after their adventures on open moors, their moss-grown mills and thatched cottages with still blooming gardens, this grey hygienic institution, set flat in unfeatured grounds, was a set-back to the imagination. If it was your work it was different. Alec liked the half-witted derelict creatures drifting about the grounds, trying their dulled wits at jobs an intelligent child of six could do better. He knew all about them; most of them had been worse and more useless before they'd been worked on. Alec had them all mapped out in his mind and meant to make them more useful yet. But he knew Sally couldn't like them. The abnormal wasn't her job and she was too healthy to be interested in it.

He began to be besieged by Sally's thoughts. He wouldn't let them in, but they clamoured at the threshold of his mind.

Sally said nothing. She kept her eyes rather carefully

turned away. When they drew up, she got out of the car with less than her usual lightness.

A moment later she was in Jane's arms. At any rate, she seemed happy enough then.

Jane's room was just as Alec had been thinking of it. Quantities of small yellow chrysanthemums against warm ivory walls, a bright fire burning; their tea spread out in front of it; hot muffins, savoury sandwiches, a great open jar of Tiptree jam.

Jane wore her yellow dress and red amber beads. Her eyes sparkled at Alec over the top of Sally's curls; and she gave him that quick firm grasp of her hand which he had been waiting for.

But she wouldn't answer any of his questions till she'd heard what Sally had to say about their trip.

Sally didn't look a bit as if she wanted to go home now. She sat on the edge of her chair, brilliant with eagerness, pouring out pictures of what they'd seen in Devon and Cornwall. Rocks and the sea, late gorse in flower, tumbled out of her by turns. She described how they'd been be-nighted on the Quantocks; and picked mushrooms on the cliffs of Kilve for breakfast. How they'd sailed round Bolt Head on a sea as smooth as June, and on another day had seen a ship nearly wrecked off it, in a gale. How a strange dog had insisted on joining them for a day's perplexing and uproarious intimacy, and then retired to its unknown home, with graceful unobtrusiveness, at night.

Alec found himself re-living these days with fresh ecstasy. Once more he felt the rigid channels of his personality break down, and the new stream of Sally run through him, swift and warm. He forgot about the hospital, and Charles. He was almost sorry when Sally checked herself at last and said:

"Oh, Jane—tell him everything! He's dying to be told

what the new man's been doing to the hospital! And about the patients and what everybody's been up to!"

"He looks dying!" Jane gently jeered. "I don't believe he'd have minded if the hospital had been burnt down in his absence."

She didn't seem in a hurry to tell them about the new man's behaviour. When Sally insisted, Jane said hesitatingly:

"You'll see for yourselves. He's quite modern. I don't think we shall find him at all obstructive to our main ideas. He's really improved the farm. He cuts down expenses while he's actually improving the quality of what's being used. Naturally there's been a certain amount of friction. People don't like being improved; still less do they like being improved away. The biggest change is that he's parted with Matron. They clashed from the first. She tried to run him, as she'd run Luke—and he wouldn't be run. I think you would have had the same difficulty in his place. At any rate, we all seem to have survived the parting."

At last Alec had a reason for anger! It was almost a mercy that Charles should have given him so good a pretext.

"What on earth did he do that for?" he demanded with fury. "A perfectly good worker—who's kept everything in apple-pie order for years! He might at least have had the common decency to wait till I got back to discuss it with me! I don't say Matron hadn't got faults—she was a bully and a bore—but we've all got something against us. Anyhow, you could always, banteringly, bully her back, and get what you wanted. She was worth putting up with; she ran this hospital like the Scotch Express! You might have written to me about it, Jane—if you couldn't stop it yourself."

"I thought I would rather talk it over with you," Jane replied, with her exasperating mildness. "There really was

nothing we could either of us do about it. Dr. Drummond
was within his rights in sending a report on the Matron
to the Committee. He told her in advance what he intended
to do. She could either resign or fight it out. She chose to
fight it out and the Committee acted on Dr. Drummond's
report. In the end she resigned, and they gave her so good
a chit that she will have no difficulty in getting another
job. Miss Sanders was made Matron in her place, and
Sister Jobson has taken on the night duty. The two deputies were a little annoyed, but they would have been more
annoyed had either been preferred to the other. There
was a good deal of talk about it, but everything seems to
have settled down now."

Alec let this sink in; but he wasn't satisfied, if Jane was.
A perverse admiration for a woman he had never admired
surged through him. He saw Charles in his mind's eye—
repellent, rigid—quite incapable of coming out of his shell
to reach a big, warm-hearted termagant, who only wanted
to be jollied, in order to eat out of your hand. A coarse
joke or two and she doubled up and gave way at once!
Charles was no psychiatrist or he'd have been able to get
the best out of a good worker. Jane ought to have stood
by the Matron even if she didn't like her; but Jane was
always so damned fastidious! What did she mean by talking as if Alec had been run by the Matron? No woman
had ever run him—and they weren't going to begin to
now, married or not!

Alec shot a belligerent glance at Sally, who was eating
her third muffin in unruffled innocence.

"She'd better not begin trying to run me!" he said to
himself savagely.

Aloud he said to Jane: "Have you seen anything of the
fellow's sister? Do they go on asking us out to full-dress
parties, and all that bunkum?"

Alec had never given Myra another thought till now,

but he found that with this mention of her her image sprang, with astonishing distinctness, into his mind's eye.

Jane didn't answer his question at once. A little frown came between her arched eyebrows which made her look like a slightly bewildered pansy. She poured out more tea and cut a cake, then she said slowly:

"I suppose I'd better tell you myself—it'll be the first thing you hear directly you get inside the hospital. It's nothing at all really. That's why it's so tiresome. It seems that Dr. Drummond's sister is Myra Anderson. I don't suppose the name means anything to you—it didn't to me; but three years ago her husband was found shot dead. There was no one except his wife in the house at the time. She was accused of murder, but acquitted. Presumably the husband committed suicide."

"Oh, but, Jane! how frightfully thrilling!" Sally cried. "Fancy keeping a gorgeous piece of news like that up your sleeve till it's dragged out of you! I always disliked her the most. But she looks so awfully like the adventuress in plays that you'd think she couldn't be one!"

"The fact of her husband's committing suicide," Alec chillingly broke in, "hardly seems a reason for calling his wife an adventuress."

Looking up, he caught Jane's eyes resting upon him in astonished disapproval.

"Why on earth"—they asked him—"are you being nasty to Sally?"

CHAPTER XV

To ENVY Jane would have seemed to be as silly to Alec as to envy his right hand. He had always taken the same sort of pride in her work that he took in his own.

Nevertheless, he found himself wondering whether she hadn't been right in thinking that he oughtn't to have given up his larger share of the hospital for the men's side.

He shrank from his first visit to his new quarters. He felt driven back, even if it was only for a few minutes, into the women's wing. Here everything was familiar to him. He knew the way windows opened and the way keys turned in locks. He could put his hand on every instrument in the spotless theatre. The nurses and the patients were built up out of his knowledge of them.

It was the swift after-breakfast hour when everyone was on his mettle and hurrying to be beforehand with routine work, in case of special emergency.

Alec watched a little shamefacedly how each old friend greeted him. Was he as welcome now, and as respected, as if he had come back their chief? If a nurse hurried by him with a mere formal greeting, and didn't stop to ask him how he'd enjoyed his holiday, his heart sank. If a patient, cleaning in the passages, deep in some incredible dream, failed to be called out of it by his eyes and voice, Alec felt as unreal and unsubstantial as the dream.

When he reached the clinical room where Jane was seeing her patients, he hesitated. What right had he, after all, to go in and bother Jane? He was due in his own wards on the men's side. Jane would be busy. She wouldn't want to see him! The place was hers now, she'd been running it a month! If she'd wanted him, she could have asked him to look in last night! And yet wasn't theirs an intimacy beyond requests or explanations? He knocked, and Jane's voice, cheerful and welcoming, took away part of his uneasiness.

She didn't look at all surprised to see him, and she behaved as if it were still Alec's office.

"You've just come in time," she told him, "to see little Miss Flint for me. It will do her good to see you. I hear she's been tearing her clothes again. While you're giving her a talking-to, I'll just run through the wards."

"I haven't any business to see her," Alec said doubtfully. "I ought to be over in my own wards. Still, if you'd really like me to——"

Carrie Flint was in a sense his special property. She had come in shattered to pieces; his skill had reached her, as a searchlight from the shore reaches a ship in a furious sea. Through her black night a beam of hope had shone.

Carrie was the youngest of three sisters left orphaned in early youth. They all three had high ideals and comfortable private means. One of the elder sisters was a famous headmistress, the other an equally famous mountainclimber. Carrie had been a gym mistress in her eldest sister's school, and spent her holidays climbing mountains with the second sister. But she had never been able to emulate the brains of Isabel or the muscles of Maud. Her sisters loved her devotedly; and they had dragged her onwards and upwards along the path which they had chosen for her, by the hair of her obedient head. Carrie had worked her hardest to please Isabel, and climbed her hardest to please Maud. She had failed dismally at examinations, and, by way of recreation, fallen into crevasses. Timid, adoring, ineffectual, a prey to secret resentment, Carrie had plodded on her exhausting way, until the inevitable collapse came. The sisters had tried all the harder to stiffen her to fresh exertion. They had poured the vitriol of moral intensity into her tired nerves, and Carrie had responded with terrific tension, until the desire to evade the ordeals which she was facing proved too strong for her. She had seen that there was only one thing she could conscientiously get out of, which would prevent her from having to face any fresh ordeals, she could go out of her mind; and this, with extreme thoroughness, Carrie had proceeded to do. Consumed by love and terror, her hunted mind found its one solution in an attempted embrace, which turned in the moment of attainment into a ferocious bite.

A knock came at the door and Carrie slid softly into the room, accompanied by her special nurse.

Jane said quickly: "Now your own doctor is going to talk to you this morning, Carrie!" and was gone.

Instantly Alec's sense of grievance left him. He forgot he was in Jane's office, not his own. He even forgot that deeper grudge that the hospital was not his, but Charles's.

"Steady, Carrie," he said, holding her back gently by the wrists and looking down at her with deep impersonal kindness.

Carrie smiled in response, her intense sly smile, trembling with eagerness to accomplish her act of frustrated tenderness.

"I hear you've been tearing your dress again," Alec said. "That's a pity! It suits you, Carrie! You look nice in pink! Doesn't she, Nurse? Try not to tear this one!"

Carrie's eyes fluttered avidly over the stout pink calico. She knew Alec was talking about her dress. She smiled harder, and dipped suddenly towards the hand that held her wrist, with bared teeth.

Nurse Christie was just in time to draw her back. "No, you don't!" she said firmly, but without harshness.

Alec's smile never changed. "No," he agreed, "you must get over that little trick, Carrie—it's better not to bite! I'm very glad to see you—and you too, Nurse Christie. You needn't whisper to me, Carrie; say whatever you like from where you are! You are better, aren't you?"

Carrie wouldn't speak, but she nodded. She stood there swaying and smiling, her one thought beating in her, automatically, like the rise and fall of a piston.

"Yes, she is better, Doctor," Nurse Christie told him. "She can sleep, and eat, and most of the time she's quite good and quiet; but not steadily quiet, if you know what I mean."

"Any work possible yet?" Alec asked.

Nurse Christie shook her head.

"Keep on trying," Alec urged. "She isn't fit for the occupational room yet, of course; but she might do something in the ward. Carrie, I'd like you to make me a present. Will you? A good strong waste-paper basket is just what I need for my new office. Do you think you could make one for me, like the big one of Dr. Everest's? Nurse will show you how."

He threw a pellet of paper into Jane's basket, while Carrie's eyes followed his hand. They came back adoringly to his face, searching it with a stubborn demand for a feeling which no one had ever shown her.

"She feels the change," Nurse Christie murmured in a low voice. "Dr. Everest's splendid with her, but she doesn't reach her. Miss Flint simply doesn't notice if she's there."

"That'll come," Alec told her. "Run along with Nurse now, Carrie; and don't forget, you mustn't tear your pretty frock, and I'd be very pleased with the basket!" He watched Nurse Christie drag her gently backwards out of the room. Carrie held out her hands imploringly towards Alec, her hunted eyes fixed on him, till the door closed.

It was nice of Jane to have let him see Carrie! A feeling of restored cheerfulness and courage swept over Alec. After all, the work was the same! He knew a lot of the men already; and he had always been more interested in the shell-shock ward than any other in the hospital. Now he'd see if he couldn't wake up that young Endicott, who'd been pushed out of the world at eighteen by the War, and never got back into it again.

Alec went through his new wards with brisk decision; and then out into the grounds to look up his working patients. Everything he did deepened his interest, but he kept to the last Arnold's occupational therapy room, which was the finest piece of work in the hospital.

Arnold was an ex-patient. He hadn't only been cured, he'd come back, five years later, a thoroughly trained and competent mental teacher, the best the hospital had ever had. Jane thought there was no one to touch Arnold, and Alec shared her confidence. Charles, of course, mightn't have the sense to see it, but fortunately Charles couldn't do much about it either way. Things that went right could go on going right. He had only the power to alter things that went wrong.

The men glanced up, casually interested, as Alec entered the room, and then turned swiftly back to their work again. But old Robson, who hadn't spoken for thirty years, recognised Alec with an enthusiasm which brought his whole sunken personality to the surface. His eyes shone with friendliness, and he lifted his hand in an old-fashioned salute. He listened with absorbed attention while Alec told him about his trip with Sally. Perhaps Robson had been a traveller in his youth, and the names of the places Alec had stopped at evoked scenes which made him forget the curtain he had drawn between himself and life. But after a time his eyes clouded over. Old Robson had a deep grudge against life, a very little of it went a long way with him. He gave a vague smile, and wandered away from Alec as if he had never known him.

"He knew you were coming back to-day," Arnold explained in a low voice. "He's been watching for you all the morning. And now, though you mightn't think it, he's as pleased as Punch! He went off his food for days when Dr. Everest took the other side; in fact, I shouldn't have been surprised if he'd petered out altogether. But she came over to cheer him up sometimes, and when she told him you were going to take over, he came round and started eating again. It's funny how the non-socials care for the one or two people they have any confidence in. It's as if the less they have to do with human beings, the more intensely they need it! All these fellows work better in company. They get themselves off their backs for a few hours of the day, anyhow! Sometimes they even take an interest in each other's jobs. There's that little chap Green, by the window. When he first came in, he sat there crying for hours, or tried to smash up other people's things. Now if he can't get his design right one way, he tries another. And you can trust him with any tool. He's made several new patterns for himself, and taught the other patients how to do them. I wouldn't be surprised if you had him cured soon. You know Travers, don't you? That tall man over there by the small table. He's our most troublesome patient; a dangerous fellow, more bother than all the rest of them put together. He's a perfectly intelligent, educated chap, but he can't leave anyone alone. Always trying on indecent tricks. Dr. Everest brought him in here, but he wouldn't work at anything, till one day she caught him watching Jackson trying to copy an old Spanish galleon, but not making much of a job of it. She said: 'Why don't you try to make a ship like that, Mr. Travers?' and before we knew where we were, he'd got the thing in his own hands and was making a three-decker galleon as good as if he'd been brought up on the Spanish Armada! He works here all day now, and whatever trouble he gives outside, we don't see any more of it here!"

Alec met the hostile, impudent eyes of the pervert across the table. Funny that Jane could make anything out of such a fellow!

"You think he really improved with Dr. Everest?" Alec asked.

The look on Arnold's face surprised him. "Dr. Everest," he answered Alec gravely, "is in my opinion one of the finest psychologists of our time. There isn't one of the men I've had in this room she hasn't improved one way or another! They aren't all curable, but they're all the better for her work among them."

Alec said nothing. He had never thought of Jane as a great doctor. He relied on her judgment. He trusted her accuracy; but greatness? He had been her chief. He had taught her most of what she knew. Generous as he was in all his feelings for her, Arnold's words were something of a shock to him. What was there in Jane which he hadn't taught her, and which perhaps he himself didn't possess?

"That's Findlay," Arnold said, after a pause. "That little fellow over there at work on a tray. He's the best worker we've got, but he doesn't get better. He's walled himself in too much!"

Alec crossed over to the man with flying hands. He saw at a glance that he was an advanced schizophrenic, living his outer life totally at variance with his inward imaginings. As he glanced up at Alec a fixed sly smile crossed the cold mask of his face. He enjoyed having his work looked at, and admired. It gave him a reassuring feeling that he could deceive everybody all round. They thought he was making trays—they little knew what he was really doing with his ruthless mind! He wanted to chain Alec's attention—here was a new doctor he had to take in if he could! He showed Alec his neat inlaid tray with watchful intensity.

All the patients were subtilely aware of Alec. They knew he was their new doctor, and each one of them was anxious to make upon him an impression of their individual importance. If only he could be brought over to their side and made to believe their false world true!

Peter, the idiot, an enormous creature with a head the size of an apple set on his gigantic trunk, came shambling up eagerly to Alec, to show him his big rag carpet.

"Peter came in here as helpless as a baby," Arnold proudly explained, "and as fierce as a gale of wind. He couldn't put his hand up to his mouth. He was thirty-three and had never fed himself. All his life he'd just sat over a stove in a tiny kitchen, nagged at by a nerve-driven mother. One day he half-killed her, and if he'd had more sense he'd have done it before! Now he can wash, dress, and feed himself; and he's as good and happy as possible, unless anyone gets in the way of that precious carpet! He might kill them then—by accident, as it were; but there's no malice in him! That boy is our youngest. Came in over a year ago. Constant fits and mishandling; very fierce and intractable he was for a bit. Now he's up to school standard and a very clever orthopædic worker. Dr. Everest has got him a job to go to outside in a month or two.

"Now that fellow Mason, who's binding books, Dr Macgregor, could you have a word with him by-and-by? He's perfectly sane, and has been for three years, and won't go out! He's an expert chemist and his money's getting low. He ought to get a job before it's too late, but the mere thought of facing his life outside throws him into a panic!"

"Send him to the office to-morrow morning," Alec said; "and Findlay and Travers too. Separately, of course. I can't talk to either of them properly here. My difficulty, you know, Arnold, is to make up my mind what we mean by sanity. When you come right down to it, who is sane? I'm sane part of the time, but mad as a hatter the rest; and so are most people I know. How do you spot the difference?"

Arnold smiled. "Probably you can't," he agreed, "because you've never been insane all the time. There is a difference, though! Mason ought to leave here, because if he stays much longer he won't be able to live in an unadjusted world. That's the main difference between sanity and insanity, as I see it. Can you get on when things aren't made easy for you, because you've got something in you that can make anything that comes along easy enough? If not, then you're better off here, where things are specially adjusted for you!"

"You mean, if I want the world my way, I'm mad," Alec said reflectively, "and if I'm content to take it on its own terms, I'm sane?"

"That's just about it," Arnold agreed quietly.

There was a slight stir through the room. Alec looked up quickly and saw Charles standing in the open doorway. A flash of anger so bitter that it startled him ran through Alec's mind.

Charles signalled to him in a friendly way across the room.

Suddenly Alec was conscious that Travers, the pervert, knew what he was feeling. The man's jeering, overintimate eyes slipped from one to the other of the two doctors.

"That's the new Superintendent!" he said aloud, and laughed mockingly.

Charles crossed the room and held out his hand to
Alec.

"I didn't know you were here," he said. "Someone told
me you were over at the Farm. I hope you had a good
holiday?"

Alec eyed Charles as a dog eyes a strange dog about
to set foot upon his private realm.

"Thanks," he said, unsmilingly, "I had a good holiday!" and turned his back on Charles.

When he turned round again, the room was once more
immersed in its tasks; and Charles was gone.

Alec felt that he could breathe more freely; but he
avoided looking at Arnold. He looked at the men instead,
with different eyes. Out of the whole hospital these were
the best material for cure.

Alec wanted to cure them, with a fierce desire; but as
he hurried downstairs to write his belated reports, which
he would have to take to Charles, he asked himself why
he wanted to cure them. Was it that profound impersonal compassion of the strong for the weak which absorbs
the whole of a man's being—except his self-consciousness
—or was it that other type of desire, as keen-witted, and
as driving, but far less pure, for proving to himself, before
the eyes of the whole hospital, that he was a better man
than Charles?

CHAPTER XVI

PASSING rapidly by the gate of Charles's garden with averted head, Alec was aware of being suddenly addressed.

"Oh—Dr. Macgregor!"

He wheeled, to face a pair of panic-stricken, appealing eyes.

"Oh, Dr. Macgregor, I'm in such trouble—can I speak to you?" Myra was looking through the gate at him, as a lost soul might look at the protective security of heaven.

His quick "Of course!" leapt to meet her need. Even in the most brutal of men a knight-errant lies dormant. It was not dormant in Alec, it was the unchecked aim of his entire life.

"Not in here!" Myra objected: "Charles might know— I couldn't—he doesn't understand. Is there anywhere you can take me?"

Alec considered a moment. It was four o'clock on a dull February afternoon. He was due back in the wards at five. He had a difficult theatre case to attend to, and was just dashing home for a cup of tea.

Sally expected him. His house was small, and full of Sally. It seemed somehow not the place for the troubles of another woman.

There was his office in the hospital, a tiny place close to the refractory ward. This, too, seemed an unsuitable background for Myra's trouble; and there was the added consideration, perhaps hardly an objection, that Charles had forbidden it. If Myra had been another man, they could have just walked up and down the road; but Myra was unsuitably dressed for a walk. She had run out of

the house hatless, in remarkably thin shoes. Nor was she
another man.

The medical quarters presented themselves to Alec's
mind. Jane's sitting-room, for instance; but Jane would
almost certainly be in there having her tea. Barnes's
sitting-room next door to Jane's would be better still, for
Barnes was on duty in the hospital and would be there
till dinner.

In the pale February dusk Myra's figure had an unsubstantial quality. Alec never noticed clothes, but he had
a vague impression that she looked, and smelled, like a
lily-of-the-valley. He could hear her quick, frightened
breathing as she slipped through the gate to his side. She
was a hunted creature. Anger surged up in Alec's heart;
that brute Charles should have protected her, instead
of adding to her terror!

They hurried, side by side, over the damp lawn, through
the open hall door, into Barnes's slightly dishevelled
sitting-room, empty except for cigarette smoke and the
slaughtered remains of the daily paper, scattered over the
floor. Myra shivered. Alec lit the gas fire, turned up a
shaded lamp on the desk, and pulled down the blinds.

She sat huddled up in the corner of the sofa watching
him. Her eyes had the quick, roving brightness of a
frightened bird's. Every now and then a fit of trembling
seized her.

Alec drew an armchair forward, and, sinking into it,
considered her thoughtfully. He was strangely aware of
her, but he did not know that she made him aware of her.
The women Alec was accustomed to had no such powers,
nor would they have used them if they had. They had
other things than men to think about; but Myra had no
other things. The way to reach men, the way to handle
them for her own advantage, when reached, was the only
lesson which she had ever learned.

Alec was a good psychiatrist and a friend to women, but his experience had been limited. His senses, though strong, were not easily roused, and there was therefore a borderland over which a clever woman might take him far, before he knew that he had entered it.

"It's very kind of you," Myra murmured plaintively. "We're strangers—I have no right—but I'm so desperately unhappy! I don't know which way to turn! I've had such rotten luck! You see, it's happened before—and each time it happens I lose my nerve—and then I have to begin all over again—and I lose more nerve. You've heard my story, perhaps? But you don't know it. No one can know it—but me! It was so awful in that empty house—after the shot rang out!" She stopped, gasping, pressing her hand over a heart that actually fluttered.

"Tell me anything you like—and nothing that you don't like," Alec suggested. His doctor's wits were roused, but they were no protection to him, for they turned Myra into a patient. She had been badly frightened, and he felt that he was bound to see her through her emergency. He was even tempted to believe beforehand that she had an emergency.

"If Charles could only understand!" she said in a low voice. "But I oughtn't to say that. He's my brother—! He did what he could—! He sacrificed a fortune for our name—for the honour of the family. Now that's done, and I'm free, as they call it, he doesn't care any more. It's natural he should resent what he's had to do for me; I could bear that. But it's having it come up—all over again! I couldn't live in London; I can't see my friends as I used to—they were his friends too—my—my husband's —and they took his side. Even if they don't think I did it, they make me responsible for his having done it. You know, perhaps—doctors do—I think—that no one knows the truth—about anyone else's married life? You like the husband or the wife, you take sides. Perhaps the one you like tells you his side—or her side. But married life isn't one side or the other, it's something both make together—which is quite different."

Alec nodded. He had been married three months, and he had heard a great deal of other people's experiences of married life, mostly poor people's, and mostly real experiences. He knew nothing whatever about married life as Myra had lived it. He thought she put the thing very fairly; and so she did, for she saw that she had to seem fair in order to secure Alec's sympathies. Men never liked women who complained too drastically of other men.

She drew a deep breath. "I've started afresh three times," she went on, "once in London, once abroad, and now—here. I can't do it again! I'd rather kill myself—as—as he did!"

"No—that's poor," Alec said sternly. "You mustn't do that!" People killing themselves, or trying to, was what he did know all about. Alec ran over in his mind the bulk of his experiences. He believed that people generally killed themselves from vanity, or out of revenge. Sometimes—but very rarely—because it was the only sane thing to do. Then they were called insane, so that they might be buried in consecrated ground. But those common-sense suicides were the exception, since common-sense usually enabled people to see some less sensational way out of their difficulties. Most suicides were mere acts of revenge. You wanted to get back on somebody who had slighted you, or if there was nobody to feel mangled by your act, back on God for having dared to expose you to the indignity of life. You were too proud to fight—that was about all there was to suicide. But that didn't stop Alec's feeling sympathy for the girl in front of him. Her motive was probably to make Charles sit up—and perhaps to bring herself before the eyes of the public again. She had done that once before, and she may not have altogether disliked it.

Alec tried to be judicious about her, but it was simpler to be sorry for her. He saw that he must try to make it seem to her not too important whether she killed herself or not, and then brush away the subject and get down to an incentive which would make her want to live.

"You'll outgrow all this worry," he said kindly. "You're awfully young—and attractive—and all that, you know; and when you come right down to it, it doesn't awfully matter what other people say. They take us much more lightly than we think. Look at the way we all go on eating our dinners—even after a funeral! Heaps of people aren't interested in newspaper drivel; they wouldn't care what came out about you. We shouldn't, for instance—I mean—Everest—and ourselves and the Hursts. It's nothing to any of us what happened to your husband. We judge people on their own merits. Of course I know you're not used to small sets of people, you'd naturally know the big social Bugs round here, but I doubt if they're awfully worth knowing! Social life is breaking up all over England now. People who find they like each other, make sets; and that's the best kind really. Don't let the past worry you. It's the dead who ought to bury their dead. I don't want to be unkind, but your husband chose his own way out of it. Even if you weren't happy together, there are other more sensible ways of breaking up a home, aren't there? You aren't responsible for the way he chose; but it would be a pity to repeat it."

Myra seemed hardly to breathe while Alec spoke. She sat with her eyes dropped, her hands clasped in her lap. Her face in the half-light was so beautiful, it took Alec's breath away. He felt she must be innocent—innocent, at any rate, of any gross wrong.

When he paused, she moved, like a person coming out of

a trance. She lifted her deep blue eyes to his. She was so near him that he could see her long fair lashes were darker at the tips. She had a honey-coloured freckle on her short beautifully cut nose. The modelling of her lips and chin and the long line of her throat were as delicate and cleanly carved as an ancient Chinese ivory.

"That isn't all," she whispered. "I'm going to be quite frank with you, Dr. Macgregor. It isn't only the past I have to get over, it's the future! They won't stop punishing me! It's true I'm young—I'm only twenty-four! I was a wife—and now I'm no one's wife. I wanted to have children—and I haven't got any children! This thing that ought to be behind me is in front of me too! It prevents my having anything—any love—any children—any decent fun! And I want them! I want them dreadfully! I want them all the time! Charles says I oughtn't to expect it. He's as hard as any stone. But stones can be right— perhaps I oughtn't to expect any more—happiness——?"

"He's utterly wrong!" Alec said gently. He was holding both her hands as he said it, though how he came to be holding her hands he couldn't possibly have said. They were odd hands to hold, pink and soft and supple, neither hot nor cold, but very much alive.

"But men—men only love women when they're happy," she whispered. "And, oh, Alec—I'm not happy!"

He murmured, "That's nonsense, too!"

She slipped into his arms as the moon slips into a cloud. She clung to him, melted into him, and blotted out the world.

The door opened and over the crushed sweetness of Myra's slender body Alec met Jane's startled hygienic gaze. It was like falling headlong into a cold pool. No murderer was ever more obsessed with the longing to know how to dispose of the body than Alec was with the desire to get rid of Myra's lively, too eloquent form.

It made everything much worse that Jane, after the first blank incredulity of her recognition, took no further notice of them. She didn't rush out. She went, quite collectedly, to the bookcase, to borrow Yellowsleeves on "Problems in Psychiatry," and, finding it, strolled out with the book under her arm, without having uttered a word.

Myra had by this time got back onto the sofa again, and broken into floods of tears. Her eyes looked enormous and brighter than ever, afterwards; but she didn't cry very long, because Alec didn't look at all touched by her tears. He was feeling infuriated by Jane, and madly anxious to see Sally. But there would be no time to go home. He must go to the theatre in ten minutes. He had to find an abscess which was pressing on a man's brain. His feeling for Myra became non-existent. He supposed he had taken her into his arms! She'd got there anyhow! And now that she was out again, he felt no more responsible for her than a letter-box might feel, once emptied of a letter.

"What on earth will happen now?" Myra demanded, a flash of amusement in her sparkling eyes. "It was that stick of a woman doctor who came in, wasn't it? Will this go all over the hospital too?"

"Certainly not!" Alec said rather crossly. "It will go no further than this room—unless you want it to. I dare say Jane will never stop despising me—but that's my business—you're all right."

"Oh, well," said Myra, as if after all that was the only thing that mattered. She took a powder-puff out of her pocket and proceeded to powder her face. She looked like a well-trained kitten at work upon a spotless ruff. After she had finished, she smiled up at Alec, a mischievous, collaborating smile.

"It's all nonsense, really!" she murmured. "But you've cheered me up no end, and I'm frightfully obliged to you.

I might even try to weather the storm here—if you'll stand by me. Will you—you and your adorable little wife—and whatever those people are called who dress in the cast-off clothes of Arctic explorers? I can spare Dr. Everest. She can hate me for ever if she wants to. Is she as jealous of your wife as she is of me? We didn't mean any harm, did we?"

Myra sprang up. She looked neither frightened nor desperate now, but marvellously full of colour. There wasn't much light in the room, but all of it was on her—on her red hair and on her thin shell-like hands and laughing lips.

"Poor Dr. Everest!" she said. "You and Charles are both so devastatingly good-looking! I'll behave properly now—at least, I think I will! You're not angry with me, are you?"

Perhaps he ought to have been angry! Alec even told himself that he was; but the feeling he had wasn't anger. It was a queer mixture of self-conscious shame and a sort of horrible eagerness. The sort of feeling a good dog has, while running after a rabbit, when he knows that he is forbidden to run after rabbits.

This particular rabbit made it even harder to be a good dog, because she actively encouraged pursuit.

Myra didn't want to find out if Alec were angry or not; and apparently she took for granted that he would stand by her. Her head reached as high as his chin. She stood on tiptoe and laid hands, as light as snowflakes, on his shoulders; then she kissed him full on the lips, a long, slow, tantalising kiss. She ran out of the room, laughing, before he had made up his mind what he was going to do about it.

The light seemed to go out of the room with her, and all Alec's eagerness. There was no sound whatever from Jane's room on the other side of the thinly built wall.

CHAPTER XVII

THE operation Alec was about to perform was difficult, uncertain, and dangerous. He had the opinion of two famous London specialists against him, taken before the patient came into their hands. They believed that there was no abscess. There was a bad psychic history and symptoms compatible with brain pressure, but which could be attributed to other sources. The case was definitely going to the bad, and Alec had pressed his opinion against theirs; and Charles's. Charles had accepted the London view that there was no abscess, and that it would, in view of the patient's nervous condition, be dangerous to operate.

"You have Jenkins and Barclay definitely against you," Charles concluded, with his intolerable air of polite indifference. "I see no reason to doubt their competence. What does Dr. Everest think?"

Jane had backed Alec, but Alec considered that it had been a tepid backing. She had merely said: "If Dr. Macgregor is right, there is a chance of saving the patient. Otherwise it seems unlikely that he can be saved; therefore I should advise an operation."

"One objects on humanitarian grounds to useless torture," Charles had gravely observed.

This had made Alec perfectly certain that the abscess was there. He had replied heatedly: "It won't be useless. I know there is an abscess. When he came in, there was still some correlation between hand and brain, and that, definitely, no longer exists. He can see a pin on the floor, but he can't pick it up. The pupils of the eyes are greatly enlarged. Jenkins and Barclay were wrong, that's all—and I'm right."

Neither Charles nor Jane made any further comment. The patient was Alec's patient, and the responsibility of proving himself right was also Alec's.

As soon as he remembered the time, after Myra's departure, a quavering feeling of uncertainty about the case took hold of Alec. Suppose after all he wasn't right?

Jane was to assist him in the operation and Charles had insisted on giving the anæsthetic himself. He was uneasy about the patient's condition, and determined to take the onus of any possible disaster. Alec would have liked Charles for this, if he could have liked him for anything.

Alec found that he was already five minutes late. He tore out of the room, down the corridor, and upstairs to the theatre.

Charles and Jane were already there. Sister Simmons, the theatre sister, had the patient on the table, and all Alec's favourite instruments were picked out and ready for him.

The shining room was pitilessly light and hot.

Alec slipped hurriedly behind the screen, washed his hands and snatched his coat, mask, and gloves, in turn, out of the sister's hands.

Jane hadn't looked at him when he came in, but, on the other hand, she hadn't tried not to. She was talking soothingly to the patient, who had already given trouble and looked as if he would give more.

Charles looked up as Alec entered. His cold eyes had said as plainly as any words, "Surgeons shouldn't be late for operations!" "He should keep his confounded sister in hand, then!" Alec thought angrily as he strode towards the table.

He didn't like the look of the patient—a bad alcoholic —flaccid muscles, congested veins, a rapid pulse, and shallow breathing. Not a good subject for any anæsthetic, however light.

Charles started giving the patient ethylchloride, chloroform and ether. The patient was a bad subject, and struggled violently. He rolled back his tongue and nearly got choked by it.

Charles managed the anæsthetic with extreme skill; but he murmured, "Be as quick as you can!"

Alec felt hurried. His heart beat hard. His nerves were ruffled. He damned Charles inaudibly for a fussy, self-important, funking fellow.

The patient kept up a perpetual thin screaming like an enraged cricket. Charles gave the signal to begin, and Alec bent over the table to make the incision. The rest of the room, and all its inmates, vanished. Nothing mattered now but the blind, inspiring search for the pocket of pus.

The sharpened steel slipped through the tissue, clean and swift as a fish's fin through water—deep, deeper—how much deeper dared he cut? The blood spurted up on either side of the blade—the flesh melted!—Ah!—here was a soft, treacherous spot! He had been right! This was the abscess, a big fellow, with the suspicion of another beyond.

Time fought him like an enemy. He cut through the thin wall dividing the two abscesses; and started cleaning them both up.

Charles said: "The patient does not look well! We must try artificial respiration!"

Alec obeyed, inwardly cursing. Why couldn't the fellow keep the patient's heart going for him? The operation wasn't a light business—but he started massaging while Charles messed about with carbon dioxide and heart injections. They got the heart started again between them; and Alec went back to the brain. It looked now as if they might get the fellow through, after all!

Suddenly the patient's screaming died ominously into a faint bubbling sound. Charles said, in a low voice full of horror: "He's off!"

Alec slipped back to the heart. He had a vague knowledge of Charles and Jane working together as if they could see into each other's minds. But the uncertain spirit of life, discontented with its dilapidated cage, had already flown.

"He's gone," Alec said grimly. "It's no use slapping a dead cat!"

"Nonsense!" Jane said sharply; but he could tell by her voice that she knew it wasn't nonsense.

Charles said nothing. Alec felt rather sorry for the fellow. The job had been his—and he had lost it. Every drop of blood seemed drained from the set mask of his face. Only his eyes were alive, leaping and burning, like tortured devils. Charles fought the limp piece of flesh, as if he held death in his hands and was putting an end to it.

"It was a third abscess, I couldn't get at, which would have finished him off in a month or two," Alec pointed out rather consolingly to Charles.

Charles never looked up from his fruitless tussle; and Jane returned to his side. She laid her hand on his arm and said gently: "It isn't any use. We have all done what we could to save him; and as a matter of fact it would have been worse for him if we had saved him." She spoke as if she had a right to make Charles listen to her—and was sure that Charles would listen.

Alec stared at them with amazement. Why should Jane talk like that to a strange man who was their enemy?

Charles's dancing, savage eyes turned towards Jane. They grew suddenly human as they met hers. They became the eyes of a beseeching child. He seemed to be imploring Jane to turn time back, and give him another chance with the fellow

Jane's eyes were full of some queer light that was like tenderness. They remained fixed on Charles as if, in refusing him the impossibility he asked, she was giving him herself instead.

Fury seized Alec. What right had Jane to look at the man in that intimate, relieving way? He had bungled his job and lost the case—let him suffer for it! Or, if this criticism was too grossly unfair, even for a man in a temper who was nevertheless a scientist, at any rate, the job had gone wrong on him, and Charles ought to face the music without any help from Jane.

Alec was sorry now that he had mentioned the third abscess. He said brutally:

"Well—it's no good crying over spilt milk, is it? I suppose things had better be cleaned up, hadn't they? Maclean, take the body to the mortuary."

Maclean took the body out on a stretcher. Somebody opened a window.

Charles disappeared abruptly, without speaking to either of them. He hadn't said a word since the patient went.

"Clumsy idiot!" Alec said in a low voice to Jane. "No nerve! All that stiff, mind-the-paint manner—and a chicken heart under it! I was right about that abscess!"

"You are wrong about everything else!" Jane surprisingly told him.

"Look here," Alec found himself saying in a savage undertone, so as not to reach the sister who was clearing up the theatre. "Have you gone back on me? Do you like the fellow—Jane? It's incredible! You've no right to! You're treating him as if he were a friend. Have you no loyalty?"

"And if he is my friend," said Jane, in a voice so low that it hardly reached him, "he is a man of honour and a gentleman. I have a right to think and act towards him as

I choose. How dare you speak of unfaithfulness to me, after what I saw this afternoon?"

"Oh, that—!" said Alec contemptuously. It was childish and absurd of Jane to think seriously of a mere embrace. Nothing led up to it—nor away from it. It was a blind accident without continuity—a mere spontaneous combustion.

But the turning of Charles's eyes to Jane's and her incredible response to it was a serious act. You did not rely on a person in a conscious emergency unless you had come near to him already in the unconscious emergencies of the blood. A heart must be near a heart to lean on it.

Obscurely Alec knew that he had a right to be angry with Jane for that mere look; and that she was wrong to be angry with him—for a complete embrace.

He followed her out of the theatre and downstairs to her sitting-room. She neither spoke nor looked at him, but she did not refuse him admittance. He went into her room, after her, and closed the door.

The room had an odd, unfamiliar look, as if it weren't the place they had always been so happy in together. Alec sat down in his usual chair and buried his head in his hands. He felt suddenly discouraged. He had been through a storm of terror. His hunt for the abscess—his race with time—and then that harrowing defeat at the end! He had minded the fellow's dying, under his knife, quite as much as Charles had. After all, the man was his patient. He had never lost a case on the operating-table before; and Jane had said nothing to comfort him!

"Faithfulness be damned!" Alec muttered, remembering the last stone she had hurled at him. "If you're such a fool as to think I care for that flaunting little bitch—because I kissed her when she asked for it—you only show what a sex-cold ignoramus of a woman you are! Sally would understand I meant nothing by it. And, after all it's Sally's job whether I kiss another woman or not!"

"Exactly," said Jane icily. "And whose job is it whether I make friends with Dr. Drummond or not?"

"Mine!" Alec shouted desperately and with deep conviction. "I hate the fellow! If you hated him, don't you know that I'd hate him too—just because you did? We're not only friends, we're partners—and he's ousted us from our job—and it's a job we care for more than for anything else on earth—twice as much because we're in it together up to the neck! I don't say it's the most intimate bond there is, but it is damned intimate all the same. Sally's my wife—she is half my soul and half my body. I don't elbow her aside for you. But you're meat and drink to me through my work! And you poison my meat and drink when you look at that stinking Maypole of a fellow as if you—as if you——" Alec's voice trailed off into silence. The words "as if you wanted to take him into your arms" stuck in his throat. He had always said exactly what was in his mind to Jane. The whole of their intercourse had been open as air, and like air it had carried all the flying seeds of their thoughts from one to the other. It did so now. Jane knew what he couldn't say. She crimsoned slowly to the roots of her hair, and then slowly began to whiten. She had been standing by the mantelpiece, but now she suddenly sat down as if she felt exhausted and at an end of her resources. When she spoke, her voice was not angry any more, but it was a little toneless and flat.

"I feel just as you do," she said slowly, "about the bond between us. There couldn't be such a bond if we didn't feel the same about it. But I don't see that we have any right to decide questions of intimacy for each other. If I am not the same to you, you have a right to resent it. But my feelings for other men or women are my own affair—and yours are, I admit, your own—and Sally's. I was angry—

perhaps I had no right to be—at what I saw this afternoon. But I was angry for Sally. However lightly you took what you did, I felt you were infringing on her rights by taking it. Why should you wish to kiss any other woman than Sally—since you love Sally?"

"Because I'm human," said Alec impatiently. "Let's have some whisky before we go on with this! God! I'm as tired as if I'd run for miles! I'll get it. You stay where you are."

It was a relief moving about the room as if it belonged to him, and getting out the bottle Jane kept only for him. The glasses and the siphon were next door in the pantry. He poured out stiff whiskies for each of them.

"Now we shall feel better," he said, drinking his off. "Alcohol has its uses, in spite of that wreck upstairs giving us the slip because of it. Personally I thought I was rather nice to Drummond over the whole business. You know I was as quick as I could be; and I mind too—about losing my patient."

"My dear, I know you do!" said Jane quietly, in her usual friendly voice. "It's beastly to lose a patient! But you weren't responsible. You operated like an angel. No one in the world could have done a prettier piece of work in less time. That was just it! Dr. Drummond did his job, too, as well as it could be done. But that black spot which lurks in all bad cases was too much for him. No one was to blame—but he was responsible. I was very sorry for him——"

"You overdid the sympathetic part of it," Alec said gloomily; but he felt less gloomy, partly because of the whisky and partly because Jane had praised him. "I resented all that sob-stuff thrown in. Women should keep their feelings out of operating-theatres."

For a moment Jane said nothing. A queer little smile

played round her closed lips and her eyes danced. "Then shouldn't men keep their tempers out of them?" she murmured.

Alec rather reluctantly found himself smiling too. He had been in a temper, now that he came to think of it! He quite saw Jane's point. After all, she had a right to be sorry for that poor devil Drummond! Alec began to feel more comfortable about the whole affair; only he needed to clear up that secondary business of Myra, with Jane, before he could feel wholly at his ease.

"It's like this about a woman," he said, leaning forward. "I can keep straight on my own feelings. The proof of it is that I did keep straight waiting for Sally—for five years. Ordinary women—and I suppose I only met ordinary women—let you keep straight. But this Myra isn't an ordinary woman. She's not only a raving, roaring beauty, she's a sort of Circe. It's her job turning you into a pig—and well she knows how to do it! I'll hand her that! She took me by surprise this afternoon, but I see now just how the thing works—and she won't do it again in a hurry. If you were me, would you tell Sally all about it?"

Jane paused for such a long time that Alec was afraid she was going to have one of her obstinate fits and refuse to answer him. She seemed—sometimes—to think that he ought to answer himself. But finally she said in her hesitating, cool, little way:

"You know what Sally would like better than I do. If you really think she would attach no value whatever to what took place this afternoon, perhaps it might be better to tell her. Men are bad hands at concealing things, and she might suspect more than what actually took place. On the other hand, if she could be upset by it, you should think twice before telling her. She seems a little out of spirits since you came back, and there is no object in making her feel unhappy over a triviality you never intend to repeat."

"What a good hanging judge you'd make, Jane!" Alec said appreciatively. "Nobody'd ever guess whether you wanted the prisoner done in or not! But you're wrong about men, they can hide a break like mine—much better than you think. It meant nothing to me, so Sally won't feel it. If it were real, I should feel bound to tell her, because then I should be feeling the thing myself, and she'd catch it from me. Being in love's like that—at least being married is; it goes awfully far in. At the same time, part of you keeps separate, unless it gets emotionally driven. Emotion leaks through at once."

"Well—I'm glad you've got it all fixed so clearly in your mind," said Jane. "Of course I'm not in love, so that I haven't the faintest idea of what leaks through or what doesn't. I merely know that on general principles people had better consume their own smoke, if they are capable of consuming it, but if some of it is liable to escape, they had much better open the whole business up."

There was nothing Alec cared to find fault with in this statement, and, as Jane seemed convinced that he was the best judge of what he thought right, he was left with the simple matter of putting his thoughts into execution.

Sally must have been waiting for him in vain for tea, and would now be waiting for him, for dinner. Jane pointed this out; and this, somehow or other, convinced Alec that he had much better not tell Sally anything.

CHAPTER XVIII

LYING at full length on the white fur rug and burying his head in Sally's lap, Alec could shut out everything except flame-coloured castles in the fire. His overstrung muscles relaxed; the operating-table, Charles's enormities, an unpleasant blurred image of himself and Myra, Jane's cold, astonished look, slipped into merciful oblivion. Sally's lap was as soft to lie on as a bank of primroses. Her breast, when he pressed himself against it, smelt as sweet as a cowslip ball. Sally never used mysterious scents, but there was always something about her like the breath of cows or the sweetness of newmown hay.

He didn't tell her any of these things. "Pig!" he muttered, "don't breathe down the back of my neck!"

Biscuit, Sally's Sealyham puppy, sat half on Alec's shoulder and half on Sally's lap, so as to catch anything that was going on. He had been christened "Biscuit" because Sally said it was a nice floating name to call, and Alec said that it was good for any puppy to learn that he could be both subject and object at the same time. Alec first threatened the puppy with a hard hairy fist, and then, slowly opening his hand, presented him with the rival merits of five fingers to snatch at. It seemed an inexhaustible game, but Biscuit suddenly fell sound asleep in the middle of it, fixing the round ball of his hind-quarters firmly into the back of Alec's neck.

By-and-by Sally would get up and make the supper; but Alec didn't want any supper just yet. He wanted to go on lying there in that warmth for ever, hearing the rain patter against the window-pane—and looking idly up into Sally's grey eyes with little brown flecks in them.

"Kiss me!" he demanded.

Sally leaned over and kissed him first on the lips, a long clinging kiss, and then with her eyelashes—a moth's kiss —fluttering against his cheek, and then on his eyes, which he obligingly shut.

"What did you do since I was here?" Alec asked, suddenly jealous of the hours which stood between them, the lonely, empty hours, in which they'd been—not each other —but their mere bleak selves.

Sally had had rather a day, she told him. She'd first done the work of the house, then washed the car, then combed and exercised Biscuit. She'd made scones for tea —but they'd heat up for to-morrow; and she'd flinched at a rabbit for their supper because of its inside, and compromised on sausages, which, though they were all insides, hadn't got to be meddled with because of their nice tidy skins, and were far quicker to cook.

"I liked everything in my day except the rabbit," Sally explained. "Only I couldn't help thinking I don't know quite enough. Would it be any help to you if I learned typewriting?"

"You'll do as you are," Alec told her. He sat up suddenly and hugged Sally so violently that Biscuit, unjustly roused, flung himself between them in a perfect hurricane of barks, and had to be slowly and soporifically scratched behind the ear by Sally, till he fell asleep again

Alec resettled himself with a long, contented sigh.

"I sometimes don't know which of us is which," he observed. "When you're rather nicer than me, you're you and when I'm nicer than myself, I'm you. But I don' know when you can be me without being less nice, whic would be rather a pity. I meant not to tell you what hap pened to me this afternoon, but I think, after all, I shall.

Sally said serenely, "Of course—you've got to!"

He had been right in thinking that Sally would understand about Myra. Perhaps she didn't exactly like it, but,
slipping his hand up against her heart, he felt its strong,
even beat and was reassured. She wasn't in the least angry
with him. She murmured "Mormon!" and then began
quite irrationally to be annoyed with Jane.

"I can't see," she kept repeating, "what business it was
of Jane's to mind what you did!"

"Oh, well," Alec explained tolerantly, "she's an incor-
ruptible feminist—that's why. You were what riled her.
She said I'd infringed on your rights. She only looked at
it from the woman's point of view. She couldn't see why
I'd been bowled over. I'm not sure she wasn't kept in a
glacier for forty years before she started breathing! I
don't believe even Freud could catch a symbol out of
Jane's dreams. She doesn't understand how little there is
in that kind of a kiss, or how it can come on as suddenly
as a shower of rain, and dry up so that it's dusty again
five minutes after! She might have known the woman
didn't mean anything to me!"

"I've read a lot about Myra," Sally said, a little pen-
sively. "The new Matron gave me a letter from the old
one, full of clippings and photographs. One was of their
Scottish castle in Skye which had to be sold; and another
of Dr. Drummond in kilts; and heaps and heaps of Myra
herself. Would you like to see them?"

"Not the least!" Alec murmured. "But tell me about the
trial. Did it seem as if the husband had shot himself by
accident or on purpose? And did it ever come out why
he'd wanted to?"

"Not exactly," Sally said slowly. "But it didn't look
like an accident. Nor as if he had shot himself at all. It
really looked as if somebody else had shot him. Only it
couldn't have been anyone else. Myra was the only other
person in the house till Dr. Drummond came."

A coal dropped from the heart of the fire with a startling crash. Biscuit jumped up and yelped. Alec, too, felt a queer sensation, as if something had dropped on him. That indrawn, secretive face of Charles's flashed into his mind. Surely it was the face of a murderer?

"Dr. Drummond," Sally said, after a short pause, "couldn't have done it. He lived too far away. She telephoned to him, but he didn't get there till after the man was dead. It was eleven o'clock at night. The servants were out, and the doors were locked. The husband lay halfway up the stairs and the revolver as if he had dropped it. But the wound was in a funny place for a man to shoot himself. Still it looked as if he must have done it, because there were only his finger-prints on the revolver. But they might have been rubbed off, and then the revolver put back into his hand when he was dead. The judge summed up rather against Myra, but she got off. Dr. Drummond's evidence of how he found the body saved her, on account of his being a doctor, I suppose. One had the feeling that the jury didn't want to hang her. It came out in the trial that she was unfaithful to her husband."

Sally told the story gently, with little pauses, and Alec could see it all quite plainly in his mind.

"I can readily believe that she was unfaithful," he said grimly.

Small flames flickered, sinister and unsubstantial, in and out of the red-hot cavern in the fire. Alec seemed to see again close to his eyes the red-gold of Myra's hair.

"It's curious," he went on slowly. "I can't help feeling sorry for her. Yet in a way to drive a man to suicide is a sort of murder. She says she feels chased, and people keeping on finding out who she is and boycotting her. Of course, if she's innocent, that's pretty rough justice. I could see she was really upset this afternoon—she wasn't fooling me over that. She looked like a cornered animal."

"I suppose you would know about a person's being upset," Sally agreed thoughtfully. "But I can't feel sorry
for her myself. You see, it's always been her husband—or
her brother—perhaps other men, too, who have got the
worst of it, never quite her."

"You can't be sure of that," Alec said, frowning a little,
"because we don't know what the worst of a thing is. They
haven't had to be her."

"But she makes nice people behave badly," Sally persisted softly; "and nice people don't like behaving badly
—whereas she seems to enjoy it. So I do rather think they
have the worst of it."

"Nonsense!" Alec said brusquely. "You don't know
that her husband was nice! Drummond certainly isn't.
And as for behaving badly this afternoon, I don't know
that I did particularly."

"Oh—well!" Sally murmured with a rueful little laugh,
"I hope you don't think you behaved particularly well!"

Alec considered this statement rather irritably. It
seemed as if a trifling thing, well over, had come back and
hit him. He hadn't meant to kiss Myra, so that the kiss
didn't matter; and if it didn't matter, it couldn't have been
wrong. He tried this form of reasoning very carefully
over in his own mind before presenting it to Sally. But
women, when they argue, never seem to go on where men
leave off. Sally started up a fresh hare immediately.

"She made you do it, whether you meant to or not!" she
asserted. "And that's the way she may have made her husband shoot himself—if he did actually do it himself," she
even more exasperatingly added.

"That man Drummond," Alec asserted, after taking
the precaution to slide the complete puppy into Sally's
lap and then sitting bolt upright, "has the face and manner of a murderer! I should like to be sure of the times in
the business. Nothing is so easy to fake, if there aren't

disinterested witnesses to prove an alibi, as time. People lie about it every day of their lives when nothing more hangs by it than not being late for a meal."

"I wonder why you hate Dr. Drummond so," Sally irrelevantly remarked. "I can't help thinking he's rather nice sometimes. You've no idea how different his eyes look when he's interested about where roads lead to; and he was awfully kind to me this morning when Biscuit got into the hyacinths by the south wall. They do snap off so, those Roman ones. He only said 'Dogs will!' "

"Anyone would be kind to you!" Alec murmured fondly; "even I seldom wish to put you to death by torture! Let's get supper—and go to bed. You can take my word for it, that man is a beast of beasts! Jane says he gave the anæsthetic all right this afternoon, but I'm not so sure myself. The patient went out under it, anyhow, before I'd had time to tie up the arteries."

He hadn't meant to tell Sally about the operation. They were practically certain now that she had started having a baby, and sudden deaths on operating-tables weren't quite the subjects for her. Still, now he had started on it, Alec told her everything, except the way that Jane had looked at Charles.

"Of course, Codgers had laid this up for himself," Alec in common fairness explained to Sally. "No perpetual tippler is safe on an operating-table. But Drummond went to pieces afterwards; and a man who can't lose without making an ass of himself hasn't got the right stuff in him. I hate a bad loser."

Sally wound her small hand in and out of Alec's long fine fingers. It was a soothing performance, but it would have been more soothing still if Sally had agreed that she hated a bad loser too. She said, after a long pause, with her head bent over Biscuit so that Alec could only see its feathery golden top:

"Perhaps he's had rather a rotten time too. He had to sell his castle. He gave up a good job to take his sister abroad; and in the papers it said Myra's husband was his best friend."

"He did stand by her, no doubt," Alec admitted grudgingly, "to save the family name. No one wants to have his sister hanged; but he's obviously let her down since. Don't you remember how he wouldn't even let her see over the hospital? A piece of petty tyranny! The poor girl's got to have some interests."

Alec paused. He wished Sally would say, "Of course! I'll take her out in the car!" or, "I'll have her over to tea, and get up a Bridge four." But Sally didn't seem to catch the silent pressure he laid upon her heart. He couldn't exactly ask for it, because of that damned kiss! Sally carefully transferred Biscuit, now so deep asleep that he merely twitched, into the heart of the rug.

Alec helped her set the table, and while they were setting it, Sally said: "Perhaps he thought she oughtn't to see people like that. I went over this afternoon, to give Matron back the clippings. On the way back through the garden little Miss Flint ran up to me. She seemed so glad to see me. She took hold of my arm, trembling all over, to tell me something, I think; but Nurse Christie dragged her away. Have they got to be unkind to the patients?"

Alec hesitated. How on earth had Miss Flint got into the big garden? Of course there was no need to tell Sally, but if Nurse Christie hadn't dragged her away, Sally would have got badly bitten. It made him feel rather sick to think of it.

"They aren't unkind," he said shortly. "Miss Flint shouldn't have been there. I don't mind your going into the hospital to see Jane, or Matron, and going through the big garden to do it, but Drummond's right about that—we don't want unknowledgeable people all over the place, without supervision. It isn't good for the patients, and might result in unpleasantness all round. Going over the hospital, with one of the staff under proper conditions, is quite another thing. But a pop-eyed reactionary like Drummond just forbids for the sake of forbidding."

This settled the matter. Sally went into the kitchen and cooked the sausages, and Alec mixed a masterly salad. They had Heinz's tomato soup first with cream in it, and wound up with bananas. Sally was just as jolly as usual, and they talked about the car, and whether they should buy a piano, and keep chickens. Before they had finished supper, they had made the chickens pay for the piano. While they were washing up, they found they could afford to go to the Riviera in the car for their summer holiday. They liked travelling better than anything, and could sleep in a tent to save hotels.

It had stopped raining when they took Biscuit for his final run. The stars were out, and had a friendly look— high up in the dark, windy sky. The air smelt astonishingly sweet.

It was rather marvellous, walking about with his own wife on his arm, and his own dog putting up imaginary cats and rabbits to divert them from noticing that he was not carrying out the last duties of the night.

A bath in the new bathroom which had pale blue dolphins on pearl-coloured tiles, soothed away the last of Alec's discontent.

Sally had undressed and was already in bed when he came into the room. She held out her arms to him smiling. The whole black day was dead. Sally, all gold and pink and white, with laughing eyes, filled up the universe.

Alec was glad, as only a doctor could be glad, that she was such a normal, healthy girl. Her body was compact and firm; she showed none of that fluttered maternal tenderness, always a little tenacious and timid, which is all some women know of love. Sally had the triumphant ardour of a bride who knows that she is her husband's world and gives it to him afresh with a satisfaction more overwhelming than generosity.

To-night Sally must have been more tired than usual, for she was the first to fall asleep.

Alec lay motionless beside her, her head upon his breast; and then the day came back. But it came back differently. He saw that it had been despicable to yield to Myra, that he had been unfair to Charles, unjust to Jane, and extraordinarily slack to go late to a dangerous operation. He realised how nearly his hand had slipped on the knife. Even if Charles had bungled the anæsthetic, he had no real grounds for judging him for it. He himself had kept the patient waiting, and perhaps added to the strain on his heart by doing so. It was true that he had been right about the abscess, but perhaps Charles had been right to fear the operation because of the man's alcoholic condition. Hadn't Alec only pressed his theory because he felt perverse and wanted to down Charles?

In the dark, with Sally's soft sweet breathing close to his ear, Alec faced up to himself. He might have been responsible for his patient's death. He had a wife he loved and should not desire another woman's kisses. He was a friend, and shouldn't grudge Jane's right to other intimacies. Thank God, anyhow, that he'd told Charles about that third abscess!

He made most excellent resolutions before he went to sleep. He would avoid Myra. He would be decent to Charles. Perhaps Jane hadn't meant anything by that look. She may only have wished, by being nice to Charles, to introduce the spirit of greater friendliness all round. If more of the same stuff came up again, he would reason with her, but not scold. They would both take the greatest possible care of Sally.

A bright March moon came striding up the sky. Sally stirred in her sleep, under its sudden light, and drew closer to him. He could see the shadowy outline of their new furniture in the room. They were all new and beautiful things, safe as his young love.

The moon, sucked under by passing clouds, vanished. The room rose black against his eyes. His beautiful new things were still there, but he could no longer see them. He had a sinister sensation, as if oblivion had laid hold of him. Then the warm weight of Sally against his breast revived him. She was alive, and more substantial than the moon, with all its light.

CHAPTER XIX

PLANS carried out alone, when you have meant to carry them out with someone else, have a mournful, second-hand feeling. Sally had prepared regal food for their picnic. The early spring day was warm and clear; one of those days, dropped ahead of summer after a long hard winter, which keep hope alive.

Sally had washed Biscuit and put on a new trousseau frock which was the colour of her hair and had no sleeves.

She hadn't liked the sharp whirr of the telephone even before she heard Alec's voice explaining that Myra Anderson had a splitting toothache. Myra was afraid of the local dentist and wanted Alec to take her to Gloucester. Charles had had to go off somewhere on a private consultation. There was apparently no one else to take Myra and she wasn't fit to drive herself. Did Sally mind if Alec drove her to Gloucester?

How could you over a telephone mind about somebody else's toothache? Face to face you could say, "Why can't she go to a local dentist?" or, "If she can't drive her own car, why doesn't she hire a chauffeur?"

Sally thought of both these things before she said in a small, subdued voice, "Of course, if you think you must!"

Alec answered eagerly—rather too eagerly: "Well, honestly I don't think there is anything else to do! I'm awfully sorry about the picnic! But we can go another day, can't we?"

Then he rang off. Sally needn't have gone by herself; but she had cut the sandwiches and told everybody she was going on a picnic; and she felt that she would rather go alone with Biscuit than explain to anyone else why Alec hadn't come.

She took the car neatly out of the garage and drove carefully through the traffic-choked intricacies of the small Welsh town. At last she was out on the broad, comparatively empty road, and could just sit still and let the world fly past her!

A special early light spread over the landscape—not very strong and transparent—like a thin golden veil; high green hedges slipped into fields, and fields into a pale blue sky. Little spires and cross-beamed cottages sprang solidly before her eyes and reeled themselves off into nothingness. Castles climbed distant hills in a blue mist; a white and silver river leapt and curved, in and out of emerald-green meadows.

Sally drew up at last at a village with an unpronounceable name, where they had planned to leave the car and walk to the foot of the nearest hill.

The sun was hot overhead. The air had grown heavy; everything smelt piercingly sweet. The new green of the trees had a bright, sticky look, and flowers in the thick hedges broke into small explosions of colour.

Sally fastened her rucksack on her back and started off sturdily. As she trudged on, the hilltop became evasive, and the nearer she got to it, the farther it moved away. When she was really near, the summit melted off altogether into a soft woolly cloud. Between the rounded breasts of two small hills she came upon a grove of young oaks leading downwards into a beechwood.

It was very quiet under the trees. You could hear birds stirring in the branches and a vague hum of insects, and far away the little crash and chuckle of a stream. But these were drowsy sounds, as if the day were half asleep and whispering to itself.

Sally stopped short. To have gone on would have been like putting her foot upon the sky. Bluebells flowed round her on every side under the pink-leaved oaks. They pierced the darkness of the wood like wandering flames.

Sally's eyes sank into them bewildered, but at rest, for their colour had no harshness in it and no monotony.

Each flower carried its blue light, a little above the ground. No wind reached them. They lay as still and untroubled as a mountain lake, but their blue was a lighter, more evanescent quality than water. Softly they melted into this green background like smoke rising from some deep, hidden fire, within the slumbering earth.

Sally sank entranced onto the nearest bank. A sweetness breathed from the army of flowers, and grew more piercing as the day drew on.

Sally's head bent lower and lower. She felt as if she were being drowned in bluebells. It was a beautiful but lonely feeling.

When Sally was a child at home, she had liked being alone, because then no one could remind her that she had a hole in her stocking or was biting her nails; but since she had been married to Alec, she had learned to love togetherness. It hadn't mattered Alec's being at work all day, because she spent her time preparing for his return. All that she did was permeated by Alec. The garden, the house, the car, were all parts of him. But this beauty which lay spread out before her now was a separate thing. It belonged to her, but it didn't belong to Alec. It made her feel as if she were a ghost.

A strange terror seized her. Suppose she wasn't going to be happy, after all? Suppose that there were worse things than being bullied and ordered about at home? Suppose that this great triumphant wave of love, mounting higher and higher day by day, could topple you over suddenly into a hollow, out of which you could never climb? Suppose that the crest of happiness was always bound to break?

Sally's mind ran back feverishly over the last few weeks. Nothing dreadful had happened. Had there been an imperceptible slowing-down of joy? Last night, for instance, she had definitely not enjoyed herself.

They had gone over to Jane's, after eating rather hurriedly a dinner it had taken Sally hours to prepare. They had talked and talked till far into the night; but Sally hadn't talked; she hadn't, after a while, even listened. It was all so technical, and when not technical rather frightening, a sort of blithe handling of terrific things. Sally wouldn't have minded so much if behind the things they had talked about there had been the protection of a God. But Alec and Jane dispensed with His protection. If they were religious at all, they were religious only about facts.

They were at work upon a gland experiment which would help them to get a certain physical reaction from manic depressives.

Alec and Jane believed it would work one way, and the Hursts, who had to be rung up about it and came over, said they believed it would work another way; and Charles, who happened to drop in, believed it wouldn't work at all.

They didn't exactly fight, though Alec and Charles were on edge with each other the whole time, but they went on arguing and arguing.

Sally couldn't keep her eyes open, and had fallen asleep at last, with her head on Biscuit's warm oblivious body. Biscuit had seen from the first that sleep was the only possible solution for a dull evening.

When they woke her up to go home, they were still arguing, and still enjoying themselves, though they hadn' settled anything. It had made her feel on a par with Biscuit.

She looked up resentfully to find him; but he had dashed off in search of rabbits. She could hear in the distance his short, explosive barks.

The wood wasn't preserved, so even if he caught a rabbit, which was unlikely, it wouldn't really matter.

Some women wouldn't care so much about dogs. If they were alone, they would comfort themselves by thinking about the babies they were going to have!

Sally tried to put up this defence, but she found it a weak one. It wasn't really a baby yet, it was more of a threat . . . When she appealed to the silent life within her, all it could tell her was: "Six months from now you won't be able to do things with Alec. Quite soon you'll begin to look horrid. All this summer—your first summer together—I will lie a hot and heavy weight against your heart!"

"I don't want to have a baby!" Sally said defiantly out loud to a shocked squirrel, who festooned himself swiftly away from anything so unnatural.

Sally's eyes sank back helplessly into the cloud of blue! If you had to have new life at all, why couldn't it be blown over you—like the light was blown over these easy flowers? How delicious to push through a green sheath, out of soft earth, to meet the sun! Ah! to lose oneself, to pass for ever away from pain and fear into Light and Colour—into anything which wasn't a human cage!

Sally gave a little trapped cry; and buried her face in her hands.

"Have you hurt yourself?" a grave voice asked her.

She looked up, dazzled and confused, and saw Charles Drummond standing above her on the sun-chequered path. Hatless, with his gold hair caught by the sun, he looked like the god of spring. Sally couldn't at once collect her wits to answer him.

He seemed to guess that Sally felt shy, for he began to explain to her, rather elaborately, how he came to be there.

After Charles had finished his consultation, someone had told him about the bluebells, and he had walked up into the hills to see them.

Biscuit, hearing a strange man's voice, tore through the wood, scattering a thousand tiny intrigues in his wake, and panting so loudly that Sally couldn't hear herself speak. She just went on looking at Charles.

She felt like a trapped rabbit, but she had a queer feeling that perhaps Charles had come to open the trap. He would have to do it without her asking him, for she found now that she had no voice at all. She was feeling very odd, and light-headed from the heat, and from having forgotten to eat her lunch. She didn't exactly want to faint, but she felt sick and shivery, and quite suddenly the golden light moving to and fro over the oak leaves flickered—and went out.

The next thing she knew she was lying quite flat with her head against Charles's knee, and finding water on her face and hands.

Charles said, "You're all right, but don't bother to talk just yet."

The bluebells streamed above her, so that she might have been quite pleasantly lying at the bottom of the sea.

By and by Charles said: "That rucksack looks as if there might be something in it!" and opening it, he discovered the regal lunch.

Charles began to feed Sally with it, and she was surprised to find that she felt quite hungry.

After a while she sat up and wondered if she didn't look awful. Bits of stick and insects had got caught in her hair

and her nose must be a shiny mess. She wondered if
Charles thought girls oughtn't to tidy themselves up in
public when they needed it, or hoped that they would?
You couldn't tell with the very nicest men which way their
niceness would take them.

Charles wasn't looking at Sally. His eyes were fixed
upon the bluebells. Perhaps he wanted to be drowned in
them too.

Sally took out a powder-puff and a glass and swiftly
tidied herself up. She looked much better now, even if he
did disapprove; but she wouldn't risk her lipstick.

"You seem to have got a long way from home," Charles
observed conversationally, but not at all as if he wanted to
know why Sally had come there all by herself.

"Well, of course," Sally replied defensively, "I didn't
plan to come alone—that just happened because at the
last moment Alec couldn't come too."

She suppressed Myra, partly because Charles mightn't
like to know about it, and partly because Alec and Myra
mightn't like to have it told. There was no harm in it, of
course, but if you said things with a shaky voice, they
sounded more important than they really were.

Suddenly, because Charles looked so awfully like a doctor, because she'd fainted on his knee and he'd brought
her round and fed her as if she were a baby, Sally found
herself saying: "I did cry out! I was afraid! In a sort of
flash it came over me that I didn't want to have a baby.
I'm going to, you know, and I do really want to—but not
just yet. You see, it rather breaks things up—the first
year you're married, doesn't it?"

"Oh, yes," Charles said quickly, "I should quite think
one might feel like that about it. On the other hand, from
another point of view, one rather likes the idea, you know.
It's the creative principle which appeals to one. If what
draws people together is a good sound emotion, it ought

to create something out of itself—with a separate life—oughtn't it?"

"P'r'aps," Sally rather reluctantly acknowledged. "But you see, when all you can be to a man is a sort of play-comrade to run round with him, and you can't run round, and when he rather likes the way you look, and you know you've got to look horrid, you mind rather! I'm not intellectual, you know; I'm no real companion to Alec. I'm just—well, I'm just his wife."

She hadn't meant to say any of this, not even to Jane—perhaps specially not to Jane—but it came out now with a rush; and after she had said it, she felt a great relief.

For quite a long time Charles just sat there, with his head turned rather stiffly away from her, saying nothing at all.

"May I smoke?" he asked her, at last. And after another long pause, while he was filling his pipe and getting it to draw properly, he took up what Sally had said, but not as if it were Sally he was talking about, rather as if they were both talking, at a convenient distance, about some abstract thing.

"This question of what men and women are to each other—or ought to be—is still awfully unsolved," he murmured. "Apparently the old idea was that you paid for—and therefore possessed—a not uncongenial chattel, who in most cases kept her position as a chattel. Your wife bore children and did a great deal of useful work about the house. Houses themselves were, of course, far more important in those days. A wife was distinctly worth her keep, and valued as such. Now we can't afford a whole string of children, and houses are less important and very much easier to run. This leaves women rather unoccupied and restless and greatly lessens their value to man. It's a transitional stage and painful for both sexes. At present

I find that men pay far too highly for women, and resent them accordingly. You don't mind my talking quite frankly, do you? Every special case has its own background, and it's rather important in looking for a solution to take in backgrounds. Women are not in any way to blame for the present state of things, and it's uncommonly hard luck on them that their jobs have been so curtailed. Perhaps they do the best they can for both sexes, by trying to fit themselves for economic independence and cultivating their sport instinct, so as to make themselves better play-fellows.

"On the other hand, one grudges them independence, when it is very seldom economic, and when they usually show quite plainly that they don't know how to make the best use of it. One still more objects to the fact that many of them are obviously out for getting men to support them —and then cheat their supporters! You don't seem to fall into either of these categories. If I may say so, you seem to me to have made a perfectly fair contribution towards your married life. You are going to have a child, and you run your home practically unaided; you work in your garden and look after your car. Nor have I ever seen a man look more satisfied with married life than your husband looks. It seems to me that intellectual conversation and games play quite a subsidiary part in most married lives. I shouldn't bother about them at all, if I were you."

Sally blushed, but she felt reassured. After all, Alec did look happy! He had put on a stone in weight since their marriage, and she knew it would cost him far more than her keep to get his house, car, and garden looked after as she looked after them.

"I never was much use at home," she explained to Charles. "I was the youngest, and I never did things as well as the others did, but I do try to do the best I can

for Alec. Only—well, you see, a person like Jane could do
all that I do a great deal better than I do it, and yet talk
to him intellectually all the time!"

Charles said nothing at all for quite a long time, and
then he murmured, so low that Sally could hardly catch
what he said:

"I don't suppose there are many women—like Dr. Everest."

"I've never met any," Sally loyally agreed. "It's funny,
though, that she doesn't mind talking to me about quite
serious things—like adrenal glands—and never laughs
at me, as Alec does, for wanting to know about them. Yet
she drives as well as Alec, and is nearly as good a doctor,
isn't she? She cooks and gardens much better than I do.
Sometimes I can't think why——" Sally's voice drifted
across the bluebells, and Charles didn't take up the com-
plicated sentence, which finished in a sigh.

The air had grown cooler. The shadows turned the bluebells into wine-dark purple. The sun no longer set little
quivering patterns on the ground under the trees. Birds
sang again, and if it hadn't been for Biscuit, the woods
would have been still more alive. Chaffinches repeated over
and over again their silvery cascade. Starlings gave long
good-natured chuckles, while in and out of the foothills a
cuckoo made wide circles of bell-like airy song, as cool as
a waterfall.

"I can't think why Alec doesn't like you!" Sally said
suddenly; but she wished she hadn't, for Charles became
a polar landscape, nothing stirred in him, and everything
abruptly froze.

"Your husband," he told her with courteous finality,
"was placed in a very difficult position by my appointment. It is hard for him to realise that I shared in his
misfortune rather than caused it."

He got up. There seemed to be no question of staying

in the wood any longer, though it was the most beautiful hour for woods.

They walked quickly back towards the village, and Sally thought Charles was going to drop her at the garage to find her own way home; but when they reached it, he said hurriedly:

"I am leaving my car here for repairs; may I drive you home? It will save my having to hire."

It was a great comfort, for Sally found herself quite extraordinarily tired. She leaned back in the seat next Charles, with Biscuit curled up like a whiting on her lap, with his tail in his mouth, while the landscape flowed past her in a blurred dream.

Charles drove well and very fast, and didn't talk at all. Sometimes he asked her a question about the road and sometimes he said what he thought of anything which blocked their path.

He was an irritable driver and did not suffer road-fools gladly; but his voice when he spoke to Sally had grown quite kind again. Still he didn't suggest their stopping anywhere for tea.

CHAPTER XX

Sally hadn't expected to find Alec at home. She had told herself, giving him as much margin as possible, "Alec can't be home much before seven!" She would just have time to rest a little, get dinner, and dress. She felt tired, but not tired enough to matter.

With what Charles had said in her mind, about the duties of a wife, Sally cooked a remarkably good dinner, and laid the table with their best blue-and-white service.

Only, when the little house was looking as immaculate as a fresh snowfall, did Sally turn her feverish attention upon herself.

What should she wear to impress Alec after he had spent a day with Myra?

Sally wasn't the daring type, and it would be safer not to challenge a comparison; but it mustn't be anything which would make her look too raw and young! To be told she was like a dear little buttercup would be more than she could bear!

She decided on a peacock-blue crêpe-de-chine pyjama suit, which had come—so they told her at the sale—direct from Paris. It had very wide trouser legs, a narrow turned-down black collar, and a thread of a black belt. You wore black suède sandals with it, and put on plenty of lipstick.

Then Sally poured lavender water all over her head; but remembering that lavender water evaporates, she searched through all her drawers for a bottle of "Toutes les Fleurs" which someone had given her as a wedding present, and which she had meant to pass on to a bazaar. It smelt heavenly by itself, but it almost seemed as if the lavender water hadn't evaporated quite enough!

Sally brushed her hair furiously for ages, and then opened the window to let the night-air hurry up the lavender water.

There was a gale blowing in from the sea; no moon, and no stars. It was what sailors call a "dirty night."

Sally caught a glimpse of herself, in the long glass of the wardrobe, before going downstairs. She thought she looked a little too much like one of those boy-dolls which never seem quite as natural as girl ones; but it was no use bothering about that now, for Alec was overdue.

She hardly touched the stairs as she went down them, and curling herself up on the divan, she started to read a book by William James on Psychology, which Alec had recommended to her. It was certainly less frog's-leggish than most books on psychology, but her mind refused to grip even the most pungent of the clear sentences.

Something was happening to the little house. It was filling, slowly but surely, to the very brim, with Fear! Fear hung in the short orange curtains, and flickered under the rosy lampshades. Fear creaked ominously on the empty stairs, and beckoned from the open doorways. All the window-panes were dark and hostile. It was warm enough still to have the windows open, but Sally had had to shut them because it was bad enough to have Fear in the house. She couldn't stand hearing the whole garden whispering and shuddering with it too!

The very divan on which Sally sat—a black divan they had splashed into the room to give its bright colours point —felt as sinister as a pall drawn over a hearse!

Sally got up stiffly and dragged herself into the kitchen to see if the joint was done. She had to take it out of the oven and move the vegetables farther away from the fire.

Still an hour late isn't so awfully much, Sally told herself rather wistfully, on a sixty-mile run!

While Sally was still in the kitchen something banged furiously against the window-pane, like the blow of a drunken man's fist. Sally's heart leapt against her side, and Biscuit bristled and barked in an agony of sympathetic fury. Still it was probably nothing but the wind. Sally only went all over the house again, to see that every window was latched and both doors locked. She looked under the beds, too, just to be on the safe side. Then she took a detective story instead of William James, and went back to the black divan again. But the detective story was as difficult to grasp as William James, except when it suddenly became unpleasantly vivid and supplied Sally with objects for her unformulated fears; and then Sally wished she hadn't grasped it!

Time hung about the room as vacant and uneasy as a schoolboy on a rainy day. Biscuit refused to settle down. He sniffed and stiffened at the slightest sound; and there were a great many slight sounds.

Sally's mind stopped making soothing excuses for them at last and began to admit their direr possibilities. Each fresh noise crept through her senses like an enemy who has found a gap in the walls of a beleaguered city. This was just the night for an escaped lunatic! The former Matron had often told Sally hair-raising anecdotes about what lunatics would do when they got out. When Sally had repeated them to Jane, Jane had said: "I have been here five years, and only one man got into the garden at night who should not have been there. It was a summer night and he did no harm either to himself or to anybody else, though I remember he picked all the geraniums in the front beds, which thoroughly annoyed the gardener!"

But that was like Jane. She never denied or suppressed terrible things; she only took the stuffing out of them and made them look bloodless and dry. Still it would be a great comfort if Jane were to walk in now!

There was the telephone; but Sally didn't like to ask her, it sounded so childish.

Suppose that blow on the window was only a try-on, and the next one went through the glass and was a man's fist, after all? Suppose that long, shuddering movement of the orange curtains meant that someone was standing just behind them?

Biscuit broke into a shrill cascade of barks, one tumbling over the other. His hair slowly rose so that his back looked like an upturned scrubbing-brush. All his teeth showed. The end had come! Sally crouched back against the wall. Her throat was dry, her eyes wide with fear! She was too frightened even to scream. Nothing happened. Then a steady, monotonous tapping began, with regular intermissions, which just gave Sally time to breathe in between. Surely this must be the lunatic!

It was no use hoping for Alec any more. Even if he came, it would be too late! It was only in books, and those old-fashioned ones, that rescuers came in time. But Jane was only a hundred yards away—at the other end of a telephone wire!

Sally put the reassuring thought away from her, with less decision.

The noises upstairs became terrific. Relays of ghosts started up in the spare bedroom. Twice Biscuit, of his own accord, dashed upstairs to investigate; and twice he came down again, churning fear in his throat. The second time Sally thought he would never come down. He had probably been ambushed, and silently destroyed! But she was too cowardly to go up and see!

The fact of the telephone became insistent and compulsory. If she was too frightened to try to save the life of her own puppy, she really ought to telephone to Jane! But how was she to reach the telephone when she was so stiff with fear that she hadn't been able to stir for over ten minutes? She said: "Biscuit!" in a hard, agonised whisper. Biscuit responded by wagging so naturally that Sally felt relieved. She managed to crawl from the divan to the telephone box; simply because Biscuit had wagged his tail!

It was an automatic telephone, which made it easier than if she had had to ask for a number. Jane's answering voice came to her from another world—cool, secure, infinitely reassuring. Sally didn't say anything about being frightened, she only said, "Alec seems rather late!" in a voice that barely shook. "Oh, is he?" Jane replied with pleasant indifference. "Well—it's a long run from Gloucester, isn't it? Perhaps the dentist couldn't see Mrs. Anderson at once. May I bring my sewing over to you, and sit with you for a little? I've finished dinner."

Sally tried to make "Yes—do!" sound less like "For God's sake, come!"

She stood for a long time at the telephone after Jane's voice had stopped, not daring to turn round. She was quite sure that the lunatic had got in, and was standing directly behind her, ready to pounce if she stirred.

The huge shadow of Jerry flickered on the wall in front of her. It happened to be her own shadow, and Biscuit saved her again, by walking through it, to see what Sally was up to. Ten minutes later she heard real footsteps—and knew that they were Jane's.

The moment Jane came in, the whole hollow edifice of Fear collapsed! There were no lunatics, no ghosts, no possible disasters! Everything turned solid and innocuous. There were only two women, sitting one on each side of the mantelpiece, with a contented Sealyham, killing lions in his sleep, between them.

Sally didn't tell Jane anything about having been

frightened. It seemed less interesting now than Charles
and the bluebells.

"I'm afraid I can't help it," Sally confessed guiltily,
when she had finished telling Jane about her abortive picnic, "but I almost like Charles!"

"I quite do!" Jane surprisingly announced. "Nor does
there seem any good reason why any of us shouldn't!"

"But," said Sally, aghast, "but, Jane—we couldn't! It
would enrage Alec so! Think how Charles came in, and
ruined everything! All our lovely plans—and Alec's work
—and upset the whole hospital!"

"The hospital doesn't seem particularly upset," Jane
remarked drily. "There have been changes, but it seems
to me to be working rather better than usual. As for Alec's
work, no one can ruin it but himself. Some of our plans
have had to go by the board, of course, but Dr. Drummond interferes with us as little as possible. In fact, he
appears to share most of our theories and to support them
whenever feasible. It is personally unpleasant for Alec to
have to play second fiddle to a man of his own age, I know,
but it is high time he got over this feeling; and it never
was Dr. Drummond's fault."

Sally listened in shocked surprise. What Jane said
might be true in a way, but it wasn't what either of them
ought to feel! Wasn't there something about Charles
which was all wrong, though she couldn't for the moment
lay her finger on it? Alec couldn't dislike anybody as
much as he disliked Charles without good grounds for it!
There was that murder hanging about in the family, for
instance. You couldn't be very nice and have a murderess
for a sister, could you? And yet that didn't work very
well as a defence of Alec's reasonableness, since in that
case Alec ought to dislike Myra more than he disliked
Charles? Unless he honestly believed that Charles had
committed the murder? And Sally doubted that.

"I really don't like Myra," Sally suggested at last, feeling that she couldn't prove Alec's theory very convincingly to Jane, without believing it herself.

"She isn't to be liked," Jane replied, with her severe lucidity, "by anybody; but that has nothing whatever to do with Dr. Drummond!"

There was a long silence while Sally tried hard to find a comfortable way of reinstating Alec without wholly condemning Charles.

"No," she began rather weakly, "in a sense, of course, you can't blame Charles. One can't help relations, I know! We had an uncle once there was something funny about. It was hushed up, and I was supposed to be too young to be told, but I always fancied it was either a cheque or else something about his cook. Anyhow, they went to live at Bournemouth and he gave up being a clergyman. Alec must feel there is something like that about Charles. Still I can't quite see why Alec likes her, can you, because, if Charles is rather off colour, she must be worse?"

"He doesn't like her," Jane said decisively. "He merely runs after Myra in order to annoy Dr. Drummond!"

It was an interesting idea of Jane's about Myra. It partly pleased and partly displeased Sally. It was nice to think Alec didn't care about her at all, and yet what other reason could conceivably be enough to make him stay away from Sally till after eleven o'clock at night—with Gloucester only sixty miles away?

"If he doesn't like her," Sally murmured her thought aloud, "then why——?"

"I don't mean to say," Jane exclaimed impatiently "that he would run after Myra if she were as ugly as a toad—obviously not! She happens to be a raving beauty with a forehead like the sliced 'Psyche's' in the Naples Museum. But one needn't pursue people because they have Greek foreheads, when one is perfectly happily married

—as we know Alec is! Alec wouldn't do it either, if he weren't madly jealous of Dr. Drummond, and didn't want to take the first way open to him of giving him a slap in the face. The hospital will have something fresh to talk about now. It is sure to leak out that Alec took that wretched woman to Gloucester and didn't bring her back till midnight!"

"It isn't midnight yet," Sally murmured defensively, "it's only ten minutes after eleven!" She wished that Jane didn't feel so angry with Alec. If it were only spite on Alec's part, his having spent the whole day with Myra seemed much less wrong. Of course it is a pity to be spiteful, but when Sally thought how splendid Alec would have been if he had only been allowed to have his own way about the hospital, she could hardly blame him.

Jane sat there darning a cobwebby stocking much too hard. She looked as if every thread she pulled were Alec, and had to be jerked back into place. It made Sally feel responsible for Alec's sins, and as if she were being jerked back too. After all, Sally was a part of Alec; and she felt more a part of him than ever when she saw how angry Jane was with him. Still the other part of her felt rather impressed by Jane's anger, and as if she were being defended by it, from actual danger.

"I wonder if I ought to speak to him about Myra?" Sally asked Jane rather dubiously. "I haven't yet. I only said he was a Mormon—and I meant that to be funny!"

"I don't know," Jane answered reflectively. "I did think you'd better not speak of her to him. If a man is doing a thing to show off, the less notice anyone takes of him, the better. But this making bad blood has gone rather too far. Perhaps it would be as well for you to point out to him that he is doing himself and the hospital no good by carrying on an intrigue with his chief's sister, when he's only been married six months. The injury to you is so obvious that you needn't mention it. He can't enjoy hurting you."

"Oh, Jane!" Sally gasped, for this outspoken Fear was worse than any that had filled the house before Jane came. "Oh, Jane! But it isn't an intrigue yet, is it?"

"What do women like Myra do with men that isn't an intrigue?" Jane implacably demanded. "I don't say that it is one yet, but it's what Myra means it to be, and Alec will be able to put up just as much fight against her as a canary against a cat!"

"I don't think you ought to say that!" Sally expostulated. "Alec's tremendously good. I doubt if Bishops are moraller than he is. You needn't look so sceptical, Jane— a kiss isn't anything!"

"A kiss," said Jane icily, "is either a perfunctory antic or a definite promise. Neither should come into consideration between Alec and Myra."

"Oh, well!" said Sally, desperately floundering in uneasy memories of long-ago dances: "nobody need be quite so clear as you are, Jane! There are betwixt-and-between kisses. But I quite agree things have gone far enough. I will say something to him. It makes it easier if you don't think he likes her."

"Of course he doesn't like her!" said Jane, with gratifying certainty. "He's like a child sucking the paint off a stick with a box of real caramels beside him. I'm sorry i I've spoken too plainly, but it's no use speaking at al unless one says what one means. Alec is a good man, know. That's part of his trouble. A good man is no matc! for a bad woman, especially when he's not quite goo enough. She wouldn't be able to tempt him if Alec wer quite himself; but at a moment when he's brimming ove with outraged vanity, she has him in a cleft stick."

Sally frowned. She didn't like Jane's way of qualifyin Alec's goodness. He wasn't really vain. Jane should ha remembered what a good athlete he was—as well as han

some and clever—and how incredibly dear! Surely, if you
could get gay without being drunk, you could flirt without
being unfaithful? People didn't always go to extremes!

At last that quick, impatient step, which always kicked
the gravel as well as trod on it! Jane, too, recognised
Alec's tread. She got up rapidly, with a neat twist of her
stockings, which she slipped under her arm.

"I shan't stay," Jane said over her shoulder, letting
herself out of the French window into the windy darkness.

Sally made no attempt to stop her. She ran to the front
door and flung herself headlong into Alec's arms. "Oh,
Alec!" she sobbed with ecstasy, "Oh, Alec!" and she heard
him answer—with his whole heart behind it—"Oh, Sally!"

He had had dinner, after all, on the road, with Myra;
that was why he was so late. But Sally forgave him even
that! She forgave him everything there was—or wasn't—
to forgive!

It was such an incredible relief to have time go on as
usual!

Alec carried her back to the divan and fed her with
pieces of overdone mutton which nearly choked her. He
poked fun at Biscuit, who went mad with belated welcome,
relief from personal responsibility, and unexpected gravy,
left over from the mutton.

When Biscuit had at last quieted down—there was a
tremendous lot to listen to—a good deal about Myra, and
the dentist, and even more about her car, which wasn't
nearly as good, though three times as expensive, as their
own little Wolsey Hornet.

When it was Sally's turn to talk, she told Alec about
the bluebell wood and Charles, and watched him with awed
delight send up splendid fireworks of artificial rage. She
had meant to make him like Charles better by explaining
about the faint and how he'd helped her. But it turned
out to be an added blot on Charles's dark career, that he

should have dared to be on the spot at all, and unspeakable cheek on his part to have brought Sally round!

To hear Alec talk, you would have thought Charles ought just to have looked at Sally—throwing her fit under the trees—and walked callously away!

Still Sally didn't really mind Charles's being cursed into a blue infinity, when she saw the gratifying torment Alec felt at her having fainted! He insisted on carrying Sally all the way upstairs to bed!

It reminded Sally of how, once, when she was a little girl, she had carried a broken doll upstairs. She had hardly dared to breathe for fear of losing some of its pieces.

Alec was equally careful. He reached the top of the stairs in safety; and he thought that all of Sally was gathered together in his arms.

CHAPTER XXI

SALLY knew that she couldn't get out of going to the staff dance. It was the first big dance to be given since Charles's appointment. Sally was a bride, the wife of one of his chief colleagues; she couldn't very well say, "I shan't like meeting Myra!" It was no use Jane's saying, "She can't do you any harm whatever if you don't let her. By not minding her, you make her innocuous." Jane always had the idea that you could move about in the world on your own feet, with your nose in the air, and come off scatheless; but you couldn't if you were in love with Alec!

It was a whole week since Alec had got back from Gloucester, and every moment of it had been Sally's. Alec hadn't seen or thought of Myra. He had been wrapped in Sally from morning till night, and when he was not actually with Sally, she had the feeling that she was tiptoeing about the hospital by his side.

She was beginning to know all his favourite new patients by name, and something about each of their cases. Alec didn't tell her everything, because he said it was no use cluttering up her mind with too much odd-come-shortness, but he told her anything which was funny, or touching, or interesting. It was a great help, because Sally began to understand sometimes what Jane and Alec talked about in the evenings; and Jane told her what the names of the different mental illnesses meant, in a way that made them sound like measles or chickenpox, not at all frightening.

But back of all this new knowledge and readjusted happiness, Sally couldn't help remembering that Myra would be at the dance.

When the night came, the hospital was brilliantly lit up and everyone was excited and alert. Sally walked across the grounds with Alec, wishing that it wouldn't seem rather cowardly and old-fashioned to take his arm.

It was a mild May night, with rain and lilac in the air; and a pale crescent moon dipped in and out of cloud-wrack like the sail of a little boat on a rough sea. Jane had helped Sally with her wedding dress so that it wasn't tight any more and her arms were free. Alec had told her she looked "topping" in it, and she must try to be satisfied with that, and in the knowledge that, after all, in a few hours' time he would be hers again.

He wasn't hers now. She was subtly conscious that he, too, felt a tension, but that instead of its dragging back his whole being, as Sally felt dragged back by hers, Alec's tension urged him forward. He wanted to go to the dance.

It hurt Sally to pass—out of the living fragrant night —into that dead, cold corridor, which was always clean, and smelt a little as if it had to be!

The new Matron received the guests at the door of the ward, with Charles at her side. The upstairs wards were always friendly, comfortable rooms; and decorated and gay as they were to-night, you couldn't have thought they had anything to do with a hospital.

At first Sally didn't see Myra. Jane waved a welcoming hand across the room, and Sally would have taken shelter with Jane if Charles hadn't asked her for the first dance.

Charles wasn't very easy to dance with, though he kept perfect time. He held his partner as if he had got to, and didn't much like it. Still he smiled down at Sally, with the same kind look in his eyes which he had had in the blue-bell wood. He asked her if she liked dancing, and Sally said, "Oh yes, awfully, but I'm a little afraid to-night!"

Charles said, "Oh!—why?" very nicely, as if it were surprising that Sally should ever need to feel afraid. "Well," Sally explained, "I'm frightened because I might so easily make mistakes! You see, I never find new people easy, anyway, and it is so important to make no mistakes with Alec's colleagues."

"I don't think you'll find it very difficult," Charles told her smilingly. "They all like your husband, and that will predispose them to like you. Brides generally succeed like wildfire!"

It was rather like wildfire, Sally thought, the way she got on with them! First Charles introduced her to Mr. Willard, the new consultant, who stood by Jane. He carried Sally off with gusto and danced beautifully.

Then Mr. Arnold came up, and, after dancing with Sally, introduced her to a lot of men, one after the other, and still she couldn't see anything of Myra.

She caught glimpses of Alec, gallantly doing his duty. First he danced with the Matron, then with the two deputy matrons, and once with Jane, and twice with Sally herself; and after that with a string of nurses, one after the other.

It was not till the middle of the evening that Sally saw Myra. She had on a daffodil-coloured chiffon, which had no back above the waist, and was so thin that you could see each movement of her body through it. It was terrible how beautiful she looked, with her red-gold hair and her long lovely limbs! She had gold sandals on her bare feet, and a gold fillet for her hair; and through the dazzling whiteness of her skin, there shone a glow like the glow from an invisible fire. The room melted away from her, until she became always the centre of everything.

Charles was dancing with Sally for the second time when she saw Myra. He said, "Shall we sit out for the rest of this dance?" and took her to a covered balcony full of flowers. Charles had had them all sent over from his greenhouse; scarlet lilies and trees of white lilac. He moved Sally's chair forward so that she sat under one of the white lilac trees, close by the window, where she could look out at the driven moon.

Charles was silent, as he very often was, but Sally wasn't afraid of his silences any longer. She knew that they weren't against what was going on in the other person's mind. She didn't want to talk herself. She could hear Myra's laugh. It had no sense in it and was high and hard, as if Myra wasn't really amused or happy, but just victorious over something. It was a cruel laugh. Charles sat so that his back prevented Sally from seeing whom Myra was dancing with. It was very nice of Charles—but she knew!

Sally heard herself say, as if the words were dragged out of her by some strange force: "Your sister looks very beautiful to-night."

"I believe she is considered so," Charles replied in a voice that seemed to make his sister's beauty negligible. "But—I am told that you are the success of the evening, Mrs. Macgregor! It was very kind of you to give me a second dance. I am not surprised that you should be fond of dancing."

Charles, when he paid compliments, meant exactly what he said; and Sally's heart felt suddenly a little warmer. She hadn't known, until after Charles spoke, how cold her heart had grown!

"I suppose you hate having to dance at all?" she ventured with a shy little laugh.

"Hate is rather a stronger word than I care to use," Charles answered, smilingly. "I find dancing rather a barbarous use to put music to!"

"Are you awfully fond of music?" Sally persisted. It was interesting—trying to explore those shut parts of

Charles's exclusive mind—and it helped her to forget
Myra. Charles didn't seem to object to her tremulous ex-
plorations.

"I can enjoy certain kinds of music," he explained;
"not very modern music, I'm afraid. Jazz leaves me particularly cold. I like early English music, and German
music as far as Wagner, whom I must confess irritates
my nerves! I like Italian classical music, and some of the
Russian operas. Among the moderns I can enjoy Debussy,
and sometimes Scriabine, and our own Elgar, but that is
as far as I care to go. When music tries to imitate a Zoo,
I prefer silence."

The leaves of one of the scarlet lilies suddenly parted.
Myra stood there, leaning forward like some lovely Bac-
chante between the scarlet flowers. Her laughing eyes met
Sally's frightened ones.

"Oh!" she said, "it's you, is it?"

Through the shaken leaves Sally could see a man's hand
at Myra's waist. Sally told the stubborn, flying thing inside her—that they had just been dancing—they were
still almost dancing! It didn't matter about Alec's hand!
The scarlet flowers closed. Alec hadn't seen Sally. They
went somewhere else. The battered, sallow moon jerked up
out of the cloud-drift, and stared in at the window.

Charles's steady voice went on—he was discussing
Haydn—or was it Handel? Sally wasn't quite sure which.
She knew they both began with an H. Mr. Arnold and
Jane came out onto the balcony. They exchanged part-
ners.

Sally danced on and on. Alec and Myra never came
back into the room again. Jane and Charles and Mr.
Arnold seemed always to come and go within reach of
Sally; and at last, when Sally thought the evening would
never have an end, the dance stopped, and the staff went
over to Charles's house, to supper.

Charles made Sally sit down at a little table, and brought her chicken and champagne. The assistant matron of the female side stood near her. She smiled at Sally, and when Charles went to look after Jane, they began to talk to each other. "I like the staff dances," Miss Watkins told Sally, confidentially. "You know where you are, if you know what I mean! And there's no responsibilities! Now when we have our patients' dances, however careful you are, or poor things they are—for I do think they try to behave their best in public—something odd may happen! Dancing may do them all the good in the world, of course, and they all like dressing up, but on the other hand, dancing may be just what will start even a mild case off!"

"They were all very good at the last dance," Sally said with a smile, "only I missed little Miss Flint. She looks so trim and light on her feet. I should think she'd dance beautifully!"

Several times during the evening Sally had thought of Carrie, and looked in vain for the little light figure among the dancers.

"Oh, she wouldn't be fit to!" Miss Watkins answered, with a shocked laugh. "It wouldn't do at all, Mrs. Macgregor!"

Sally felt quite unreasonably upset and cross at this answer. She bit her lips to keep from saying something rude. Why shouldn't poor Carrie be allowed to dance? She could easily be stopped taking her clothes off—if she began to! If some people could have on as little as Myra—— Again she heard that high, shattering laugh! Myra had come into the room, and Alec was still with her. The assistant matron moved away, and Charles took her place again; but it wasn't any use his standing there and talking about Mozart. For Sally saw two things quite plainly: one was that Alec and Myra had never been apart

since she last saw them two hours ago; and the other was
that they had both been drinking. They were not drunk,
but they were excitable and silly, and Alec stood too near
Myra. She was like a flame, Sally thought, that ran out
at men, and licked them up!

The rest of the evening seemed to consist of cold chicken
which Sally couldn't swallow, and laughter that was like
being cut to pieces by broken glass. Alec wasn't steady on
his feet by the time they went home. The Hursts and Jane
went with them to the door, and by behaving as if nothing
could happen, they almost succeeded in making Sally believe that nothing had!

But when they had gone and Sally and Alec were alone
—Alec kicked Biscuit!

Biscuit had been barking rather a lot. It was fearfully
exciting for him to be let out at four o'clock in the morning, especially after a night of more than mortal loneliness. When Alec called to Biscuit to come in, he ran excitedly round and round them, and tried to bite their
slippers. Alec said, "Damn the dog!" and kicked him.
Then Sally knew that something horrible had happened at
the dance!

CHAPTER XXII

LYING on her face in the sand, where she could feel the full heat of the sun pouring through her body, Sally became conscious of her own weight. Middle-aged people, she thought, must feel as she did when the lovely lightness of their youth had gone, and all their taut springs slackened. But they didn't all look unhappy about it. The slowing-down of their blood made them perhaps relinquish lightness and speed, without the bitter grudge Sally felt, at twenty-one, lying beside Jane's erect, unchallenged figure.

Jane had everything. She wasn't old yet. She had health and work, and that poise of her inner being which made her independent of the heart's crushing claims. She had Alec, too, in a sense that Sally had never had him. It didn't make any difference to Jane's Alec that he ran after a silly woman with a murderous heart. The life of his mind was clean. He had not betrayed Jane with Myra! But Sally he had betrayed!

While she lay there, hiding her eyes from the light, she felt as dry and lifeless as a grain of the hot sand which slid through her idle fingers. Her back was turned to the sparkle on the azure sea. The soft crash of light summer waves irritated rather than soothed her senses. The blue frame of the cloudless sky hung above her bowed head like the bars of a cage.

She felt like a young knight who, full of life and ardour, sets out for the jousting green, only to be struck down by the first blow of his adversary. Abashed and broken, wishing that he had been slain, he must crawl off the field, leaving his high hopes in the dust.

It was all very well for Jane to sit there and be sorry for Sally! Jane, for all her thirty years, knew nothing of what Sally felt. She had never cast her body like a coin into the Fountain of Trevi, as passionate earnest of its desired return! Jane had never had a man wake to her— as the earth wakes to the sun! Nor known what it was to be robbed of her warmth and light, and forced, like a dead moon, to go travelling on for ever in the frozen dark! Jane had lost nothing—knew nothing—was no comforter!

"Why mayn't we kill ourselves?" Sally heard herself saying the words with astonishment. She had not meant to ask Jane anything.

In the silence that followed, she knew that Jane wanted to meet her eyes; but she kept them down, and went on staring at the fruitless sand.

"Sally, my dear," Jane said at last, "you are being very badly treated. But you are too big a human being to lie down under it. Death is no solution. And you are not vindictive enough to want to use it as a weapon. I firmly believe that in a year's time you will be able to look back and laugh at the idea of Alec's caring for anyone but you. He cannot care for Myra Anderson in any serious way. Such women are their own antidotes. Only light men are in any real danger from light women! We know that Alec isn't really light. In a few weeks, if you can be patient, you will have nothing to worry about. Why not go home for a bit—let him find out for himself why—and see what comes of it. In a week he will be at your door!"

"And I should know that you had sent him there!" Sally said to herself bitterly. To hear Jane talk about Alec was like having water described to you when you lay in a burning fever. Besides, the Alec that came back—if he ever came back—wouldn't be her happy bridegroom any more. What was the use of a shamed lover?

Jane didn't go on talking, but she didn't turn her mind

away from Sally. She sat there alert and silent, till something in her silence opened the door of Sally's heart.

"I suppose you always knew that love didn't last?"
Sally said reluctantly, after a long pause. "Or else you
can't think love—which a silly fancy can cut through like
this—is real?"

Looking up to see why Jane made no answer, Sally
surprised a strange look on Jane's face. Her grey eyes
weren't cold any more, they were kind, with a deep private
kindness. A light wavered over them like the sunlight
sparkling over the sea. The light met Sally's eyes for an
instant, and vanished.

"I see no reason why love should not last," Jane said
slowly, with her usual lack of emphasis. "I am sure that
yours and Alec's will! A 'region cloud has hid him from
your sight'! One cannot speak of anyone's love as a static
thing, or give it a separate entity. It is as great or small
as the heart that contains it; and as constant as the whole
human being is constant. Once, when I was unhappy, I
wrote a poem about love. It is bad, of course, because I
am not a poet, but it said something which I still believe.

> Not a thing
> Nor a force,
> But Light
> At its source.

"The sun can be obscured; it cannot be put out."

"One can go blind," said Sally sullenly.

Jane made no answer. Sally remembered, with a flicker
of compunction, that Jane's lover had been shot for cowardice. This must have been hard for Jane, but, after all,
dead lovers are safe, they cannot be untrue!

"I wouldn't have minded Alec's being a coward!" Sally
thought to herself. "I could have forgiven his being shot
for anything. He would still be mine."

Perhaps Jane, in the long silence that followed, touched upon this thought, for she broke it at last by saying: "I know this must seem to you irreparable. But nothing in life is irreparable! Alec has an illness from which he will recover; and when he has recovered, you will be happy once more."

"Nothing will ever be the same again!" Sally cried passionately. "I don't know that I even want him back. I've stopped wanting things."

Jane made no reply. Perhaps she did not altogether believe Sally's statement. Perhaps she thought there was another way of looking at life than as a means for carrying out personal desires. Sally waited for Jane to say something silly like this, but Jane merely went on, saying nothing.

Slowly the sun grew less hot. The sand sparkled more. The returning tide broke closer to their feet, leaving a glistening wake.

Sally sat up and faced the sea. Across a strip of wet beach, where a wave had just broken, a seagull shuffled clumsily over the shining sand. Its body looked unstable and heavy, till, suddenly struck by the nearness of their alien presence, it rose and floated on wide, silvery wings, into the blue air. Sally followed its long flight with a bitter grudge.

"There isn't anything to be done about it!" Sally said at last. "I shan't go away! Being at home now would be too awful! Mother would be so pleased I'm going to have a baby! Besides, I'd rather be near you. I'll stay and see what happens. I don't talk to Alec about it—and I don't try to find out anything. I always know when he lies to me—and he lies most of the time now, but in a kind way. Besides, I think he half-believes his lies. It is like an illness. But it's an illness that he needn't have! Being married is much worse than you think, Jane, for whatever the other one has or does is catching. You can't get away from it. I always know when he has been with Myra."

Jane said tentatively: "Yes, I suppose so. I imagine being married is both better and worse than one thinks."

Sally nodded. It made her feel better that Jane should admit her wider range of experience. Her body too felt lighter with the decline of day. Everything was just as awful, she assured herself, but she began to want her tea.

Jane, when Sally told her that they might as well have tea, drew out the picnic basket with alacrity and gave it to her. Perhaps Jane had been wanting her tea too!

While they were eating it, Sally suddenly remembered something, which had run in and out of her mind ever since the dance.

"Jane," she demanded, "I want Carrie Flint to come to tea with me one day! Can she?"

Jane's eyes met hers in blank bewilderment.

"Carrie Flint!" she exclaimed. "Why ever in the world——?"

"I know," said Sally impatiently. "That's what Alec said too. But he agreed that if you let her she might come! I must have something to think of outside my own life, or I shall go off my head! And I'd like to try and see if I can't help that poor crushed thing! You said she'd been awfully bullied and badgered at home, didn't you? Well, you know, I was too—so that I shall understand her all the better! I want her alone—without that aggravating nurse who keeps clutching at her."

Jane said nothing for a minute or two. She went on looking at Sally, with a look that seemed to probe past the defences of her benevolent intention into Sally's angry heart.

For Sally was very angry! That was really why she wanted to have Carrie Flint to tea!

Here was another crushed, sat-upon, defrauded human

being! Not clever enough to stand clever people, and so shut up for it! Ah! they were kind to her, no doubt! Just as Jane was kind to Sally herself—fathomlessly and maddeningly kind! And here was Sally, understanding the weight of just such kindness, and capable of lifting it from Carrie's broken mind! If Jane and Alec were going to have a game of their own, without Sally, and talk for hours over their mended patients, why shouldn't Sally have a mended patient of her own, that neither of them was able to reach?

Jane said at last: "Sally, madness isn't what you imagine. It is an illness which only trained people can understand and help. Carrie is getting better. In a year perhaps she may be well again. One can't, of course, be certain, but when there has once been definite improvement on certain lines, one can confidently hope for recovery. Alec discovered how to reach her, and he has done a great deal towards making her recovery possible; but I simply can't understand his agreeing to her going to tea with you—as she is now. It won't do her any good. It will merely confuse her. She is always worse when she has to see her sisters."

"Yes, but I'm not her sisters!" Sally persisted excitedly. "She likes me! She wants to see me! I know I could do her good!"

Jane relapsed into a disconcerting silence. Sally felt surprised and rather flattered at the effect she had produced on Jane. It wasn't perhaps quite truthful of Sally to tell Jane that Alec had agreed about Carrie. What had really taken place was that Alec had said: "What utter nonsense! Ask Jane and see what she says!" But anyhow he hadn't refused point-blank.

"I hate to say 'no' to you," Jane confessed at last. "Naturally I want you to have whatever could interest you just now, especially if Alec thinks it feasible. But I honestly don't think Carrie would even enjoy it. Can't you wait for a few months? I quite see your point about doing her good—but she isn't yet in the right state for being done good to—not like that, I mean! Her mind is like an iceberg coming up out of the sea. Most of it is invisible, and there isn't standing room yet for anything to light on."

Sally frowned, but she was beginning to feel better and better. She was overpowering Jane, who obviously hated to refuse her, or to let her have Carrie!

"Can't you ever be wrong about a patient?" Sally asked rather rudely.

Jane flushed. She had a pride which was afraid of infallibility. She said quietly:

"Yes, of course! I can very easily be wrong—but I don't think I am wrong about Carrie. There are many unmistakable signs about non-social patients which can't very well be misunderstood by any practising psychiatrist."

"Alec always says that all the patients are human beings, and can be treated along the same lines as other human beings," Sally said obstinately. "I think he likes trying fresh things better than you do!"

Jane's eyes widened in hurt surprise. She hadn't expected Sally to want to wound her; but she ignored Sally's taunt.

"I can't in any case allow her to come without Nurse Christie," Jane said steadily. "I am responsible for what she does, and she might do most unexpectedly tiresome things! I warn you that a tea-party won't do her any good. It won't do her any definite harm, of course, or I should refuse to let her go to you. But it may make her feel that she is unhappier than she really is! I can't understand quite why you so much want to have her."

Jane had given in! Never before had Sally felt herself

a match for Jane—not even when Jane wished her to feel it. Jane had given in; and she wasn't at all comfortable about it! Sally had had to feel uncomfortable often, and it was good, she felt, for Jane to have to feel it once!

Jane began to put the tea-things away in silence, burying the scraps in a neat little hole in the sand.

The sun was sinking, a great golden ball cut flat by the line of the darkening sea. Jane's eyes were fixed upon it; and having finished packing the basket, she sat with her hands in her lap, as if there were nothing else but the sun to dispose of. She seemed to have given up—or to have discovered—why Sally wanted Carrie Flint to come to tea with her.

A vague discomfort penetrated Sally's feeling of triumph.

"I do really want her, Jane," she explained. "I have quite a definite feeling that I could help her!"

"Definite feelings about questions which seem not very important in themselves are not always to be trusted," Jane said gravely.

Sally thought this over in silence. It was one of those tiresome remarks which Alec and Jane often made—as if they knew more about one than one knew oneself! Sally felt that neither of them—especially not Jane—had any business to know what one felt like, or why one felt like it! It was just another of their unfair advantages! She hardened her heart and said:

"Well, it's settled, then. You think I'm wrong, of course, because I don't agree with you. But I can't help that. I believe I can do Carrie good—and I mean to try."

Jane accepted her defeat meekly; but she gave a little sigh as she turned to follow Sally off the beach, as if she didn't believe a person could do another person very much good by being cross about it.

CHAPTER XXIII

SALLY couldn't help wishing that Carrie Flint played games. In a game you got to know people without fuss. You needn't be polite when there was a ball to hit—and talk always flowed more satisfactorily if taken unawares.

Sally had meant to have tea in the garden, and perhaps take Carrie for a run in the car afterwards; but the rain had come down in torrents all day, and meant to go on coming down. There was only Biscuit to fall back upon. People always either liked or disliked dogs; and then the dog himself could be counted upon to contribute something towards the conversation. Biscuit was looking his best. He had just been washed and his coat was a glorious lathery white. He would probably bark a good deal when Carrie and Nurse Christie first came in, but though not one of those soppy dogs that wriggle ingratiatingly to the feet of strangers, he didn't really mind them unless they wore blue aprons and reminded him of butchers.

Sally filled the room with blue flowers, because she had heard Jane say once that blue was the most restful colour for nerves. She arranged a group of delphiniums by the window—very tall and stately—and ranging in colour from the darkest gentian to the milky azure of forget-me-not. She put a large bowl of violas in the middle of the tea-table; and made four kinds of cake and three different kinds of savoury sandwich.

Preparing for Carrie was a great relief, and drove away a little of the ache from Alec's absences.

Alec wasn't very nice about Carrie's coming to tea. He broke into a storm of inexplicable fury. Still Sally rather enjoyed watching his hollow friendliness explode into vituperation. She liked it less, however, when he rushed to the telephone to expostulate with Jane. What would Jane say? Would she let him know that her consent had been wrung out of her by a trick? There was a long, uneasy pause while Sally strung herself to face exposure. Then Alec slammed down the receiver and said that Jane was a damned fool and didn't know her own business. Sally breathed a long sigh of relief. Alec changed his ground after that, and said he couldn't be expected to come home for tea—with patients all over the house! Then he went out and banged the door behind him. Men with bad consciences seldom make good excuses; but Sally rather preferred Alec's banging doors to kissing her. He put more of himself into it.

Nothing had happened to prevent Carrie's coming to tea; and that was the great thing. It was four o'clock and nearly time for her to arrive. Sally stood by the open window watching for her. She thought the raw air felt chilly, and went to the fireplace to light the neatly laid fire.

How awful it would be if it should smoke and there was nowhere to sit except the kitchen! That was the worst of having only one big living-room; if anything went wrong in it, there was nothing to fall back upon! But the fire did burn; and Sally went back to the window again.

At last two figures emerged from the hospital, and hurried across the grounds in mackintoshes and umbrellas.

Sally was glad to see that Nurse Christie wasn't holding on to Carrie. Carrie flitted along sideways, with that light, surreptitious urgency, which Sally had noticed before, as if she wanted to pass through the air unseen. Her hurrying figure was at once purposeless and intent! How defeated and driven she must feel—to want to go so fast without knowing why—or where! Nurse Christie had several times to catch up with her and start her off afresh towards their little house.

At last both guests stood in the hall. Biscuit rushed out and barked, and Carrie drew back and trembled. She was apparently one of those people who don't like dogs. Still she didn't seem to mind Biscuit after he'd stopped barking. Biscuit was rather funny about her; after the first casual sniff, he completely ignored Carrie's presence, though he devoted a good deal of rather friendly attention to Nurse Christie.

Carrie stood in the hall between Nurse Christie and Sally, smiling her fixed shy smile, and not attempting to do anything but drip. Nurse Christie had to take off Carrie's mackintosh and goloshes, as well as her own; but when Sally turned to lead the way into the sitting-room, Carrie followed so quickly of her own accord that it was quite uncanny to find her so close to one's shoulder.

Nurse Christie slipped an arm in Carrie's, and without exactly drawing her away from Sally, prevented her from coming any closer.

Sally had meant to take Carrie into the kitchen with her to help bring in the tea. She thought it would break—not the ice, for there was no ice—but the strange feeling of tension which hovered in the air between them; but meeting Carrie's vague eyes, so like the shining, unconscious eyes of a bird, she decided not to suggest it. It would be so dreadful if Carrie were too vague, and dropped something which broke!

When Sally had brought the tea in, she asked Carrie if she liked flowers. One could see it was no use asking her about dogs! Whenever Biscuit passed Carrie on one of his meretricious errands—which brought him nearer and nearer to the savoury sandwiches—she trembled! She hadn't even that elementary knowledge of dogs which would have told her that Biscuit, besides having accepted her presence, was wholly concentrated upon windfalls from the table. After he had satisfactorily settled down as near as he could comfortably allow himself to the sandwiches, Carrie's smile deepened, but she still didn't answer Sally about the flowers. Her face looked more and more like a mask behind which her real life was lived, so that she really had no interest to spare for outside objects. She didn't seem to see even the sandwiches or the cakes.

Nurse Christie, without undue pressure, succeeded in persuading Carrie to sit down between them. Sally drew out the smallest of a nest of tables and put Carrie's tea on it, close to her, and offered her a choice of the feast. Carrie sat motionless and entranced, like something made out of wood. Suddenly, without warning, she swooped over the table, gathered up half-a-dozen sandwiches, ran off with them to the corner of the room, and hid behind a curtain.

Nurse Christie laughed a little apologetically.

"I'm afraid she won't eat in any other way," she said. "She'll come back when she's finished. I hope you don't mind?"

Sally had to say, "Of course not—if she likes to eat that way. But what about cake later on?"

"She may come back for that," Nurse Christie said cheerfully, "if we just go on talking. Dr. Macgregor thinks she was too much noticed and criticised when she was a child, and perhaps specially at meal times. He told us never to draw attention to what she does about food, and then he thinks, in time, she'll get over it."

So they went on talking. Nurse Christie was rather a nice girl, after all. She played hockey and had been at the same school at Eastbourne as one of Sally's friends. Mental nursing wasn't a usual profession for girls of her class, she explained, but she had always had a fancy for it, and it was great luck she had come to such a good modern hospital. She had learned a lot from Dr. Macgregor and Dr. Everest. "It's a comfort," she told Sally, "that they work so hand and glove together. It makes everything go with such a swing, and there's none of that cut-off jealous feeling you often get between doctors in a hospital. Your husband visits some of his old cases on our side, and Dr. Everest some of hers on his, so that we get the experience of both."

That "cut-off jealous feeling"! The unintentional words drove Sally back into her haunted mind. What was Alec doing now? With whom was he squandering their golden hours? She still saw Nurse Christie's pleasant, open face. She heard her talking; but the words meant no more to her than the patter of raindrops against the window-pane.

The curtains at the other end of the room stirred. Carrie came from behind them, and hovered in circles, nearer and nearer to the table.

Nurse Christie looked up, and quietly took the cake-knife, onto her own plate. Carrie darted forward and pounced on the nearest cake, and hurried off with it once more behind her curtains. She made a lot of crumbs on the floor, and passed through the delphiniums without so much as a glance at them. It was quite plain the flowers meant nothing to her, even though they were blue!

After she had finished eating, she came out again and went—with the same little oblique movements—towards the fireplace. She didn't seem to want to get warm, but she looked at the flames as if she loved them. Nurse Christie got up quickly, and once more persuaded Carrie, though this time it was more difficult to persuade her, to sit down between Sally and herself.

Sally began to feel rather glad that Nurse Christie was there. She had a strange idea that Carrie wanted to put the live coals out of the fireplace onto the floor. It was an absurd idea, but Carrie's expression seemed so intent upon those flickering flames!

Now that she was back at the table again, her bright gaze fixed itself once more on Sally's face. The cake—the fire—Sally's face—she seemed to want to associate herself with each in turn, without knowing how to reach a point of contact.

"I am so glad you were able to come to tea," Sally said gently, for it was for her, she quickly reminded herself, to produce the contact. "Do you remember me?"

Carrie stared silently on.

"I don't expect she does really," Nurse Christie interposed. "But of course she likes to see an outsider. They all do. It's a bit of an event for them, and then in some queer way they feel that people in the outside world are stronger than they are—and yet not looking after them or bothering them as we have to! So it's an advantage for her to meet you—if you know what I mean!"

Sally nodded. She could put the thought of Alec away from her now. This was what she had been longing for, to be able to help Carrie, because she was the stronger!

"It was in the garden," Sally went on. "Don't you remember—ever so long ago? You asked me to stay with you, but I couldn't then. You said you had something special that you wanted to say to me, and I said I'd try to see you again, and then you could tell me anything you wanted to tell me?"

Carrie's lips parted. Something in Sally's voice—in her eyes, perhaps—resting on Carrie with the eager pity her heart felt—communicated itself to Carrie. "Do—do stay!" she said urgently. "Do—do let me——" She made a quick little movement towards Sally, but Nurse Christie's hand drew her resolutely back.

Carrie broke off suddenly and smiled her little secretive smile. She had started trembling, but not a frightened trembling, like Biscuit had aroused in her. It was an eager trembling.

"Do let her go!" Sally exclaimed impatiently.

Nurse Christie shook her head. "No, I mustn't," she said quickly, flushing apologetically, to soften her refusal. "I'm so sorry, Mrs. Macgregor, but I mustn't! She doesn't really want to say anything either."

"Ah, but that's nonsense!" Sally protested. "I can see that she has something tremendously on her mind! It's just on the tip of her tongue—you can see how she's trembling with eagerness to say it!"

"She wants to do what she knows she mustn't," Nurse Christie said guardedly.

Biscuit, who had been lying perfectly quietly under the table, got up and came close to Sally's knee. His hair stood erect and he started growling.

"I must kiss you! I must kiss you!" Carrie cried.

Sally didn't much like being kissed by a strange girl, but she thought they were all making rather a fuss about nothing, so she leaned forward towards Carrie. There was a sudden scuffle; Biscuit snapped; Carrie screamed; and Sally saw what Carrie had wanted to do.

"She would have bitten me!" Sally exclaimed in horror.

Nurse Christie, who had pulled Carrie back in time, and was now holding her fast, agreed a little breathlessly: "I'm afraid she would! She starts kissing, and then it turns into a bite—so one can't let her begin! She doesn't mean anything by it—and she's not at all excited, so it's quite all right! She doesn't do it nearly as often now, and she's so much better—in all sorts of ways—that Dr. Everest thought I might bring her! I didn't like explaining about it before her—for fear of putting it into her head—you never know whether she's understanding what one says or not! You didn't seem to know—but I'm so sorry!"

"No, I didn't know," said Sally. She leaned back in her

chair, feeling a little queer and faint. This, then, was the
reason they'd made that fuss about Carrie's coming to
tea! But they might have told her! Perhaps they would
have told her if she hadn't been going to have a baby!
Doctors always muffle things up so. She felt curiously conscious of the baby—not as if it were a mere physical bur-
den, but as if it were something precious to be protected.

"Thank you! thank you!" she said quickly to Nurse
Christie. "It was all my fault. I shouldn't have had her
her—I made her want to!"

"It doesn't matter a bit," Nurse Christie said soothingly. "She didn't touch you, and there's no harm done.
She's settled down nicely. She won't give any more trouble
—will you, Carrie? When she's quite got over all her foolish tricks, she can go all by herself into the big garden!"

Biscuit settled down too. He jumped onto Sally's lap
and tied himself up like a whiting. He even pretended to
be asleep, though his eyes were open and his ears cocked.
Nurse Christie took one of the violas out of the bowl and
put it on Carrie's knee. Carrie picked it up at once and
began tearing it to pieces. She tore it very softly and
tenderly, as if destruction was a form of caress. After she
had finished tearing it, she helped herself to fresh violas
and went on tearing. She seemed quite contented. Nurse
Christie said: "You don't mind, do you?—it will keep her
quiet."

Sally had to say she didn't mind, though it hurt her to
see the delicate velvet petals torn into shreds.

"Then there isn't anything," she asked Nurse Christie
in a low voice, "on her mind? That time in the garden,
she didn't want to tell me anything—even then?"

"Well—I don't think so," Nurse Christie said consideringly. "She talks and talks to herself for hours sometimes, but not reasonably—not to expect answers. Her
mind doesn't connect yet with anyone else's—except for

a flash sometimes, with Dr. Macgregor's. She knows him
all right, and she listens to what he says to her, and re-
members it afterwards. You can't say she exactly answers
him, but she may before long. At first when she came she
was very unhappy, and angry too. She was brought in
like that, but it soon died down. She's quite quiet now—
except when her sisters come to see her. She goes off then
sometimes for a day or two."

"And then," Sally asked in an awed voice, "when she's
'off,' what is she like?"

Nurse Christie hesitated. "Well, then you have to be
careful," she explained, "or she might hurt herself, or
anyone who came near her. One has to watch her all the
time, of course; but she's quite controllable in her present condition. Your husband says her whole trouble is that
she's been too good for too long!"

Sally gave a queer little sigh, and Carrie echoed it.
Their eyes met over the heap of torn violas, as if they
knew they had something in common.

A quick step sounded on the gravel outside the window. Alec was there, though Sally hadn't expected him.
He said he'd found time to run in for a cup of tea after
all.

Carrie gave a quick cry of delight and flitted eagerly
towards him. He caught her by the wrists, smiling down
at her with his kind schoolboy eyes. "Well, well!" he said,
"and how's the little tea-party going?"

Nurse Christie got up and said, "I think it's time we
went back now," and, firmly slipping her arm into the
reluctant Carrie's, drew her out of the room.

Sally shook hands with them both at the door; but Carrie was looking over her shoulder at Alec, and didn't even
see what was happening to her hand.

Alec only stayed ten minutes. He ate the sandwiches
and praised them. He praised the flowers and the cakes,

and the fluffy whiteness of Biscuit. He even said that it was quite a good idea having Carrie to tea, after all.

Before he went back to the hospital, he mentioned casually that he'd been invited to dinner by an old patient of his, who had turned up in the town. He might be late coming home, and Sally wasn't to sit up for him. He kissed her good-bye without looking at her.

Sally stood in the open doorway and watched his tall, upright figure darting through the bright curtain of the rain.

She had had Carrie to tea now; and there was nothing left to look forward to.

When she couldn't see Alec any longer, Sally shivered a little, and went back into the sitting-room to sweep up the torn violas.

CHAPTER XXIV

HALFWAY across the grounds Alec felt an overpowering impulse to turn back. He would tell Sally it was all over! There wasn't any old patient! He would come back to dinner and never see Myra alone again! He swerved half-round, but was brought up short by a counter-impulse. Giving up Myra was easy, but to give up to-night wouldn't be easy! You can't slap a woman's face the moment she has granted you her favours! Myra must have her due—her drive, her road dinner, and half the summer night! Then he would be able to say to her: "You wanted this, and you've had it, and it's over! Now I go back to my wife!"

It wasn't as if he had to consider Myra's feelings. Feelings, apart from physical excitement, weren't involved on either side. Myra would bite her lips and laugh, get a little drunk, and go on to the next man! And Alec would have learned his lesson! No more light women! Only that one achieved, increasing intimacy which satisfied him, body and soul! Sally was safe already in his heart of hearts. He had never meant to be unfaithful to her. Unfaithfulness had happened to him, like a fall from a horse. Damn it all! How Jane despised him! She hadn't said a thing. She hadn't even taken the trouble to change her cool cordiality into anything colder. But he knew! He hadn't worked with Jane for five years not to know the difference between her trust and her distrust! She had believed in him! Her loyalty had been slowly given to him, but it had gone deep. Her faith had been an element—salt and buoyant like the sea—on which Alec had felt himself upheld. And now it was withdrawn! Worse than withdrawn!

Jane had given her faith to Charles. That was the real inconstancy. Not a single unforeseen act, but that deliberate turning of the indispensable heart!

The sense of his ill-treatment drained out remorse. He was in the hospital now, and all thought of darting back to Sally was over.

In his tiny office he was like a captain on his bridge, surrounded by broken and treacherous seas! He knew his way through each emergency, but even here he couldn't escape the torment of his subserviency to Charles! His was not the ultimate command.

A message lay on his table.

"Colonel Endicott to see his son."

The struggle in Alec's mind broke off. Jane, Sally, even Charles faded out, and left the image of young Endicott reigning supreme.

Alec had a theory about young Endicott, who wasn't young any more. He had come out of the War, in his extreme youth, shell-shocked and mindless, and had lain ever since like an insect pinned to a board. Alec's theory was that his father was behind the whole thing, not the mine which had merely blown up young Endicott's astonished body. Well, here was a chance to see if he was right! He telephoned through that he would see Colonel Endicott in his office and take him on to the ward afterwards. A few moments later a lean, elderly man with a soldier's straight narrow back and neat shoulders, entered with abrupt decision. Under beetled brows his blue eyes, touched by a fundamental innocence, were as bright as mountain flowers.

Colonel Endicott stared hard at Alec, as if he could judge all he wanted of a man in one straight glance. He was, Alec said to himself, the usual hide-bound military type, to be counted on for disciplined deeds, but never to be counted on for imagination or for tolerance.

Still the old man's heart was broken—whatever he'd managed, probably innocently, to inflict, had reacted on himself. His lean, long face was wrinkled and chiselled with the blow that had fallen on his only son. He had brought young Endicott up on his iron code and according to his terrific standards. The boy had been crucified against his father's pluck! But the father, too, was a victim of the same inflexible standard.

Alec's wits, aroused to meet him, drove back his antagonism. He couldn't go on being angry with a tortured man, even though the man reminded him most unpleasantly of Charles!

"Dr. Everest has told me about you," Alec said, as soon as Colonel Endicott had accepted the chair he pushed towards him. "She takes a great interest in your son's case. Now that he is under my care, I do also. I have got the benefit of her year's work over him. But you know she only had a year. He has been more or less in the same condition for nearly fourteen years, hasn't he?"

Colonel Endicott nodded. He refused a drink, he waved away cigarettes. His expression said, "This is a disagreeable business, but I need no anodynes in order to go through with it!" He didn't want to hear Alec's theory. He didn't want to have his feelings either spared or roused. Still less did he want to be plunged into the indecent irrelevancy of thought; though he must endure what the fellow had to say, since he was a new doctor and had a right to say something.

"I suppose you consider my son's case hopeless?" he said gruffly, turning his eyes away from Alec out of courtesy, so as not to surprise unfairly an answer to the only question which interested him.

"We never say hopeless," Alec assured him. "Experience has taught us that there are always unknown factors likely to break in. Science advances very slowly on psychological lines, and we have frequent set-backs; but it is never static. I have known cases of very long standing clear up most unexpectedly. Still I should be unfair to you if I let you indulge in false hopes. After so long a period of practical unconsciousness there must be brain deterioration. Dr. Everest has given you her view of the case, I don't suppose it differs materially from my own. We have a ward full of shell-shock cases here, more or less severe, none quite so deadlocked as your son's. In my opinion shell-shock has nothing physical about it. It is simply a state of mental conflict where the desires are so evenly matched that neither can yield to the other. You have perhaps seen such a thing in a serious dog-fight. The jaws get locked, and neither dog can break away from the other, even if it wants to."

Colonel Endicott frowned. He disliked having his son's condition compared to a dog-fight. This fellow was worse than the woman doctor! It had shocked him to the core to have a woman doctor for his son. But he had got used to her. She held her tongue and was competent. In fact, the only improvement he had ever noticed in his son's case —and he had noticed everything—had been while he was under Jane's care.

He grunted.

"Men trained as your son must have been trained," Alec went on, "and then exposed to a series of unimaginable shocks, are liable to such breakdowns. There is nothing, in their past experience, to help them to meet the demands made on them in modern warfare, and they have a code so developed as to refuse them any natural exit."

Colonel Endicott didn't know what the fellow was getting at, but he suspected him of something lawless.

"My son had the usual standards," he said sternly, "of an English public school boy. His War record—until this shock—was what I had expected of him. I don't know what you mean by 'natural exits.' The boy couldn't run away! He'd have been, very rightly, shot, if he had."

"His record was terrifically good," Alec objected. "He volunteered for every stiff job going. He simply couldn't show funk, and no sane man with his experience could have escaped it. Cowards don't get shell-shock in its severest form. It is your overstrained, ambitious hero that goes completely to pieces. The normal man escapes because he only does what he has to, the coward escapes because he's not useful enough to depend on, but the hero—well, my experience of most war heroes is that they get smashed up, or take to drink. The more fixed and built up to a pinnacle a character is, the more driven by ideals and preconceptions, the harder job it is to adjust it to startling occurrences. The hero can't give up being a hero, and beyond a certain pitch his nerves won't let him go on being a hero, so we get shell-shock."

"Hum!" said the Colonel grudgingly. "What you say sounds very fanciful to me. I thought there might be—buried up to the chin, and what not—and probably knocked about the head by clods of earth—a certain amount of structural damage?"

"No," Alec told him, "I understand there was no structural damage in your son's case, nor any form of pressure on the brain. Every possible examination has been made and every known physical means of improvement tried. You can go over the case notes if you care to. We have got the preliminary ones from London here, and we made the other tests ourselves. Fortunately, he doesn't suffer. The whole of him, including his power to suffer, has gone into the one act of locking. What we are trying to do is to detach any thread of consciousness we can get loose from the central conflict. Some of the lighter shell-shock cases in the ward have got a lot of consciousness detached, and can live a more or less useful life in consequence. Some have even been cleared up altogether. I wish I could hold out such a hope about your son. All I can promise is that we shall follow the faintest clue we get. Dr. Everest has told me all the facts you were able to give her. I understand your son was an only child, that his mother died in early infancy, and that you brought him up yourself?"

The Colonel nodded.

"The more you can tell me yourself the better," Alec urged. "You come to see him every week, I know. Well, study him all you can on these visits and report to me anything fresh you notice, or wish to have done for him."

"I am much obliged to you," Colonel Endicott said stiffly. "I will, of course, give you any information that is in my power. I went into my son's case very thoroughly with Dr. Everest. She gave me no direct encouragement; but since my son was under her care I have noticed one or two slight signs of improvement. He definitely knows me, for instance. For some years after the shock I felt that he did not. Also he makes some faint physical attempts to assist and co-operate with his nurses. My son was always most considerate to his inferiors, and I should expect what consciousness he had to be directed towards saving people trouble. I live near here in order to visit him. The hospital authorities have afforded me special facilities for seeing him. Dr. Everest wished him placed in a public ward. I was averse to this at first, my boy always liked being alone; but I must admit that the improvements date from his having been put with the other patients. I do not think there is any suggestion for his comfort which has not already been made, and carried out. I understand that you have made no changes in this respect, and I am grateful to you."

Colonel Endicott paused. "Dr. Everest also told me," he said at last, "that my son does not suffer. It is difficult for me to believe this."

He had reached the core of his adversity, and without expecting to dispose of it, he could not forbear trying to get what help there was. Science, he told himself, had nothing to do with pity. Objective facts can be reassuring, without being impertinent. This fanciful fellow might know of some such redeeming fact!

Alec, watching him, realised both what the father wanted and how he feared appearing to want it. He said casually and as if they were both dealing with an abstract thing:

"Of course one cannot prove scientifically the cessation of pain. It would be useful if we could invent a thermometer which registered it. But by watching an accumulation of similar cases, most psychiatrists have arrived at the same conclusion. We feel convinced that though intense mental suffering may lead up to the condition of shell-shock, once it has taken place all sensation dulls down. The more complete the shell-shock, the more entire will be the absence of sensation. The physical tremors and contortions have no spiritual counterpart. The reflex actions of shock in an animal take place, as you know, even after death. Your son's condition is a lesser death. Shell-shock was his escape from a situation which had become unbearable. For such an escape one has to pay a price. Your son paid the price of his whole consciousness for it. He cannot regret paying it, because regret is part of the consciousness which is no longer there."

"You have explained it clearly enough," Colonel Endicott admitted. "But personally I don't agree that there is such a thing as an unbearable situation. I suppose there must be some weakness in the character for such a breakdown to take place."

Alec shook his head emphatically.

"On the contrary," he said, "I should suspect a misdirected strength. We are all human, Colonel Endicott, but we haven't all learned how to allow ourselves to be human. When we refuse to accept our limitations, Nature, who is a stern realist, pays us out. It is to men who try to be supermen that this sort of thing happens."

"Then, according to you, my son is being punished for his pluck," Colonel Endicott said severely, standing up and facing Alec with his long, belligerent stare.

"If you like to put it that way," Alec agreed. "My own way of putting it would be that he is being punished because the inventive genius of mankind has taken a wrong turn. We have preferred to study the art of physical extinction rather than that of self-development. In the late War some of us saw that we had outrun the constable; but we have not yet turned back."

"Ah!" said Colonel Endicott severely, "so you're a pacifist, are you, young man?"

Alec laughed good-humouredly.

"I sometimes wish I was," he admitted, "but I've got my share of the fighting instinct. Still, I wouldn't pit it willingly against machine guns or poison gases."

"My son was not like that," Colonel Endicott said proudly. "He did his duty and faced whatever weapons were to be faced in its execution. I am glad you think this visitation was not due to weakness on his part. Dr. Everest was good enough to reassure me also upon the same point; but without doubting her competency as a doctor, in which I have grown to have great confidence, I rather suspected that as a woman she might desire to let me off cheap. As you can easily imagine, I have no such desire. If my son suffers I should wish to share his sufferings."

"I have told you what I believe to be true," Alec said firmly. "Nor do I know any psychiatrist of note who doubts it. Your son died for what you call his duty, if you will allow me to say so, just as certainly as if his body was no longer here."

Colonel Endicott turned towards the door. He thought this a flowery way of putting it, but the phrase stuck in his mind and comforted him, as Alec had intended that it should. He found that he didn't mind the idea of having this fellow look after his son, after all, even though he seemed to be a pacifist!

Young Endicott lay at the farther end of the big shell-shock ward. His bed was by the window looking out over the garden. His eyes were turned towards the door. When they reached his bedside, Endicott, the father, looked down at his son without speaking. The son was a big hulk of a fellow, blue-eyed like his father, shaking, helpless, most of him gone. He did not smile as he met his father's eyes; neither of them smiled. For a moment or two the tremors of the son became more violent. His father drew a chair up, and sat down in it, with his back to the ward.

Alec stood at the foot of the bed and talked to young Endicott easily and lightly. It was impossible to say how much young Endicott understood, but Alec's voice already had a steadying power over him. The tremors dwindled to their normal proportion. After a few moments the Colonel drew a newspaper out of his pocket and began to read it. He sat there by his son's side every Sunday afternoon reading his Sunday paper from cover to cover. Sister Headly brought them a special tea, and the Colonel helped his son drink from a feeding-cup. He liked doing this, and Sister Headly told Alec—when he joined her across the ward—that the son liked his father's feeding him. On one occasion, when the Colonel had been detained, the son refused his tea till his father came.

"I think," Sister Headly explained to Alec, "that he knows Sundays, even when we don't tell him. I don't know how; perhaps like dogs know when you're going to church. Sundays you can see him watching the door. On week-days he always lies with his eyes straight in front of him. Later on his father will start telling him things. I don't go near them if I can help it, but when I had to once, the Colonel was telling him how many shots a hole he took to go round the golf course! Captain Endicott can't talk, of course, but he moans a lot, as if he wanted to, and words come out sometimes, though I don't think there's much meaning to them. Dr. Everest liked him to be talked to, as if there was."

Alec nodded. "Talk to him as much as you have time to," he agreed, "and let me know if there's anything from him which can be twisted into an answer. It's a cruel business!"

Alec was in no hurry to leave the ward. He knew what he should meet, when he went outside, into the corridor again. Were these two, father and son, so unlucky after all— packed tight in their neat little boxes—unalterable fixtures? Alec himself roamed an uncertain universe, anything might happen to him! Anything might happen to Sally through him! Not that anything would! He looked at the clock.

It was nearly time for him to start off to meet Myra. They considered appearances a little. He would take his car to the bottom of the hospital road before she joined him. He left the ward telling himself that he wasn't sure whether he was going or not. He wasn't forced to go. Still, it would be a shabby thing not to! Fortunately, Sally wasn't one of those set Jane-ish women, who either can't forgive at all, or forgive like a churl with rancour and self-applause. Once it was over, Sally would see her way not to take any more notice of what had happened; and he would see his way to showing her that there'd never be any more of it. Together they would wipe out Myra and start quite afresh.

It almost seemed to Alec, as he hurried down the corridor to get his car, as if they had already started quite afresh!

CHAPTER XXV

ALEC felt as if he were a figure in a nightmare; nothing fitted and everyone tried to detain him. The night sister wanted to see him about a case that threatened to go "off"; an engineer had to have a poisoned thumb lanced; he had his case notes to write up. At last there was nothing left but to glance in at the laboratory and verify a test.

If only he could get out of the hospital unseen! At first he thought the laboratory was empty. The light was on, but neither the Hursts nor Charles were in its spacious precincts. Then he saw Jane in the distance bending over the table. She looked up when Alec came in and faced him, implacably courteous but determined.

"I wanted to see you for a moment," she said.

As she walked towards him down the long, narrow room, he noticed something different about Jane. She looked younger and indefinably softer, as if some strange transfiguring power had passed into her blood.

"I can't stay a minute," Alec said hurriedly. "I'm frightfully late for an appointment as it is. I only looked in to verify a test." He was conscious of the blood beating hard in his temples. The door slipped out of his hand; and closed itself behind him. It made him feel trapped.

"It's Sally," Jane said. "What is the matter with her, Alec?"

Anger seized him, so hot that it seemed to leave a taste upon his tongue.

"What should be the matter with her? I left her all right at tea-time!" Alec demanded.

Was Jane going to challenge him with Myra? Dared

she enter the forbidden chaos of his mind? He hoped she would. Let her say what she thought of him, break up the cold region of distrust—and treat him as man to man!

Her eyes fixed on his were not scornful; they were puzzled and anxious, but they did not accuse him. They had never accused him. That was the cause of his anger. Jane had judged without condemning him!

"Sally isn't all right," Jane told him in a low, strained voice. "There's something very badly wrong with her. This business about Carrie Flint—it's serious!"

Alec's hot-driven mind allowed itself an instant's collected thought. She wasn't going to drag out Myra, after all, then! Curiously enough, this knowledge made him no less angry with Jane. It was an offence the more that she wouldn't let the skirts of her mind touch the subject which possessed him. Still he had only to control himself for a minute or two, then this savage, held-back feeling would be released! He would be on his way to Myra, and what Jane thought about it, and wouldn't say, would cease to matter to him. He tried to remember Sally's face after that damned tea-party. But all he could remember was the rain, and Biscuit darting out into it, white and barking, to spoil the effects of his bath!

"Carrie Flint!" he stammered, meeting Jane's eyes with an effort. "Yes—I suppose Sally has rather a maggot in her head about Carrie. Why on earth did you let her come over to tea? Still, the party went off all right! I ran across to see for myself. There were no bones broken!"

"I had to let her," Jane said with ominous gravity. "That is what is so extraordinary, Alec; if I'd refused to let Sally have Carrie to tea, Sally would have broken our friendship."

"Broken your friendship!" Alec exclaimed incredulously. "Sally couldn't have meant that, Jane. Why, she adores you! Surely you're exaggerating!"

He felt a queer sick feeling at the pit of his stomach. What was there behind that strange insistence of Sally's? Break her friendship with Jane in order to have a mad girl to tea? Surely the two women were inseparable? Lately Sally had been with Jane every moment of the time Jane wasn't on duty! But Jane didn't exaggerate! She stood leaning against the table, within a few feet of him, her hands in her pockets, anxious but unemphatic.

"I don't think I am exaggerating," Jane said, after a pause. "She wanted to see Carrie so much that she didn't care what happened. But she wasn't sincere. I mean her anger with me was sincere, but not the reason she gave for wanting to see Carrie. It is a dangerous state of things when a person, so sensible and friendly as Sally, puts on a mask. Nurse Christie had a very bad time over the tea-party. Carrie nearly got quite out of hand. She felt the tension. What is at the back of it? There must be something."

The eyes of the two psychiatrists met and searched each other warily. "You mean," Alec said slowly, "that Sally is using Carrie as a stalking-horse for something in herself?"

"I don't know what she's using her as," Jane answered, "but I know well enough that she is preoccupied with something that is very bad for her. I can keep Carrie away from her, of course. I can truthfully say now that it isn't good for Carrie to see her. She's been restless ever since, and tries to get out of the ward every time the door opens; but I cannot, by refusing Sally the use of Carrie, prevent what she's trying to use her for. Nor can I discover what this strange compulsion is. Her mind is shut to me."

"Women get odd notions in their heads," Alec said uncomfortably, "at these times. She's four months gone now. Her pregnancy is physically normal. But what goes on in the mind—— Look here—I've got to be off. I shan't be back before midnight. To-morrow I'll get to the bottom of it. Can you go over and sit with her till I get back?"

"I am in charge of the hospital," Jane said, with a flicker of impatience, "as you know; we can't both leave it at the same time."

"Well, there's your friend Drummond," said Alec grimly; "couldn't he for once do a little job of work and sit in the medical quarters till one of us gets back? You could do the rounds and go over after them."

"The Superintendent has his own duties to perform," Jane said, with a cold flash in her grey eyes. "If I asked him any such favour, he would very properly refuse."

Fury repossessed and released Alec. He didn't care now what Jane did. Still, the ghost of Sally somewhere in the back of his mind, wanting something or other from Carrie Flint, refused to be dismissed. He controlled himself sufficiently to say:

"Young Barnes would eat out of your hand. Why not ask him to take charge? Everything's fairly quiet to-night. That Jones woman is nearly off again. But Sister is on the lookout for her. He's only got to sit there in case he's called up."

"The juniors can't take charge at night," Jane said, with controlled exasperation. "You know they can't, Alec. Besides, Barnes has an abscess in a tooth and has gone to bed with fomentations, aspirin, and a detective novel. He might just as well be out. Do try to be sensible. I'd have Sally over here with me, but hipped as she is, I shouldn't care to let her cross the grounds alone. Can't you run over and fetch her yourself? I'll keep her here till you come back. I don't care how late we sit up."

The word "hipped" applied to Sally hurt Alec so sharply that even the drive of his desire to get off slackened.

"What d'you mean by 'hipped'?" he demanded angrily. "Do you mean I leave her alone too much?"

Jane's eyebrows lifted expressively. Probably that was one of the things she meant, but it wasn't—and Alec knew it wasn't—one of the things which she would ever say.

"I mean," she said steadily, "that on the last evening you were out till midnight—I think you were at Gloucester, a fortnight ago—she telephoned to me. There was so much fear in her voice that I ran all the way across the grounds. When I got to your house, I thought Sally was going to faint. She looked scared blue; and what was worse than her looking like that was that she never told me what had frightened her. She pretended she just wanted us to sit and talk."

"Why on earth didn't you tell me before?" Alec asked savagely. "Why have you kept this up your sleeve till now?"

"I don't think that the subject of Sally has come up between us since then. Nor should I have told you now," Jane said, looking away from him for the first time, "since it seemed to me to be Sally's own business to tell you what she chose to tell you, if I did not think she is now in a condition which actually requires your care."

"I can look after my wife for myself, thank you!" Alec flashed out at her.

Jane turned away from him and walked over to her test-tubes. There wasn't any reply she could have made; yet, as Alec stood there glaring at her back and her bent head, his whole soul craved for Jane to turn round and show fight! He could go now. She wasn't detaining him. The urge inside him was as strong as ever, and yet he lingered. He watched her long neat fingers manipulating the retort. How delicately shaped her wrists were, how precise and balanced her every movement! How accurate she was! How damned right! How divinely cool!

"I'm sorry, Jane," he said, half under his breath.

She heard him. Without turning round, she said, "That's all right, Alec."

"Do what you can about Sally!" he called out, banging the door behind him.

He was safely away now. No one else spoke to him. He dashed out of the hospital, swung into his car, and tore down the drive.

There was no moon. A thick blanket of cloud shut out the stars. If he could only drive fast enough not to have to think! His heart lay like something bound and drugged beneath the mounting waves of his desire. Neither danger nor pity reached him.

The car leapt madly along the lighted funnel of the road. Rain dashed at the wind-screen; darkness solid as stone hemmed him in on either side.

Half a mile from the hospital he automatically slowed up.

A slim, muffled figure stepped out from the hedge. Myra had waited for him, after all! That driven, maddened craving fell back appeased. The light wavered over her red hair, sparkling with raindrops.

She jumped in beside him, cursing at him for being late, but laughing while she cursed. She smelt like a lilac tree.

The car released itself and sped on. Everything was behind them now except speed and darkness.

Far away, in another life, and as fortuitously as a cork flung up by the sea, Alec saw young Endicott lying gagged and shaken, at the end of the long ward.

He wasn't like young Endicott, he was safe. Honour hadn't held Alec. He had run away.

CHAPTER XXVI

JANE finished her job with unruffled precision. It was no use putting annoyance into test-tubes. Then she went back to her quarters. Alec had no business to thrust his deserted wife at her, as if his emergencies were a natural part of her evening's leisure. But Sally, alone and frightened, while her husband was making love to another woman, could not be dismissed.

It was a night with all the winds of heaven loose and wandering. Gusts raced down the chimney, the long French windows creaked and rattled, high voices whined through frightened trees. Six months ago, on just such an evening, Alec had dashed in to tell Jane of his defeated hopes. It was not very comfortable to sit there and think that he had worked them off on Sally! Would it have been better, after all, not to have urged him to stay on?

Jane rang Sally up. There was no answer. Sensible child, she had gone out for the evening! There was nothing to be worried about, then, after all, for Jane was sure Alec would break off with Myra, if not to-night, certainly soon. His violent delight would have its violent ending. Nor need she feel any compunction about Myra. They would be well rid of each other.

Jane curled herself up in an armchair by the fire and took up a book of poetry. She read:

> "I know my mind, and I have made my choice.
> Not on your temper does my doom depend!
> Love me or love me not, you have no voice
> In this, that is my portion, to the end."

This was the way to take Love, when it came and drove its terrific flood over the startled heart!

There was no way of getting rid of what she felt for Charles; but Jane made up her mind that, behind the high walls of her being, this overwhelming visitant could be both controlled and concealed. Jane wanted to get away from the personal element in love! She needed no human sharer. The earth could share her secret and give it back to her in every sunset, storm, or bird's brief song. She could be just as proud of loving a satisfactory human being as of being loved by one. In fact, as love is a more thorough and active process than being loved, she could be prouder. It would be a weak God who needed her love. A strong God is his own defence.

Charles liked her. Let her but remain steadily and coolly his friend, and he would talk to her often; rest sometimes in her room; laugh with her over their dry kind of jokes, and help her to bear the disappointments of their arduous profession. Her life would be the richer for his occasional cool companionship; and Alec need not feel defrauded. In time, perhaps, Jane would learn how to bridge the gulf between the two men, and act as their interpreter. Sally, too, liked Charles. It would be wonderful if they could all four of them be happy together! Jane's mind shifted back to Sally. She felt curiously uneasy again. It was horrible to think of what Sally was going through just now. Sally must know that Alec was with Myra. Whom was Sally with? What was she doing to keep their images at bay? Had that silly tea-party with Carrie Flint helped or hindered her? It was odd that Sally hadn't rung Jane up after it, to let Jane know what she felt!

The telephone bell rang out with a startling clatter. Jane stretched for the receiver with her finger on the page of her sonnet; because, although she was thinking about Sally, she had gone on reading about Charles.

"Drummond speaking. May I come over for a few minutes?"

The book slipped out of Jane's hand onto the floor. Charles couldn't know that the little pause before she answered him was to keep her voice from sounding too breathlessly pleased!

"Yes," Jane said politely.

Telephones were better than knocks on the door; they gave you time to fly to the nearest looking-glass and do what you could for a face which looked, Jane thought judicially, rather better than usual!

There wasn't any disorder in the room to remedy, except to pick up the book and put it back in the bookcase, lest Charles, taking it up, should come upon that too frank betrayal. Poets, when they write of love, give themselves and everyone else away!

Jane read over three times a sentence in the "British Medical" without making head or tail of it, before Charles knocked at the door.

By the time he had lit his pipe and settled down, to discuss the women's work in the laundry, Jane's heart was beating no more rapidly than usual.

"Have you seen Mrs. Macgregor lately?" Charles asked, after rather a long, but quite comfortable, pause.

"I usually see her every day," Jane replied consideringly, "but this morning she telephoned to say she couldn't have time to run over. I saw her yesterday, though. Why?"

Charles's eyes met Jane's and held them.

"I didn't think her looking quite up to the mark," he said questioningly.

"She isn't," Jane answered precipitately. "She is anything but well just now. I am exceedingly worried about her."

It was curious that Charles had brought up the subject,

but it was a great relief. One need never be careful what
one said to Charles, because he always put so much carefulness into the way he listened.

He was silent for quite a long time after Jane's con-
fession of anxiety. At last he said, more slowly than usual:

"It doesn't usually do much good talking about things,
but perhaps we'd better. It's Myra, isn't it?"

"Yes," said Jane, "it's Myra. It has been on my mind
to ask you if you could do anything about her, but I
hoped it wouldn't be necessary. Besides, it's very doubtful
if third parties can do anything about other people's love
affairs, however undesirable, except look away from them
—isn't it?"

"Need we call this a love affair?" Charles asked, raising
his eyebrows scornfully. "I should have thought it something much simpler."

Jane evaded Charles's contemptuous eyes.

"I hoped it would come out all right by itself," she said
hurriedly. "I still do! Dr. Macgregor isn't really like this
He's a seriously constant person. This business with your
sister isn't quite what you'd think it is. I mean I don'
believe it has much to do with her. When a proud mar
loses his job—or a job he had expected to make his—h
has to take it out of somebody. His heart hasn't changed
It's set on Sally. This is a sort of angry fling, and I thinl
it's nearly over, but anything that is done to end it ough
to come from him."

Charles smoked meditatively.

"Ought," he said at last, "generally has a catch abou
it. Please don't think I am judging Macgregor or tha
I have the slightest wish to intervene on my sister's ac
count. She is twenty-eight, and because she finds it a con
venience to stay under my roof I have no right whateve
to interfere with her little amusements. But we live in
community here—and can hardly ignore each other's diff

culties. Mrs. Macgregor is very young, and she was very happy. I share your anxiety about her present condition, and I feel a little responsible as to its cause. I should be sorry to see her sacrificed out of consideration for her husband's feelings. If he really cares for her, he, too, might prefer that her feelings were considered rather than his own."

"What should you propose to do about it?" Jane asked, a little stiffly.

"Personally I shall try to expedite my sister's return to the Riviera," Charles said, with a faint smile. "I may, however, fail, because she may not consider the inducements I have to offer sufficient. It is impertinent for me to suggest any action on your part; but if you ask me, I must admit that I should, in your place, speak with the utmost plainness to Dr. Macgregor. Men should always run away from a danger they cannot overcome. He appears to attach considerable value to your opinion. I presume that he would have given up his appointment here on my arrival had you not steadily opposed his resignation. You acted for his good, no doubt. Could you not do so again, by giving him—the opposite advice, now?"

Jane listened in silent discomfort to Charles's unusually long and fluent speech. Had she wished not to interfere with Alec because, if she had spoken to him about Myra, he would never have forgiven her? Why did Charles wish her to interfere? He was not an interfering person. She had had a right to point out Sally's danger to Alec—and she had pointed it out! But had she any other right?

She frowned, and wondered whether it was any use weighing motives when desires were behind motives! What had she really wanted most—to save Sally or to keep Alec? She had wanted both; but was to want both really to want neither? She said, after a pause:

"I did speak to Dr. Macgregor to-night, but not about

your sister. I thought if I could make him see that Sally was seriously unwell, he would act on that and give up your sister. Surely it would be better if it came like that?'"

"Yes," said Charles drily, "it would undoubtedly be better. Still, when one has acquired considerable influence over another human being, one has also acquired the responsibility of speaking disagreeable truths to him, when not to speak them is to connive at a catastrophe. The way to avoid the one is to avoid the other."

This was almost a quarrel. Jane would have supposed, if she hadn't known that Charles was wholly impersonal in all his human relationships, that he was angry with her. It seemed almost as if he resented Jane's friendship with Alec! But of course, Jane told herself, he couldn't be resenting it.

Charles was only angry because he thought her moral cowardice was endangering Sally!

Well, perhaps it was. One can easily confuse moral cowardice with a high-minded refusal to interfere; just as one can sometimes fail to distinguish between moral indignation and a tyrannical desire to order another person about! But whether Charles was right or wrong, she couldn't bear his being angry with her. Her heart began to beat with terrific insistence, as if it was locked up in a strange room and wanted to get out, and she felt a ridiculous desire to cry. Even if she was in the right, she didn't want to stay there, if Charles didn't think she was!

"I will speak to him to-morrow," Jane said at last in a low voice, "if he hasn't broken off with your sister—after he's seen Sally."

"Please don't consider anything I have said of the slightest importance," Charles said, with distant gentleness, "unless you yourself agree with it."

They were both silent for a long time, but the tension which had risen between them had died down.

Jane lifted her head and looked at Charles. His profile was turned towards her and he was gazing contentedly into the fire. The storm clamouring round the house gave the stillness of the room a secret quality. To be in it together was to be more alone with each other than they had ever been before.

"I have been worried about Sally all day," Jane said at last, "but not on your sister's account, though I suppose if Sally were happy it would not have happened. What I'm worrying about is a strange fancy that Sally has taken to one of the patients."

Charles bent forward and listened, intent and silent, while Jane told him of Sally's tea-party with Carrie Flint.

When Jane had finished, Charles said consideringly:

"Has it ever struck you that perhaps Sally—I mean Mrs. Macgregor—feels herself in some way allied to Carrie Flint? Couldn't she feel that Carrie Flint's deeper injury is a counterpart of her own? It looks to me as if she might be making a protest—a sort of unconscious warning to superior people: 'Look at this—it is what happens to girls like me when they get knocked about too much!' "

"Superior people?" Jane asked, glancing at Charles in surprise. "What superior people do you mean?"

Charles hesitated.

"Well, aren't we rather superior," he murmured, with a wry smile, "to poor Sally? I mean I'm afraid she might think we were. Learned—more experienced—and a good deal older? Of course Myra is the immediate cause of this particular mess, but—I may be quite wrong—I've only spoken two or three times to Mrs. Macgregor—but I rather gathered that she feels intellectually flattened out by our superior wits."

"Oh, I don't think so," Jane said, after a brief pause for reflection. "We're all three—Sally and her husband

and I—such tremendous friends. Sally says whatever she likes to us, and has her own way about most things. He is madly in love with her. I don't think—till this knock-out came along—that she was conscious of any feeling of inferiority. By the by, she likes you."

Charles bowed a little stiffly, but his eyes smiled.

"Her feeling is reciprocated," he said gently. "I like Mrs. Macgregor very much indeed. That is why, I suppose, that I happened to notice how off colour she looked. Is she alone to-night?"

"Mercifully—when I rang up an hour ago—she was out," Jane said. "I mean," she added, hurriedly correcting herself, "mercifully—because Dr. Macgregor was obliged to leave her alone." The hot colour rushed up into her face; she could have bitten her tongue out for that "mercifully"!

Charles took no notice of Jane's momentary confusion. He emptied and filled another pipe before he spoke; then he said:

"We don't need to pretend, do we, that we don't know what the obligation was? In our profession we call that kind of obligation a 'compulsion neurosis,' don't we, and we lock people up till they get over it?"

Jane refused to meet Charles's mocking eyes. She couldn't bear to admit, even to herself, far less to Charles, that Alec was with Myra.

"I rang up Sally," she said colourlessly, "to ask her over—here. I didn't like her coming by herself, but I had no one to send. Dr. Barnes has an abscessed tooth and has gone to bed; so that I was relieved to find that she had made her own arrangements for the evening. I don't know where Macgregor is."

"I haven't an abscessed tooth," Charles suggested, with a smile that had ceased to be sardonic. "You could have sent me!"

Jane held her breath. She daren't meet Charles's eyes, for fear he should see how pleased his words had made her.

She knew instinctively that Charles would not have told many people that they might have sent him anywhere!

"I could ring up again and see if she's come home," Jane suggested.

"I think that would be wise," Charles agreed.

Jane rang up. There was still no answer.

"Do you know what friends she would be likely to be with?" Charles asked Jane.

"The town is too far off for her to have gone there without the car," Jane said consideringly. "Macgregor has taken that. I suppose only the Hursts—or possibly Matron."

Charles looked across at her, but said nothing. Jane rang up first the Hursts and then the Matron, but Sally was not with either the Hursts or the Matron.

"Perhaps, if you wouldn't mind," Jane suggested diffidently, "it would be better to run over and see if she isn't at home! Someone may have picked her up in a car, of course, and taken her out for the evening, but just to be on the safe side—— Here is their latchkey."

Charles took the latchkey. In taking it his fingers closed over Jane's. His touch was a blinding sensation. "It was an accident," she told herself with angry severity, quickly dismissing the blissful panic of her senses.

It would take Charles five minutes to reach Sally's. Two minutes passed. Time seemed to have forgotten his job and to be waiting in the room with Jane. Two minutes more; then the telephone bell at last, and Charles's voice:

"Will you put Dr. Barnes in charge of the hospital and come over here at once. There has been an accident—I don't quite know how serious. Better bring some pituitrin with you."

After Jane said "Yes," he rang off. He knew she wouldn't say more than "yes."

Jane ran upstairs to Dr. Barnes's room, and shocked the pleased surprise off his swollen face in a few seconds; packed a medical bag, and, without waiting to put on a coat, ran breathlessly through the noisy darkness.

Charles met her at the door.

"She fell downstairs," he told Jane briefly. "Nearly five months pregnant, isn't she? It'll be the deuce stopping this hæmorrhage. Have you the pituitrin?"

Jane found Sally lying on the sofa where Charles had carried her. Sally's wide-opened eyes stared, with an unnecessary fixity, at the lamp. Her face did not look like Sally's face.

"There's some definite internal injury, I'm afraid," Charles murmured. "Better take her over to the theatre, hadn't we, and see what's up? I wish I could get Jones—the gynecologist—over from Gloucester, but its the deuce of a long drive so late at night! It would take all of three hours, and we must stop this hæmorrhage before then."

"Without Alec?" Jane asked, with lifted brows.

Charles nodded.

"We might have to operate immediately," he said. "Well —I suppose we can risk another half an hour!"

Jane sat down beside Sally. Her conscious mind never left Sally, or what she could do for her. Her back was turned to Charles, but she was aware of his presence. It was like sharing a watch, in a storm at sea, with the captain.

CHAPTER XXVII

Fog rolled up on all sides of the car like foam blown off the edges of a wave. Myra, huddled beside Alec, was fast asleep. Her bright hair was the last colour he saw, and the shape of his own hand on the wheel was the last shape, before the fog swallowed everything.

Half the short summer night was already gone. There was no traffic and no sound. The car raced through the blanched darkness like a mechanical toy. Alec could neither see nor hear, but, deprived of the use of his other senses, he could smell and taste the fog with the keenness of a man after a long fast. Fortunately, he knew every dip and curve of the road.

This being swallowed up suddenly in a fog was an odd thing to happen to him to-night! Though it often did happen, with the clouds stalking the small round Welsh hills, and getting drawn under into the valleys when the wind fell.

How quickly, Alec thought to himself, earth and man can sink out of sight and form into chaos! How little what one had thought solidity could do for one! Half an hour ago the long-slumbering twilight still hung on the hills like a jewel on the curves of a woman's breast, and half the night ago Alec was still sure of himself; sure of being able to handle the situation he had provoked; to break with Myra; to set himself right in his own eyes!

All his life he had been one of the clear thinkers and direct actors. He had never shuffled or vacillated, or said one thing and done another. He had not counted on that

baffling reach of the unconscious—that fog-bank—silting
through his clear thoughts, drowning them out, and bringing him to shame!

His brain was pitilessly clear now; though he was still,
he supposed, a little drunk; not very, for he was not the
kind of man to take charge of a car unless he could control it. But was he sure he wasn't? What kind of man was
he, after all?—this sworn lover, who had been false to his
bride!

His brain separated itself from him and refused to
supply him any more with flattering elucidations. His desire, having unclenched itself, no longer blinded him.

It was no use blaming Myra. Beyond pushing her away
from him when she lurched up against him, she had already ceased to exist as a conscious thought.

How had it happened, then? What was it Alec had
missed within himself? At what point had he dashed past
the signals of his fixed intent?

His inveterate honesty dragged up the whole of that
sunken hour. They had driven to a harmless enough country club attached to a golf course. There were rooms to
stay in, and a good dance place. They had danced for a
long time, with drinks between. At dinner he had said just
what he had meant to say: "We've got to cut all this out,
you know, from now on. I mean to be true to my wife."

Myra hadn't said anything. She'd looked across the
table at Alec and laughed. Then they'd drunk some more.
But Alec had a strong head, and wasn't drunk.

After dinner they had wandered about a wet garden.
Alec couldn't remember anything particular about the
garden, except that the moon looked like a tarnished silver
coin chucked into a tattered black shawl. The rain had
stopped. There was an empty summer-house. Were Myra's
lips, the scent in her hair, her soft warm body pressed
against his own, enough to turn him? No! Men were not

faithless to loved wives because other women were more desirable! He knew that mere physical contact would not have been enough.

Damn that wind-screen! The car leaped over some obstacle on the road and nearly overturned. How could anyone drive on a road that looked like dandelion fluff and felt like wet steel?

Any amount of summer nights, stiff drinks, and provocation to the senses wouldn't have driven that cold-blooded fish Charles off his course! Nor Alec either—if he hadn't wanted to be driven off first!

The fog tasted raw on Alec's lips and confused his hot, tired eyes. But let him get the thing clear once and for all, and he'd willingly take the nearest precipice!

Which was the better man, he or Charles?

He would examine his own field first, where he knew his work! The hospital respected Charles, but they both loved and respected Alec. All the other doctors were spoken of by name, but when the nurses or patients meant Alec, they still spoke of him as "Our Doctor."

Alec knew that he could get quicker to the root of the patients' troubles, even than Jane. His laboratory work was as brilliant, if less controlled, than Charles's. He hadn't the time Charles took (with all his patients and a wife to go back to) for such continuous checking!

Their work as surgeons was equally good. Alec had seen Charles do some rather pretty things in the theatre, but he could do as pretty!

Charles was a good organiser, no doubt, and he had shown more modernity and breadth of vision than Alec had given him credit for. But Alec had no reason to doubt his own powers in either direction. No! their work was equal enough. Jane could not think Charles a better psychiatrist. But wasn't he muddling things up? He couldn't be jealous of Jane?

Jane having turned up in his mind, reminded Alec, not for the first time to-night, of young Endicott, Jane's favourite patient. Funny how he kept seeing him, lying on his bed, gagged and pinioned by his distracted will, with eyes in which suspense had lain frozen for fourteen years! It was as if the fog narrowed into the white-tiled corridor of the hospital, and the car shut between its walls was careering towards that one ward!

Well, Alec knew he was right about young Endicott! Tie a man up in any strait-jacket like that damned antiquated code of his old father's, for instance, instead of bringing him up self-reliant and free, to make his blunders young and find his own feet, and you were equipping him for disaster if he ever met anything formidable enough to cause one! But wasn't any compulsion a form of strait-jacket? That was the point, then! What had Alec's own compulsion been? He dismissed that funny idea of jealousy. Perhaps what Jane had once laughingly called his "sunny vanity" had been to blame? Charles—lucky chap!—had no compulsions. He didn't care about being admired. His pride saved him. He acted—as he meant to act—unvaryingly just. Alec, with a judgment equally good, had submitted his judgment to his desire. It was his vanity, then, which had swallowed him up like a fog, and made him dishonest to Sally!

The word "dishonest" jarred Alec's whole being, as if he had brought his car up against a rock. Truth was the breath of his inner life. It made him so miserable that he thought "This must be right!" and drove on, with more care. He said to himself savagely, "I must take this woman back safely, or I'm being dishonest to her too."

His work was safe, because his work was honest. But this business about people, this thing which he had always prided himself on—for he was successful in all his personal contacts—was this all a sham? Could you be too successful—too popular—too much respected and loved? Could this warm bath of being so much liked all round draw the strength out of the sinews of your will? From that first flash of Myra's eyes on his, she had provided food for his vanity, and from the first flash of his eyes on hers, he had accepted it! God in Heaven! hadn't he had enough without? To be loved by Sally, to be admired and respected by Jane—what more could any man want?

But vanity was never satisfied with "more"; it asked for everything! People like Myra said: "I'll pretend you're perfect—while we're acting exactly as I like!" It was a kind of game. You ceased to act as they liked, and they thought you the Devil, and went about, as a rule, saying so. He knew their tricks well enough! The hospital was full of people who had played themselves off the stage by their own vanity.

Well, he had learned his lesson, and was man enough to take it! He'd got off pretty cheaply, too, all things considered! To-morrow he would eat dirt—tell Sally he was sorry, cut out Myra, and reform his manner to Charles. He found himself feeling oddly lenient to Charles, as if a score had been wiped out between them. Charles had had something to complain of lately, and hadn't complained, and shouldn't have anything more to complain of in the future. Then, Alec told himself, he would go into that funny Carrie Flint complex of Sally's and clear it all up! Better take her off, perhaps, for a week-end somewhere! A little bathing would do them both good! They might take a tent and sleep out on the shore. Biscuit would like that! One day—but not for a long time—he would talk it all over with Jane, and see what she had to say about it. Jane had had no sex life, and knew less about a man's temptations than a dead frog; but that wouldn't matter, because it wasn't the sex appeal which had downed Alec! He'd have stood that all right. Myra had suddenly whispered, "You're so wonderful!" Well—then of course he'd had to be wonderful! Just about as wonderful, he now told himself grimly, as a performing flea! Still, that was better than thinking he'd made love to Myra because he was jealous of Jane!

He drew up with a jerk before a solid shadow. An instinct told him these were the gates of Charles's drive.

He tried to rouse Myra, but she only stirred and clung closer to him. He got out of the car and turned on his pocket torch. He would have to get the girl out of the car somehow—not an easy job from a low two-seater!—when she went as mushy as a rotten tomato.

It was odd to think there had been any enticement in the soft, heavy figure he half-dragged, half-carried up the drive! He dumped Myra on the steps of the dark and silent house while he looked in her bag and found her latchkey. She hadn't been fool enough to forget it, that was something! He opened the door quietly, and shoved her inside as if she were some kind of overdue parcel. The servants could find her there in the morning if she didn't wake up first. That was her lookout. His obligation to Myra ended, once she was safely at home.

He had some difficulty in finding the car again. The fog was thicker than ever. Once inside the hospital gates, and he wouldn't bother about putting it into the garage!

There was no particular hurry about getting back to Sally now, but it took what seemed an endless time to reach the hospital gates. He rang up the sleepy porter, muttered his name, and, leaving the car to take care of itself, plunged impatiently into the fog.

He had told Sally not to wait up for him. But when he reached his door and heard Biscuit's welcoming bark, he saw the lights downstairs were fully on. He let himself in and began saying, with savage severity, "I thought I told you not to sit up for me——" For however honest he meant to be, his conscience was too bad to allow him to be tender. But neither Sally nor Biscuit ran out to receive his reprimand.

Alec, still more enraged at this lack of welcome, flung open the sitting-room door.

After the dense fog outside, the light in the little room confused him. Biscuit dashed against him with a paroxysm of nervous barks.

Was that Sally's figure, rigid and still, lying in a heap on the sofa?—and Jane, standing straight as the flame of a candle, her lips parted, her eyes trying to tell him what her voice couldn't?

Alec stood swaying in the open doorway, his hand automatically stretched out to stroke Biscuit, his mind refusing to take in what he saw.

Jane said something at last, but he couldn't hear what it was. His soul and body were frantic now with the demand for Sally. He pushed something out of his way— he wasn't sure if it was Jane or furniture—and was on his knees by the sofa.

Sally's face was strangely contorted; she lay there staring up at him with bright, unseeing eyes.

"Sally!" he shouted, "Sally!"

An unknown voice answered him, very faint but pitilessly clear: "I'm Carrie Flint! I'm Carrie Flint! I'm not Sally!" the voice said.

Sally's stiffened head turned slowly towards him till her teeth met in his arm.

CHAPTER XXVIII

JANE looked as she used to look when she awaited his decision in the wards. Her attentive eyes steadied Alec. He freed himself gently from Sally: "Tell me," he said to Jane, "as near as possible, what you think took place."

"We are not quite sure," Jane answered. "Dr. Drummond found her at the foot of the stairs. He thought she had fallen from the top and struck her head against a stair. There may be an internal injury as well. There is some hæmorrhage. She has not been really conscious since. Dr. Drummond is in the kitchen now, telephoning to the hospital for a stretcher. We thought you might like to take her over to the theatre for a thorough examination. There is a spare room in the medical quarters where we could put her up afterwards."

Alec nodded. The broken-hearted lover and the guilty schoolboy had sunk alike below the level of his consciousness. He was himself again, but he dared not look beyond the freedom of action.

"I must speak to Drummond," he said quickly. "Look after her till I come back. This—" he looked down at Sally. Her face still had its fixed, distorted look. "This isn't consciousness!" he muttered.

Sally's tiny kitchen was spotlessly clean. The blue-and-white tiles shone with impeccable splendour; but she hadn't had time to clear away the little salad supper she had been eating by the window. She had had tomatoes and lettuces. They were set out on a blue-and-white tablecloth, with a glass dish of raspberries in the middle. Sally hadn't eaten much, Alec noticed.

Charles stood with his back to the door, telephoning.

He put his hand over the receiver, and turned his head as Alec came in. Charles's eyes were completely emptied of any personal issue. He spoke quicker than usual, as if to save Alec the trouble of having to question him.

"The theatre is ready and they are sending over a stretcher," he said. "I'm speaking to Matron. She has volunteered to look after Mrs. Macgregor. She is a first-rate surgical nurse, isn't she? She says it won't interfere with her work at all to have a night on duty again. The theatre nurse is about too, in case we want her. Is there anything you wish to add?"

Alec shook his head. The Matron was his friend, Sally would be safe with her, and, if she went on thinking she were Carrie Flint, no one else in the hospital would know it.

Charles finished telephoning, and turned back into the room. "No doubt Dr. Everest has already explained to you," he said, "how I found your wife? The examination I made was purely superficial. I formed the opinion that there was concussion and that there might be a further—internal—injury. There is hæmorrhage. Her condition, of course, is a bad factor in a fall. How far advanced is her pregnancy?"

"Four," Alec heard himself say. He had a strange feeling, as if he were being tried for his life and had just pleaded "guilty." The word "wife" on Charles's lips stung him like scalding water. But he was obliged to admit to himself that, if he had to take this facer from his enemy, Charles at least had added nothing to the brutality of fact.

"Should the question of an operation arise," Charles went on, after a slight pause, "which of us do you wish to have in control of the case? I am at your disposal, of course. Or would you prefer calling in a surgeon from Gloucester? They have a good man there, I suppose—but would take some time getting him over."

Alec dismissed Gloucester with a wave of his hand.

Men shouldn't operate on their wives. They did, of course, occasionally. Cold-blooded fellows with complete self-confidence, and no nerves. Perhaps he himself would have preferred to—but not after an evening with Myra and seventy miles of night-driving through a fog! He could trust Jane implicitly; she was a safe, but not a brilliant, surgeon. She would run no unnecessary risks; but if a risk should be necessary, would it be fair to ask her to run it? She loved Sally.

He hated to trust Sally's life to Charles, but he had seen the fellow operate on a gastric ulcer a month ago. It had been an intricate, tedious, alarming job, and Charles had done it beautifully, as if he were cutting out a paper pattern. Sally's life was a bigger question than Alec's hatred. He couldn't risk not trusting it to Charles!

"Thanks," he said stiffly. "Perhaps you'd better. I'll assist. Dr. Everest can anæsthetise."

"It may not be necessary," Charles reminded him with grave considerateness.

Charles's manner was as unobtrusive, and without emotional context, as that of some casual stranger. Yet Alec felt conscious of an alliance between them. It was as if he had met a fellow-countryman in a railway accident abroad —a decent fellow, who would make phenomenal efforts to cut you out of the wreckage, and yet could be counted upon not to come round afterwards with the hat! However much Alec hated Charles, he recognised that he was —emotionally speaking—a decent fellow.

Both men heard the tramp of the stretcher-bearers with relief.

It was already dawn. The fog had been whipped clean out of the empty sky. A little wind tugged at the skirts of the trees. Night still lingered in the fields; and long black shadows stretched from the hospital walls across the vivid summer grass. The sky was a light colourless grey, and over the clear outlines of buildings and trees brooded a curious hush. It was as if there was a pause in the strange business of living, which day had not made up its mind to break.

Jane walked close beside the stretcher, which Alec and Charles both helped to carry. Sometimes Jane walked ahead of them, and Alec, with his eyes on the ground, saw her neat small feet in evening shoes and stockings, drenched through by last night's rain.

The door of the hospital had been left open. No one spoke as they made their way through the long shadowy corridors. The sound of their shuffling feet reminded Alec of men marching along the interminable roads of Flanders towards the guns. It wouldn't be long now before he knew if he had killed Sally.

The theatre was ablaze with light, and very hot. Matron and the sister had everything in readiness. The stretcher-bearers tramped off. Alec lifted Sally onto the operating-table. Charles disappeared behind the screen. Jane prepared her anæsthetics. Alec did not look at Sally while she was in his arms.

The Matron and the theatre sister between them began to prepare her for the examination, and Alec turned away to wash his hands and put on gloves.

Everyone knew his job; and there really wasn't any difference in doing it, whether your whole heart was at stake or you were going on afterwards to the pictures with Sally.

Something inside Alec registered everything without feeling it. He would have said he was not anxious—except for the clock. That big blank china face had something sinister about it. You knew, watching its blankness, that those small black pointers on its face could hold, and could not be kept back from holding, the passage of a life.

Both Charles and Jane must have been quicker than usual. Alec wasn't in any hurry for them to begin, but they had begun. The hæmorrhage was not alarming, but it was continuous.

Jane said: "Sally has a heart like a rock!"

That was satisfactory! If Jane was contented with the anæsthetic, Alec could keep the whole of his mind free for watching Charles.

Charles, with his sleeves rolled up to shoulders, bent low over the operating-table. His firm slim hands ran over Sally's body as a good violinist handles a violin. After a moment or two he looked up and met Alec's eyes.

Alec had seen what Charles had seen. They would have to operate. Sally could not keep her baby; she might not keep her life.

Charles said a word to Jane, who made no answer; but changed the lighter anæsthetic to chloroform. Then Charles stretched out his hand for the knife. He was a neat, rapid surgeon. It was a pleasure, Alec thought, to watch him. Alec felt as detached as a railway porter with his eyes on a train. But he was ready for each moment's need before it took place. His mind was in direct communication with Charles's mind. He hardly needed Charles's occasional curt comments or explanations. He followed and endorsed Charles's every move, as if he loved him. "The damage is to the placenta. I'm afraid I shall have to detach the fœtus," Charles murmured. "You might get the pituitrin injection ready."

Being a doctor was a convenience. A road you had trodden over and over again held fewer surprises. The patient on the table was not Sally; she was a field of gradually narrowing possibilities. This thing Charles did here, this chance he dared to take, this certainty which closed an avenue either of escape or of danger, hadn't anything to do with the body which was part of Alec's heart. Everything was mercifully familiar to him. Only the element of time was missing. Usually Alec was aware of time, in an operation, as a swimmer is aware of the sea while wholly occupied with the main business of swimming. But this business of operating on Sally had no beginning and no end.

He did not say to himself, "Now this has begun!" or, "This must not take longer than so-and-so!" or, "This must be approaching the end!"

Occasionally Jane said casually, "Heart satisfactory!" or Charles grunted.

The patient made no sound; she lay quietly asleep, like a child in its mother's arms. You knew she wasn't dead, because there was that unmistakable atmosphere of urgency, which belongs to life. The light and silence in the room seemed parts of one another.

Then the theatre sister began to breathe audibly. It was a thing, Alec felt, she ought to be more careful about. One shouldn't have to notice her breathing. The Matron made no sound. She was one of those blessèd, infrequent women who appear exclusively in the act of solving a problem. She took up no room, and, when you didn't want her, she wasn't there.

There was a good deal of hæmorrhage now, and it didn't show any signs of stopping.

Neither Charles nor Jane made any comment on the hæmorrhage.

That was, of course, the question, and had been all along. Alec hadn't asked it before, but now that it was all over, and he could risk looking into his own mind, he found himself asking if it would never stop?

Charles laid down the knife. His hair, usually wavy,

was straightened out by the heat. Great drops of sweat stood out on his forehead and all the way down his white muscular arms.

He said, "That's that!" rather grimly, and, without looking at Alec, went behind the screen to wash his hands.

Time had gone on after all, because the sun was pouring into the theatre, putting out the lights.

Alec and Charles together carried Sally into the medical quarters and put her in the room next Jane's. She felt very light. Then they left her to the Matron and went down into Jane's sitting-room for a drink.

They had been up all night, and in an hour they must be ready for their day's work.

Charles threw open Jane's long French windows as if the room belonged to him, and, leaning his head against the lintel, looked out into the garden.

"Shall I telephone for someone to take your place, Macgregor, for a few days?" he asked. "We might get help from Gloucester, or Saint Mary's, Stowe."

Alec shook his head. "I should prefer to work," he said shortly, "in any case."

Charles drank his whisky and stepped out of the window onto the grass. It was apparently his intention to slip away without another word to either of them.

"Look here, Dr. Drummond!" Alec said sharply.

Charles swung round and looked at him.

"I'm awfully obliged to you!"

The words seemed wrung out of Alec almost against his will. He didn't know whether to hold out his hand or not. If Charles knew that a few hours ago Alec had pushed his drunken sister into his house and left her, hoping that Charles would find her there in the morning, would he wish to shake hands with Alec?

Of course Charles might never find out, or, if he did, he mightn't blame Alec for the way Myra carried on; but it was a moot point whether Charles would wish to shake hands with a man who had wanted to put him at a disadvantage!

Charles settled the question by holding out his hand and grasping Alec's with a firm, warm pressure. His eyes, meeting Alec's, had something so strangely alive and friendly in them that Alec felt tears spring to his own.

After Charles had gone—and he went very quickly without having said anything—Alec turned back blindly into the room.

"Jane!" he muttered, "Jane!"

He was aware of stumbling towards her slim, erect figure; he heard her say quickly, "There, there, old boy! there, there!" and then he found himself on his knees beside her, with his head on her lap, sobbing as if the sides of his body would break. He could feel the mercy of her cool, steady hands pressed firmly against his burning head. They rested on him like the absolution which he had not asked for; and which she could not give.

CHAPTER XXIX

CHARLES stood at the foot of his sister's bed, and considered her with dispassionate gloom. The summer light shone on her red-gold hair, and on her innocent azure eyes, uplifted to his—as if no disagreeable consciousness had ever troubled her. Myra's self-respect easily re-launched itself, through physical means. Once she had had a bath, slipped on her lemon-silk pyjamas, and eaten a good breakfast, the memory of the night before became an agreeable but distant after-glow. No one could have believed—to look at her—that she had been picked up dead-drunk in the hall at dawn, and carried upstairs to bed; except perhaps the man who had carried her there.

"Well—you seem all right now!" Charles said, with a sigh of disgust.

"I am all right," Myra responded complacently, returning his gaze with calm serenity. "Why shouldn't I be? Of course I don't quite remember last night. I'll admit I was blotto. I suppose you must have helped me up to bed?"

"Yes," said Charles; "this time the servants didn't have to know. I came in at dawn and found that some chivalrous male escort had deposited you in a heap in the hall."

"Dawn, did you?" Myra murmured nonchalantly. "What were you doing out at that hour? Better not enquire, I suppose! But you might have done something to make yourself look tidy since! You look as if you'd either not slept at all or slept in your clothes! I can't think why you will wear such disgustingly shabby trousers!"

Charles took the hardest chair he could find, moved it nearer the window, and sat down on it.

He glanced about him with distaste. Wherever his eyes

rested, there seemed to be soft things: divans; cushions; relaxed dolls; silk rugs; books with embroidered covers; vague disintegrating scents and colours. It was a relief to look out on the hardness of the gravel path.

"I haven't slept very much," Charles admitted. "I got a bath and a shave before I had to go back to the hospital. I think Mrs. Macgregor is dying."

Myra flung back the bedclothes with a dramatic gesture and sat bolt upright in bed. "You think—what?" she gasped; "that little thing dying! That dear little thing!"

"You seem to take quite a friendly interest in her," Charles remarked, with weary irony. "Yes, I doubt if she will live. She went out of her mind suddenly last night, and threw herself down rather a steep flight of stairs. She was four months pregnant, and injured herself so severely that I had to operate. I thought she would pull through, but the hæmorrhages won't stop. She is twenty-one. It is rather a pity."

"Out of her mind—but why?" Myra cried. She flung a newly lit cigarette onto the nearest ash-tray; fastened her hands round her slender knees, and gazed tragically at Charles.

"Some women dislike having their husbands taken away from them, I believe," Charles suggested drily. "Perhaps Mrs. Macgregor is one of them."

"Oh, but she couldn't have been such a damned little fool!" Myra expostulated. "I didn't take him away from her—not in any real sense! Neither of us meant anything at all serious! One has to do something in such a dead-alive hole as this! He told me last night that he meant to go back to his wife! My dear boy, you simply must save her! Why on earth aren't you with her now? Don't leave her in that Dr. Everest's *papier-mâché* fingers! I'm sure she would love to do her in! She is one of those venomous women with the cold passions of toads! Poor little Sally!

I had no idea she was going to have a baby—what a dreadful complication! Why didn't Alec tell me? I must say I think doctors are terribly callous! Did you make a hash of her operation, Charles? You ought to have got a really good surgeon over from Gloucester. You are only supposed to be a psychiatrist, aren't you?"

Charles gave a wry smile. He had not thought Myra could still annoy him; but she had not lost her power. He felt the old outraged, slightly flabbergasted sensation he used to have in the nursery when Myra had destroyed the treasured Palace he had built of bricks, and somehow or other succeeded in getting him blamed for his carelessness. He had never been able either to justify himself to authority, or to restore his shattered dream. Even now he had to remind himself that he was no longer in the nursery and had outgrown the need for self-justification.

"Her husband is with her, at the moment," Charles said at last, with controlled patience. "It's going to go hard with him if she doesn't recover!"

"Yes, I suppose it will," Myra agreed philosophically. "But then, of course—sooner or later—he'll settle down and marry Jane. From what I hear, they've always wanted that!"

"Hear—and from whom?" Charles demanded with increased exasperation.

"Oh, the Matron you sent away told me all about them —and lots of other people mentioned it to me—it's a well-known fact. But of course you wouldn't hear of it! Why should you, darling? Nobody would ever dare to tell you about a human relationship. I suppose that's why you're so fond of your tortoise—because even if the poor thing had a passion, it couldn't produce anything—by itself, could it? I expect Sally knows that Jane is her enemy! I was quite fond of her, myself, though she does dress so badly!"

"Myra," Charles said sternly, fixing his eyes on her wandering ones, "do you deliberately deceive yourself— or are you trying to deceive me? You know perfectly well what happened last night, and why Mrs. Macgregor—who also knew it—should go to pieces under it! If she dies, you will have committed—another murder."

Myra's face went white. Her eyebrows met in a fierce crease on her soft, unlined forehead. Between narrowed lids she shot a glance at Charles, vivid with hate. There was a long silence. From the garden floated up the peaceful sound of a lawnmower. It was a hot morning, and the cut grass smelt sweet.

Charles felt suddenly tired, and as if nothing, not even telling people the truth, was worth the trouble.

"You are a fool, Charles," Myra said at last, coolly lighting a fresh cigarette. "Why do you want to make me angry? I really am sorry for the poor little thing; if I did upset her by going off to dinner with her husband—I'm still sorrier! It certainly wasn't worth it!—and I'll do whatever you think best to make up for it! Tell me, my dear, what can I do?"

"To make up for it?" Charles asked incredulously. "Nothing!"

He had never been able to make Myra see that her power to hurt was greater than her powers of reconstruction. Long ago, after she had spoiled one of his childish joys, when his infant control had snapped and he had wept, Myra had instantly become the soul of generosity and consolation. She could not do enough to compensate him for his irreparable loss—and she had thought him cruel when he had refused to be comforted.

"You know," said Charles, with a faint smile, "there are things you can't get round, Myra! Death happens to be one of them."

"I think, Charles," Myra said, with dignified reproachfulness, "that it's a little unkind to upset me so if I can't do anything to help the poor thing! I had meant to stay here with you, through July and August, and only go to the Riviera for September and October, but I could change my plans and join a motor tour or a cruise, or something, if you thought it best? I really would do anything to be of use to them!"

"It had occurred to me that you might go away," Charles said reflectively. "If she dies, it would be very hard on Macgregor to have to see you again, and, if she lives, I'd like to be able to tell her that you were gone. By the by, it would be a great convenience to me personally, Myra, if you could remain permanently away. I do not think we are suitable house-mates!"

"Oh, Charles!" Myra cried with genuine dismay; "how can you be so cruel? We've only got each other!"

Charles looked at her thoughtfully. There were moments when he hated Myra, with a cold vigour that surprised him. But could he hate her, with such concentrated bitterness, if he didn't care for her? If she wasn't, in some odd way, part of himself? And when he wasn't hating her, didn't he find her sometimes a very engaging companion? She knew all his habits, she even considered them important—after her own. She took off his shoulders—with easy skill—some of the minor burdens of living. She shared his memories and his manners. Could he cut out of his heart that absurd old loyalty, that half-shamed admiration, which made him feel how clever it was of her always to be able to get away from her disasters? To be so unscrupulous, so selfish, so wilful and so arrogant, and yet somehow or other never to have to pay for it! While he, who was at the worst only proud, had had to pay for it all the time! Myra broke through Charles's reflections by flinging herself back onto her pillow, in an agony of tears.

"Oh, Charles!" she sobbed, "I've only got you! Don't

you see—none of the others count! How can they—they don't know! and you know everything—and yet you care about me! You do! You do!" She seemed to be quite certain of it, though she went on sobbing.

Charles noticed that it wasn't her usual clever crying —crystal tears running down undisturbed, cool, pink cheeks—she was crying now with her face all screwed up like a monkey's. She meant these tears. Charles waited till Myra grew quieter; then he said:

"I'm sorry. I've thought this out rather carefully before making up my mind, but we're definitely unsuited to each other. I don't think you need my protection any more, and anyhow you'll find plenty of other men to give you theirs. But please don't think that I shan't continue to take an interest in you. I suppose I always shall. If you needed me—got ill—or into any critical difficulties, I should continue to come to you, and try to help you out of them. Isn't that caring? These people you like to spend your time with, and who have such violent passions for you, wouldn't, I take it, do as much for you in the long run, would they? Besides, I dare say some of them expect you to behave properly—I don't!"

"No—of course not!" Myra said, wiping her eyes, and sitting up in bed with a little snuffle or two which wrung Charles's heart; "that's just what I mean! I only amuse myself with them! You're the only real person in my life, Charles, now that mother's dead!"

Charles got up; he did not want to talk about his mother to Myra. "Then you'll go away, I take it," he said firmly, "as soon as you can make your arrangements. I quite see the sudden change of plan may upset your finances. If you need any extra money, let me know. I can let you have some."

"No!" Myra said quickly. "I've saved lots staying here as it is! I can manage perfectly!"

This rather surprised Charles, who knew that Myra never had enough money, and was quite incapable of having saved any under any circumstances. After all, Charles thought to himself, she had good blood in her. A better woman might have been more grasping.

"Charles," Myra called suddenly, as he reached the door, "don't leave me in that terrible cold-blooded way of yours! Even if I've got to go away for good—come back and kiss me!"

Charles shook his head. He felt a brute, but the kind of brute that he had to be. "I'd rather not, thank you," he murmured; "but don't forget what I said—if you need me, I'll always come to you!"

He shut the door on the sound of her voice. No doubt she wanted to have some kind of last word; to hurt him again; or to show him how hurt she was herself. But he couldn't go on with it, or he might have had to let her see that she had hurt him.

CHAPTER XXX

THE light through the early summer leaves made tiny golden patterns on Jane's hands, and on the pale pink satin bedspread stretched over Sally's knees. Sally's face was in the shadow. There were deep blue hollows under her shut eyes, and no colour at all about her except the colour of her hair.

There had been so many crises, Jane thought sleepily, that not to have Death just round the corner was almost too sudden a relief—you kept wondering what there was to wake up about. Even now, though she knew that Sally was going to live, there was that further, more intricate question: when Sally came out of the long sleep which had so nearly passed into a final sleep, would she be Sally? The few murmured words she had spoken from time to time had been menacingly the same: "I'm Carrie Flint! I'm Carrie Flint!"—and always that fixed look, as if over her soft, round, innocent face she had pulled a hard mask. When she sank into deeper unconsciousness, the mask had slipped off, and she had looked—as she looked now—like a tired child.

Jane's heavy eyelids lifted as she looked once more, to reassure herself, towards the bed. How easily Sally slept now! Poor Alec—who could not sleep at all! The worst of the bitter bad business was his sudden collapse, after the blood transfusion which had saved Sally. He would have died then, if Jane had let him. But she and Charles, between them, had kept them both alive. Beautiful cases, really, Jane thought with sleepy satisfaction; one couldn't have had a better illustration of what Science could

achieve, with the clean tenacity of youth for its material!
They had both had wounds which weren't the size of a
door, but that would have sufficed to let Death through if
Charles and Jane hadn't stopped them up! One had just
had to watch, like a cat at a mouse-hole, and take any and
every ghost of a chance there was!

The hospital hadn't suffered either, though it had been
a terrific business, fitting things in; and there'd been rare
snatches of talk with Charles, which had shown them the
swift reliable workings of each other's minds. There
weren't very many of these moments; snatched between
jobs; but they had a new, strange quality about them—
a breath of fear! It didn't make them—for Jane—any less
precious—rather more! It was as if, while she was letting
the clear, innocuous waters of a stream run through her
fingers, she found, left behind, wet and sparkling, a hand-
ful of precious stones! She couldn't throw them back into
the stream again—and yet dared she keep what might not
belong to her?

It might be chance that gave that breathless quality to
Charles's voice while he was alone with her. Or she might
be imagining the deliberate effort she felt he made to turn
away from her his too happy eyes.

Probably his eyes weren't happy—Jane admonished herself so sharply that she woke right up—but merely relieved
at not having had the two Macgregors die on his hands.

Jane gave a little start and leaned forward. Surely Sally
was awake! She was looking at Jane with unflickering,
conscious eyes.

"Jane," she whispered, "I feel—rather funny! Have I
been ill?"

"Yes," Jane said consideringly; she took Sally's wrist
between her fingers. "You've been pretty ill, my dear, but
you're nearly all right now, thank God!"

Perhaps Jane thought "thank God" sounded too emphatic, but Sally took no notice of the emphasis. It was Jane's heart, not Sally's, that was beating extra fast.

Sally said nothing for a moment or two. Her eyes roamed about the unfamiliar room, with interest but without surprise. She had been in it three weeks, without knowing anything at all about it.

Jane had made it as pretty, and as like Sally's own room, as she could. The pink satin bedspread over the bed was Sally's. On a little table, where her eyes could rest on them, stood a great bowl of yellow roses; and her own photograph of Alec.

Biscuit, who was going the rounds with Alec at the moment, came in and out regularly. There was a tall orange lily which Charles had sent over from his conservatory. The air, blowing through the bright curtains, was full of garden scents.

"Would you like me to telephone to Alec?" Jane asked. "Funnily enough—or perhaps not so funnily, when we know how he cares for you, he's been ill too; but he's up again now—he could come over?"

"Not—just—yet," Sally said, with little pauses between her words. Her voice trailed off uncertainly. Her eyes rested questioningly on Jane's face. She was so weak that she probably couldn't feel anxious, Jane thought, even about Alec; but the question in her eyes showed that she had something on her mind, which she'd be the better for getting off it. On the other hand, one didn't want to put any more on it than she already had. It was difficult to know quite what to say—when there was so much!

Jane got up and gave Sally some milk with a dash of brandy in it, but when she had sat down again, the question was still in Sally's eyes.

"Myra," Jane said, feeling her way uncertainly, "went away the morning after your accident. You fell downstairs and got concussion; that's what makes you feel weak now.

I don't think she's ever coming back. Not that it would matter if she did. She didn't matter, you know, Sally, in any real way—ever—even before your accident. If any man ever had only a single idea, and that idea was a woman, then Alec has only one—and you, Sally, are that one! He's hardly eaten or slept till he knew you were going to get well!"

"I've been as bad as that, then?" Sally said thoughtfully, and she gave a little sigh—not of displeasure, Jane thought, but rather as if she were relieved.

"Might I ring him up now?" Jane persisted gently. "You oughtn't to talk much just at first. Save yourself a little for him!"

"I've not been talking," Sally reminded Jane.

Jane put her hand down from the receiver. It wasn't going to be so easy, this first merciful return of Sally's consciousness! She had hoped that Sally, in the overwhelming joy of seeing Alec again—back in her eyes and her heart—would take with comparative acquiescence her other losses. But it was as if, having thought of him with such piteous concentration that her mind, fixed on him, had splintered under the strain, Sally couldn't now regroup her desires about his image. Or perhaps Sally felt that she wasn't strong enough yet to stand the emotion of seeing him? It would be—you couldn't help it, after all they'd both been through—a terrific emotion! And as long as she wasn't craving for him, she was better without it. But there was something which she was craving for! Her eyes still gazed unwaveringly at Jane, demanding—what?

Jane said to herself: "She must ask me. Whatever it is, she must herself ask it! I daren't tell her more than she wants to know!"

The clock ticked steadily on. A scent of newmown hay

blew into the room. In the distance they could hear Dr. Barnes and Dr. Harding playing tennis.

"Is it—is it gone?" Sally whispered.

Jane knew now what she had to say. "Dr. Drummond had to operate, Sally. It might have been a good deal worse. You can have a baby some time or other—but not just now, of course."

The pulse under her fingers ran quickly, checked, and went back to its steady normal beat.

Sally turned her eyes towards the open window and sighed a little quavering sigh, as if something half hope, half fear, had gone away from her for ever. From where she lay she could see the chestnut trees on the lawn, and the bright flickering of birds' wings, slipping in and out of leaves, darkening the light and setting it free again in little spurts of gold.

"You must all—be very tired," Sally said after a long pause, "looking after me!"

"Well," Jane said cautiously, "you certainly gave us a lot to do at first; but it was really quite easy as far as the work went. Matron and Alec divided the night, and we got a nurse down from Bart's for the day. Dr. Drummond was your chief doctor."

"And the hospital?" Sally asked.

"That was quite easy too," Jane boldly lied. "Alec did most of his own work; and what was left over got fitted in somehow. For a few days, while he was ill, we got another man in; but Alec went back to-day. So you see there's nothing whatever for you to worry about. In fact, your illness did one rather wonderful thing—it brought Alec and the Chief together. They don't say anything about it, but one can see it perfectly well. Twice they've had long talks together in my room in the evenings, when I've not been there."

"I expect they were just waiting for you"—Sally said softly—"together. Jane, did you save my life?"

Jane felt rather taken aback at this question. It was, she thought, irrelevant; but no doubt Sally's mind slipped about here and there, like a minnow in a stream, without certainty. Consciousness couldn't flow back quite intact after such long disuse.

"No," Jane said reflectively, "I don't think I did. It depends what you mean by saving a life. The three of us took all the care of you we could, of course. There's very seldom any actual dramatic moment in an illness. If you had one, it must have been the Chief's business—or perhaps Alec's. You had a good deal of hæmorrhage, and when it stopped, Alec thought you ought to have some more blood; and he gave you his—quite a lot of it. I think that saved you. Dr. Drummond perfectly approved of the idea, though we were rather anxious about Alec's giving it—in the middle of everything. However, he had his own way, of course. It left him rather weak for a few days, but he's all right now."

This was a subjugation of truth on a larger scale than Jane ever remembered making; but she felt justified in making it. Alec looked a wreck, and had very nearly gone out altogether, like a spent match, from sheer heart-break and shock. He'd had a bad collapse after the transfusion, and Jane had had her work set pulling him round. The memory of those hours haunted her yet. She kept them out of her clear eyes by an effort, and smiled cheerfully at Sally.

Sally, however, didn't smile back. Her mind made another of its queer plunges up-stream.

"Did you lose—your three brothers—in the War—as well as the—the other man?" she asked. "It was an awful lot to lose, Jane—all at once!"

"The man I was engaged to," Jane answered. "Well,

yes—I did lose them all. But it was so long ago, Sally.
You needn't worry about it. Time doesn't change loss,
but it quite mercifully lessens the pain element. In fact,
beyond knowing that I've missed a good deal by not having them alive, I feel very little the worse for it. I dare
say that sounds heartless, but pain, once gone, is gone for-
ever. One hasn't to let one's life get wasted by what happened yesterday."

"No," Sally agreed after a long pause; and then, as
if it had something to do with it, though Jane rather
missed the connection: "I suppose people can matter too
much!"

Jane laughed a little uncertainly. "Perhaps to me," she
said, "they hardly matter enough! Still, you and Alec
matter, Sally! You have no idea how glad I am that you
are getting well!"

Having said rather more than she meant to let herself
say, Jane took up a book. "We won't talk any more," she
said, "till you've rested a bit—and then you can see Alec."

Sally shut her eyes obediently. She hadn't asked about
her own relations, and didn't, of course, remember that
her mother and father had been in again and again. They
were in the town still, and must be telephoned to later on.
They were anxiously waiting for Sally's return of consciousness; but they hadn't had the further anxiety of
knowing that it might, when it did return, not have been
Sally's! How much Sally herself knew of the menace which
had come again and again to her lips in her faint mutterings through the last three weeks, and which had never
weakened while her life slipped farther and farther away
from her, none of them had been able to guess. It might
never come back, and she might never know through what
dark paths her soul had strayed. How near they had all
been to going to pieces didn't bear thinking of! Jane
shivered. She mustn't let herself dwell on it, nor on the

strange words that Alec had said under the harrow of his grief—"It wasn't only Myra!—I never gave her myself —I couldn't drag it out of your hands to give!" He had taken them back afterwards—or said, anyhow, that she mustn't pay any attention to him. He had to blame something besides himself—or die of sheer shame. He was like that—poor Alec—exaggerated and dramatic! Still, he nearly had died of it! Both he and Sally had been too sure of their happiness; they'd made it the stuff of their days, and not a side issue! What a mercy it was that—however absurdly happy her private heart insisted upon being whenever she thought of Charles—Jane was too old to have a love affair of her own! Many women don't think themselves too old at thirty-two, but maturity is much more an affair of what you do with time than of how much there has been of it! If you could do as much with time, Jane thought, as she herself could, you needed no other occupation.

Sally moved restlessly. "Jane—?" she said. Jane looked at her attentively. "I want to speak to Charles!"

"To the Chief?" Jane demanded in astonishment. "Before speaking to Alec? Must you?"

Was the whole thing going to go wrong again from a different direction? Surely Sally would have the sense to realise that impatient young husbands must come first?

"You said he saved my life," Sally reminded her.

"Well—of course—in a sense he did," Jane admitted. "But he wouldn't mind about that. It was all in the day's work to him—saving your life. He'd hate awfully to be thanked for it."

"Still—I want to see him," Sally said obstinately.

It really wasn't good for Sally to talk any more—but, on the other hand, it was still less good for her to worry! Alec needn't know she'd asked to see Charles first! Charles was her doctor, and might come in to see her anyway before the night. Jane stretched out her hand to the telephone and rang up Charles. She had done it often enough before, but she still couldn't help the uncontrollable shock of joy it was to hear his voice! He always spoke on the telephone rather lower than usual, as if he were reassuring the person at the other end into the act of listening.

"She wants to see me? Oh, I'll come at once, of course." Then a pause, and his voice again, casual and yet significant, because of the pause. "You'll be there?"

"Yes, I'll be in her room," Jane said after a further pause. She too must govern the spirit out of her voice, and not let it plunge, like the ecstatic birds she had been watching, into the light!

Jane met Sally's eyes again as she hung up the receiver.

The odd part of it was, although Jane had told Sally everything, Sally's eyes still seemed to be questioning her.

CHAPTER XXXI

It was rather an ordeal for Charles to go into a room where he knew he should find Jane. Still, it was better if he knew beforehand that she was going to be there, for then he could take precautions against looking too pleased. He had given up trying not to be pleased. If he had been a vain man, it might have occurred to Charles that Jane too had to take precautions; and that sometimes her precautions failed.

He admitted to himself that Jane must like him. One could not be so good a colleague without a sense of comradeship. But then Jane appeared to be a born colleague. She was equally successful in her relationship with Alec. Perhaps—Charles told himself—she was even more successful.

Charles opened Sally's door with a guarded expectancy, and looked away from Jane; but he had seen her before he looked away. She stood by the open window, her hand on the back of her chair.

Of course it was only natural that she should look pleased at Sally's having come round. Her eyes sparkled, her cheeks, which were rather too thin after all the crises they had been through, were a lovely colour. Her lips parted as if she were going to speak; but she did not say anything.

Charles murmured: "May I come down and see you later on, Dr. Everest?" He would have to report to her, as well as to Alec, on how he found Sally.

Jane said, "Oh—yes!" with a sort of little breathless sigh, and slipped past him to the door.

After that it took Charles a minute or two to remember what he had come for. He had to remind himself that Jane's having left the room did not empty it.

Sally lay on the bed with her eyes shut, but as soon as Charles had sat down opposite her, she slowly opened them, and fixed them on his face.

Charles had not been able to find out much about Sally's condition from Jane on the telephone, because he had realised that Jane was speaking in Sally's presence. He had asked, "Is she herself again?" and Jane had said "Yes." But that only meant that Sally was no longer masquerading as Carrie Flint.

Charles satisfied himself that Sally's pulse was a great deal stronger, and, after meeting her grave absorbed look, turned his eyes away from her.

"Well," he asked gently, "how are you feeling, Mrs. Macgregor?"

"I suppose I am going to get well?" Sally asked in a low, toneless voice.

"Yes," Charles said. "I don't think there is any doubt of it. Don't you want to?"

"No!" Sally said, in a still lower voice. "Not very much But it was kind of you, all the same, to save my life! You couldn't have known that I would rather have died."

"One doesn't really save people's lives," Charles said with a slight frown. "One does the best one can, and then all sorts of other things help decide—the patient's will to live, for one thing, Mrs. Macgregor."

"You must have done without that!" Sally whispered.

Charles made no reply. He had been puzzled all along about Sally's case. Had she been driven out of her mind? Or had she perhaps run out? Charles's opinion of the case had differed from his two colleagues'. He had thought Sally's condition more hysterical than mental. He did not think that she was consciously Carrie Flint, but he believed that the shock had precipitated her into an escape she had already longed for.

"You may not wish to tell me," Charles said at last, after a long pause, "why you don't want to live, but if you do wish to, I might be able to help you a little—and I should respect your confidence."

"Yes, I know that!" said Sally. She gave a long sigh. "Only I thought you knew," she whispered.

"I knew you had had very good cause to be unhappy," Charles told her, "but I also knew—or thought I did— that the cause had been removed. Whatever momentary fancy your husband may have taken to my sister was of the slightest possible description, and died the moment it touched the reality of your illness. I have always wanted you to know that my sister's power, though very potent for a short time, is extremely ephemeral. I think the power of very selfish people—however beautiful—always is."

"Oh, your sister——" Sally murmured. "That—that wasn't really it!"

Neither of them said anything for a time. Charles continued to look out of the window, and Sally lay very still, watching him. At last she asked: "Do doctors and nurses always know whether a patient's conscious or not?"

"No," said Charles, "not always. But there are fairly positive tests, if one cares to try them."

"When I was ill," Sally explained, "I heard people say things—not you or Jane, or—or Alec—but the nurses."

"Nurses," Charles said, with a faint expression of disgust, "are sometimes careless, and seldom accurate. I think I should discount whatever you heard them say."

"Not always," Sally insisted; "not when you know yourself the thing they say may be true. They said Alec only got well—because of Jane!"

"After the blood transfusion?" Charles asked consideringly. "Dr. Everest is an excellent doctor. I don't see why you should mind her efforts having been successful with your husband, any more than he should mind the little I was able to do for you having been successful in your own case! You were two ill, but exceedingly healthy, patients; there is really not much more in it than that!"

"They said—other things," Sally went on after a pause.

Charles did not ask Sally what the other things were. Nurses were the deuce! Fancy discussing a husband before a patient! Fancy daring to discuss Jane at all!

"But," Sally went on slowly, "I shouldn't care what they said—if I hadn't known! I dare say they don't know, Charles—I mean Alec and Jane—it's too deep—it's like real unconsciousness! But you can't live with them as I've lived—and not know! Besides, I've—applied tests!"

Charles turned his head and looked gravely at Sally. "There really aren't any," he said gently, "for—for that! At least, I don't think there are—not any infallible ones! One sees what one looks for—and Fear is a very blind guide. I am an outsider, Mrs. Macgregor, and I don't think your husband is in love with Dr. Everest. I think he is in love with you. The relationship between congenial fellow-workers is an intimate one, but the other—well, I should suppose it was beyond all calculation! Remember I too have watched your husband. I too have watched them—both! It was necessary, before I took over the charge of this hospital, to know and trust my two chief colleagues. I should not have asked them both to stay on if I had not satisfied myself that the relationship between them was a —reasonable one."

Sally gave another long sigh, then she said: "But it isn't unreasonable for Jane to be stronger than I am—and for Alec to—to care for her strength more than he knows he does! She decides him, Charles; I only please him! That isn't quite enough for a wife!"

Charles took some time to think this over. It was a

statement which lacked the exaggeration of jealousy.

"But—even supposing that his confidence in Dr. Everest helped him through his illness," Charles said at last, "I cannot see that it should interfere with your future life. You wouldn't have liked your husband to die, would you?"

"Yes, I should," Sally replied unexpectedly. "Then I should have died too. We'd both have been together. To be together and not together—that's what hurts so! To be dead—wouldn't hurt at all!"

Charles took this reply in silence. There was something direct and sensible about it which appealed to him. On the other hand, was not Sally building up out of her admiration for Jane a false feeling of her own inferiority?

"Do you blame Dr. Everest—for what you imagine this state of things to be?" Charles asked her at last.

"No," Sally said quickly. "I love Jane, and I know she wouldn't hurt a hair of my head. She'd give up Alec if she thought I minded! But I don't think she knows what she does to Alec. She had a dreadful tragedy when she was only eighteen, and it made her think that she was finished with love. But you aren't finished with love when you're eighteen—if you ever are! I don't think she wants husbands. It isn't that way she feels about Alec—it's deeper."

Charles turned his head away again. He did not know how to answer Sally. He believed that what she said was true. He had not expected Alec to pull round, after the collapse which had followed the transfusion. Jane had sat up with him all that night; and he had pulled round. There was something between them—no mere physical tie! Jane didn't want husbands! What then did she want? Men's wills? Their spiritual essence? What had she taken from Alec—which Sally missed? What did she take from Charles? Was she only one more instance of the power instinct in women?

He had always feared it! It had never deceived him

when women used the charms of their sex to support it;
but Jane had deceived him! She had been as sexless as an
invisible wind; and she had worked the havoc of a hurricane! He must think this over later! His duty now was
to help Sally, for without confidence she would make a
poor thing of her life—if she recovered at all!

He turned back to her with faintly smiling eyes.

"Do you remember anything else," he asked her, "about
your consciousness or your unconsciousness?"

"You mean," Sally whispered, "who I was?"

Charles nodded.

"She got hold of me!" Sally said, with a little frightened
gasp. "She was me! I couldn't help it! I don't know what
happened! Only—when I woke up just now—she wasn't
me any more. Could it—could she come back?"

"It was a mistake," Charles said firmly. "You thought
what was quite untrue. You persuaded yourself—from
fear, I think—that it was true! You were not altogether
to blame for such a mistake, because your husband had
made you profoundly unhappy. When one is unhappy, one
frequently broods oneself into unhealthy states of mind
as well as of body. In this unhappy state the perfectly innocent relation of your husband and Dr. Everest took on
the—anything but innocent—appearance of the relation
between your husband and my sister which was being held
up before your eyes. This is at an end now, and therefore
you must bring your unhappiness to an end. Only one
reality remains. Have you seen your husband yet?"

"No," Sally whispered, "no—not yet!"

"Ah!" said Charles, with increasing cheerfulness; "when
you do, all this nonsense will subside. He's been pretty bad
—and he's got better—as he got ill—for your sake, not
Dr. Everest's! Don't you want to see him? If anybody
saved your life, he did. It's his blood you're living on now!"

"It'll make me cry!" Sally whispered.

"Probably," Charles said drily; "but that won't hurt you. Your having given way to your fears, however natural they were, has caused a great deal of trouble all round, and I'm not sure that you don't rather deserve to cry. But don't cry too much. The right thing for you to do now is to get well—and believe in your husband. He's had his lesson. You can safely trust him now."

Charles got up and went to the window. He stood with his back to Sally, gazing out with unseeing eyes upon the dancing figures of Dr. Harding and Dr. Barnes, who were popping up and down on the bright green lawn in the sunshine, with shining white tennis balls and slashing rackets. He remembered them for a long time—without having noticed them.

Sally was Charles's patient. It was his duty to give her hope enough to live by. He had given her all the hope he had, and left himself hopeless.

He heard Sally saying: "Oh, Doctor!" and went back to her bedside.

She was smiling for the first time, though her eyes were full of tears.

"Send Alec to me then!" she murmured.

"You've talked enough," Charles said sternly, "for the moment. I shall ring for your nurse. She can give you some light nourishment and then you must rest for an hour. After that you can see your husband for five minutes. I should suggest your not crying for more than four of them!"

"I won't," Sally promised him. "It's such a pity," she added, as he turned to leave the room, "you don't make love to Jane!"

Charles stopped short, without looking round.

"It's the very last thing," he said grimly, "that I feel inclined to do!"

CHAPTER XXXII

CHARLES came in quietly, shutting the door noiselessly behind him. He stood in front of it, as if he repudiated the friendliness of advancing any farther into Jane's room.

Before he spoke, Jane was conscious in every nerve of his anger. She felt like a ship trapped in an ice-floe. The words, "Isn't it wonderful about Sally?" had been on her lips to greet him with—and she still spoke them; but they came from her lifelessly, as if the point of her joy had suddenly been blotted out.

"You mean," said Charles, with punctilious irony, "that it is wonderful she should retain her sanity after what she has been through? I agree with you. It is indeed wonderful!"

His eyes, fixed upon Jane, blazed with icy contempt; his voice was so low as hardly to be audible.

Jane had been writing reports at her desk opposite the open window when Charles came in. The light from the setting sun streamed over her. As she turned to face him with her back to the golden stream, she thought that Charles looked as if he were made out of darkness. What could he mean that was so cruel? What had she done to make him despise her? For this coldness, which seemed to flow round her physically, slowing the beating of her heart, must be Charles's hate.

Jane was afraid to know what he had against her, because she could feel that he must be right! So deep was her reliance on him, that he was to her both law and law-giver. She had no advocate within herself if Charles should condemn her.

For a moment she tried to pretend that nothing had happened, as a man might try, helplessly and without any means of defence, to fend off a mortal blow.

"It is extraordinary," she said, taking up this question of Sally which lay between them still. "Her concussion has acted like twilight sleep. It seems to have rested and freed her inner consciousness from its obsession. I could hardly believe it when I looked up and met her freed eyes."

"You have the delusion, then, that you are fond of Sally?" Charles asked mockingly, with raised eyebrows. "I must confess she seems to share it! She spoke of you with the deepest affection. She isn't aware, you see—as I am—as I had supposed so intelligent a being as yourself must be aware—of the grave wrong you have done her!"

"The wrong I have done Sally?" Jane asked incredulously. It was no use trying to pretend any more. The blood checked at her heart and drained itself away from her very lips. "What wrong have I done her, Dr. Drummond?" she forced herself to ask. "Why are you so angry with me?"

Her pride fought hard to keep the last words back, but something stronger than her pride broke through to claim his understanding.

Charles's anger was out between them now, like something alive and dangerous in the room, which she couldn't appease or escape from.

"It seems absurd," he said, with cold disgust, "that you should ask me such a question. Can you doubt the wrong you have done her? My sister Myra used sex to bait her trap with. You, with your deeper vanity, used your wits. Both of you used what weapons you had to destroy the happiness of a man who happened to attract you, and take him from the woman he had chosen to share his life

with. Both of you cheated! To me, the more transparent
ruse of mere physical beauty was the lesser dishonesty.
Sex by itself is too patent a snare to do a sensible man
any great harm. You, with your self-control, your mask
of uprightness and decency, have done a far more deadly
thing. Your little friend upstairs is too innocent to know
what it is. She only feels instinctively that she cannot hold
her own against it. She would only rather die than keep
up this unequal combat!"

The words, "I don't know what you mean—what combat?" sprang to Jane's lips, but did not pass them. She
was too scrupulously honest a woman to want to excuse
herself lightly. She must go below the level of her immediate consciousness, and search for some stricter test
than her own sense of guiltlessness. Was she wholly innocent? What was Alec to her? He was a great deal! She
had been aware of the flowing of her life into him—not
once, but many times. She, who had barriers between herself and the whole of mankind, had, for Alec's sake, again
and again let down those barriers. She knew that she had
deliberately saved him by her strength; but to do this—
what had she taken from him? All that night after the
blood transfusion, she had kept Alec alive. In his collapse
his eyes clung to her, his spirit leaned on her. He had not
asked for Sally.

Jane had not noticed this at the time; the mere terrific
emergency of keeping his heart going had occupied all
her faculties; but it came back to her now as strange that,
though he believed himself to be dying, Alec had not once
asked for his wife. She reminded herself of the cry he gave
when he saw Sally change into Carrie Flint before his eyes.
Did not that cry contain the whole of his heart? The next
moment he had looked up at Jane; she had felt his mind
stumble and recover itself—by what he found in her eyes.

Hadn't one a right to give one's friends that much of oneself? What boundaries should we set between ourselves and another soul?

Charles moved restlessly. She was aware that she had left him so long unanswered that he must have thought that she acquiesced in his condemnation. She said hesitatingly:

"It is true that we have had, Macgregor and I, a very deep friendship—is that inexcusable—impossible between a man and a woman—without wronging a deeper relationship? What makes you think that I have tried to take him away from Sally—for this is, I suppose, what you do mean? I love Sally, as I love her husband. I have never consciously stood for an instant between them. When he was—I will not say attracted by your sister Myra, but pulled off his balance by his jealous misery over your appointment, so that he became vulnerable to any outside excitement—I risked his friendship to stand by Sally. I cannot think that I failed her. Not willingly, at any rate. It is true I may have acted mistakenly in giving way to her wish to see Carrie Flint, but, even looking back, I don't know that to have acted otherwise would have prevented her obsession. Carrie Flint was only a pretext—and if she hadn't been available, Sally would have found another instead. When one is tormented beyond one's strength, one invents a scapegoat—even if it comes to dividing half of oneself against the other half: as I see it, Sally's personality shaken to the core—split. There was a side of her nature which corresponded to Carrie's, and this got the upper hand of the sane, wise child, who is also Sally. If she recovers now, and he is himself again, I see no reason why there should be any further difficulty for either of them."

She stopped breathlessly and raised her eyes in a final appeal to Charles; but the anger in his had not lessened. He said:

"You are far too intelligent a woman not to be able to justify yourself satisfactorily, but you must know, as well as I do, that we use our wits to fulfil our desires. Our reasons follow our preconceived images of ourselves. There are two points in your defence which weaken it—to an objective observer. Why was Macgregor jealous? Do you really think that it was only my appointment to this hospital which threw him off his balance? And why should Sally choose Carrie Flint for her scapegoat? Sally has no great opinion of herself, perhaps, but she can hardly have supposed Myra to have been her moral or intellectual superior. She was outshone by you; and your friend Macgregor was jealous of you. You know, perhaps, why you liked to make him jealous—I do not! And it is unbearable to me to have been used in such a relationship! Either you must resign from this hospital or I must!"

Jane was so overwhelmed by Charles's anger that for a long time she sat frozen and still, with her head bent, staring at the heavy fingers on her lap. What did he mean by "unbearable" to him? How had she "used him"? Her conscience was clear from that particular charge, at any rate! She could have laughed aloud at the thought of "using" Charles, for whom she would have used every power and ounce of virtue that was in her, without hope of return.

She said at last, without lifting her head: "I will resign, of course." That much, at least, she could do for him! Charles had repudiated her! Somehow or other she had come between him and his work, in a way which he resented. Their friendship must have been unreal to him, or he would have trusted her enough to tell her sooner what was wrong. He despised her, as he did all women, believing that she wanted from him and Alec, both, an admiration which set them at loggerheads with each other—and with life!

Had she wanted it? She would have to think this out, when Charles had taken away from her the mocking force of his anger. While he stood there despising her, she could neither breathe nor think. She could only keep quite still, like some poor hypnotised animal whom fear holds in a trance, till death strikes—and releases it.

Even if she had wanted Charles's admiration, hadn't she given him hers in return? Alec had had, for five years, her equal comradeship. Charles—if he had wanted them —could have had both her body and her soul. What wrong, then, had she done either of them? Whose was the weakness which had betrayed them all? What was that question in Sally's eyes?

Jane would have liked to ask Charles what Sally had said to him, but she couldn't ask him anything. She couldn't even look at him. When he had gone perhaps her brain would be freed, and she could think things out for herself. Her whole being waited for Charles to go.

He said, after a long pause: "I accept your resignation." But he still stood there. Perhaps he expected Jane to explain—or to excuse herself further. But she could not explain, because she did not know what she had done that was unfair or wrong. If she had acted differently from her former self, it was because her former self was no longer there, but had become merged in Charles. She could not say, "Any difference Sally and Alec have found in me— or you either—is because I love you!"

"I have never met a single woman in my life," Charles said at last in a low, even voice, "who was not so bitten by her own vanity that she was not prepared to let any man down rather than forgo the tribute of his capture. I made a mistake when I came here; I thought you were above such predatory habits. I see instead that any good qualities you may possess, you use as bait to draw men to you, and to cheat other women. Your little friend upstairs made very few claims upon life—but you have robbed her—even of those few!"

The words cut their way into Jane's heart. They cut so deep that her heart itself rose up to defend her. Let him down? She would let him torture her to death rather than let him down! She would have died a thousand deaths rather than weaken him! Didn't he know that even when his voice cut at her like a whip, she would rather hear the sound of it than any other sound? If she had cheated Sally, she had done so inadvertently—for Sally had nothing which Jane wanted to possess! She couldn't say, "I have never tried to capture you! I am captured! I have never tried to mislead Alec—because, if you like to call it mislead, I was, and am, misled by you!"

She therefore said nothing at all.

Perhaps her lack of remonstrance may have touched Charles a little, for he said, less icily, after a long pause:

"Please don't think Sally gave you away—or shares my opinion of you. She spoke of you with the highest praise and affection. She wanted to see me—to thank me for saving her life; and as she thanked me, the truth forced itself out of her, and she said, 'You couldn't have known that I would rather have died!' She won't die, of course. She will get quite well; and in time perhaps she and her husband may be able to make something of their married life together—that is, if they are left alone."

"I will leave them alone," Jane said.

Charles made no response to this, unless his still staying in the room was meant for some form of response.

He must have stood there for nearly five minutes after Jane had said, "I will leave them alone." Then she heard him give a curious little baffled sigh—and that was the last of Charles.

He went out of the room, shutting the door behind him, and walked rather slowly down the passage till the distance swallowed the last sound of his footsteps.

Jane would never hear him come to her room again, nor would she ever see his face, except as she had seen it while her eyes were fixed upon her empty hands.

CHAPTER XXXIII

JANE rose slowly to her feet. She felt as if she had been ill for a long time, and couldn't move about very easily.

Barnes and Harding were still flitting to and fro about the tennis court in their white flannels. The earth lay flat and green to the horizon's edge. A deep band of violet cloud swallowed the sinking sun. From its invisible presence shafts of transparent gold streamed down towards the earth, Jane counted six long shafts. She thought to herself: "I shall always remember this sunset—and Dr. Barnes and Dr. Harding skipping about on a sort of cloth-of-gold, whenever I think of Charles—but I shan't remember Charles at all! I can't even remember him now!"

A thrush's voice rang out close to the open window in a mounting ecstasy. He was a fearless, happy bird, and all the untinctured joy of earth was in his ringing notes.

Jane found that tears were pouring down her cheeks. She did not struggle with her sorrow. It seemed to her as inevitable as the lessening light across the fields. The past had swallowed up all her early comradeships, but death seemed a lesser catastrophe than the loss of these living friends. It was not only letting them go, it was the fact that they would still be there, and that she must let herself be driven away alive from them! The cruel thrush kept on singing against her loneliness.

Barnes and Harding finished their game and walked towards her, swinging their rackets. She brushed her tears hastily away, and set her face in its usual lines of aloof repression.

Harding must have won, she supposed, or he wouldn't look so happy; and Barnes looked happy too, probably because he saw her standing at her open window.

It would look rude if she ran away from them. She wondered with secret irony if Charles reproached her for Barnes's fruitless devotion. All poor Barnes asked of her was to be used by her; and all Jane asked of Barnes—was not to have to use him! Anything more unsought for and unwanted had never been thrust upon any woman!

They stopped in front of her, and she asked politely about their game; then, as they still stood there, she relented to Dr. Barnes. Perhaps it would hurt him less, this business of her going away, if she let him help her.

"I want to pack some of my books," she said, turning to him. "Would you help me bring my packing-cases down from the attic?"

His eyes flew to hers. His whole soul was in the question he dared not ask. Dr. Harding, unfettered by any scruples as to Jane's privacy, expressed it for him with gleeful impertinence:

"What's all this? What's all this?" he demanded. "Not going away, are you?"

Jane did not trouble to answer him. She lifted insolent eyebrows, and with a light shrug of her shoulders turned back into her room.

Dr. Barnes followed her, stammering his eager consent. Jane rewarded him when he had finished helping her by giving him her limited confidence.

"I am going away for a time," she explained, "rather unexpectedly. I may not come back; and I don't want to talk about it, or have it talked about. That is why I asked you instead of anyone else to give me a hand with my boxes. I shall pack them to-night, and I shall be immensely obliged if you would send them on after me."

"Of course I'll never say anything!" Dr. Barnes ex-

claimed agitatedly. "Only if—only if I could stay and
help you pack—or anything—!"

Jane shook her head. "You have already helped me,"
she said kindly before she shut the door on him.

Probably Charles would have thought she oughtn't even
to have said that! Fortunately, Dr. Barnes took no advantage of her limited kindness. He did not even ask her
when, or where she was going! If only Alec didn't look
in, Jane thought, she could get away safely. It wouldn't
do to have to speak to anyone as real to her as Alec. It
might break down that passive, mercifully unsubstantial
feeling which came upon her while she packed. She would
give everybody as little trouble as possible. Barnes could
forward her heavy luggage, and as soon as she had finished packing it, she would slip out, with a suitcase, into
her car, and drive off alone to London.

She would leave affectionate non-committal notes behind her—to Sally and Alec; and she would run over to
the men's side and see Arnold. She would like to see the
men's workroom for the last time, and carry away a
memory of the most hopeful side of her work.

The men's garden was the shortest way into the hospital.
She let herself in with a private key. It was so beautiful
an evening that most of the men were outdoors, rambling
about the grounds. The smaller garden was full of the
more impulsive cases. Maclean and Dawson were both on
duty in it. The moment she stepped into it, Jerry stopped
her with one of his eternal complaints.

Jane looked into his haunted, angry eyes with her usual
gentleness. Poor fellow! Everything was an enemy to
him. No thrushes sang for him, and no syringa spilled its
piercing sweetness into the twilight! All the summer's
loveliness besieged his stubborn heart in vain!

Two men were quarrelling in a corner by the wall. A
very demented schizophrenic ran from tree to tree, touch-

ing each of them in turn with his light, helpless fingers;
and then started back with dramatic concern, as if the
trees were threatening to attack him. A kindly idiot sitting
in the last patch of sun smiled up at Jane. She went past
him onto the verandah. She stopped for a moment at the
shell-shock ward. It was empty except for young Endicott.
The patients were still out in the grounds. Sister Headly
had gone to her supper; and the nurse was away on a
momentary errand.

Young Endicott wasn't expecting anyone. He lay as
usual, staring and twitching, in his corner near the open
window.

Jane moved softly to his bedside and laid her fingers on
his strong, unused hand. She thought he knew her, but,
though his eyes gazed up into hers, he did not answer
her smile. Her sorrow dissolved and lost itself in her longing to unloose his knotted consciousness. To look into his
astonished, baffled eyes, even though you knew there was
no pain there, was like seeing a man held down by vicious
weeds under the weight of water.

Jane said in a low voice, "Mr. Endicott! Mr. Endicott!"

The touch of her hand on his, the sound of her quiet
voice, reached young Endicott. His eyes quickened to
meet hers. He raised himself a little, as if whatever she
wanted to do for him, he wanted to help her to do. He
actually muttered, "It's you—Doctor!"

Jane thought, with a sudden flash of hope, "If he can
get as far as this, he will go further." And then she remembered that she would never see how far he could get.
Sorrow came back, like a mist before her eyes; but she
smiled through it at young Endicott.

"I am *sure* you are going to get well, Mr. Endicott,"
she said firmly.

He made a sound as if he were trying to agree with

her. Then the weeds dragged him down again; but she felt the hand she held still press her own. He was alive, then— in the real meaning of life—he wanted to communicate! She was glad to be able to carry this much of him away with her!

By the time Jane reached the workroom, the men had left for the night; but Arnold was still there, tidying up unsuccessful efforts, and arranging fresh work for the next day.

"I had a moment to look in and see how you were getting on," Jane said a little breathlessly. "I am sorry to be too late to catch the men at work."

She sat down by the open window and asked Arnold about each of the men in turn. After a while she was conscious that he was looking at her with a concern which had nothing to do with what they were talking about. He broke off suddenly and said, "Have you had bad news to-night, Doctor?"

Jane didn't feel annoyed with Arnold, as she would have felt with Dr. Barnes, for asking her such a personal question. She felt that Arnold had gone so far down into the human consciousness that what might have sounded personal from anyone else was impersonal to him. He had reached a level where all souls were the same.

"In a sense I have had bad news," Jane told him. "I have had to make up my mind to leave the hospital to-night."

Arnold finished tidying up a newcomer's tangled efforts at basket-making before he answered her.

"Well—! it's been worth it, hasn't it?" he said at last. "You'll feel that more still later on, perhaps. What you've been able to do here—has been solid. It won't break up. Do you remember Peter when he first came in? Poor angry lump—such a nice fellow now! Findlay and Travers, too, they're shaping well. And that boy Johnstone's going out

to-morrow. You might look him up to-night before you
go and say a word to encourage him. He'll be all right, I
think. But he can't quite feel sure his fits won't come
back. I don't believe they ever will, and if they do, it
won't matter as much as he thinks. He'll be able to face
them. After all, that's the main thing, isn't it?"

Jane said nothing. What if you had provided yourself with the wrong things to face, didn't that undermine
your courage? Need she have had to stand under the icy
hail of Charles's displeasure if there had been no vanity,
no self-centred blindness in her relationship with Alec?
Need she be haunted by the wistful pleading in Sally's
eyes—that question without words which she could not
answer?

"The work," she said in a low voice, half to herself and
half in answer to Arnold's unaggressive silence, "is of
course the same wherever one goes. But one has interested
oneself so deeply in this particular place that it is hard
to leave it. I find one's colleagues count for a great deal,
too!"

"Yes," Arnold agreed consideringly, "I think they
should. There is no bond stronger than that of a congenial fellow-worker."

They were silent for a time. Arnold spread out Peter's
carpet, and sorted his wools for the next day's work. Jane
looked out of the window across the men's gardens towards
the empty tennis courts.

Her mind, which she tried to keep firmly away from
the thought of Charles, obediently concerned itself with
Arnold. He was a curious fellow; how could he have ventured to come back to the scene of his terrific illness—to
stand on the very spot his mind had turned into sheer
nightmare? Any other mental hospital, where he hadn't
been a patient, would surely have been easier? She turned
her head to meet his eyes. They rested upon her with a

piercing and incurious kindness. It was as if he wanted his sympathy to reach her without the consciousness of any cause for it.

She found herself saying: "It's not so much leaving that I mind—as being afraid of myself in new surroundings. One is more supported than one knows by kindly, familiar things."

"Don't be afraid of yourself," Arnold said urgently. "That's a dangerous thing to be! If one is afraid of oneself, one is liable to do oneself and other people harm! I know that by experience!"

Jane thought this over carefully: "But too much self-confidence," she suggested, "surely that's worse all round?"

"One knows what one can do," Arnold said hesitatingly, "if one has taken the trouble to do it! One needn't have more confidence in oneself than that. You see, one can't divide oneself from other people; and if one hurts or distrusts oneself, one risks hurting and distrusting other people! When I was mad, I started out by hurting myself—and when this went beyond a certain point, I found it a relief to hit out at other people instead. I put myself into them, and then what I hit at didn't hurt me so much. Of course I shouldn't have started hitting if I hadn't been afraid. I suppose one never hurts anyone unless one is afraid of them—and the less afraid one is—either of oneself or of anyone else—the more sane! Isn't that the way you look at it?"

Jane nodded. Had that been her trouble—that always she had been a little afraid—both of herself and Alec? Hadn't her fear shut Alec out from the very things that would have made their relationship harmless? She hadn't treated him as an equal—nor Sally either! She had fenced them both off from her deepest emotions. What she had liked in them—what she had taken from them—had al-

ways been their need of her! No wonder Charles's fiery
pride, suspecting her hidden arrogance, had turned away
from her!

Her cheeks burned at the affront to him. That must
have been what he meant when he had said: "I thought
you were not one of those women with predatory habits,
but I find you are!" It is predatory to meet people's
needs—to cater to their weaknesses, and to fence them off
from your own! With a pang of dismay Jane admitted
to herself that her reserve had been a form of cowardice.
She drew herself up to face this new enemy, and asked,
with a dry smile, as if after all it was rather a joke, "And
what does one do when one finds that one has been a
coward, Mr. Arnold?"

He was silent for a long moment—waiting perhaps for
her self-contempt to die down. She did not know what he
thought of her, but she was aware that whatever it was,
his kindness would be deeper than his judgment.

"You know that as well as I do," he said at last. "One
only gets over cowardice by trusting oneself more! The
cure for cowardice—perhaps for conceit, which is only the
other half of it—is confidence! When I was ill, the first improvement I made was due to the doctor who let me have
the tools I could have done him in with! I remember to this
day the way it took all the gusto out of planning to do
him in! One has to mix in with people more, too—before
one gets much courage. The way I look at it now is that
there mustn't be any private worlds! Letting oneself be
cut off by pride—or shutting oneself up completely in a
dangerous intimacy—or hiding because of fear—well,
those things aren't the escapes they look like. There is in
all of them a sort of solitary confinement—even in the
intimacy; one's got to belong to the outside world as
well! Then one's all right! I don't mean that one need go

about talking—but one mustn't keep the best of oneself up one's sleeve. One must stand open to life!"

Jane thought this over. "Dr. Macgregor does that," she said at last. "Sometimes I've thought too wide open!"

"Well," Arnold admitted with a smile, "he hasn't quite got himself in hand always. His desires act on him like compulsions. I suppose one's got to learn to hold oneself in, before one gives oneself out. But he's a satisfactory doctor. I think he switches his compulsions off when it comes to his work."

"And the new Chief"—Jane asked, turning her eyes back to the darkening lawns—"he—hasn't any compulsions!"

"Ah! well, there you get the opposite difficulty," Arnold agreed. "The new Chief can do what he doesn't like almost too easily. He's one of those fellows who cuts off an arm or a leg—almost before he needs to—so as to get into Heaven maimed, when perhaps if he'd had a dash more patience, he'd have found himself there with all his limbs intact! They tell me, too, that he doesn't like women. That's a bad note! I should say—shouldn't you?—that he must be rather afraid of himself not to like women?"

"I don't know," Jane answered rather sadly. "Lots of men hate women now-a-days. It seems to me rather natural. We're too much over their horizon. It was a man-made world, and now we're asking to go shares in the making. One can understand, I think, that a very capable and able man should distrust us. Particularly as many of us are not very trustworthy, and assume an equality which is not always there. Besides, the new Chief may have his private reasons for disliking women!"

"There are no private reasons for disliking a whole sex," Arnold objected. "To come to terms with Mother Eve is to come to terms with life itself. A man—or a

woman either—is only half alive if he doesn't accept the
other half of the apple! Besides, it turns marriage into a
dog-fight! You can't have any decent union without
equality. One needn't bother about individuals letting one
down. What is it Nietzsche says: 'In the end man experiences only his true self.' It's the way one takes what one
goes through, not what one goes through, that is to be
trusted or distrusted!"

Jane said doubtfully: "That's a nice idea, but doesn't
it free one rather too easily from all responsibility? Isn't
one rather more of one's brother's keeper than that? Not
to be able to do anyone else any harm sounds too good to
be true!"

"Oh, one can still do harm!" Arnold admitted, "but not
more harm than other people let one! Influence is always
a compact. When you come to think of it, you can't do
anyone more good than he'll let you either! No patient in
this hospital, for instance, can be cured if he becomes in-
accessible! The private world is complete then, and has
unhitched itself for ever from mankind."

Jane was silent. This business of intimacy with other
human beings—had she ever solved it? Had Charles?

She was thirty-two, and she had never given herself to
any man. Her friendship with Alec was the greatest intimacy that she had ever known, but it was incomplete. It
was not physical, nor had it ever reached a place where
Alec was as much at home in her mind as she was in his.

Jane was afraid of Charles. If she hadn't been afraid
of him, she could have reached him with the truth. She
could perhaps even have said, "Look here, you and Sally
are all wrong. I'm in love with you!"

But the bare idea of Charles even guessing that she
loved him had made her willing to accept any other doom.

If she could have thought Charles liked her—well, liked
her really—beyond his gentle respect and friendliness, she

might have run even that risk. But how could she think
so? How dared she think so, of a man who distrusted and
disliked women? Wasn't it only because he wasn't attracted by her as a woman that he had given her his
friendship? And now that he thought her to be attractive
to another man, he had simply swept her aside with contempt.

"And I'm not! I'm not!" Jane thought to herself, with
exasperated amusement, "I'm not even attractive to Alec!
Only to Dr. Barnes!"

Then she remembered that she must do her packing.

She got up with a sigh, for she liked the big quiet room,
full of twilight, and Arnold's friendly, impersonal talk.

She held out her hand to him and said: "Well—in a
sense we've parted before, when our work together had to
stop; but this, I'm afraid, is a more final parting. You
are one of the colleagues I shall miss most!"

Arnold took her hand in a firm, warm grasp. "I don't
suppose I shall miss you at all," he rather surprisingly
observed. "I've built all I know out of what you've taught
me. Besides"—he paused a little, walking with her to
the door—"I don't suppose you will go—unless you want
to!"

Jane wanted to know what he meant by this, but she
found that she dared not to ask him.

CHAPTER XXXIV

"WHAT the hell are you doing with those books?"

Jane, looking up from her packing, saw Alec standing in the doorway glaring down at her with astonished eyes.

"Another angry man to deal with!" she thought to herself dispassionately, squatting back on her heels. She had hoped to be spared Alec, but it seemed that she wasn't going to be spared anything! She said, after a pause to give herself time:

"You've seen Sally, then?"

The angry surprise in his eyes lessened. He came into the room, shutting the door after him, full of the relief he had thrust aside for the moment.

"Yes," he said, "I've been sitting with her all this time —not talking, of course, only smiling every now and then—to get her to smile back. It's a miracle the way she's come round. Good Lord—I don't deserve it!"

"I don't think that you do particularly," Jane agreed rather acidly.

Alec came and looked into the crate before which she knelt.

"You haven't answered my question," he demanded. "What are you doing with those books?"

Jane's mind rushed hither and thither in circles, like a coursed hare. Should she say she was going to sell them? Nonsense! Why should she sell her books? Alec knew she had plenty of money! Should she say she was going to have them rebound—or sending them all to a sick friend? Neither of these projects sounded likely. Were any lies more than a moment's respite at Alec's expense? Wasn't

that what she'd always done for him? The mean, easy way
she shielded him from any trouble which he'd be the better
for facing?

Of course she didn't want to dash his joy in Sally's recovery, but how could she help dashing it? What had she
got to do with any joy of his which could be dashed?

She sat back on her heels again, and looked up into his
questioning eyes, with sombre directness.

"I'm going away," she said at last, "because Charles
thinks I'm bad for Sally."

Well, it was out now—and he could make what he liked
of it! She hadn't deceived him in order to spare him!
She'd trusted both his judgment and his pluck! And she'd
spoiled his miracle—if a miracle can be spoiled!

He looked at her with blank incredulity.

"What the bloody hell," he exclaimed explosively, "has
Charles to do with us? And what utter balderdash, anyhow! What harm have you ever done Sally? She very
naturally thinks the world of you!"

"Ah, thinks!" said Jane. She felt as near despair as
she was ever likely to get. "What do thoughts matter?
They are of some importance to a job of work, perhaps—
but not when you're trying to get round a human boggle!
Sally was more unhappy than Myra could account for.
That's Charles's idea—and it is a fact! We were a lot too
clever—or a lot too selfish—please yourself what we call
it—to see what was upsetting her. She didn't like any
other woman meaning as much to you as I did—and quite
right too!"

"But you didn't mean anything to me at all!" Alec
wildly asserted. "Not in that way, Jane!"

"There isn't a 'that way'!" Jane answered wearily. "I
once thought there was too, but that's been our mistake.
Any way of being too important in another person's life
is all wrong. And when you are—you've got to get out of

it. So I'm damned well going! And it's midnight, and I want to finish my packing and be off. Let's say good-bye, Alec, and try to think the best we can of each other to the end. What I owe you I'll always remember, and what you owe me, you'd better set to work and forget as soon as possible. Most of it was all wrong!"

"What rot!" Alec said, tossing all the books out of the nearest armchair and sitting down in it as if he intended to stay there for the rest of the night. "I never heard greater rot in all my life! You pay too much attention to Charles. He's a nicer fellow than I once thought him, and I'm everlastingly obliged to him for what he's done for Sally, but he's talking through his hat when he says you upset her. She adores you! The trouble with Charles is, he doesn't understand the affections. He's a sort of Saint Simon Stylites—sits on a pinnacle above us all, and dangles those long legs of his, and thinks he knows it all! He knows damned little! There's nothing much to learn on top of a pillar—except dangling!"

Jane felt herself flushing angrily.

"Well, Charles may, or may not, know what he's talking about," she said, with studied calm, "but anyhow he's dismissed me!"

"He's done what?" roared Alec, springing to his feet. "Why, the fellow's blind—stark—staring mad! He ought to be locked up! I'll go over at once and tell him what I think of him!"

"If you dare to say a word to him about me," Jane said, barring his way with a cold gleam of her eyes, "I'll not only go away, I'll never see or speak to either you or Sally again! I mean what I say, Alec!"

He flung himself down again, took out a cigarette and smoked it, in angry spasms.

Jane went on packing. It was not an easy job, and would have been the better for a little more attention. The larger books ate into each other, the smaller ones baulked at the shape of intermediate spaces. Her hands felt curiously clumsy.

Alec said at last, with that kind of reproachfulness she most dreaded: "I thought you cared about me, Jane—but you don't! You only care about your own bloody pride!—or else you'd let me have it out with Charles. It's my business as much as yours! How do you suppose I'd get on without you? Just run over in your mind what you've done for me. I don't mean this recent stuff—driving injections into me night after night, without a wink of sleep, to keep my old engine going—nor half my work done for a month, as well as all your own. Emergency marks of friendship haven't the pull a chronic relationship has! Five years is rather a lot of a man's lifetime; and it's five years we've had—of the best and closest partnership there is. From the first I wasn't your boss. We were equals; and we've been happy equals. We haven't competed, we've shared. If I had a tough case I couldn't see round, I brought it to you; if you had one you couldn't, you brought it to me. Who do you think is going to take your place with me—or mine with you? If you let Sally spoil our job together, I shan't be able to forgive her—not though she's like the blood in my veins! If you let Charles spoil it, I'll find a way of paying him out which he'll be sorry for to the end of his life! I don't care a damn whether I'm vindictive or not. I'm going to hold on to the best thing I have in my life—or know the reason why! I dare say I've deserved the rough time I've had over Sally, but I don't deserve this. It wasn't you I betrayed with Myra!"

"That's damned true," said Jane grimly. "And it wouldn't have mattered if you had! I was safe—and Sally wasn't; that must have been an endearing thought to her!"

"Look here," Alec said, sawing the air with his finger and leaning forward till his head was six inches from Jane's. "Just let's get this thing quite straight from the start. What made Charles think Sally was upset by you?"

Jane moved as far back as she could get in the circle of surrounding books; but she couldn't get rid of Alec's more insidious approach to her mind. What had Charles said? If she'd got to let that out into the room between them, what more mightn't follow? It is not easy to limit a confidence to a familiar friend.

"He didn't tell me all there was of it," she said after a long, breathless pause. "At least, I don't suppose he did. But I had noticed something funny before he spoke. Sally wanted me to send for him before she sent for you. Of course I said to myself that she was pretty weak, and might be funking the thing she wanted most. Still, it was odd, when she had something on her mind, she didn't want either of us to know. Anyhow, Charles went to her and I came down here. By-and-by he followed me."

The room narrowed to the terrible watchful hostility of Alec. He made Jane feel as if she were a matador waiting for a bull to charge. She'd got to slip in past his horns and drive the knife home, into the right spot, quickly, before he turned, and had her! But which was the right spot? There was no pity in the eyes that watched her.

"Charles said Sally told him that she didn't want to get better," Jane said in a rush. "Well—she knew Myra was over. What else had she got to face? I always knew there was something more than Myra—behind that Carrie Flint dodge! Myra couldn't have made her feel like Carrie Flint. I did!"

"Well—suppose we put it to Sally," Alec began with dangerous reasonableness. "When she's a bit stronger, I mean; and get her to say straight out what she does feel.

Babies on the way make women rather odd sometimes—
and Myra on the top of it was enough, Jane! You don't
need to undermine what we've all lived on, because of a
censorious old misogynist, green-eyed from the start!
You're just a little half-seas over from lack of sleep and
strain all round, or you'd see this thing quite differently.
When you're over-tired, you shouldn't make plans."

How wise he sounded—how considerate, and safe; and
yet whose hand but his had pulled her over this precipice?

"What we've been living on," Jane said relentlessly,
"has got to be undermined! I see that—quite as plainly
as Charles sees it; and I see why. It's not my pride that I
like better than you, it's my independence, and your own!
It isn't being strained that makes me see quite clearly
now that that's where we've both been wrong. It's what
Sally, as your wife, has a right to resent. I respect her for
resenting it, and I advise you to do the same. Otherwise
the same trouble will crop up later on—in some other
form. What I'm going away for is to be able to work
without you—and for you to be able to work without me.
When I was first surprised by Charles's accusation, I
thought it was worse than I now think; I mean I thought
we ought to do something final and irrevocable; but that
was only shock, and one's impatient desire to get to the
end of pain, and find oneself maimed—but beyond emotion! Well—I see straighter now, and I'm glad we've had
this talk—and can perhaps meet again and have others;
but I'm going to go away!"

"For Heaven's sake, stop this Queen Guinevere and
King Arthur stunt!" Alec rudely asserted. "You can't be
both—and you happen to be neither—and I've never
played Lancelot round you! By-the-by, are you in love
with me by any chance?"

This was too much for Jane. An overwhelming gust of

laughter took possession of her whole body. She rocked herself to and fro with it, while the tears ran down her cheeks.

"No!" she managed to gasp out into Alec's frightened and astonished face. "Thank God, I'm not!"

"Oh, well," said Alec rather reproachfully, "you might have been, you know! Women have! But you needn't carry on like that, anyhow! It was important to know! If you're not—and I'm not, I don't see what the hell Sally has got to mind about! and I believe—knowing Sally a damned sight better than you and your Charles know her—that she neither did, nor does, mind our work together!"

"Don't call him my Charles," Jane said, still rocking with laughter; "that's funnier still. You and Sally are the only people who are each other's. Let's keep to our particular point. Something upset Sally—something more than Myra, and more than a healthy girl having a baby by a man she loved should have been upset. Well, what else was there to upset her? Nothing else but our eternal talks above her head! Those evenings—you ought to have been alone together! And we sat here instead—till one or two o'clock in the morning—talking shop, while Sally went to sleep on the floor with her head on Biscuit; and I—God forgive me!—thought how comfortable and happy we all were together! Alec, if you hate me for the rest of your life, I won't blame you; but if you don't want to make me hate myself—and you too—for God's sake let me go, and make no more fuss about it! The more fuss you make, the more clearly I see what blind and brutal fools we've both been—and called ourselves psychiatrists!"

Jane thought that she had silenced Alec once and for all. She had disturbed him. He flung his third cigarette stub across the room, missed the grate, got up and trod it out, and said: "Damn everything!" After that he sat down again, as if something new and satisfactory had just occurred to him.

"I see what you mean," he said, with his dreadful, plausible charm. "Isn't that where we've come out, then? Have we got to chuck the thing we care for most, and do most good by—remember that, Jane, we've done a power of good together, far more than either of us could have done apart—just when we see for the first time how to steer clear of trouble? I tell you what we'll do—we'll give up our evenings!"

Jane stared at him incredulously. Here was this man back again at his old stumbling-block; this innate belief that you could combine the smooth with the rough! And she'd always let him! She'd taken the rough and allowed him to think he'd had it, with the smooth! But she couldn't take it way from him this time—even if she would! She said gently:

"Look here, old boy! We mustn't duck from under. If I stay, nothing is really changed for Sally, she is still sharing you with me. But if I go away, she has what she ought to have, and I've still got something to look forward to. In two or three years' time you're dead sure to get a superintendentship. Well—if by then you've worked all right by yourself, and I've worked all right by myself; and Sally wants it, and you're both solidly happy—if you send for me to join your staff then, I'll join it! You've taught me all I know. It's no use your saying we are equals. We weren't, anyhow, for the first four years. You were my master—and even now you are too much my master! That's got to go—the overplus—and your overplus of me! But the rest needn't. Don't you see that my going away is partly selfish? It's to save the rest. Humanly speaking, I've nothing else in the world to live for, except your friendship and Sally's. Help me to save it."

Her knife had gone home at last! Alec got up and

walked blindly about the room, touching the silly things she hadn't packed yet. She was as safe as she wanted to be. She felt about, for more books, to put into the crate.

He came over to her and dragged her by the wrists onto her feet. She knew he wasn't disagreeing with her any more. He put his hands on both her shoulders and shook her a little.

"Jane," he said, "I can just forgive you! Promise me, though, that no matter what heroic maggot you've by then got into your brain, when I send for you you'll come to me?"

She bit her lips and said: "Don't, don't!"

He was too near her—and too kind! She put her head down suddenly onto his shoulder, and cried with silent sobs that tore her to pieces, but without tears. She felt both comforted and estranged by Alec's nearness.

By-and-by—for she went on sobbing in the most helpless stupid way for quite a long time—he pushed her gently into the empty armchair, kissed the top of her head, and left her.

CHAPTER XXXV

CHARLES walked rather slowly down the long white-tiled tunnel, towards the laboratory. There were some test-tubes he wanted to look at, before he went to bed. He felt calm and unhurried. He had put an end to all his frightened ecstasy. He would never again have to exercise the preventive self-control which stood between him and bliss!

Unfortunately, his work in the laboratory was not quite so absorbing as he had expected it to be. Charles tried to force his mind back to the safe region of the abstract. That question of the sugar tolerance test for melancholia, for instance, could be carried even farther. It was closely bound up with Carwin's theory of adrenal glands and the emotions; and was a definite material proof of a psychological event.

It was difficult to overestimate its importance, and it might lead to other still more vital discoveries. But it did nothing to clear up a steadily increasing discomfort at the back of Charles's mind. Would a woman, who only cared for power over men, have given in as readily as Jane? Was it guilt that had made her sit there so stunned and still, with her hands in her lap, refusing to lift her eyes to Charles's face? She hadn't even said good-bye to him, nor let him touch her hand.

After all, they'd been good friends! They'd liked each other! It must have been rather a shock to Jane to lose his good opinion!

Charles began to wish that he could have put things to her in a way that wouldn't have forced her to feel that

she had lost it. But at the time he had felt too angry to
wish to spare her feelings.

That was the worst of a dispute with a woman! If he
hadn't been angry with Jane, he couldn't have sent her
away!

She had said something or other, quite intelligent, in her
own defence, but that had only made it worse. Charles
had not been accusing Jane of lack of intelligence! He
knew that the innocent seldom make good excuses! Still,
he wished he could have known before he left her what
Jane felt about being sent away. It would have come out if
she had lifted those stubbornly cast-down eyes!

Charles's experience of women's emotions was strictly
limited. He had generally been able to gauge his mother's
feelings by his own. She was a milder, more tolerant edi-
tion of himself. Then there was Myra; her feelings Charles
had never been able to judge at all. He only knew that
they seldom were what Myra exhibited. She built up incredible lies into self-congratulatory virtues. This had
made Charles suspect all women's mental processes. He
thought they only did good work because they were vain;
and he believed that they only told the truth if it suited
them.

He ran his eyes with disconcerting regret over Jane's
table in the laboratory. How scrupulously careful and accurate her work always was!

He wished he need not be reminded of her honesty!

Perhaps hospital administration would be more absorbing than chemical tests, and have less to do with Jane?

Charles could have done his work as well at home; but
he didn't want to go home. He went instead to his new
office, and buried himself with relief in administrative details.

He was unaware of how long he had been working when
he was roused by a sharp knock at the door.

The last thing he wanted was to be confronted by the human element. But before he had time to deny himself, the door was flung open and Alec stood before him.

"If you aren't too busy," Alec brusquely demanded, "I want a talk with you!"

Charles murmured something ineffectually self-protective, and swung his chair away from his desk. He supposed he would have to listen to Alec, but he needn't talk. It had cost Charles too much to improve his relationship with Alec, for him to risk throwing it away in order to suit his own convenience; so he drew out his pipe, crossed his legs, and managed to keep his eyes dispassionately amiable.

Alec sprawled comfortably in a big leather armchair opposite Charles, and, waving a cigarette about in an excited manner, began immediately upon what was in the forefront of his mind.

"I've seen Sally! It's tremendous, isn't it? How do you account for her having come round, in a flash, as Sally? Not a hint of that cursèd delusion left! I doubt if she as much as knew she had it! I want to hear exactly what you think about her?"

Charles's eyebrows went up and sank again. He was prepared, within limits, to speak of Sally. He realised that Alec had a perfect right to ask him about his wife.

"I never took quite so serious a view of the mental side of her illness as you and Dr. Everest did," Charles explained slowly. "Once we had fought through the physical symptoms, I expected her to come round all right. Her delusion always seemed to me more in the nature of an hysterical outburst than a mental illness. Don't misunderstand me; I don't think that Mrs. Macgregor is at all an hysterical type; but we are all likely, if the emotional pinch becomes too severe, to run ourselves off the rails. Mrs. Macgregor's unconscious mind is healthy—that is the main difference between an insane and an hysterical patient, is it not? In the case of the insane, it is the unconscious mind which is unhealthy, and recovery from delusion is therefore much more dubious. But in an hysterical case the conscious mind, for reasons of its own, has driven itself into its delusion, and any physical release—like that of your wife's concussion—gives it time to get over its protest. I expected her recovery to be both instantaneous and complete."

Alec didn't like the word "protest," but he didn't take it up. Charles didn't try to rub it in, but he didn't feel particularly inclined to let Alec off all round.

"Look here," Alec said, leaning forward and fixing Charles with his intent and eager eyes, "what you say sounds all right, and I'm inclined to agree with you—but is her recovery complete? The delusion's gone—Sally is Sally, of course—but is she lively enough? I didn't expect her to be any stronger, but somehow or other I thought she'd be more glad to see me! She—she cried a bit when I first came in. She said it was joy, but I couldn't quite swallow that—she didn't look so particularly joyful!"

"Well"—Charles answered with careful deliberation—"we know that she was not happy when she went off, and beyond being unconscious, I hardly see that she has had as yet anything to make her feel much happier?"

"Myra's gone!" Alec urged, with no carefulness at all. "Sally knows that. She knows I don't care a damn either! She knows that I've come back to her, the same as ever, if you like to put it that way. I don't admit personally that I ever in any real sense left her—but she wasn't to know that, of course. I behaved like a cad—and that's next door to being one—but not quite the same door, is it? Why shouldn't things be all right, then? And what on earth has the girl got left to cry about?"

Charles frowned. He did not wish to enter into this subject at all. Why shouldn't people keep their emotional crises to themselves? When he spoke it was more slowly still, and with increased formality.

"I think Mrs. Macgregor found herself in rather a difficult situation for a young married woman. It has not perhaps been fully cleared up yet. By-and-by she will realise that it is safely over; and no doubt, as she grows stronger and you can talk more to her, she will become reassured by your own attitude. I thought both her mental and physical condition highly satisfactory, considering what she had been through!"

"Now," Charles thought to himself, "I've gone as far as I need. Surely the fellow can read between the lines, and hold his tongue about the rest!"

But Alec continued to gaze at Charles with the restless, reckless eyes of an impetuous Irish terrier.

"My attitude!" he repeated, with a grin. "D'you mean my attitude about Myra, or are you getting at my 'attitude' about Everest?"

Charles stiffened from head to foot. His eyes froze, his eyebrows shot up into his hair. He felt as if he were biting on iced steel. He neither could nor would speak of Jane to Alec. If Alec forced him to listen to anything about her, he would make it as difficult for him as possible. He dropped his eyes to the floor, knocked out his pipe and put it back on the desk, and clasped his hands tightly round his knees. The impression that he succeeded in giving was that, while his clothes remained upon the chair, he himself had already left the room. But Alec took no notice of Charles's physical evasion.

"I've promised Everest," he went on rapidly, "not to try to persuade her to stay on—nor even to ask you to! She'd never speak to me again if she knew I was bringing the matter up. But I've a perfect right to come to you

about Sally, haven't I? And if Everest's mixed up with
what you think about Sally—well—you can see for yourself we've got to thrash the subject out! Is it—or isn't
it—Everest—that you think is upsetting Sally?"

There was a long silence. A murderous rage flooded
Charles's mind. Killing Alec would have seemed to him an
excellent way of finishing the conversation; but his reason told him that it would not have been conclusive. Somehow or other he must get the subject of Jane away from
Alec's intemperate advocacy.

"Dr. Everest's leaving the hospital," Charles said at
last, "is, if you will allow me to say so, her own affair—
and perhaps a little mine!—not yours, nor that of Mrs.
Macgregor."

"Nonsense!" Alec said, shaking his finger in front of
Charles's disgusted eyes. "You can't get out of it that
way! People don't have affairs that aren't their most intimate friends'! Besides, Everest said you'd sent her away
because of Sally! She didn't say she was going away of
her own accord! or because of a personal flare-up with
you! If you are dismissing her because of Sally, you've
got to take our point of view into consideration! God
Almighty can move in a mysterious way His wonders to
perform, but a fellow-man has got to have reasons, and
he's got to give them when he's asked for them! Mind you,
Dr. Drummond, I'm not urging you to keep Everest on!
She wouldn't stay on—whatever you said to her now!
That's the worst of her! She's so proud, she can't forgive
herself, and so scrupulous, you can convince her of sin as
soon as look at her! You must be off your nut to suspect
her of having been unfair to Sally! I've been unfair, I
know—but Everest couldn't be unfair!"

Charles sat as silent and immovable as if he had been
turned into stone. How dared Alec defend Jane to him?
How dared Alec know so much about Jane as to be able

to defend her? How dared he tell Charles what Charles already knew? But anger was not the deepest of Charles's hidden emotions. For the first time Charles found himself falling under his own condemnation. How dared he have placed Jane in a position where Alec would be obliged to defend her? In order to get her out of this, she must be spoken of, but not necessarily as if Charles felt anything about her. The way to extricate them both was to show no sensation whatever.

He spoke at last, tonelessly, and without looking at Alec.

"Dr. Everest is a very able woman," he observed. "In addition to her having gifts which few other women possess, she happens to be your friend as well as your colleague. Does it not occur to you that the continuous intimacy, caused by your work, as well as by your similar tastes, forms a situation which it is difficult for a young wife to accept? Mrs. Macgregor is a very diffident person, and that implies that she is very easily discouraged by the pre-eminence of other people. Surely there is no reason to attach blame to anyone in order to see why it is as well for Dr. Everest to find another field for her undoubted talents?"

"You mean," Alec asked bluntly, "that because Everest is Everest she's got to be kicked out of her job? And you really think that would be a relief to Sally? And if Sally should be relieved by such a thing, you think our married life wouldn't suffer because she'd been relieved by it? My good chap, you know as much about human relationships as a hard-shelled crab! If there's one thing more despicable than giving cause for jealousy, it's being jealous without a cause! I'd rather Sally died than let us all three down like that!"

Charles stirred uneasily. Put like this, it did sound rather unfair! But he thought Alec too ingenuous and violent to realise the dangerous power which Jane used over him. If Alec had guessed it, Jane would have had no power. Only at the instant when Charles himself had felt her power had he been able to break it—at the cost of finding a stone had taken the place of his heart! But he could not defend himself by giving Jane away. He would have, therefore, to accept Alec's thinking him unfair.

After a long pause Charles said with rigid unconcern:

"You probably know what Dr. Everest thinks better than I do, but I was under the impression that she had acquiesced in the wisdom of leaving here. Needless to say, she will receive the highest possible testimonials, both from Dr. Armitage and myself. Should it have to appear that anyone is to blame for the change, I will see that no discredit attaches to her. As far as your wife is concerned, she has had nothing whatever to do with my decision. She has no idea that Dr. Everest is leaving us, and had she known, I am sure her protest would have been as marked as your own. Nevertheless, in my opinion Mrs. Macgregor will be much happier and better for feeling that she has your undivided companionship."

Alec got up and walked to and fro about the big room he had once expected would be his own. He didn't answer Charles at once. He seemed to be fighting something in his own mind.

Charles was acutely conscious of Alec's struggle. He thought with regret of how good a fellow Alec was, and of how hard it must have been for him not to use his many admirable qualities in command. It must seem as if Charles was trying to take away from him everything Alec had, as well as what he might have had. The main things in his working life had been his hope of directing the hospital and his companionship with Jane; and both these things Charles was forcing him to renounce.

At last Alec broke their long, constrained silence. He flung back his head aggressively: "It seems to me a little odd," he observed, "considering that you're the head of this hospital, that you don't think more about the good of the work than you do of our private relations to each other. When all's said and done, we've worked together like a pretty well-matched pair. You must have been satisfied with us, mustn't you, or you wouldn't have kept us on? There is not a woman in England who can touch Everest as a psychiatrist, and if you believe that male patients should have men doctors, you might also bear in mind that female patients frequently do better with women doctors! Arnold, who's a pretty good judge of what he's talking about, thinks Everest the best psychiatrist he's ever worked for—and I'm damned if I'm not inclined to agree with him!"

Charles made no immediate reply. Could he possibly be accused of putting a personal matter before an objective one, he asked himself? Had he overlooked the good of the hospital in order to end a situation which had grown emotionally intolerable to him? If only he could be alone to think things out in peace, and not forced by an aggressive intimacy into a feeling of such intense antagonism that it blinded him to the chastity of fact!

"I offered to resign myself," Charles found himself confessing, "if Dr. Everest did not agree that it was best for her to leave the hospital. I do not think I have allowed my feelings to influence me. It will be, as you say, difficult to replace her; and impossible to find another woman who is as good a doctor. I should not look for one. I think a completely male staff will work better in some ways, but not in all. One must measure disadvantages against each other. It is part of the difficulty of the situation that Dr. Everest is exceptional in every way."

"If it's true that Everest upsets Sally, your leaving her to it wouldn't have been much of an improvement, would it?" Alec ironically demanded.

"I should at least not have to be responsible for a position I could not approve of," Charles said with an effort to remember why it had seemed perfectly logical for him to go, if Jane didn't, in order to benefit Sally.

"You seem to me," Alec informed him, "to be taking a header into the Victorian Era! What the devil has anybody else's private life to do with you?"

Charles felt surer of his ground now. He replied firmly: "My duty is to see that my colleagues are suitable people for carrying on an arduous, exacting task in the best possible conditions, without extraneous emotional strain. The last five months have not been, in my opinion, devoid of danger to the working of the hospital."

"If it's our moral natures that have been menacing the hospital," Alec volunteered, "I hardly see why you've pitched on Everest to sack! Her morals are starched throughout, and your grey matter must have misfired, if you haven't found her so. You sent your sister away—and I think you did right there; the other culprit is myself."

Charles felt himself, with a vicious reluctance, to be slowly crimsoning. "I do not think any man respects Dr. Everest more than I do," he said, as if the words were being dragged out of him by forceps. "You have no need to justify her character to me. What has been dangerous to all of us—and chiefly to your wife—has been your daily co-operation and deeply intimate friendship with an exceptional woman; even though your wife has shared this friendship. It has placed her in a position in which, consciously or unconsciously, she has felt herself to be inferior. You, as a psychiatrist, should know how dire this belief can be to any human being."

"Ah!" said Alec, with satisfaction, "now we've got it! What you're accusing Everest of—and getting rid of her for—is intellectual adultery, isn't it? I don't say you're wrong, mind you! It's what might happen to any intelligent cold-storage woman like Everest, without her being aware of it, but you're wrong in this particular instance— or, at any rate, you're out-dated. And do you know why you're wrong?" Alec swung round and, standing directly in front of Charles, stared down at him with grimly humorous eyes. "If you weren't so damned certain of your correct intentions, you might be less blind to your own and other people's feelings! As it is, you seem to overlook the fact that you and Everest are both madly in love with each other—and could put the whole thing right by admitting it!"

Charles was so startled by Alec's statement that he simply grew more crimson, and said nothing. After a long pause he turned his eyes away from Alec's mocking ones and said with cold distaste:

"You let your imagination run away with you, Macgregor!"

"No, I don't!" Alec told him impatiently. "I've never had any imagination! But like all psychologists worth their salt, I have two other faculties—intuition and observation. I've known you were in love with Everest ever since that fellow petered out under chloroform. I wasn't quite sure about her, though I thought there was something funny about her! You can generally tell that a woman's in love when her looks improve, when there's no particular reason why they should—especially after thirty! However, I found out for certain to-night that it was you. She's crying fit to break her heart over you now! That's what made me come here. If you marry her, you see, the whole thing gets cleared up. Even you could hardly think her bad for Sally—if she was your wife!"

Charles switched his chair round to his desk, with his back to Alec. He felt that he ought to be very angry; in a sense he was very angry with Alec; but he was so many other things besides angry that he daren't let Alec see his face. He wanted to bury his head in his hands; to fly up into heaven; to sink beneath the floor; but not to be looked at, or spoken to.

"Well!" Alec said, turning away towards the door, "you can do what you like about it now! I've got it off my chest, anyhow! I can assure you I wasn't any too keen about the idea at first! Everest has meant a lot to me— a lot she can't mean in quite the same way if she's another man's wife! Besides, I suppose she loses her job if she marries you! Still, there it is—it lets out Sally—if she ever did have that maggot in her head about Everest— and I suppose it'll make Everest happy! I didn't ever expect her to marry, somehow. She always seemed to me rather immaculate—like the Virgin Mary without the Child, if you know what I mean; but I suppose she's like all other women really—she'd rather let holiness rip, to set up a home of her own! Well—I'm off to bed now! If you want to catch Everest before she's off, you'd better look slippy. I think she means to do a bolt, once she's stopped crying!"

Alec went out and banged the door after him.

When his footsteps had died away, there was no sound left in the sleeping hospital.

A long time passed. Charles sat motionless with his head buried in his long, sensitive hands. Alec's words burned on in him. He did not accept them because Alec had said them, but because of a muffled witness in his own heart. Why had Jane sat so still under his accusations, and never lifted her eyes to his face? An angry woman wants a man to see that she is angry with him. Why had Jane always been so easy to be with? Charles knew that other people did not always find Jane easy. When she looked at Charles, she was beautiful, and yet she was no beauty. Supposing that she had no wish for power, but was simply subject to a power which controlled them both?

Charles had only to go on sitting where he was, and Jane would go away. His life would be his own again; but did he want perpetual loneliness? He had acquiesced in being in love with Jane. When he woke up in the morning, his first thought was, "I shall see her to-day!" and when he fell asleep at night, the last thing the eyes of his mind rested on was her image.

But it was one thing to have grown used to being in love with Jane, and quite another, and a far more disturbing thing, to grow used to the idea of Jane's being in love with him! It was so overwhelming a shock that Charles wasn't altogether sure that he even liked it! If it was true, he would have to marry Jane, and to marry her, though one side of it felt like the Kingdom of Heaven, was a most perturbing prospect! He would have to give up his single, undivided life!

Had he dismissed Jane from the hospital wholly to save Sally—or because unconsciously he was staving off the terrific business of mutual love?

Other men accepted the necessity of a shared life with easier minds. Passion driving them made short work of their fears. But Charles's passions didn't drive him. He was always in control of them. He could, at a pinch, give up anything he wanted. But could he give up anything Jane wanted? If what Alec had said was true, how cruel she must have thought Charles—and a little silly too—forcing Alec down her throat like that! Jane's pride, which Charles respected as much as he respected his own, had of course prevented her from showing him that he needn't be angry! Perhaps it had also prevented her from guessing why he was angry? She might have thought him over-

flowing with righteous indignation, or compassion on
Sally's account, and not guessed that his was the fury of
a jealous heart? Charles had been cruel to her because
he was afraid! He had been afraid of her feeling for Alec.
Well—now he wasn't afraid of it any more, so there was
no more need for him to go on being cruel.

He still hesitated. He didn't want to go back to her
room, where there had been all that anger; and all that
pain; and where Alec had seen her tears! He decided to
wait for her somewhere else, where he could be sure of
seeing her before she went away, but not where it would
seem as if he meant to stop her. When he saw her, he would
know what the whole of him wanted; and be able to think
of how he was going to tell her what it was. He knew already that Jane would never want anything but the whole
of him.

He rose quickly to his feet; his entire being felt conscious of release. But he hadn't released himself! It was
Alec who had released him! Charles hadn't thanked him.
He never would thank him; but he realised, before he
left his office, that in the long duel of jealousy and generosity, which they had fought out together, this revelation
from Alec had been rather a fine stroke.

CHAPTER XXXVI

WHEN Jane had finished packing, she sat down at her empty desk. She wrote a note of concise instructions to the Matron, with a sentence of cordial farewell at the end; another to one of the sisters about a difficult case; finally, a letter to Sally full of the warmest tenderness and the vaguest plans. She put her keys in an envelope and addressed it to Charles: that, she thought, was all.

She glanced round the room, where she had lived and worked for six years, with a curious empty feeling in her heart. It had never been very much furnished, and, except for the gaping bookshelves, it did not look much barer than usual. There was nothing she minded leaving in it, except perhaps the chair where Charles had always sat. She let her hand rest for a moment on the back of it. She would never see his spare, erect figure at ease in it again, his long limbs spread out and that look of strength held back—of beauty unregarded! She would never be able to watch the tension melt out of him while her friendly irony freed both his wits and his gentleness. These things were over. The room could witness them no more. Nor those discussions with Alec, vivid, alert, and so deeply congenial that half the short night through they had fought out their differences, oblivious of the long day's work ahead. All that unfettered friendliness—that reach and flight of the mind over a world of unsolved problems—must be relinquished now. She knew that she would never find such colleagues again. Their talk had been all the furniture the room needed. It had been Jane's life. Compared to one of those shared adventurous evenings, memory would be like a dried flower in a book, with all its scent and light pressed out of it!

She drew her mind away forcibly from that bleak spectacle to more practical difficulties. Alec would have to do double work for a bit; and so would Dr. Barnes. Charles would soon find somebody to take Jane's place, though he might curse her for leaving her job in the lurch: still, he would probably feel more relieved than oppressed at being freed from the sight of her!

She gave one last look round, clicked out the light, and stepped out of the long French window into the darkness.

Jane had never liked going through the grounds alone at night. It was the only time in all the twenty-four hours when she thought of those nightmare minds, and their possible escapades, as personally dangerous. She used to be frightened of their faces in the dark. No one had ever guessed her secret fear till Charles came. Not that he had said anything about it, but whenever it happened that Jane had to cross the grounds at night, Charles had always turned up, to stroll across them with her.

This last time she must manage alone. She felt absurdly terrified. Twigs snapped under her feet, little causeless winds sighed hoarsely close to her ear. There were stars, but no moon, and the stars did nothing to break up the darkness; they only stabbed it wider awake. Her suitcase weighed heavily on her arm. Bushes crouched like figures ready to spring. The gravel crunched revealingly under her light feet. There were sounds, too, that had no reassuring significance. If she switched on her torch, what it didn't show her moved nearer. Still she reached the garage in safety at last. There was a light in it which had no right to be there! It was the kind of thing that would happen on a night like this! Everything she had wanted to avoid had pursued her; and now she was to wind up with an escaped patient!

For a moment Jane felt that she couldn't face it. After all, her work was over! She had only to go down to the lodge, wake up the porter and tell him the light was on and he'd better ring up the night inspector at the hospital and see who had got inside!

The next moment she had opened the garage door—for the habit of attending to things herself was stronger than any fear—and found Charles.

It was more frightful than any lunatic, to have to face him again.

He stood in front of her Morris Cowley with his hand on the open door.

"Get in!" he said, a little impatiently.

Jane got in. Charles took her suitcase and shoved it into the back of the car, and then slipped into the driving-seat beside her.

"I have a key for the lodge," he told her reassuringly, "so we needn't wake up the porter." He seemed to think no other explanation was necessary.

Outside the gates he took a direction away from the town.

"I am going to London," Jane managed to say mildly. Charles grunted.

Jane did not press him. After all, it didn't matter much to her whether she went to London by a longer or by a shorter route. She didn't want to get there, and she had made no plans. What did matter to her was that she knew Charles wasn't angry any more.

It was curiously peaceful to be driven through the soft warm darkness, with Charles at her side. There was no traffic on the road, and no sound except the mutter and buzz of their engine; but there was a great deal of life in the air. Moths flew up and bumped themselves to death

against the glittering facets of their lamps. Not a bad
death if you were a moth, Jane thought sleepily. Little
trailing winds full of moisture brushed their cheeks.
Scents came like music into the mind. Searchlights made
quivering pools of opal in the dark sky above them. Now
and then a startled animal flickered by; a cat's eyes burned
amber in the ditch; or a rabbit leaped in and out of their
small field of light, with a frightened flash of its white
scut.

"Dr. Drummond," Jane ventured at length to ask him,
"have you been sitting up all night?"

"Why not?" Charles answered rather crossly. "You've
been up, too, haven't you?"

"I've been packing," Jane told him, just to keep it well
in his mind that she was really off.

Charles made no answer, but his crossness was a
friendly, companionable crossness, remote from the frozen
seas of his anger.

Jane leaned back farther in her seat and let the warm
night flow over her like water. Her sense of peace was
deeper than any mere rest from physical fatigue. She was
at peace because she trusted Charles, and knew that her
trust was returned.

He hadn't changed his mind about her being bad for
Sally. He had only more and more realised that Jane
would agree with him about it, once she had seen his
grounds for saying it. She had shown him her agreement
by acting instantly on his verdict and by not making any
kind of fuss.

Charles's honour was at peace now in his heart, because he knew that Jane's was safe. She was no longer
damaging his self-respect by pulling away part of his trust
in her.

The wind that blew against her lips tasted salt. She
roused herself to say:

"But we aren't on the London road, Dr. Drummond. Isn't this the way to the sea?"

"There is no reason why you shouldn't go to London later on, if you choose," Charles replied cryptically. He seemed to be presenting her with an alternative without letting her know what it was.

Jane thought about the possible alternative for a long time, but she came to no conclusion except that they were really getting nearer and nearer to the sea.

Suddenly Charles stopped the car.

"We may as well get out here," he said, "and sit in the sand-dunes. It'll be dawn in a few minutes."

Jane got out and stumbled a little. She would have fallen if Charles's light touch had not steadied her.

All round them there was a thinning out of darkness, and now that they were standing still, she could hear the waves. The sand was heavy under their feet, but they hadn't far to go before they had the dunes at their back and were facing a grey moving darkness, broken every now and then by a white line of foam. Jane couldn't see Charles, but she knew that he was close beside her. She heard him give a little sigh, as if he were profoundly pleased about something. She wondered if Charles meant this to be the end—a happy end rather than an unhappy end—of their companionship—but still an end? Or did he mean it to be the beginning of a new life together? She had no means of knowing how deep his feeling for her was. Other women guessed when men were physically attracted by them; but Jane, unless her attention had been disagreeably called to it, never knew.

Charles moved restlessly and sighed again, less peacefully this time. Jane felt an impulse to put out her hand to him, as a mother might to quiet a child; but wasn't that the trap she had fallen into with Alec? Men shouldn't be treated like children! She held herself quiet and aloof.

"You needn't go away, you know, unless you want to," Charles said at last. "Why shouldn't you stay on—if you don't mind staying on—with me? That wouldn't upset the others."

Now that he had actually said what they both wanted, it sounded, to Jane, unbelievable. Did he really want it? Had he suddenly felt in his reaction from his unjust anger that he was depriving Jane, both of her job and of her friends, so that he must offer her some kind of substitute?

He liked her, of course. He wouldn't be such a fool as to propose marriage without liking her; but was he the sort of man who really wanted marriage?

Jane knew him to be, at heart, a solitary. It would be unendurable, she thought, to violate his privacy, or to let him violate it, for the sake of kindness.

She hesitated to answer him, and while she hesitated the sea came, out of the pale darkness, to their feet. The shadowy ridges of the waves bent over each other, flattening themselves against the oncoming waves, and sending up a shower of snow-white spray. The dawn wind stripped the sky bare of stars. Jane could see through the thinning darkness the shapes of the low dunes and the roundness of the sea.

She could see Charles at last. He was leaning on his elbow, his chin cupped in his hand, gazing straight in front of him. He was hatless and still wore the grey flannels he had worn all day. The responsibility had gone out of his face, and all its rigidity. He looked as he must have looked in his boyhood. Her own heart beat so hard that she was afraid she would not be able to reach the end of any sentence she began. She said: "Charles!" It was the first time she had ever spoken his name, and she hoped it would be answer enough. But apparently it wasn't enough, for Charles said rather impatiently: "Well—?"

"It seems to me," Jane began again, "that such an

awful lot of things have been happening lately—one on the top of the other, so that it must have been dreadfully hard for you to know what to do about us all! It would be quite natural for us to make a mistake—while we're still so upset! You aren't just thinking—this would be the best way out of it, are you?"

"That is the last thing I should think of marriage!" Charles answered drily. "I should think it was the worst way out of anything—as a way out, I mean."

His voice still had an edge of resentment, as if he were talking to someone who ought to know, by intuition, what he meant, but when he came to the end of his answer, his voice, just perceptibly, shook.

Jane paid more attention to this than to what he had said. It suddenly struck her that Charles was frightened —more frightened than she was; it made her speak with a greater plainness than she would otherwise have spoken.

"I don't know what you really want," she said gently; "that's the only thing that makes it hard for me to say 'yes.'"

She could feel that the body so near her own had slipped from tension into peace. He did not touch her, or try to take her into it. She was in it. She was, she realised with an astonished joy, his peace.

For a long time neither of them spoke. At last Charles put out his hand and, without looking at her, touched hers. It was the lightest, gentlest touch, and after he had touched her, he instantly withdrew his hand.

"It's so stupid," Charles said, with a little laugh, "to be so afraid of what one feels, isn't it? But you see I'm thirty-five, and I've never let myself feel—this feeling before."

"Our being such good friends," Jane suggested, "isn't that a help?"

"No," Charles murmured, "not exactly—not as much as you'd think. It will be—afterwards."

Jane nodded. She herself felt that there was no great hurry.

The world grew lighter and lighter every moment. Time slipped over them, without the consciousness of time. The dawn wind had no chill in it; it stirred the long grasses by their side, and carried on its wings the tonic wildness of the sea.

"Did you," Charles demanded suddenly, "think you were so awfully right—when I said those—when I was so angry, I mean?"

Jane thought this over carefully. "I wasn't sure," she said, at last. "Just at first, you see, it was difficult to get sorted out in my mind what I did feel. I had so thought of them both as a sort of beautiful duty! Not that I didn't enjoy, and like them, and feel awfully grateful to them— for their liking me! You mustn't think I was as hideously arrogant as all that! I dare say I needed them more than they needed me—till you came, I mean! But still, to be told I had been bad for Sally was rather a mouthful! But after you'd gone, I saw it! Bits of it, I mean, kept on floating up into my mind! At first I couldn't see anything—except that you were angry!"

Charles laughed softly. "I wasn't only angry," he said. "I was jealous! It's not a nice thing to be! I was furious with you for making me feel it—even now I'm not sure that I've quite forgiven you! And instead of helping me out of it, you drove me away with it!"

"Well, but, Charles," Jane said defensively, "you had sacked me, hadn't you? I couldn't very well do much to entertain you after that!"

"You needn't have sent me away!" Charles asserted, fixing her with eyes which danced with laughter. "I didn't want to go! You must have known I didn't—I stayed and

stayed! But you wouldn't even look at me! Your hands
in your lap were the unfriendliest hands I'd ever seen.
Your eyelids were like the shutters jewellers draw down
over their jewels, to keep thieves out!"

Jane listened, astonished. She had not known that
Charles could say such pretty things—without saying
them!

He looked away again, though he was still smiling, and
trickled the sand, which had suddenly become yellow,
through his fingers.

The long dune grasses bowed and quivered towards the
sea. A sandpiper fluttered close by them, as light as a
blown leaf.

"I don't think I could very well tell you to do anything," Jane reminded Charles, "either to go or stay!
You were my chief! I could only like—or dislike—what
you did. I thought when you had gone away that I should
never like anything, very much, again."

Charles turned towards her, and drew her close against
his heart. She felt his kisses on her eyes, and hair. She
had no separate life; clinging to him, she felt like a wave,
drawn back into the sea. She could not tell which it was,
his heart or hers, that beat so hard against her side. His
loneliness had ended, but she had not taken it away from
him. She had entered into it. Her hands moved blindly
towards his head and drew it down against her breast.
The long sigh he gave was like the happy sigh of those
who enter into a final rest.

At last he moved away from her. "There's something
I've got to tell you," Charles said quietly. "In one way
—now—it doesn't matter—we never need tell each other
anything! But when one knows one needn't, one finds one
can! It's about Myra. I had not meant ever to speak of
it to anyone else. But—you aren't anyone else, are you?
It has weighed on me rather. You see, I had to do what

I didn't like doing. I faked that evidence in Myra's favour, to prevent her being hanged! She had killed her husband. I don't quite think she meant to. It's so difficult to say, isn't it, even what reasonable people mean to do? And Myra's not reasonable. She's as impulsive as one of our patients. Of course I think all impulsive people should be patients, but in that case, there would be too few of the rest of us to attend to them! Some cast-iron, puffed-out lobster of an old Colonel gave her a pistol. I suppose she'd made him think it was to defend her honour. A man who would rape a woman, or a woman who wants to be raped, are always rather particular about chastity. They speak of it as if it were some sort of sweet to be preserved. It is absurd to suppose you can attack honour by violence. You can only attack a body by another body. Still—anyhow—the damned old fool gave it to her. I suppose—Peter—that's my friend who was her husband—was still in love with Myra. I sometimes blame myself for not having done more to try to prevent the marriage—but I did what I could. I said to him once, 'I don't think you'll like being married to my sister.' However, he would marry her. He came in one night, before his illusions had completely crashed, and found her with her lover. He told the man off pretty quick; and then I expect he gave the rough side of his tongue to Myra. He was a straight speaker. She got this toy out and waved it about, threatening to kill herself—and he laughed at her. It was his way of hiding that he felt pretty sore, no doubt. Besides, perhaps he already knew that she wasn't the kind to do herself any physical harm. She turned it on him then, and he said: 'You couldn't hit a haystack if you tried to!' I expect he did say that, for of course I have only her evidence as to how things happened, but that sounds like Peter. They were his last words. What is it careless housemaids say when they break things?—'It came off in my hand.' Well, Myra said her fingers were on the trigger by accident—she didn't even know it was a trigger, but it went off, and shot him through the heart. He was standing on the landing near the top of the stairs, and went over in a heap, halfway down them. She thought he was doing it to tease her. She was pretty scared when she found out what she'd done; but she had the sense to telephone to me.

"When I got there, I rubbed off her finger-prints, and before *rigor mortis* had set in, I got his onto the pistol instead. When I'd staged the whole thing to look like an accident, I coached Myra what to say, and rang up the police. I didn't want to get her off particularly, but I had to think of my mother."

"Of course you had to get her off," Jane said gently.

"Well, anyhow," Charles said, stretching out his hand towards hers again, "that's that! I thought I'd better tell you, in case you minded. Some people might!"

Jane laughed. She took his hand in both of hers and laid it in her lap.

The sea was the colour of light steel. A thin line of light quivered over the horizon's edge, and, growing broader, shot a sudden path of gold towards the shore.

"We'll get breakfast at rather a nice place, ten miles away," Charles told her. "It's pretty early still, but I'm famished, aren't you?"

Jane nodded. She hadn't been aware of hunger before, but now she was aware of it as a new, savage pleasure. She looked at Charles, caught his eye, and laughed.

"Will you ever like women?" Jane asked him, when they were on the road again, the car running along as smoothly as a mounting bubble.

"No!" Charles replied firmly. "Why should I? I've resigned myself to you. That ought to be enough."

Jane told him what Arnold had said about them both.

"He's an intelligent chap, Arnold," Charles acknowledged, "and I dare say he's right. I've been rather strangled one way and another by women all my life. That was what made me nasty to you. I was afraid of you, but I'm not now. Are you still afraid of me, by-the-by?"

Jane considered this question carefully. She had disliked other men often; but never feared them. Charles she had never disliked, but from the first moment she saw him, she had feared him. She wasn't afraid of him now, but when had she stopped being afraid? Only a very short while ago!

"I've always been rather afraid of you," Jane admitted, "till I knew that you were afraid too—and then I saw what it was—we were both afraid of love."

"Not very sensible of either of us," Charles said, putting on speed, "seeing that it was about the only thing we needn't have been afraid of!"

CHAPTER XXXVII

It was quite like a second honeymoon! Sally leaned back in their Wolsey Hornet with Biscuit curled up on her lap, and Alec, capless and grinning with irrepressible joy, sat in the driver's seat beside her.

Charles and Jane, the Hursts and Matron, all waved them off from the hospital gates. It was a sunny October day, with that tart feeling in the air which is like the first bite of a good apple.

Everybody had been frightfully kind to Sally ever since she'd been ill, and Sally felt it was a little ungrateful to feel so much relieved at seeing the last of them. She couldn't say that she hadn't had plenty of Alec, either, while she was being nursed at Jane's. He'd rushed in and out, in a tearing hurry, every hour or so, gazed at Sally with avaricious intensity; kissed anything he could get hold of to kiss; and agreed to everything that Sally had asked him. Still, you couldn't call that being with a husband!

Sally didn't know what Alec had really thought about anything. Stupendous facts like Sally's being ill, and losing their baby, or Jane and Charles being in love, couldn't be cleared up by a joke and a few kisses!

Jane had told both of them about Charles, but not together—separately. She had told Alec downstairs in the post-mortem room of all places; he'd said it was so like Jane! And she had told Sally much more quietly and fully, after Alec had left Sally for the night, and before she went to sleep.

Alec had bounded in quite cheerfully next morning with the news.

"Marvellous idea for both of 'em! 'Love, when we met 'twas like two icebergs meeting!' Apologies to Ella Wheeler Wilcox—she had it 'planets'!" Alec had exclaimed; but that might have meant anything!

Of course, no doubt tact was all right, or there wouldn't be so much of it about when anyone was ill; but when it came to using tact on your own wife, so that whenever Sally wanted to find out anything, Alec became vague and reassuring—it was quite dreadful! Besides, of course Sally could see through Alec, as if he were a crystal doll!

Biscuit was the only person who behaved naturally in the sick-room. It was really quite a comfort when he bit Charles's shoe under the bed! Sally wanted it bitten because Charles had refused to let Sally go home before coming away—even for one night! He'd been charming about it, but quite inflexible.

"Directly you come back," he'd said, "of course; but Jane'll get you anything you want now. Take the little holiday first."

So damned soothing! Of course the words "Carrie Flint" had never been mentioned by any of them!

"Are you all right?" Alec asked in his new, cautious, exasperating voice.

"No!" Sally said, with vicious emphasis. "I'm human, and I'm all wrong! And I want to be!"

She felt slightly better after this outburst. Apparently Alec did too, for he chuckled; and the car bounded forward as if it too felt freer, with Jane and Charles—just for the moment—safely out of sight!

"It isn't as if they weren't nearly perfect!" Sally told herself reprovingly. "They've both been dearer than dear. I don't know that I'd exactly die for Charles, but if he

did die, I'd water his grave, quite regularly, with my
tears! As for Jane—of course she always was my best
friend as well as Alec's—and now she's been more my best
friend! She's gone quite human, and looks much better
with my kind of lipstick on! We can talk for hours together, too, now—about whether the best cotton sheets
are nicer than the worst linen, and what men like about
their underclothes! She doesn't go off into intellectual
trances any more either! And I must say, even if Alec is
right and she is an iceberg, she's like an iceberg stuffed
with burning lava about Charles! And it's all very well
for Charles to pretend he doesn't like it when I say nice
things to him about Jane—a child of two wouldn't be
taken in by him! Still, when other people are in love,
one doesn't particularly want to be with them—not, anyhow, if one's in love oneself! This going away now will
be better than our honeymoon! For then I had to remember that Alec thought I was an angel, and now he knows
I'm not, so I needn't try to behave like one, and it'll all
be quite perfect!"

Sally gazed tranquilly at Alec's profile. As a profile
it wasn't perhaps anything very Apollo-ish. Still, it was
a nice lively face, with a nip to its jaws, and most ex-
pressive eyes.

Alec had been pretty ill and his cheeks had gone rather
hollow and colourless, but a little sunburn and plenty
of North country food would soon make him look all right
again.

Matron had said that Alec and Charles were the too
best-looking doctors she'd ever seen—and she'd seen heaps
and heaps, because of the War, as well as in all the London
hospitals. "Look at their figures," Matron had said;
"and the Chief's features! And Dr. Macgregor's always
being so alive!" And besides Alec's particularly good

mouth and chin, there was the way he flung his head back
and strolled along as if life was as easy as passing through
an open door.

No wonder the nurses were all quite silly about them
—poor things!

When Sally and the Matron were alone, they simply
gorged on personalities; and by now Sally knew more
about the hospital than Alec and Jane would ever know,
let alone Charles!

"What's the matter with my face—smut on it?" Alec
demanded. "I can't return your glances in this traffic,
but I can feel your eyes going through me like a gimlet!"

"Well," Sally said threateningly, "now we're alone,
p'r'aps I'm going to be a gimlet! I don't know quite what
I'm going to be yet—my soul has just begun to stretch
its legs. Hasn't yours?"

"Not yet," said Alec significantly. "It may by-and-by."

"Yours is an easier stretched soul than mine, anyhow,"
Sally told him reassuringly. "Charles said we were to stop
off at Chester for the night. *Don't let's!* Let's push on
to Shap Fell."

Alec began to look careful again.

"Oh, no!" he said. "You're just shoving that in on
me, because you know I like doing a mileage! You haven't
been in the car for more than two hours at a stretch since
you threw that fit! We'll have to go slow!"

"We'll go to Shap Fell to-night," Sally said firmly.
"It isn't mileage, and this air is food and drink to me!
I'm as strong as a horse. And we *can* and *will!* I like Shap
Fell! And I want to send them a wire, from there, to-
night! We don't need to stop off anywhere, except in a
hedge. I've got food enough in this hamper under my feet
to feed us and a family of wolf-hounds as well—let alone
a small Sealyham!"

"Something seems to be the matter with you!" Alec

said, with an appreciative grin. "You've been hideously spoilt since you were ill—I suppose that's it! I shall have to start beating you like a carpet."

"Well, I haven't said anything for a month," Sally observed resentfully, except 'Better, thanks!' and 'How frightfully good of you!' and 'May I sit up for a little now?' and things like that. I can see quite plainly that husbands and wives ought to live alone together under one roof, where they can kiss—and knock about—without having to pretend not to like to each other!"

"Well—I could have told you that before," Alec replied. "Hideous police court cases always start with a husband or wife going off to stay with a friend, or else they take a holiday together in seaside lodgings (shared, no doubt, by curates), and do each other in with a bootlace on the beach! That's why I chose mountains. There never seem to be any bootlaces about in Scotch mountains!"

They speeded up and shot through Chester. Alec found a wood for lunch, where Biscuit could stalk imaginary lions, and find himself baffled by actual rabbits; and Alec and Sally could lean against a small tree, and each other.

Sally, who had hitherto been applauded for eating dubiously a few forkfuls of chicken, now dashed through boiled eggs, stout ham sandwiches, and forests of lettuce, without turning a hair!

They reached Shap Fell at six. The short October day was nearly over. The bare green curves of down stretched endlessly away into each other—rhythmically, like great chords of music.

The downs were empty except for harebells and wandering sheep. Sunset still lingered in the sky. Tufts of ragged golden cloud climbed up into high blue spaces. The air smelt of frost and clover without there being any of either.

All day long the air and the sun had run through the

Moss Hotel. It wasn't only that the Wordsworths had stayed there—William and Dorothy—and had never really gone away; Sally felt as if she too were a sort of Wordsworth, standing in a clean, low-ceilinged, white-washed room, and knowing it was hers and Alec's!

All rooms were theirs again, and all lilac fells with keen air blowing over them, so that you could breathe double!

After they'd eaten pounds and pounds of cold roast beef with mustard, drunk hard cider, and nibbled at a cheese, which William and Dorothy too must have thought better for mice—Alec said sternly: "You'll go straight to bed now!" And in a sense Sally had gone straight to bed.

She knelt on the floor and looked out of their bed-room window while Alec and Biscuit put the car away and talked to everybody for hours, including sheep. The sky was bare of cloud, and the moon rolled up suddenly over the side of a round fell—like a thin golden plate.

Stars couldn't get enough darkness to twinkle in. Their pale little meek faces poked out of the sky like primroses out of a mossy bank. Flocks of sheep came pattering up, making a sound like a heavy shower of rain.

At last Alec came to bed. They weren't either of them at all sleepy, so they left the blinds up; and the moon, and the fells, and the sheep wandered in and out of their room all night.

Sally drew Alec's head onto her breast and slipped her arm under his head so that they could be comfortable again. The air that came in at the window was frostier and more honey-sweet than ever.

After just being happy for a while, Sally said:

"Alec, there're lots of things I want to know. Tell me—d'you mind about Jane?" Her heart slowed for his answer.

He must have guessed it was a grave question, for he didn't hurry over it.

"Mind about her——?" he said at last. "It all depends on what you mean by mind! Just at first I felt rather knocked over. Joseph must have felt——that piece about the angel——a bit rum——however much he thought of Mary! All the more, probably, if she'd never cottoned particularly to him! Not that I wanted Jane for myself, mind you! If you'd set us on a desert island for sixty years, we'd have walked off intact! I'd as soon kiss the Venus of Milo as Jane——a damned sight sooner! Good God! it makes the roots of my spine cold even to think of it! But that's Charles's lookout. I can't imagine him making love either——if it comes to that——can you?"

"I dunno!" said Sally reflectively. "He might do it rather well in his way. He's more human with women than he is with men, I think; and he's nice to look at. Rather like a Greek statue that's sweated itself stringy ——if you know what I mean! Jane likes that stringy kind best. Their marrying won't interfere with your work, will it?"

"No!" said Alec grimly, "nothing will——now. I kept at it when you nearly died on me! I thought it well over. If you did die, should I kill myself? People do for a lot less than that. I knew I'd done you in, you see. I couldn't get away from it. You were a healthy girl——the sort that has babies as easily as a duck takes to water. Besides, I wouldn't have cared to live if you hadn't. It wouldn't have been any fun. But I made up my mind I would live, because, when you come to think of it, there aren't many good psychiatrists, and all those poor crocks are just as human as we are! Heaps of 'em can be cured; and quite apart from that, what we learn on them helps to keep other people sane. You see, Sally, modern life isn't a thing we've any of us quite got the hang of as yet. We're in for big changes. Not only in our conditions, but in ourselves. Any of us who know this, or have learned how to deal with people who come croppers, ought to keep on deck. A man like me, who's made the worst sort of croppers himself, he'll be as useful as any! One night, when I thought you were going out—and Charles thought so too—only Jane didn't, I said to myself: 'Well, now I'm damned if I don't cure that little Carrie Flint, anyhow!' That was funny, wasn't it?—because just at first I wanted to strangle her at sight!"

"I'm glad you thought that," Sally said earnestly. "Alec, I want to tell you all about how it happened now. I couldn't before."

"Not to-night," Alec swiftly interposed. "You'll get all tired out! Let's just love each other!"

But Sally was inflexible. "If I don't get it off my chest now," she said, "I never will. I can somehow to-night. It isn't only our being alone at last. It's the air, and the moon, and a lot of things I was thinking about on our drive. I know when I can, I must. Charles said to me: 'Don't force yourself to tell him, but when you feel it come, don't keep it back.' Well, Alec, I feel it's come."

"All right," Alec said, drawing a deep breath, "fire ahead!"

Sally was sorry for him. She knew that it was going to hurt him to hear what she had felt, and all the more hurt him because Charles had told her not to keep it back; but she loved Alec enough to know that hurting him was best. It would clear up for both of them the dark places in their hearts which should be filled with light.

She drew his head closer against her heart and kissed the ear nearest to her lips.

"I'd been feeling queer," she began, "for a long time,

not unhappy quite, but dulled down—like a sleepy bear. I don't know that I knew what it was, but I don't think even then that I thought it was wholly Myra. That was a more ordinary kind of pain, like catching your finger in a door. If I hadn't gone stupid first, I think I could have tackled Myra. She wouldn't just have crumpled me up."

Sally felt Alec's head press deeper into the softness of her breast, as if he was trying not only to shut out her voice, but the very air he breathed, and live only in her heart.

"It's all right!" Sally said consolingly. "It's all over now, and this soon will be—and then we can go on loving. Where was I? Well—I wanted to get something done—on my own—better than Jane! I wasn't satisfied to be just what I was. I wanted to be everything to you, and I could feel all the time I wasn't. I seemed to be melting away like a wax doll in front of a fire. When Myra came along too—I just went out altogether! That day when Carrie Flint fluttered after me in the garden, I felt 'Ah! here's someone at last that wants me! Poorer than I am! Jane hasn't understood her!' And I was glad. I wanted to get her away from Jane! I wanted to make her better, of course—but not really to help her—only to be grander than Jane. Wasn't it silly of me, and spiteful too! Charles says you ought only to want life itself, and life for itself; not what you can get out of it—and people the same way!"

"Charles is damned right," Alec said in a muffled voice. "But, Sally, you might have known you were everything to me! I hadn't got to think about you! That was the worst of it. You were in my blood! If you'd only cater-wauled—or kicked me—or turned nasty and run away —I'd have dropped Myra like a hot potato! But I ought to have seen I'd taken the guts out of you, so that you couldn't stop me, because you hadn't the courage left. I'd used you up."

"Yes, in a sense you had," Sally agreed softly, "you and Jane together; but I oughtn't to have let myself get used up! Jane told me to go away. But I didn't want to owe your coming back to her! If she'd only told me about Charles instead, I would have run away!"

"Yes, she wasn't enough of a '*Mensch*,'" Alec agreed grimly. "She has her faults too—like the rest of us. And so has that damned Charles!"

Sally knew Alec wasn't as savage as he sounded, and she didn't try to stop him, for she felt, "P'r'aps it's nicer for him feeling savage than sad!" She kissed his ear again —and even bit it a little, to reassure him, before she went on.

"Well, that was how Carrie began, and it just simmered on inside me till the tea-party. Of course I saw then that I couldn't do what I wanted! It was quite true what Jane had told me, but I hadn't believed; Carrie wasn't get-at-able! But I saw, too, that in spite of the fact that I couldn't make her understand anything, Carrie felt just what I did! There was a pull between us. In some strange way, we both knew that we belonged to each other. It was quite horrible, because I saw that what pulled me towards her was her madness! Alec, I wanted to be mad, too!"

Alec groaned.

"Yes, but I see now," Sally reminded him, "that you can go into your mind—just as well as you can go out of it! And it was because I had never gone into my mind before that I went out of it! I used just to dance about on the top!

"Where was I?—Well, I wanted to go mad because I saw what a nasty thing it would be for you and Jane if

I did. And I wanted to be nasty. That's why I'm telling you about it, because Charles said that I shouldn't get really well—and you wouldn't either—till you knew I'd been as nasty to you as you'd been to me! He said the trouble with most married people was that one of them was a victim and the other a brute—and that it was much more comfortable if they knew that each of them was a little of both!

"That tea-party evening, after you'd gone to Myra, and Carrie had gone back to the hospital, there was that thunderstorm—do you remember? Rain and an awful wind. I went upstairs to shut the windows because of the rain coming in on the new carpets. I don't know that I was particularly frightened. I just felt rather tired and odd. But after I'd shut them I heard someone call me— quite distinctly—'Sally! Sally!' And then I was frightened. Biscuit heard it, too, for he was with me; but he didn't bark as he usually does, he whimpered and crouched flat. I heard the voice again: 'Sally! Sally!' from downstairs.

"I went to the top of the stairs to see who it was; I still thought it might be Jane; but Biscuit wouldn't come with me.

"There at the bottom of the stairs stood Carrie Flint! I know it wasn't her now, for Charles says she never left the hospital. But I saw Carrie Flint. She stood there, looking up at me, and smiling that queer little lost smile of hers. She said, 'I'm going to have your baby. I'm Sally now—and you're Carrie Flint!' I put out my hands to stop her coming up—and then it was as if I suddenly went down the stairs into her! I didn't feel as if I were falling, but going—going—away from myself! I don't remember any more till I saw Jane looking at me over the top of a book."

Alec started shivering as if he would never stop. Sally

held him closer against her heart. At last the shivering stopped, but he didn't say anything.

Sally could see out, over the top of his head, into the night. The honey-coloured moon was alone in the sky; no clouds or stars were visible, only the endless curves of the fells stretched their firm dark shadows into the silvery light. It was too beautiful for Sally to feel very sorry for either of them.

It was all right now—better than all right—as bad things were when you had once had them, and knew what they meant.

"I suppose," Sally said after a long pause, "I really wanted to get rid of that baby, and that was what made me invent Carrie Flint's coming to fetch it. But it was real at the time. Alec, I want a baby—most awfully now —in quite a new way. We can have one, can't we?"

"Charles's operation going right made it possible that we could," Alec told her. Sally could hear the effort in his voice. She thought it very brave and nice of him to give all the credit to Charles. "He did a wonderful operation on you," Alec explained; "it makes my hair rise now to think of it! It awfully nearly didn't come off. You see, you'd lost so much blood—there was a time when we thought you couldn't cope with it. But we worried through somehow. I made them do the transfusion on the chance.

"They're better people than I, Sally—it's right you should know it; but they're not better doctors. You see, Jane does everything right as rain, but she's so determined to do it perfectly that she has to stick to the rules. She hates to go outside what she knows. Charles does too— though he stretched a point over your operation, I will say that for him. But there are times when everything breaks down and there aren't any rules. Well, I can go on then, when other people would stop. I don't tell you this just to boast—but you see I got the lot of us into trouble just by comparing myself with Charles and feeling sore about his getting the appointment. I was pretty near dead with shame when I faced up to it; but I've got out of that too now, because shame's no use—it takes your eye off your job—only I thought I'd like you to know. I am rather a good doctor!"

"Ah, but I do know!" said Sally swiftly. "I've known all along. They're not better than you, Jane and Charles! They're just different! They couldn't do anything at all they thought bad—even if it wasn't!-But you could; you could do anything in the world that it was necessary to do! I dare say Matron isn't a very clever woman, and I know her father was a pastry-cook, because she told me so—but she knew about you and the others. She said, 'I think the world of the new Superintendent now, and Dr. Everest I always have, and shall—but that doesn't mean I don't love your husband, Mrs. Macgregor. I love him as if he were my own boy that got killed in the War.'

"You see what I mean? You go outside yourself more, and they go inside themselves more, and p'r'aps they're tidier, Alec, inside and out, than we are; but we needn't bother about that, need we? And whenever you feel badly, you can remember how nasty I was, and that ought to be a comfort to you!"

"You weren't nasty!" Alec said indignantly. "You weren't nasty enough! But you can turn nasty now as often as you like—and it'll be a great help if you can, you see, because I brought you here, after all, though I'd made up my mind to stop at Chester! Anyhow, I'm glad you don't think Charles such a devil of a fellow as all that—I don't mind about Jane—so much! We'd better go to sleep now, I suppose!"

"Oh, no—not yet!" said Sally. "Oh, Alec!"

"Oh, Sally!" Alec said; and then they became incoherent and melted into each other like the silent downs.

Sally didn't think any more for hours, till she heard by Alec's soft, quiet breathing that he was fast asleep. She turned away from him then, nearer to the air and the darkness, which had covered up even the moon. Alec was just as much hers in the darkness as in the light, near or far; but he wasn't everything any more. That was one of the things Charles had told her the last time he'd seen Sally alone. "No one is everything, and everyone is something! Only it's probably safest for us to be most things to ourselves and by ourselves—it works better!"

Charles could say that, though he was so awfully, awfully in love with Jane that he could hardly bear it! And Jane with him! Not that they would be any happier than she and Alec were—now; but they would be safer than she and Alec used to be! Because they had those high walls—as well as the rushing togetherness!

"If I have a boy, I shall call him Charles," Sally said sleepily to herself, "and if I have a girl, I'll call her Jane —and I think I may be going to have both! And now we can all be as different as we like and yet be happy together!"

And then quite suddenly Sally thought of Myra. She felt very sorry for Myra. All of them had come out all right except Myra; and Myra had had to go to the Riviera instead.

THE END